WELL READ AND DEAD

ALSO BY CATHERINE O'CONNELL

Well Bred and Dead

WELL READ AND DEAD

A HIGH SOCIETY MYSTERY

Catherine O'Connell

HARPER

NEW YORK • LONDON • TORONTO • SYDNEY

HARPER

WELL READ AND DEAD. Copyright © 2009 by Catherine O'Connell. All rights reserved. Printed in the United States of America. No part of this book may be used or reproduced in any manner whatsoever without written permission except in the case of brief quotations embodied in critical articles and reviews. For information address HarperCollins Publishers, 10 East 53rd Street, New York, NY 10022.

HarperCollins books may be purchased for educational, business, or sales promotional use. For information please write: Special Markets Department, Harper-Collins Publishers, 10 East 53rd Street, New York, NY 10022.

FIRST EDITION

Designed by Justin Dodd

Library of Congress Cataloging-in-Publication Data is available upon request.

ISBN 978-0-06-167325-2

09 10 11 12 13   OV/RRD   10 9 8 7 6 5 4 3 2 1

For my father,

George B. O'Connell Jr.,

who always encouraged idealism

Two things sustain me. Love of literature and hatred of the bourgeois.

—GUSTAVE FLAUBERT

WELL READ AND DEAD

Prologue

I fell in exhaustion onto the sloping lawn behind the Martha's Vineyard cottage, the pungent scent of burning leaves filling my nostrils and the melancholy crash of the surf echoing in my ears. Henry crept up beside me on the dewy grass wearing a mischievous smile. He had dismissed the gardeners hours earlier, and we had passed the time ever since diving headlong into the mountain of crisp autumn leaves they had left behind. Like a couple of children playing, we took turns charging the pile and flinging ourselves into space, laughing gleefully as we floated back to earth through the downy mattress of withered leaves. Though we were celebrating the first anniversary of our marriage, each day with Henry still held new surprises. He had been able to coax out an impetuous side of me I never knew existed.

When we had finally tired of our game, we raked the flattened leaves back into a tidy haystack, and Henry applied a match. Leaning back on the cool grass in contented silence, we watched our handiwork smolder and flicker before erupting into flames, illuminating the evening sky in a bonfire worthy of Savonarola himself.

I closed my eyes and thought hungrily about the two unsuspecting lobsters that awaited us in the kitchen. The fire spit and crackled and the pungent smell of smoke grew stronger. As waves of heat caressed my body through the chill autumn air, Henry drew closer and brushed my eyelids with his fingertips. I tipped my chin upward in anticipation of his kiss. But instead of feeling the soft insistence of his lips upon mine, my desire was met with a sting of pain when a flaming leaf spiraled from the sky and landed squarely on my cheek.

My eyes flew open as I cried aloud and flicked the ember from my face. It took me a second to get my bearings. I wasn't in Martha's Vineyard after all, but rather in my Chicago penthouse, a thousand miles and light-years away. And Henry was still dead. It had all been a dream. But my throbbing cheek was no dream, and neither was the smoke. It rose above me in variegated layers, floating alongside the orderly rows of my bookshelves. I was on the library floor with the wavy pattern of a Persian rug dancing in the periphery of my eye. My head ached like a cracked egg, and when I reached around to the back of it, my touch was met with a sizable lump covered in warm, sticky dampness. I put my hand in front of my face. My fingers were wet with shiny red blood. I grimaced to think I was wearing winter white.

I tried to sit up, but a blinding flash of pain forced me back to the floor. Turning my head ever so gingerly, I sought out the source of the smoke and found it in the corner of the room where wide tongues of flame were spewing forth from the copper wastebasket. Like a serpent climbing a tree, the flames slithered up my bookshelves and lapped the spines of my rare editions before flaying them, leaving charred black curls in their wake. *Great Expectations* and *Vanity Fair* reduced to ashes. *Nana, Anna Karenina,* and *Madame Bovary* violated in the same despicable manner. As the flames moved laterally, they fed their insatiable appetite with mysteries and biographies and histories alike. With each fiery lash a whip cracked against my own flesh. I watched in mute horror as Henry's collection, the words so treasured by him, were devoured. *Canterbury Tales. Don Quixote. Scruples.* Gone in an instant.

The conflagration built in intensity, spreading out like an octopus in all directions. One fiery tentacle dropped to the ground and zipped toward me across the hardwood floor, changing its course upon reaching the rug. In my befuddled state, it occurred to me I had best take action soon or succumb to the same fate as my books. Fighting past the immobilizing pain, I grasped the edge of my desk and pulled myself to a seated position. A butterfly of burning paper alighted on my sleeve, singeing my jacket and threatening to set my shoulder-length hair afire. I frantically slapped at the flame and attempted to stand. The room careened about me like a carnival ride, causing me to fall back onto my derriere. Rolling onto my hands and knees, I found this position to be easier. Numb with fear, I crawled on all fours through the open French doors and into the hall.

The smoke was roiling out of the library, but for the most part it clung to the ceiling, leaving the air in the hallway relatively clear. As driven as Lot's wife, I turned and looked back into the burning room. The east and south walls were completely aflame as the fire gorged itself on paper, wood, and furniture polish. Only the bookshelves on the west side of the room remained untouched.

The Great Gatsby was on those shelves. The first edition bore personal inscriptions to Henry's grandmother from both F. Scott and Zelda, who had been frequent guests at her Park Avenue parties in the twenties. Henry had given me the book as a gift on our wedding day, adding his own inscription beneath that of the Fitzgeralds':

To my Pauline, whose green eyes outshine the light on Daisy's dock. Forever, H.

That book meant more to me than anything.

The fire had attacked the ceiling, and rivulets of flame were skimming along the crown molding like a string of Christmas lights being turned on. I calculated my chances of beating it to the west wall and the dire consequences if I didn't. Death. Or more frightening, disfiguring burns. Was the book worth the price? The words of Seneca danced a pas de deux in my brain. Life is short. Art is forever.

Abandoning all rational behavior, I pushed back the pain and got to my feet, running unsteadily back into the room. Propping myself against the shelves with one hand, I reached out with the other to claim my prize. But my hand froze midair as my mind's eye labored to comprehend what it was seeing. There was an empty slot between *Tender Is the Night* and *Collected Short Stories. Gatsby* was missing

I searched the surrounding shelves. Surely the book had been misplaced. It couldn't have simply disappeared. The flames grew more insistent, pressing me from behind like an unwanted suitor. Realizing there was no time left to look, I gave up and groped my way back through the smoky room to the exit.

What met me there was something from one's basest nightmare. The French doors had been closed. I grabbed the handles and shook them, but the doors didn't budge. I shook harder and they still held firm. Something was blocking them from the other side.

With the smoke growing thicker by the second, it was getting difficult to breath. I leaned against the doors and pounded on the glass for help. The fire took a breath and surged toward me, searing my face as I turned into it in search of something that might help me break through the glass. My eyes fixed on a cloisonné vase resting on the side table beside the club chair. I reached out for it, and the hot metal burned my hands. Mustering every bit of available strength, I heaved the vase at the door and heard the blessed sound of shattering glass as one of the panes gave way.

Reaching quickly through the broken glass, I found what had impeded my exit. An umbrella had been placed through the two handles. I slid it out, and the doors flew open under my weight. I stumbled into the hallway, taking in grateful breaths of the fresh air with each step.

Then something jumped onto my back, something alive. It ripped my jacket and tore at my hair. A swift blow from behind sent me crumpling to the floor. Lying there helpless as a rag doll, I fought to retain consciousness. But the effort proved too much. The world slipped away, and I could hear Henry's voice calling to me from the murky depths of a Martha's Vineyard fog.

1

The Odyssey

My plastic surgeon assures me that not only will the burns heal entirely but that since they were only first-degree my skin might become smoother and younger looking than before. Frankly I'd rather have had the chemical peel. Cosmetic issues aside, it's the internal wounds that trouble me more. Are they also first degree or will they prove beyond healing? I suppose only the balm of time will tell. In the meantime while waiting to see the final results, I seldom stray from bed as I replay the drama of the last months over and over again. Though all the warnings were laid in front of me, they were too close for me to see them. Now each time I revisit the drama, it becomes clearer who the players were and who were merely chorus. But unfortunately, like all Greek tragedy, the outcome is always the same.

In retrospect, it may have been a *bit* excessive for a party of one to charter a hundred-and-twenty-foot yacht just for herself. At sixty thousand dollars a week. Plus gratuity. But my frivolity at the time was not without justification. Having chosen to spend the autumn in Europe while my penthouse underwent a renovation, I happened to be in Portofino the day a group of pathetic zealots commandeered four airplanes and crashed them into the twin towers of the World Trade Center, the Pentagon, and a field in Pennsylvania, killing untold numbers and propelling us mentally back to the Middle Ages. In the weeks following the disaster, nearly all my friends overseas decided to return stateside, turning the mood abroad so somber that I contemplated returning home myself. The problem was that with my apartment under construction, I had no home to return to.

That's when Gianfranco entered the picture. I was strolling along the dock, wrestling over what course to take next, when I came upon him standing in the shadow of a sleek Benetti with the name *Herakles* stenciled in gold across her ample stern. With his tall, muscular frame draped in nautical whites, his sandy brown hair falling in loose curls along his face, and the regal profile of a Roman coin, he cut quite an Adonis-like figure. I stopped in pretense of admiring the yacht, and he engaged me in conversation, lamenting in broken English that his autumn charter had just been canceled. The Americans who had hired the *Herakles* for a tour of the antiquities were now too frightened to travel overseas. Perhaps I might be interested in such a charter? A quick tour of the vessel ensued, and my dilemma of how to spend the next months was solved. I chartered the orphaned *Herakles* myself. And felt rather patriotic about it, I might add. What better way to show the terrorists that Pauline Cook was not about to buckle under to their agenda of fear than by continuing to lead a full life?

I rushed back to the Splendido to settle my bill—a sum equal to the budget of a small third-world country—and soon thereafter my seven pieces of luggage and I were delivered dockside by the hotel's car. An hour later, I stood beside Gianfranco on the bridge of the yacht with a warm September breeze brushing my shoulders. As we watched the gentle hills of Portofino recede in the afternoon glow, my *capitano* assured me that I would never regret choosing to take this intimate tour.

"I will *take-a* you places you only dream *of-a* visit," he promised.

And take me he did. We hadn't made twenty nautical miles into the Adriatic when Gianfranco turned the wheel over to his first mate and escorted me belowdecks where he proved his sublimely tuned and tanned body to be more than seaworthy. For the next two and a half glorious months, certain all my interests at home were being looked after by competent parties, I gave little thought to the present-day world and immersed myself in the ancient one with Gianfranco as my captain, companion, and tour guide.

Together we explored the farthest reaches of the Hellenic and Roman empires. We visited Ilium, where the ill-fated Trojans made the poor choice of accepting the Greek's four-legged gift. We traipsed the ruins left by the Minoans at Knossos, often thought to be the lost civilization of Atlantis. We traveled to Actium where I felt the ghosts of Marc Antony and Cleopatra stir. When the weather grew cooler, we sailed south to Alexandria, the site of a library that once held 400,000 priceless scrolls whose ashes were now but dust in the wind.

And while the *Herakles* put in at one port after another, Gianfranco continued to *put in* at all points in between, a pastime I enjoyed as much, if not more, than the touring. Having breached the dreaded half-century mark over a year ago, I reveled in having a young paramour, though I did wonder what he would say if he knew he was making love to a woman nearly fifteen years his elder. Fortuitously, time had treated me well, and my skin did not reveal my age. This was the mixed blessing of growing up as a redhead who had to take shelter from the sun or risk looking like a beet. The summers of my youth were spent cowering beneath wide-brimmed hats and beach umbrellas while my peers cavorted gaily in the sun. Now while those same peers paid the price for their earlier freedom, having their faces pulled back to gather up the crevices carved out by youthful indiscretion, I gloried in the delayed benefits of my exile.

I had also been blessed with a trim figure, a benefit that comes along with standing five foot ten in one's stocking feet. And since I never bore children, there were no untoward stretch marks to be dealt with either, though I must concede each year the drapery of my body seemed to hang slightly lower. But this seemed to matter naught to my young lover, who claimed his preferences ran to mature women, explaining that the *ripe-a pear-a* has the sweetest taste and finest perfume while an unripe pear is *hard-a and no taste-a so good.*

And so this semiripe pear reveled in the attentions lavished upon me between islands. So much so, I actually toyed with the idea of bringing him to Chicago for a visit. I envisioned his lean, vigorous body in a tuxedo at the Amici of the Literati fundraiser, or wearing Brooks Brothers at the oh-so-staid Chicago Club, while my peers looked on in envy. Sunny Livermore would positively turn emerald as her corpulent husband tugged at his tight shirt collar with one of his cigarlike fingers. What did it matter that Gianfranco's English left much to be desired? I would simply introduce him as a count.

That notion was put to rest the day in late November when we motored back into Portofino on an ash-colored sea. Standing quayside was a raven-haired young beauty who hardly qualified as a pear. Ripe or otherwise. Apple would have been the better fruit metaphor, and a rather ripe apple at that. An apple whose child-swollen belly tugged at the seams of her dress. When she saw Gianfranco on the bow, her full lips broke into an ear-to-ear smile, and she began waving wildly. Beside her a shiny-eyed bambina jumped up and down shouting at the top of her lungs. "Papa! Papa!" So that's what *il capitano* was trying to tell me as he zipped up his pants for the final time. He looked at me sheepishly and shrugged. Then he leapt off the boat and swept the little girl into his arms while somehow managing to embrace his very pregnant wife at the same time.

If there is regularity in the universe, as the ancient Greeks believed, it is this. Men are bound to stray. I thought of Henry for the first time in months and wondered if he had ever been unfaithful to me in our thirteen years of marriage. Then I thought of how utterly close we had been and decided he hadn't. A surge of melancholy swept me, and I found myself missing my deceased husband more than ever.

Though somewhat wounded by Gianfranco's antics, in an odd sort of way, it was good to have a definitive end to the relationship. My dreams of bringing him home with me were only illusions; he could never have fit in my world. And since I abhor adultery—not only for moral reasons, but because it's nearly always a losing proposition—that put an end to the affair in my mind. Making a mental note to verify all men's marital status in the future, I wrote out a final check to my philandering captain and wished him and his family well. Gianfranco raised my hand to his lips and kissed it in a formal, polite manner while his smiling wife looked on.

"*Grazie, signora, grazie,*" she said, plucking the check from my outstretched hand before her husband could take it. It was clear she never suspected him of compromising himself with a woman of my advanced age. As far as she was concerned, he had spent the last few months earning their grocery money.

I suddenly felt older than the ruins I had spent the autumn visiting.

My bags were loaded into a waiting Mercedes, and the driver took me to Genoa, where I boarded the next flight to Paris. There is no better place to lick one's wounds than the City of Light. Besides, the red chiffon Dior gown I had purchased early in September would be ready by now.

2

And Then There Were None

It was in Paris that my real problems began to unfold. I checked into the Hôtel de Crillon, the only hotel in Paris as far as I'm concerned, with its staid public rooms and seventeenth-century tapestries. Maurice, the concierge, informed me he had some messages for me. Quite a few of *zem* in fact.

"We *'ave* been *'olding zem* for you, Madame Cook," he said, smiling graciously as he pulled a stack of cream-colored envelopes from his desk. I couldn't fathom who would know to look for me at the Crillon since I had only just that day decided to go there myself. My curiosity piqued, I graciously took the messages from him and carried them to my room. The very moment the bellman unloaded my last piece of baggage and the door clicked shut, I took a seat at the Louis XIV desk in the sitting room and slit the top envelope open with a mother-of-pearl letter opener. The message was from my broker, James Slattery. It dated back to early October.

Mrs. Cook: Urgent you contact me as soon as possible. Call anytime, day or night. J. S.

I tore into the next envelope in the stack. It, too, was from James. It was dated the following day and bore the same message as the first. I was to contact him as soon as possible. And so read the next message. And the next. And the next. James had left a message every day. Some days two of them. Right up to the present date.

The sangfroid of impending doom chilled my veins. My eyes flicked to the marble fireplace where the antique clock on the baroque mantle read three-thirty. That made it eight-thirty in the morning in Chicago. A call to the States found my ever-efficient broker already at his desk.

"Oh, Mrs. Cook, where have you been?" he moaned. "I've been trying to reach you for months."

"What is it, James?" I asked.

"I couldn't find you anywhere," he continued. "I tried the Connaught, the Splendido, the Grimaldi, the Villa d'Este. You weren't anywhere you were supposed to be and no one knew how to reach you." He sounded somber and weary, like a surgeon with some very bad news to deliver. I pictured him sitting in his sixty-second-story office, turning his chair toward the Chicago skyline and combing his fingers through an imaginary hairline as he prepared to drop the bomb. "There wasn't a thing I could do without your permission. I had to sit there and watch it hemorrhage, and not be able to do anything about it."

"What are you talking about? What's hemorrhaged, James?" My voice remained calm even as talons of fear clawed at my spine.

"Enron. The energy company you put all that money into. They've gone into bankruptcy."

The blood pooled in my ears as hysteria bubbled up from within me. Somewhere in the back of my mind a funeral dirge played. My hands turned to ice, and I felt myself getting lightheaded. I was glad to be sitting as I feared I might faint. I took slow, measured breaths in a futile attempt to still the hammering inside my chest.

"Could you repeat what you just told me, James?"

"I'm sorry, Mrs. Cook. Enron is history. Your stock is worthless."

"James," I chastised him, amazing myself with my self-control. "When you told me to buy Enron, you told me it was a no-risk investment. In fact, as I recall, you called it a 'slam drop.'"

"Slam dunk," he corrected me. "It was. Then. How was I, we, the entire investment world, to know they were cooking the books?"

"What do you mean, cooking the books? How cooked were they?"

"Burnt beyond recognition."

This was not the sort of answer I wanted to hear. Surely this could not be the total disaster he was making it out to be. "Well, I still have all those other stocks you recommended. Don't tell me they're all in bankruptcy."

"That's the problem. There's been a huge market adjustment since Nine-Eleven. Enron just helped to pull a lot of it down."

"How bad is it?" I asked pragmatically.

I cringed at the length of his pause, the same way one cringes waiting for the cosmetician to tear the cooled wax from the bikini line. "It's bad. You've lost ninety percent of your portfolio."

The pain of hair being ripped out by its roots is excruciating, but fleeting. This was pain that would linger. My first impulse was to scream in agony, but I feared drawing hotel security. I clapped my hand over my mouth and listened to the voice of my broker repeat over and over, "Mrs. Cook, are you there? Mrs. Cook?"

When I finally did speak, the voice that emerged sounded alien to me. "James, if you knew this was happening, why didn't you sell those stocks?"

"I couldn't do it without your approval," he replied. "It wouldn't be ethical."

I hung up without saying good-bye, placing the phone gently in the cradle with the restraint of a reformed alcoholic at an Irish wake. I didn't care to hear another word from James Slattery, and I was afraid of what might come out of my mouth if I said another word to him. The world's only ethical broker would understand.

Moving in a trance, I went into the bedroom and seated myself on the edge of the bed. I took my shoes off and put my feet up, admiring the matching floral pattern of the bedspread and the wallpaper and drapes. I studied the intricacies of the carved ceiling and the ornate crystal chandelier that hung from it. I wanted to think about anything other than the spectacularly bad news James had just delivered. While I'd been off committing adultery—albeit unwittingly—nearly twenty million dollars of my money had evaporated. Nine-tenths of my portfolio! That left me with little more than two million dollars in my account. Hardly enough to live on! I thought about the check I had just written Gianfranco for the charter. I thought about the Dior gown waiting to be picked up and paid for. I thought about the complete remodel of my penthouse that had taken place in my absence. The estimates alone ran in the hundreds of thousands, and those bills would be due upon my return.

Turning my head into the pillow, I felt bitter tears come to my eyes. Was it in my stars to forever be financially insecure? Somehow it didn't seem fair. Like Humpty Dumpty, my nest egg had plummeted from the wall and shattered on the ground. All the king's horses and all the king's men certainly couldn't put this mess back together again.

3

Kidnapped

As luck would have it, first class on Air France was overbooked, so Maurice booked me in *l'éspace affaires,* which was probably a blessing in disguise in light of my newly discovered financial distress. But regardless what class one flew, travel to the States had changed dramatically since my trip over nearly three months earlier. It was a different world in the aftermath of the terrorist attacks. Security at Charles de Gaulle was so dreadfully slow I could have swum home more quickly.

Onboard the plane, the changes became even more evident. Though the flight attendants tried to put up a good front, they were skittish to the point of being paranoid, lending an atmosphere of doom to the travel experience. The gravity of the situation was really brought home to roost when lunch was served, and I unfolded my napkin to find a plastic knife. Now I'm all in favor of security, but honestly, if one wants to wreak havoc onboard an aircraft I can think of far more imaginative ways than waving around what amounts to a glorified butter knife in the first place. A pair of stiletto heels, for instance, could be a far more dangerous weapon. No wonder so many of my contemporaries were taking to buying their own aircraft. At least one could board in a reasonable amount of time and eat with proper utensils.

After lunch I tried reading the copy of *The Corrections* I'd picked up in the duty free, but my mind kept looping back to my hideous financial situation, making it impossible to concentrate. I finally took an uneasy nap with the book open on my lap, and woke to the sound of the captain announcing that we were preparing to land. After descending through a long and ominous bank of window-streaking clouds, the plane touched down into a damp and drizzly Chicago afternoon. As we taxied to the gate, my thoughts shifted away from my financial situation and turned to my cat. My dear friend, Whitney Armstrong, had been watching Fleur in my absence, and I was anxious to get to Whitney's and pick her up. I thought of how comforting it would be to climb into bed tonight and have her curl up beside me. It almost made me forget my money worries.

After satisfying an immigration agent that I proved no terrorist threat, I obtained a couple of luggage carts and wheeled them to the carousel posted for my flight. A roving customs agent noticed my two carts and asked to see my customs form. His eyebrows shot up to his hairline when he saw the dollar amount I had declared. After all, I had made some serious acquisitions while overseas, including the Dior gown, which was elaborately folded and tissued into a piece of luggage entirely its own. The agent drew a bright green ring around the bottom line of my form and pointed at the red "something to declare" lane across the room. He instructed me to report there after claiming my bags, as if I wasn't already familiar with the procedure. Customs agents only had to take one look at me and it was "Could you step this way, ma'am?" Having learned the high price of a little dishonesty, I now filled out my customs declaration with complete accuracy. Well, almost complete accuracy. One still had to leave a small omission here and there just for the challenge. Such as the Chanel handbag I was carrying, another last-minute purchase in the duty-free halls at Charles de Gaulle. Certainly no one would pay it any attention in light of all my other declared purchases.

The carousel began turning, and the customs agent moved on to his next victim. I waited for my bags. Uneasiness started creeping upon me as bag after bag fell onto the belt with nary a sign of Monsieur Vuitton. When the carousel stopped, I had yet to claim a single piece of my luggage. Was it possible that my bags hadn't made it onto the plane after being tagged for special handling, especially after the outrageous fees I had paid for the bags' being overweight?

Yes, it was possible, and to make matters worse, because of the green ring on my declaration form, I still had to go through the "something to declare" lane. Without my luggage. The young female agent levied a hefty duty on my purchases despite my explanation that none of the declared items was in my possession, and I couldn't be certain they ever would be. When I tried to argue the point, the smug young bureaucrat noticed the Chanel handbag. She added it to the final tally with a penalty for failing to declare it. I should have known better.

I hired a limousine and had it take me directly to the Armstrong mansion on Astor Street. I may have been arriving home without my clothes, but I had no intention of crossing the threshold without my cat. Fleur was my touchstone. The last thing Henry had given me before his death, she had been the one consistent thing in my life ever since. Men had been sporadic, friends at times unreliable, and finances fickle, but Fleur was always there with unconditional love. I hoped she wouldn't be too angry with me for this extended desertion, but she had been left in the best of hands during my absence. No one loved animals more than Whitney.

Instructing the driver to wait, I walked up to the front door and rang the bell. My ring was answered by Surrendra, the Armstrong's Indian houseman. Whitney had adopted Surrendra on a trip to Mumbai after she discovered him living as a squatter in the zoo. As kind and unselfish a person as one could ever hope to meet, Whitney was always picking up strays, be it dogs or people. But in an environment where the best of friends had stepped up from stealing each other's nannies to stealing each other's British butlers, Whitney's instincts regarding the young Indian had paid off. Despite the handicap of a clubfoot, Surrendra had turned out to be the perfect servant: efficient, proper, unceasingly faithful, and, most important, invisible.

"Good afternoon, Mrs. Cook," he said uneasily, holding the door for me. I stepped inside and immediately sensed something odd about the house. Surrendra stood quietly before me studying the floor, his slight frame hunched with fragility and his sandy brown skin ashen-looking in the glimmering light of the Venetian chandelier two stories overhead. Finally, he said, "You were not expected."

"I realize I should have called beforehand, but I only just decided to return home yesterday. Is Mrs. Armstrong in?"

Surrendra flinched as if a fishbone had just lodged in his throat. Pushing back a thatch of dark hair from his forehead, he peered over his shoulder surreptitiously before turning his gleaming black eyes back on me. "Madam has gone," he whispered.

"A shame," I said flippantly. "I was hoping to find her in. Well, no matter. I'll catch up with her later. I've come to collect Fleur."

"No, Mrs. Cook. You don't understand. Madam has gone."

"You mean she's out of town? Well, bully for her escaping this dismal weather. Then could you just get Fleur for me?"

Now Whitney's loyal servant looked like he had just been handed a one-way ticket back to Mumbai. He dropped his head so low his chin nearly touched his concave chest. Then he let fly with some most unpleasant news. "The cat is gone, too."

"What do you mean, the cat is gone?" I demanded, understandably confused. "She took Fleur with her?"

He nodded and said, "Mrs. Armstrong left last week. With the cat. And the dogs. We have no knowledge of where she has gone."

Then it dawned on me what was so unsettling about the house. The silence. Visitors were generally greeted by Monet and Amitié, Whitney's two Yorkshire terriers, little rats of dogs that scampered about one's feet making incessant yapping sounds like a chain smoker clearing his throat. Pampered beyond belief from the satin ribbons in their hair to their custom-made diamond collars, they led a life even I envied. Their meals were cooked by the Armstrongs' personal chef, and on the chef's day off, Whitney ordered in their dinner from the best restaurants in the city. If reincarnation exists and I have any say in where I might resurface, I would lobby to come back as one of Whitney's dogs.

I stared at Surrendra dumbfounded, trying to sort through this unexpected turn of events, when the sound of leaden footsteps on the landing above drew my eyes upward. The salt-and-pepper gray head of Jack Armstrong came into view at the top of the winding stairs.

"Who's that, Surrendra?" he demanded, peering over the railing. When he saw it was me, a weak half-smile came to his lips. "Pauline. Thank God you're back." He quickly descended the steps, a tall, distinguished figure in gray slacks and a cranberry cashmere sweater with a *Wall Street Journal* tucked under his arm. He stopped in front of me, his stern hazel eyes appraising me through the lenses of his tortoiseshell glasses. There was a slackness to his lean, etched face and firm jaw that I had never seen before. In a gesture highly unusual for him, he hugged me tightly and held on to me. Then Jack Armstrong, tough, self-assured magnate of the country's largest lingerie empire, worth scores of millions more than I would ever hope to see, rested his head upon my shoulder and began to cry. Out of the corner of my eye, I could see Surrendra quietly retreating down the hall.

"She's left me," Jack sobbed, like a child who has just learned his puppy has been hit by a car. "Whitney's left me."

I stood awkwardly trapped beneath his rain of tears, uncertain of the protocol when an icon of American industry is having a breakdown. I gave him reassuring little pats on the back until his tears finally ceased. He released me and straightened up, pulling a monogrammed handkerchief from the pocket of his perfectly creased slacks and using it to wipe his tear-streaked glasses and face. "I'm sorry," he apologized in a voice cramped with pain. "That's been building up in me for some time. This is the first time I've cried since she left. Seeing you brought it to a head."

"That's all right, Jack. I understand," I comforted him. Though I really didn't understand yet, and wouldn't for some time.

"Please, stay for a while," he begged. "I need to talk to someone."

He sent Surrendra out to dismiss the waiting limousine, and we went into the solarium at the back of the house, the room Whitney called her refuge. We sat down on two rattan couches amid a rain forest of her tropical plants. Despite the gloomy drizzle on the domed skylight, the room was cheery and the sound of the corner waterfall lent a soothing tranquillity to our surroundings. Surrendra appeared magically with a tray of coffee, tea sandwiches, and wine, and faded back into the shadows.

Jack picked up a silver-framed picture of Whitney from the cocktail table. She was stretched out on a chaise longue in silk pajamas, all blond hair and long legs and bulbous breast implants, her rose-petal skin luminous, her large brown fawnlike eyes serving to make her look the tiniest bit frightened.

"I spend a lot of time in this room since she left," Jack began, putting the picture down and pouring himself a cup of coffee from the heavy silver service. I wavered between coffee and the Puligny-Montrachet, and finally opted for the wine. Though I was tired and jet-lagged, it would help me sleep when I got home. The sandwiches sat untouched.

"Tell me what's happened," I prompted him.

"That's the problem, Pauline. I'm not sure what happened," he said. He'd regained his composure, and his voice held its usual businesslike tone. "Whitney had been acting oddly in recent weeks. Cool. Distant. Not her normal self. She'd become argumentative, too. Now you know yourself that Whitney is about as nonaggressive as a woman can be. But she had gotten touchy. And even stranger, political. She kept trying to engage me in political conversations."

"And what did you do about that?" I asked, as surprised as Jack was. To the best of my knowledge, Whitney's political involvement was limited to raising funds for the animal shelter.

"I tried to change the subject. Lord knows I didn't marry Whitney for her politics. I married her for her lack of them. But she would insist on these discussions and they would invariably lead to another fight. It's ironic, the thing that drew me to Whitney was that she didn't require any mental demands." He sighed wistfully and continued. "And worse, she usually pays so much attention to me, and, well . . . she wasn't. Not the way she normally would." Another wistful sigh. This one stronger. Jack didn't have to elaborate for me to recognize the attention he was lacking was of a physical nature. Whitney had told me about Jack's impressive libido. "I blame myself in part. She really started to change after she joined the book club."

"Book club? Whitney was in a book club?" This revelation came as a bigger surprise than Whitney's interest in politics. The only things I'd ever seen Whitney read were *People, Vogue,* and *Vanity Fair.* And I think she only bought *Vanity Fair* for the covers.

"Yes, and I was the one who pushed it. I just wanted her to be a little more—well, you know—acceptable to the other women. I had no idea it was going to be like she ate the goddamn fruit from the tree of knowledge. Anyhow, after one particularly bad fight last week, I had to go to New York overnight for business. When I came back she was gone. Surrendra said that she left in the middle of the night while he was sleeping. She left me the day before Thanksgiving. She took Monet and Amitié and just disappeared."

"And Fleur," I added with a heavy heart, my own loss brought painfully back to mind. "Have you reported this to the police? Maybe she didn't leave of her own accord. Could she have been kidnapped?"

"That was my first thought. But then I decided against it. For one, she took the animals. What kidnapper would take the animals?"

I thought it over. It was unlikely that a kidnapper would take pets, especially annoying creatures like Monet and Amitié, but it wasn't unheard of. Grandmother's friend Biffy Rothstein's toy poodle was held for ransom back in the forties. It nearly caused a divorce because Stuart refused to pay at first. Biffy even accused her husband of orchestrating the event himself, and I think she took those suspicions to her grave, even after the culprit was caught trying to pawn Froo-Froo's diamond collar a month later.

"Jack, you said, 'For one, she took the animals.' Is there a 'for two'?"

He rested his coffee cup on the table and leaned back the way a man does when he has some great piece of wisdom to impart. Nowhere did I see the person who had broken down in front of me earlier. His face turned cold and his voice resumed a corporate air. "She left her engagement ring. Put it on my bureau next to my watch case where I couldn't miss it. If she were kidnapped don't you think the kidnappers would have taken the ring?"

Surely they would have taken the ring. I would have taken it! Twelve carats of faultless canary yellow diamond from Harry Winston, set in platinum with a pair of VS trillions on either side, it was exquisite. So exquisite I had to push back the green-eyed monster every time I set eyes upon it. Though Henry had always been generous with me, he had never graced me with anything half so magnificent. In fact, the material goods that Jack Armstrong lavished on Whitney served to just further prove how much he adored her. He fulfilled her every desire with never a question about the price of the ensemble, the piece of jewelry, the service. Whitney had more handlers than an Arabian. Every wife in Chicago society longed to know what her secret was.

Of course I knew what her secret was, though I could hardly share it. There was something about Whitney that was more unnatural than her implants. And that was her gender. In her earlier life, Whitney had been a man. As far as I knew, only her husband, her doctor, and I knew about it. So she was able to keep Jack physically happy in ways that only a former man could understand. In fact, she had shared a few pointers with me once, moves that still cause the tips of my ears to redden at the very thought of them.

My silent nod confirmed my tacit agreement with Jack that if Whitney had been taken under duress, the ring would have accompanied her.

"Pauline, I've got to get her back. I've never known a woman like Whitney," he added, his mask softening and his face falling slack in misery again.

"Of course you haven't," I agreed, feeling no need to point out he had just stated the obvious. "Have you given any thought to hiring a private detective?"

His face showed relief at having someone he could be candid with about the sensitive nature of Whitney's history. He lowered his voice and drew close since one could never be certain where Surrendra might be lurking. "Of course I've thought about it, Pauline. But how can I hire an outsider? You just can't know what these people might do if they learned about Whitney's former life." I had to agree. The delicate issue of Whitney's past was not the sort of thing a titan of industry would want to see exposed. Aside from her previous, well, maleness, she had also shared with me that she had once had a drug problem. Those sorts of things could spell disaster on the business pages and certainly wouldn't bode well for club memberships.

Misery cloaked Jack's face again, nearly causing my own heart to break at the thought of his devotion. I got up from my chair and took a seat beside him on the sofa. Keeping enough distance between us so my action would not be misinterpreted, I took one of his large manicured hands into mine and squeezed it sympathetically. "Jack, if there's anything I can do, let me know. Anything at all."

For a moment I thought he might cry again, but instead he came out with an offer that nearly knocked me to the floor. "Pauline, there is something you can do. Find her for me. I know if I could just talk to her I could get her to come back." Then he added words mellifluous to one who has just lost a fortune. "I'll give you five million dollars if you can find out where she is. I know you don't need money, but you could give it to your favorite charity. You're the only one I can trust."

I couldn't quite believe my ears. The very notion that Jack Armstrong was offering me a reward to find his wife was positively absurd. My first thought was I would do anything I could to reunite them, but I wouldn't take money for it. Then I had my second thought. I thought of how five million dollars would go a long way toward stemming the flow of my bleeding financial artery. Not to mention finding Whitney meant finding Fleur. But as I was no detective, I had no idea where one might start on such a mission, and in my jet-lagged state I was in no condition to make any major commitments. What I needed most was to go home, climb into bed, and face the world tomorrow.

"Jack, I don't know what I could do," I said, getting up, "but I'll think about it."

He stood up with me and took my hand. "Pauline, there's one other thing. Let's keep this between us. I think it's for the best right now that no one else know."

4
The Inferno

Jack insisted that Surrendra drive me home. I stared out the Bentley's window at the choppy gray lake to one side of me and the wind turning people's umbrellas inside out on the other, and was grateful for the luxurious warmth of the car. As the early rush hour traffic crawled along Lake Shore Drive, I got the distinct impression Whitney's loyal servant wanted to tell me something by the way he kept clearing his throat, opening his mouth as if to speak, and then snapping it shut without a word. Finally, I could take it no longer.

"What is it, Surrendra?" I asked.

"Well, Madam, it's just that . . . " He hesitated as if he were thinking about leaping from the car into the icy lake beside us rather than come forth with what he had to say. "There was much fighting before Madam left. I thought you might want to know this."

"Thank you, Surrendra," I replied, replaying what Jack Armstrong had already told me about the two of them arguing. "All couples fight. It's nothing out of the ordinary."

He cleared his throat again, as if he had something to add but wasn't sure if it was a good idea. Then he let it go and said simply, "Yes, Madam."

He drove in silence the rest of the way to my building, a vintage co-op constructed in the heyday of the first stock market boom. It is located on the very short, pricey, and prestigious stretch of beachfront property known as East Lake Shore Drive. And while words couldn't begin to describe the vacuum created by the absence of my cat, I was still anxious to see how my "spare no expense" renovation had turned out. I hoped when I walked in the door, the astronomical amount of money sunk into crown moldings and wainscoting, imported marble from China, new wood floors, and custom-made cabinetry would feel like money well spent. Even if I wasn't quite sure anymore how it would be paid for.

Surrendra pulled into the circular drive and stopped beneath the porte cochere. Jeffrey rushed out to meet the car. The most efficient of the building's doormen, Jeffrey was a blond, curly-haired specimen of masculinity whose triangular physique, even under the cloak of his hunter green uniform, brought to mind much of the statuary I had seen in Greece—the torsos in particular. Though Jeffrey was always polite and never too familiar, I had a sense he would have gladly taken me in the storage room off the lobby—given the opportunity.

"Mrs. Cook!" he exclaimed, a peculiar look coming over his face when he opened the door and saw me. "You're back!"

While I got out, his face remained locked in the same strange expression. "Are you all right, Jeffrey? You look like someone has stepped on your toe."

"I'm fine, ma'am," he replied, shutting the door behind me. "No bags?"

"Don't even ask."

Surrendra drove off, and Jeffrey escorted me through the revolving doors into the lobby. It was quiet in the dark-paneled room, as it nearly always is in a building with only thirty residents. Usually friendly and loquacious, Jeffrey was oddly quiet as he accompanied me to the single elevator and reached inside the guilded doors to push twenty for the penthouse. Then he stepped away quickly as if he knew the elevator cable was frayed and he didn't want to be anywhere nearby when the elevator plunged to the basement. I held the door open and stared at him.

"Are you certain you're all right?" I asked a second time.

"Well, it sort of depends on what you call all right."

"Whatever is that supposed to mean?" I demanded, growing ever more mystified by his behavior.

"I think you'd better go up and have a look for yourself," he replied, giving me a 'you're going to be none too happy' look as the elevator doors closed on his comely face.

What greeted me when the door opened onto my private foyer made me wish the elevator *had* plunged to the basement. What I could see of my residence was little more than a shell. There were wires hanging from the ceiling, gaping holes in the walls, and piles of sawdust everywhere. Certain that I had landed in the third ring of hell, I followed the sound of Eastern European music down the hall to what had formerly been my powder room, where a sluggish-looking creature was laying imported Italian tile on the floor. He looked up at me with watery blue eyes, blinking away smoke from the cigarette that dangled from his lips. A heap of cigarettes in the corner attested to an expensive habit.

"Who's in charge here?" I demanded, none too happily.

"Missus?" he said, raising a thick eyebrow. His accent bespoke one of the former satellites of the Soviet Union, though I could hardly venture a guess as to which one.

"I want to know who's in charge here," I repeated. "Who is your boss?"

"Ah, boss. Mr. McKay. In master bedroom."

"Mr. McKay? Who on earth is Mr. McKay?" I huffed aloud as I made my way through the war zone of a hallway to the room where I had whimsically hoped to sleep that evening. The room was empty, the furniture having been put in storage right after I left the country. Going into the bathroom, I located the person I assumed to be Mr. McKay. Or rather, I located his lower half, a pair of legs wearing paint-splattered work pants and heavy boots sticking out of the bathroom cabinet.

"Mr. McKay?" I called, doing my best to keep a civil tone. When there was no response, my civility took leave of me, and I shouted, "MR. MCKAY!"

A pair of broad shoulders squeezed from the cabinet door, followed by a dust-coated face set among waves of long, dusty hair. With sharply chiseled cheekbones, a strong, square chin, and a nose that fell straight from his dust-covered eyebrows, I was reminded of yet more statuary. A pair of turquoise eyes blinked at me quizzically before the statue shimmied the rest of the way from the cabinet and climbed to his feet. I towered over him in my high-heeled boots, though I still would have been taller than he was in my stocking feet.

"Can I help you?" he asked.

"I fear I may be beyond help. My name is Pauline Cook and this disaster area happens to be my residence."

"Oh, Pauline. I'm Tag McKay, your new contractor." He held out a dusty hand and, thinking better of it, wiped it off on his paint-speckled pants before extending it again. I ignored it, crossing my arms defiantly as I lowered my eyes a couple of inches toward his.

"New contractor?" I spouted, justifiably confused. Before I left the country my decorator and I had conducted an exhaustive interviewing process and settled upon Djordjevich Brothers to do my remodel. The firm was not only renowned for their use of old-world artisans, but their ability to finish a project on schedule. Adrienne French had used them at her Barrington mansion and the results were nothing short of a mini-Versailles. "What happened to my old contractor?"

Ignoring my slight, Mr. McKay met my eyes without flinching. He was clearly not in the least bit intimidated by me. I took an immediate dislike to him. "Nine-Eleven happened, that's what," he replied coolly.

"Nine-Eleven? Oh my god, Mr. Djordjevich wasn't . . ."

"Nothing like that. But just so happens a week after the attacks a carload of Djordjevich employees got pulled over for speeding. None of them had good papers. With the feds so jumpy these days, they ended up deporting the whole carload of them. And then most of the rest of the company. Sent 'em all back to Serbia, including the Djordjevich brothers themselves."

Was the fallout from those terrorists ever going to end? First stocks. Then cutlery on airplanes. Now highly skilled artisans plucked from their host country and sent back to the old world.

"And where, might I ask, did you come from?"

"Your decorator called me in. Lucky for you he caught me between jobs."

"Lucky for me," I echoed dully. I might have become a bit snippy after that, but I blame it on jet lag. "I want to know why we aren't any further along than this."

"Your cabinets were delayed. The cabinet maker was deported, too. We finally got them this week."

"Well, that's just the cabinets. What about the rest of the work? This place is a shambles."

"Until we set the cabinets, there isn't much we can do. We can only rough in the plumbing, can't finish the tilework, the granite . . . Do you get the idea?"

The only idea I was getting was that I didn't like his impudent manner. I was about to give him a piece of my mind and remind him who would be signing his checks when the elfin figure of Bharrie Williams sashayed into the room. The moment he laid eyes on me he recoiled as if he had just stuck his hand on a hot radiator. His pasty face grew more drained-looking than usual, and his algae-colored eyes bugged out from behind the narrow red frames of his designer glasses.

"Eeek, Pauline. What are you doing here?"

"This is my home, or at least it used to be," I informed the feminine side of my decorating team. "Can you please explain what's happened here?"

"It's not my fault, Pauline. Blame the terrorists. They've been deporting people left and right. I did the best I could. I tried calling you, but you weren't following the itinerary you gave me."

I made another mental note to check in during extended absences in the future.

"How much longer is this going to take?"

Bharrie toed at something on the floor. I noticed he was wearing a pair of pull-on slippers. Since nothing but the finest Italian leather ever touched Bharrie's *petits pieds*, I imagined he had left his loafers at the door. After all, why should he sully them in the mess that used to be my home? He collected his thoughts and looked back at me. "It's not really as bad as it looks, Pauline. We finally have everything we need on site and Tag has his men working overtime. Now that we've got the cabinets in, we should be finished in this room in no time. The kitchen, the other baths, the painting . . . it shouldn't take more than . . . " He looked to Mr. McKay, who was kind enough to finish for him.

"We're looking at another six weeks."

"Six weeks? *Six weeks?*" I was aghast. That would take me through the holidays into the middle of January. Where was I supposed to go for six weeks? It was all too much for my jet-lagged mind. I needed some place to lay my weary head this very evening. "I'm too exhausted to talk about this right now. I don't suppose there's a working phone anywhere in this disaster?"

"In the library," Bharrie responded sheepishly. "But you can use my cell." He held out his phone, but I stormed past him and down the hall, past paint-stained scaffolding and exposed wires. Bharrie followed me in hot pursuit. When I reached the library, I pushed aside a sheet of plastic protecting the French doors and went into my inner sanctum. The book-lined room was the only part of the apartment to remain untouched during the renovation. The library had been Henry's favorite room, and it housed the collection of first editions and rare books that had been among his greatest treasures. With its masculine furniture and floor-to-ceiling bookshelves, it reminded me so much of him that I couldn't bear to change it.

I picked up the desk phone and dialed the Drake Hotel down the block. The turn-of-the-last-century hotel, with its sedate public rooms and high-coffered ceilings, bespoke the elegance of another era, and I often employed it to house my overflow guests. I asked to speak to Silvio DeLuca, the general manager. While I waited for the operator to connect me, I covered the mouthpiece and asked Bharrie, "Where the devil did you find that horrible McKay?"

"Pauline, I had to scramble to get anybody on such short notice. You can't begin to believe—"

I cut him short as the efficient voice of Silvio DeLuca came on the line, his Castilian-accented English as smooth as Spanish olive oil. I explained my dilemma and that I would be in need of his finest suite, possibly for the next six weeks.

His pause warned me of more bad news to be delivered.

"Unfortunately, Mrs. Cook, we have no suites available at the moment.

In fact, I'm filled to capacity. Every hotel in the area is filled as well with Christmas shoppers. I can put you in my finest suite on Monday."

"Silvio, this is an emergency. I simply must have a room this evening. You don't expect me to sleep on the pavement with the street people, do you?"

Another pause and then, "Give me a moment, please." I was put on hold to one of Bach's Brandenburg concertos and had moved on to Beethoven's "Ode to Joy" when the general manager finally returned to the line. "Mrs. Cook. I have some good news. I have been able to locate a room for you. A last-minute cancellation. Unfortunately, it is twin-bedded and faces the alley. I am sorry but it's the best we can do under the circumstances. However, after three days we can relocate you into our finest suite."

I was far too tired to fight any more losing battles. I asked him to hold the room for me and hung up. Then yet another unpleasant thought entered my mind.

"Bharrie, where are all my clothes?"

I could hear him swallow. "Still in storage with your furniture, Pauline."

Of course. Why should it be otherwise? I looked at my watch. It was just after six, and the windows of my library were a wall of black. Though I had gone from tired to overtired, it was necessary to do some quick shopping before checking into the hotel. I needed to buy something to sleep in that night and fresh clothes for the morning. There was no way in creation I would be putting on the same clothes tomorrow that I had been wearing for the last twenty-four hours. I spoke to him in much the same manner I had spoken to Jack Armstrong before vacating his premises.

"Bharrie, I'm beyond thinking right now. We'll have to discuss this contractor later. Right now, I'm going shopping."

He followed me into my dusty foyer, where I left him standing in his pull-on slippers.

An hour later I walked out of Barney's with several bags of survival clothing: sweaters and slacks, silk pajamas and bathrobe, the necessary lingerie, a Versace suit, and a pair of low shoes. I had spent a small fortune on clothes I wasn't even sure I was particularly fond of, but I had to have something decent to wear until Air France located my bags, or I was able to get some of my clothes out of storage. Now to the Drake. Where I would be sleeping in a standard room, twin-bedded no less.

My mind was in a fog, so much had changed in such a short span of time. I was in essence homeless, without male companionship, and both my cat and one of my best friends had gone missing. I thought about my seven wayward Vuitton bags. My Dior gown. My clothes and furniture and six-hundred count Frette sheets in storage. I thought about the cost of the remodeling project and the balance that would come due upon completion—if that day ever arrived. I thought about Enron and bad stock choices and the substantial fortune I had lost.

Weighed down with my bags, as I stood in the gale-force wind on Oak Street, trying desperately to hail a cab, I was suddenly gripped with panic at the thought of what tomorrow might bring. Could things get worse?

It was then that I noticed the red neon sign in the window above the dry cleaner across the street. Like a siren, it beckoned to me.

PSYCHIC READINGS BY MARIA.

5

The Interpretation of Dreams

For the absolute life of me, I'll never know why, but I crossed that street and went up those stairs. Carrying all my shopping bags, no less. When I reached the dimly lit landing, a button glowed next to a solitary door. Before I had a chance to push it, the door was opened by a woman who couldn't have been half my age. Her eyes were so black she had no visible pupil, her hair blacker still, her smooth skin tinged with olive. She wore a gray sweatshirt that said DE PAUL UNIVERSITY and a pair of new blue jeans. "May I help you?" she asked.

"*You're* Maria?"

She nodded, and her narrow lips rose subtly at the corners.

"The psychic?"

"That's right."

I studied her carefully. I'd never visited a psychic before, but she certainly didn't look the way one might imagine a psychic to look. I expected she would be a little more gypsy-like, with gold hoop earrings and a scarf tied around her head. This girl looked like a college co-ed, far too youthful to even make up interesting lies. My first impulse was to turn around and walk back down the stairs. Then the huge sense of disconnection returned. It was either the psychic or the psychiatrist.

"I'm here for a reading," I said.

She smiled in a Mona Lisa-esque way and led me into a surprisingly cheery room. It was decorated with Victorian furniture and doilies, a pair of red velvet sofas and lamps draped with a toile-like material softening the bulb's glare to a warm gold glow. Through the large picture window, I could see people below scurrying with their heads lowered into the wind. In the corner of the room, a gray cat was sleeping upon a red and white heart-covered pad in a red wicker cat bed, its small rib cage rising and falling in rhythm with its breath. My heart pinched with pain as I wondered if Fleur was safe, and where she would sleep this cold, cruel evening.

A small kitchen opened off the room where a man with his back to us sat smoking at a narrow table. He was reading a magazine and did not so much as acknowledge my existence, flicking his cigarette nonchalantly before turning the page. Opposite the kitchen, a small cubicle with glass doors was sectioned off for privacy. Through the leaded windowpanes, I could see the room was filled with religious icons, crucifixes, and statuettes of Jesus and Mary and saints unfamiliar to me. I put down my bags and followed Maria into the little room. She closed the door behind us, indicating I take one of the chairs on either side of a café table. She sat in the other.

"May I ask why you want a reading?" she inquired.

"I've never had one. I'm merely curious."

In truth, it was ironic that I was there. I was the ultimate skeptic, putting no stake in horoscopes or lucky numbers or black cats. But at this moment my life was such a shambles, I wanted some glimmer of hope that things would look up. I wanted to hear something positive. It didn't matter if it was hocus-pocus or not, I needed a raison d'être.

She studied me with probing eyes. Then she asked to hold something of mine. I still wore my engagement ring, but on my right hand—not wanting to discourage any potential suitors. I took it off and handed it to her. She studied the four-carat marquis diamond and nodded approvingly. Then she rubbed it between her palms so rapidly I half-expected it to disappear. Her head fell back on her neck and she closed her eyes as if in a trance. When she opened them, her face was very sad.

"The one who gave you this is no longer living," she said.

"That is correct. My husband died nearly thirteen years ago." I was unimpressed. Since she had seen me take the ring off my right hand, it would not take the world's greatest powers of deduction to put that one-and-one together. However, her next words were truly a challenge to non-believers everywhere.

"You are having many problems with construction."

Though I was flabbergasted, I tried not to blink.

"This construction is upsetting your well-being. I see that clearly."

She rubbed the ring again. "Oh, my. Everything is in flux. I see now why you are visiting me. There is too much happening in your life, much of it not good, most of it out of your control. And that is very difficult for you. You need to be in control."

She peered into my face. "You are very out of balance."

Sitting up straighter in my chair, I wondered if I should feel insulted.

"If you want to be happy, you need to find balance," she continued. She clasped her palms tighter around my ring and drew her knuckles toward her mouth, blowing on them. "You have undergone many losses in your life, the biggest one some time ago. Of the recent losses, some are important, some not so important. It's up to you to figure out which is which."

Losses. Of course there were losses. I recounted them yet again. Henry years ago, but more recently my money, my cat, Whitney, my Dior gown. I wondered if Gianfranco counted for anything.

The psychic went on to tell me more about myself, but they were the sort of things that could generally hold true of anyone. That I believed in fairness, though I went to great lengths to disguise it. That a search would bring a great revelation. That my health would be good except for the emotional effects of my raging hormones.

I asked if that meant I could opt out of this year's breast-flattening mammogram.

"You must do as your doctor tells you," she replied.

She moved on to fresh territory. "I see travel. Sometime soon. Someplace cold."

So much for psychic powers. This was one prediction that would not come true. There was no way in creation that I would leave Chicago in the dead of winter and go someplace cold. Michigan Avenue was bad enough with its gale force winds blowing one's breath back down one's throat. If I left town it would be for Palm Beach or St. Bart's.

She closed her eyes again and concentrated, tilting her smooth forehead toward the ceiling. When she opened her eyes, they shone brightly.

"You are going to find your soul mate," she said, adding, "He is a man who comes from great means."

Now I was a believer. "Is he tall? He must be tall."

Eyes closed again. And then open. "I see you looking up to him."

She drew closer to me and searched my face. "You have beautiful eyes, Pauline. Like a cat." And then she gasped aloud. "You have a cat, or perhaps you've lost it. Yes, you have lost it. The cat is safe, but you must find it."

This took me from believer to true believer. Perhaps there were no accidents in the universe. Perhaps there was a reason I had stumbled onto Maria this blustery damp night.

"My cat is with a friend," I said. "Would you be able to tell me where my friend is?"

The psychic shrugged. "I would need to hold something personal of hers to even try." She handed my ring back to me, a none-too-subtle hint that our time was finished. I slid it onto my finger and stood up, still numb with astonishment that she had known about Fleur.

"That will be one hundred and twenty-five dollars," she said.

"Do you accept credit cards?" I asked.

"Of course," she replied with a laugh. "I don't think I could stay in business if I didn't." She took my card and ran it through a machine. A receipt printed out, which she handed to me to sign. I scribbled my name on the chit, and she looked at it studiously. "I do handwriting analysis, too," she informed me. "It's just as I said. You are a control freak."

Maria walked me back to the entrance, past the kitchen where the man was lighting a fresh cigarette. "My husband," she said fondly to his back. "I just can't get him to quit." She opened the door and touched my arm lightly in farewell. Then she rapidly drew her hand back, her dark eyes growing round as if she had glimpsed into Hades.

"Pauline!" Her grave tone bore little resemblance to her soft-spoken voice of earlier. "Beware of those in rags. There is much danger for you there."

6

The Scarlet Letter

One would think that after nearly twenty-four hours without rest, sleep would come quickly. But that was not to be the case. As I lay in the dark upon the narrow bed in my claustrophobically small room, my mind wouldn't stop racing. I thought about Maria's predictions, ticking them off one by one. That I would meet my soul mate. That he would be rich and tall. Though it all sounded nice, I couldn't help but think her act was staged. For example, her warning about danger from those in rags. That was a safe enough prediction in a major city fraught with street people. But I had to admit it was eerie that she knew about Fleur and my construction problems.

One more point in Maria's favor. I did have a need for control.

One against. I'd be damned if I was going anyplace cold.

A restless sleep finally descended on me and when I awoke, thin gray light had worked its way along the seam where the drapes met. The glowing numbers on the clock read six in the morning. This is generally an uncivilized hour for me, but knowing I wouldn't be able to get back to sleep, I got up and showered. Then I ordered some room service and called Elsa, the only other person I knew who would be awake. A confirmed insomniac,

Elsa Tower stays up into the wee hours of the night working and is back at her computer at dawn. Just recently a grandmother, her husband joked that their two now-grown children had been conceived in the only two hours they had shared in bed together since their marriage.

Elsa writes a society column for *Pipeline*, the rag the entire Gold Coast awaits with baited breath on Monday mornings, hoping to have gotten some good ink. It is Chicago's shiny sheet sans the shine. A little newsprint on the fingers holds no threat to Midwesterners. Having come from money herself, Elsa started writing her society pages as a butterball of a debutante at age eighteen, and so enjoyed it she carried the tradition into adulthood.

And though she's a very dear friend, one still has to be guarded around Elsa. She considers herself a journalist, but sometimes I think there is a bit of sadist in her that likes to see people squirm. A little round pixie who nearly always wears a hat, her impish appearance can be deceiving, often leading people to assume she is a kind person. And she can be one of the kindest people one could hope to meet—when it suits her. But cross her and one will discover that inside Elsa beats a malicious and vindictive heart. What one shares with Elsa one must be prepared to see later in black and white, though I do believe I am one of the few people who can tell Elsa a secret and have it remain so. But only after employing the caveat that "this is between us." Otherwise, she will consider whatever she is told to be fair game.

I met Elsa when I moved to Chicago from back East to marry Henry. She made such a fuss over us, one would have thought we were royalty. Elsa had a particular fondness for my husband. Perhaps it was his roguish good looks or his pedigree of being third-generation Cook, one of Chicago's most noted families. Or maybe it was just that he always had a good word and ready smile for everyone. Regardless, like nearly everyone else, Elsa held Henry in such high regard that it spilled over onto me. We had remained fast friends even after his death.

Elsa picked up on the second ring, always quick to grab the phone before some caller with a juicy tidbit could change his mind and hang up. She waxed enthusiastical at my return.

"Pauline, I'm so glad to hear your voice. Everyone's missed you terribly, though you haven't missed a thing at this end. It's been the doldrums until the last week or so. Thank God the holidays are upon us."

"That is easy for you to say, not being one of the homeless," I said.

"Whatever do you mean by that?"

I informed her of my construction crisis and the room shortage at local hotels. She sounded mortified. "Darling, come and stay with us. I hate to think of you holed up in a hotel room the entire month of December."

The only thing I could think of worse than my current twin-bedded situation would be sitting down to breakfast across from Elsa and Max in their Lincoln Park townhouse. Max has never had an opinion that he could keep to himself and I'm not sharp enough in the morning to guard myself around Elsa. It would be a free-flow of information.

"Thank you for the offer, but I'm going to move into a suite in a couple of days. I imagine I can tough it out until then. Besides, I really feel the need to stay where I can keep an eagle eye on my disaster area down the street."

"You poor dear," she sighed. And then, "What are you doing for lunch? I'm meeting Sunny and Marjorie at the Tavern Club. We'd love to have you join us."

Sunny Livermore and Marjorie Wilken were but two of the A-list members of Chicago society with whom I shared a frequent, but ofttimes uneasy, association. Arriviste Sunny's bourgeois upbringing could make her so stunningly boring at times that I wanted to die. Marjorie, while well-educated and from the finest of backgrounds, was such a lush that lunch could often be embarrassing. But no matter. Since I wasn't a member at the Tavern Club, no shame would be leveled upon me. Besides, lunching up high with a view of the city's skyline certainly beat being holed up in a hotel room with a view of the alley. I told Elsa I'd love to join them.

My next call was to Air France in search of my luggage. After four transfers, followed by fifteen minutes of "La Marseillaise," I finally connected with a sympathetic human who regretted terribly that Madame's luggage had been lost. She assured me that they were searching for it, and upon learning its status they would inform me *immédiatement*. I sighed and hung up, thinking forlornly of the three months of accumulated purchases I might never see again. I couldn't bear to think of the Dior gown.

✳   ✳   ✳

Over a Caesar salad, I recounted my overseas adventures and the more educational aspects of my trip, adding that a couple of months at sea can be
most helpful in distancing one from the travails of this postterrorist-attack
world. With Elsa's eagle ears in attendance, I had to be especially careful
what I said or risk reading next Monday:

> *What colorful widow has just returned from her tour of antiquity where she
> found things far warmer than those cold, hard marble statues?*

Instead of:

> *Just back from a tour of antiquity, Pauline Cook reports that two months is
> hardly an adequate amount of time to gain a full appreciation for what the
> Greeks contributed to our Western civilization.*

"And you were the only person on this yacht?" Elsa probed too know-
ingly, her cherub cheeks still rosy from the cold, her impish blue eyes alert
beneath a white mink crown, a hat that had come from a long-established
box on her closet shelf, no doubt. She wore her commitment to hats as faithfully as she wore the chapeaux themselves. They were her small attempt to
resurrect the style of an era sadly gone by the wayside.

"The only passenger," I corrected her. "There was crew, of course. I took
most of my meals with the captain, who was also an excellent docent, I
might add."

"I would think that might get a bit dull over two months. That is, unless
you had some other stimulation," said Elsa, shooting me an all-knowing
glance over the rim of her teacup.

"You'll have to give me the name of the charter company," an oblivious Sunny Livermore piped up as she poured more Perrier into her ice-filled
glass. She picked out the lemon floating in it and gave it a squeeze with her
unfashionably long fingernails. She was wearing a pink angora sweater with

a fur-trimmed collar and cuffs dyed to match her dark hair. The color was definitely at odds with her olive skin. A fall shouldn't wear pink. The sweater was stretched across her immense bosom like the skin on a grape. "I can't think of anything more stimulating than a personal tour. I think Nat would really enjoy something like that."

"Personally, I hate anything to do with water," Marjorie Wilken added dejectedly as she poured from her own bottle of Perrier. One of the worst dipsomaniacs I've ever had the pleasure to know, the only form of water that Marjorie usually took was in the shape of ice cubes. But before we sat down, Elsa had given me a whispered heads-up that Marjorie had finally quit drinking after doing something wretched enough to finally shame her into it. There hadn't been time to learn exactly what it was, but I did know that it had to be something particularly horrific. When one had the means that Marjorie and her husband had, one was practically immune to public opinion. Their marriage was very much in the French style. They had each enjoyed numerous affairs over the years, but they stayed together through it all. The fortune was not to be separated. It was to stay in the family. Oddly enough, Marjorie had gained weight since taking the pledge, and she looked the better for it. Her usually pinched cheeks had filled out, making her look a decade younger, though the gaps between the buttons of her silk blouse suggested she had best not put on another ounce. For the first time in ages, her hazel eyes were clear instead of pink. "I get bored to tears on water. Put me in a city anytime."

"Well, enough about travel," said Sunny. "It's time to talk about the Amici of the Literati gala. New Year's is a little over four weeks away and I still need to sell tables."

Oh, Lord, I thought. Had I known this lunch was about the Amici benefit I would have bowed out. A firm believer in richesse oblige, I was on the board and had contributed generously in the past to this foundation whose mission was to keep reading alive, not only among the proletariat but the upper crust as well. But in my post-Enron state, I was feeling the pinch, and the tables at the gala started at ten thousand dollars apiece, with sponsors' tables going for twenty-five. In her never-ending quest to elevate herself, Sunny had taken on the role of chairwoman for this year's gala, a private showing of *A Midsummer Night's Dream* in the Shakespeare Theater followed by dinner for five hundred at Navy Pier. I knew she would be looking for me to buy a table. I filled my mouth with a forkful of Caesar in hopes of staying out of the conversation.

"What about the unsinkable Mrs. Armstrong?" asked Marjorie. "Isn't she supposed to buy one of the sponsors' tables?"

"She is, but she's done a disappearing act. No one's been able to locate her. It's very strange. Besides the table, I really need her help. She's a co-chair of the decorating committee."

"Whitney Armstrong as a reading advocate is such a delicious oxymoron," said Marjorie, staring with disdain at her water glass.

"Tell me about it, she's in my book club," Sunny concurred, rolling her eyes in a superior manner.

"Whitney's in your book club?" I asked, nearly choking on a piece of romaine. Jack had mentioned Whitney had changed after joining a book club, but I didn't know it was Sunny's book club. I knew the women in that group, which included my downstairs neighbor, Joan Armitage, and none of them had ever said a good word about Whitney. Though they had plenty else to say about her.

"Jack called me and asked if she could join. He said he would pledge fifty thousand to the Amici. How could I say no? Luckily she's only shown up a few times. When she did, the things that came out of her mouth made me wonder if we had read the same book. Honestly, I have no idea what Jack sees there."

"The same two things we all see. And envy," Elsa said, always quick with witticisms.

"Well, Jack also asked that I put her on some committee for the Amici, so I put her on decorating. I figured what harm could that do? She could hang a few ribbons, pick out flowers, donate some more money, things like that. Then she goes and disappears. The woman is a total flake. I haven't talked to Jack, but according to that strange Indian houseboy of theirs, there's some illness in her family. Still, can you believe she would just run off without contacting anybody?"

"Hmmm," said Elsa. "Something is rotten in Denmark. Surrendra told *me* she had gone to the Palm Beach house to oversee the new landscaping."

"He should get his story straight," Sunny opined.

"I smell a rat," said Marjorie.

In keeping with my promise to Jack, I remained stone-silent. Elsa glanced around the table with that all-knowing look.

"My guess would be she's getting some work done. Why else would anyone vanish into thin air? Though I'm surprised she'd chance it this close to the holidays."

I could already see the words in *Pipeline*:

What glamorous blonde, already sharing conjugal bliss with a husband more dedicated than any we've seen in recent history, is so committed to keeping things right that she's off making sure everything stays high and tight? How's that for love?

"That was grueling," I said to Elsa the moment we hit the elevator after lunch. As I feared, Sunny spent the rest of the meal trying to enlist my services and my money for the Amici benefit. I finally agreed to help with the decorating committee, but only committed to buying two of the thousand-dollar tickets instead of a table. I could tell this irritated Sunny. I've served on enough boards to know the number-one caveat. Give, get, or get off. At present my finances were too compromised for the "give" part of the equation and I didn't have the energy for the "get." The "get off" was looking to be the most appealing option.

"So what did Marjorie do that finally got her to sober up?" We had all seen the various faces of Marjorie, from her use of language beyond the pale to falling asleep at state events—with her face buried in the potato gratin, no less. This had to be something that really stretched propriety to its limits.

"Well," said Elsa, a happily wicked smile adorning her face. "It seems that Harold Jr., "Hootie" they call him, brought a few friends home from Andover for a long weekend. There was lots of booze flowing and Marjorie got soused, as usual."

"Nothing new there," I commented.

"Yes, but after most of the party went upstairs to sleep, Marjorie and one of Hootie's little friends stayed up for a nightcap. And there they were the next morning with their arms entwined, stretched out in the altogether on the zebra rug in front of the fireplace."

I thought about a naked Marjorie and her son's equally naked college friend sprawled out upon the black and white stripes. Disgraceful. Yet impressive. There had to be a twenty-five-year difference between the two. I raised an impassive eyebrow.

"I've heard of worse," I said.

"It gets worse," Elsa countered with a wink. "The friend of Hootie with whom she was entangled happened to be his girlfriend."

"Ooooh, that is unfortunate," I said, cringing.

"Even I couldn't write about it," said Elsa, giving her mink-covered head a final shake as the elevator doors opened and we stepped out into the lobby.

7
Bleak House

After lunch, I decided to stop at my building for a fresh look at the war zone that was my home. As the taxi pulled up, I was surprised to see a bag lady had parked herself in the parkway beside the barren bushes. She was huddled under a mound of dirty old clothes and a length of plaid blanket, her face hidden by the rim of a filthy baseball cap. Rags, will you? Naturally the psychic's words came back to me. But this tragic bundle of humanity, while unsightly, didn't appear to be any threat. I rode the wind past her and into the lobby.

"Jeffrey," I said. "There's a strange woman outside on the curb."

"Is she back? I'm sorry, Mrs. Cook, she started coming around the other day, and she's peskier than a fly. I keep shooing her off and she keeps circling back. I'll take care of it right away."

He headed outside to sweep the woman from the sidewalk, and I headed up the elevator to my apartment. This time the doors opened onto a much calmer scene than they had the day before. Since it was a Saturday, the workmen's tools were idle and there was no music. I padded down the quiet halls and looked into each room.

Upon examination, things weren't as bad as I first thought. They were worse. The kitchen was a mere shell, the living and dining rooms ghosts under tarp, the bedrooms and baths a disaster. The room closest to completion was the master bathroom, and that was because not only did it have cabinets but the tub and shower had also been installed. As I stood in the center of the mirrorless room and studied the patched walls, a sense of hopelessness overwhelmed me. I walked back into the empty bedroom and stared at the space my bed normally occupied, where I would stretch out at night to read with Fleur purring contentedly upon my lap. I wanted life to return to what it had been before my trip. I wanted my home. I wanted my cat. I wanted my money.

Letting out a melancholy sigh, I headed back down the hall to the library to sort through the mail that had accumulated in my absence. Thankfully, the bills had been sent directly to my accountant while I was out of town, so there were no money matters to attend to. Christmas cards had already begun arriving, gold-leafed and engraved, many of them with family photos replacing the Madonna and child that had been the mainstay of my youth. There were also invitations to weddings and Christmas parties and fund-raisers. I accepted the best of the Christmas parties and declined all of the weddings, buying myself a year to present a gift, in which time half the couples would separate anyway, if history was any gauge. I declined all the fund-raisers with the exception of the Amici of the Literati gala, dutifully writing out a two-thousand-dollar check. I responded for two persons, both hoping to find an appropriate date and that my gown would have turned up by then.

A pink envelope yielded a card announcing the birth of Sandy St. Clair's first grandchild, Marie Caroline, seven pounds, three ounces. A photo of the baby was attached to a pink ribbon. As I looked at the infant's crinkled-up face, practically interchangeable with any other baby in the moments after birth, an unpleasant realization swept over me. My college roommate at Radcliffe, the woman I once shared clothes and secrets and boyfriends with, the woman who had married far, far better than I but had to put up with incessant philandering, was a grandmother. It was just one more thing to make me feel older than my fifty-one years. I gave Sandy St. Clair's wrinkled, hairless granddaughter a final look and hoped her parents would prepare little Marie Caroline for what was to come. Then I scribbled out a congratulatory note and put a reminder in my file to send a sterling silver teething ring from Tiffany's to the toothless creature.

Leaning back in my chair, in the shadow of Defoe and Milton and George Eliot, I felt completely disenfranchised. Here were all these people celebrating life-affirming events, marriages of their children, christenings of grandchildren, and I didn't even have my cat. I wondered if Henry and I had made a mistake by not having children.

It wasn't that we planned not to have children, but just the same we never really tried. As the only child of estranged parents, I thought of childhood as a lonely time. When I was five, my father nearly bankrupted us and then left Mother for a wealthy widow with a home in Palm Springs. One of the walking wounded, Mother would date men she cared little for, sometimes going off on trips with them for weeks, leaving me in our New York apartment in the care of our housekeeper. Grandmother had cut my mother off for marrying my father, and that didn't change after he left us, which forced Mother to often go begging to her for our very existence.

Though we managed to keep up the best of fronts, we were always sorely lacking when compared to those around us. Forced to buy my clothes at inexpensive shops, Mother would sew labels from Bergdorf Goodman or Saks Fifth Avenue into the garments so the girls at Foxcroft, and later Radcliffe, wouldn't know my shame. I don't know if it was because my green eyes reminded her too much of my father, but she often seemed angry with me for no good reason. It wasn't until she was sick and dying that she relented and gave me the love she had withheld from me as a child. But by then the breast cancer had destroyed her, and it was too late. I was twenty-three when she died.

I met Henry Hamilton Cook III the next year. Growing up in a strong, loving midwestern family, rich enough so that the money spread like creamery butter between heirs, he accepted my selfish ways and understood them. From the very day we met at a party in the Hamptons, things between us had clicked, and we seldom spent a day apart afterward. He called me his Scarlett O'Hara, down to the green eyes, all backbone and no fluff. I suppose that did describe me. I asked nothing of anyone and had little patience for falsity, which was why my own circle so often irritated me.

Though my marriage had been exceedingly happy, that hardly made up for the fact that at thirty-nine I was suddenly left alone. Thankfully the last stages of brain cancer are swift, but the steps up to the demise are frightening. Getting lost in the house, forgetting the simplest of words, unable to remember how to drive or, worst of all, one's wife's name. Not to mention making a series of financial mistakes that had left me nearly destitute upon his death. Thankfully, I had been saved from the throes of that black death when a friend left me a substantial fortune.

But now my life had come full circle again. I was alone and in a financial undertow. Like trying to grip glass with one's fingernails, I was back on the slow slide to poverty.

Suddenly, it was all too much. The stiff upper lip I so prided myself on began to quiver and then cracked. My eyes welled with nasty tears that spilled onto my cheeks in drops at first, but soon grew into rivulets. Before long, my body was heaving with massive sobs. Like a child having a temper tantrum, I pounded the desk with my fists and screamed out at the injustice of it all. After finally exhausting myself, I laid my head on the desk with my right cheek flattened against the wood, waiting for my breathing to return to normal.

The sound of footsteps coming down the hall nearly caused me to jump out of my skin. I bolted upright to see Mr. McKay standing in the doorway. At least I was fairly certain it was Mr. McKay, though I couldn't have sworn to it, he looked so different from the man in my master bathroom the day before. He had cleaned himself up, his shoulder-length hair a shining brown and his face both clean-shaven and spatter-free. But it had to be him. His height gave him away.

I swiveled my chair around so that my back was to him, and wiped my eyes with my hands. I was humiliated that a paid employee should see me in such a state, even if he was, in part, to blame for it. "Haven't you ever been told it's not polite to sneak up on people?" I said with my back still to him, trying very hard not to sniff as I pulled a handkerchief from my purse. Giving my face a final dab, I blew my nose and turned to face him.

"I'm sorry to disturb you. I called out, but I guess you didn't hear me. I just came over to pick up some specs I left in the bathroom." He looked at me studiously. "Are you alright?"

The breath I released turned fatalistic. "I imagine so. It's just that . . . it's just that . . . " and then I lost it altogether. "It's just that I want to come home." Once the words were out, the tears came again, flowing like lava from Mount Vesuvius. He stood awkwardly in front of me as if he had been hewn from stone, a mute witness to my breakdown. I was reminding myself of Jack Armstrong at the Astor Street mansion the day before.

"Look," he said when I had finally calmed enough to hear him speak, "if you're really that freaked out, I'll see what I can do about speeding things up here. Maybe I could even get you back in for Christmas."

A ray of light cracked the gloomy horizon. My tears slowed. Though carols and punch were out of the question, there was the possibility I might ring in the New Year in my own residence.

"That would help immensely," I sniveled, embarrassed but encouraged.

"I'll put a few extra guys on and we'll bang this out as fast as humanly possible. But I gotta warn you, it'll cost you a lot more."

"Money is no object," I lied, smiling through my tears. "Just get it done."

After he left, I felt better. Maybe the cry had been cathartic, but a new determination sprung alive in me. There would be no more crocodile tears cried by Pauline Cook. I was a woman in my prime—well, sub-prime—and I was capable of taking care of myself. I thought about Jack Armstrong's offer. If money were no object, as I had told Mr. McKay, then I had to have more of it. And like the proverbial thousand lawyers at the bottom of the ocean, five million dollars would be a good start.

8

Common Sense

I awoke at seven in the morning to the sound of a ringing phone. My irritation at being awakened at such an ungodly hour was lessened by the French-accented voice of an Air France agent telling me that my luggage had been located. However, my irritation returned when she informed me that for some unknown reason, the bags were in Singapore. They were being sent back to Paris and from there she guaranteed they would be placed on the first flight to Chicago. She apologized for my regrettable experience with Air France and hoped that I would still consider them in my future travels. Though it was discouraging that my bags weren't even in the Western Hemisphere, I hung up with new hope that my Dior gown would show up in this lifetime.

Shaking myself the rest of the way awake, I recalled my new mission in life—to find Whitney and Fleur and collect Jack's five million dollars. The question was where to begin looking for a missing person, especially one who might not want to be found. I decided I needed some kind of professional advice, the sort one might receive from a police official. I only knew of one person in this line of employment, a very coarse and off-putting homicide detective named Jerry Malloy. We had met the year prior when he was investigating the possible murder of a friend, and though it was a vast understatement to say he was crude, he had proved to be adept in his business. He had given me his card back then, and told me to keep it in my wallet in case I ever got into a jam—his words, not mine. Figuring this could be considered as much a jam as anything, I unearthed his card and tried reaching him at Area Three headquarters. A recording told me he wasn't in, but he had written his cell phone number on the back of the card, so I tried that number next.

The sound of a football game in the background told me I had reached him either at home or at a bar.

"This is *who*?" he asked after I had given him my name. Evidently I had not left as indelible an impression on him as he had on me. I attempted to jog his memory.

"Pauline Cook. I was a friend of Ethan Campbell. Do you remember now?"

There was silence as he opened his mental address book. I envisioned him the way he looked upon my first encounter with him, dressed entirely in black, his murky green eyes staring out at me from a pockmarked face framed with thinning brown hair. If he wasn't smoking a cigarette at the moment, he was pursing his full lips as if he were. I was beginning to lose faith in our paid protectorate as I waited for him to place me. After all, how many other women have brightened the interior of that dingy police station with peach Escada. Then I could almost hear the lightbulb pop up over his head. "Did youse say you were Pauline Cook?"

"That I did," I replied.

"Tall redhead. Snappy dresser. You live on LSD East, right? In that fancy joint with the four-way views."

"That is correct," I confirmed, although I didn't think he would find my "joint" so fancy in its current state. But I was glad that my peach Escada had not gone unnoticed after all. I had paid a fortune for the suit.

"What's up, Pauline? Another friend croak himself?"

Normally I would have been appalled at such callousness, but such was the nature of this particular beast, and I needed him. "No, another friend has not suffered an unfortunate death, thank you. But a very dear friend has disappeared and I thought perhaps you might be of some assistance in helping me find her."

"Ain't my department, Pauline. You need to speak to missing persons."

"This isn't your typical missing persons situation. I'm fairly certain she's missing on purpose. It's a rather long story, but to get to the point, you are the only policeman I know and I was hoping you could spare me a bit of your time."

"I'd love to help youse out here, Pauline, but homicide ain't exactly no picnic like auto theft or B and E, and my time's at a premium. Why don't'cha hire a private dick?"

"This is a situation that needs to be handled discreetly. I just need some advice. Would it be possible that I buy you lunch tomorrow? You do eat lunch, don't you?"

His voice perked up. "Lunch? Where were you thinking?"

"Your choice, Detective. Wherever and whenever is convenient for you."

There was a pause and the sound of an exhaled breath told me he had just lit a cigarette. Then I heard the roar of a crowd. So he was in a bar. "Tell you what," he said. "I gotta be in the Loop tomorrow to give a deposition. Should be done bout twelve. How's about the Italian Village?"

A perfect choice, I thought. The restaurant was an institution in the Loop, a rarity in these days of rapid change. In its third generation of stewardship by the same family, it consisted of three separate restaurants, two moderately priced, the third expensive.

"Shall I make a reservation at the Village then?" I asked, referring to one of the less expensive restaurants.

"I was thinking more like dat fancy restaurant dere."

"Vivere. Very well. I'll make a reservation for noon then." I hung up wondering why a homicide cop preferred a gourmet lunch to spaghetti and meatballs at a fraction of the price. But as he was my sole connection to the dark side of life, if he was able to help me locate Whitney, then the investment would pay back many times over.

Though it is generally not my practice to arrive anyplace on time, the next day found me arriving at the Monroe Street restaurant at a quarter to twelve.

I didn't want to risk losing my guest by not being present upon his arrival. But he was already there and was standing on the sidewalk in front of the restaurant, delivering a last fix of nicotine before entering the smoke-free zone inside. The wind funneled between the buildings was so strong it felt it might blow the hair off my head, so I went inside the revolving doors to wait for him. He spun through a minute later, his black leather jacket unzipped as if it were a mild spring day.

We stepped into the terrazzo-tiled foyer of Vivere. The high-ceilinged restaurant was decorated in a manner that combined elegant materials with high-tech style, giving one the sense of being in an Italian spaceship. Fred, the ever-present maître d' and one of the few in the city who still recognized the importance of his customers, greeted me by name. He seated us in a two-person booth where we could speak freely, away from any prying ears at nearby tables. Fred handed us menus and a wine list the size of the Bible before discreetly disappearing.

Detective Malloy picked up the wine list, and I gulped as he opened it to the Brunellos. "What's dis? A wine for five hundred bucks? Marone. Too bad I can't drink on the job."

"That is a shame," I lied, greatly relieved.

He slapped the wine list shut and switched to his menu. After perusing it quickly, he closed it and announced, "I don't know about you, but I'm starving." He stuck his hand out and brushed the sleeve of a passing waiter. "Hey, could we get some service here?" The waiter graciously ignored the slight and took out his pad. We ordered, he the osso buco and a Coke, I the grilled sea bass and a glass of Soave. The waiter left, and I turned directly to business, explaining that a good friend was missing, along with her dogs and my cat, and that I desperately needed to find her in order to find my cat. His first question was the obvious one.

"What about her husband? Why ain't he the one asking these questions?"

"They fought. He thinks that's the reason she left and that she's still mad. He wants to apologize and would be eternally grateful if I could find her."

He cocked an all-knowing eyebrow. "Yeah, he'd be grateful all right. Does the guy got any dough?"

"Quite a bit of it, in fact."

"Den she ain't around no more to find. Take my word for it."

"I beg your pardon?"

"Look'it, Pauline," he said, pouring a liberal amount of olive oil onto his bread plate and dredging a piece of focaccia in it. He stuffed the bread in his mouth and gave it a few rudimentary chews before continuing, gracing me with a partial view of his food as he spoke. "He's got a lot of money and she up and leaves? Never happens . . . never. She ain't going to leave where her bread's buttered. Now she might leave him in the visible way, you know, file for divorce and all. But to go off without a trace? Unheard of. He's offed her."

He was so adamant, it gave me pause. Then I recalled how grief-stricken Jack Armstrong was. Enough to offer me five million dollars to find his wife. "I don't believe that is the case," I retorted.

"Lemme repeat. He's got a lot of money?"

I nodded.

"Then she's dead. And so are the dogs, no doubt, and your cat. Probably couldn't stand having them around either. I'm just surprised whoever this guy is hasn't filed a missing persons yet. They usually do, and then they're all weepy and they're like, 'Oh, I miss her so much, where could she be, how could this be happening,' when on the side they've got a little number half their age with big tits and a tight ass and lungs that could suck a . . . well never mind. You get the picture."

"How could I not get the picture, you draw it so vividly. But I can assure you, there is no other woman in this case."

He nodded complacently as if he were placating a child. "Yah, yah. Who is this guy, anyway? Maybe I should be talking to him."

"I'd rather not say. I've promised him I'd be discreet."

He tented his fingers and pressed them to his lips, leveling me with his eyebrows. Then he gave me an ironic smile. "Right. Just as well anyway. We're up to our eyeballs in shit as it is."

The waiter brought two salads, and Detective Malloy started eating at a pace that exhausted me to watch. I layered a few pieces of green onto my salad fork and had barely taken a bite before he'd consumed his entire salad.

I stopped eating and rested my fork on my plate. "Tell me this. If you were to start looking for someone who might not want to be found, where would you start?"

"Like I already told you, Pauline, I'm not missing persons. But a real good start would be her family. Lots of women go and hide out dere. Do you know anything about her people?"

"Very little," I replied. In fact I knew next to nothing. Once she had made reference to being raised in Houston and that her father had worked on an oil rig, but that her early upbringing had been hardscrabble. She'd never said anything more than this.

"Well, I'd find dem first. Den you might consider gettin' her phone records. Especially cell phone. You can learn a lot about a person from who dey call. In fact, if I'm wrong and this babe's not dead, den she's having an affair. The records would show her calling him a lot. Dese unrequited lovers—they just can't get enough. Dey can't help talking to each other about a hundred times a day. Then they wonder why they get caught."

"Where can I get her cell phone records?"

"Well, if it's true like you said and the husband is so concerned, I'd start with him. He's paying all the bills, right? In fact, he should be happy to hand them over to you."

The food arrived and he dug in. He might have been just as well served with a shovel as a fork, eating vigorously with nary a word between bites. Thank the lord. I'd hate to imagine the visual had he opted to speak. I picked at my fish and contemplated what he had said about Jack Armstrong. I simply couldn't picture Jack doing any harm to Whitney. But the detective's idea to get the phone records seemed a good suggestion. The question was how to get those records. Did I go directly to Jack Armstrong and ask for them? He'd want to know why, and what if we looked at them together and found out she did have a boyfriend? Jack was already tormented enough. Besides, if he used the records to find Whitney himself, that might preclude me from receiving the reward. There had to be a way to get those records without Jack knowing about it.

Detective Malloy had taken a break from eating and was staring at me.

"Sorry to be such poor company," he said, wiping his face with his napkin.

"I was starved. It's already been one hell of a day. Dis morning had a guy in pieces in a Dumpster. Reeked like hell. Must'a been dere since Friday night. I gotta tell you dis story. Everyone's standin' around holdin' der noses, and Bill Spector, the lead on the case, wants to know if anybody can make the guy. So Spec—he's wearing gloves, of course—picks the head up by its ponytail and holds it up for everyone to see. This guy is one ugly son of a bitch. He asks if anyone knows who he was. Everybody shakes der heads. Nope. Don't know the guy. Never seen him."

The direction the conversation had taken was not doing much for my appetite, but what could I do? This was, after all, my guest. He turned his attention back to his osso buco, cutting into it so deeply that the knife scraped the bone. He stabbed a piece of meat with his fork and raised it to his lips. Then he started laughing so hard he had to put it back down on his plate.

"So Spec puts the head back into the can and what happens next? One of da vice guys goes, 'Hey, wait a minute, lemme have another look.' So Spec holds the head up again and O'Reilly stares at it like he's really contemplating. Then he goes, 'Nah, never mind. Guy I knew was taller.' "

He continued to laugh at his gallows humor until he noticed I hadn't even cracked a smile.

"You mean you don't find dat funny?" he asked, as if anyone who didn't find a severed head amusing should have their own still intact one examined.

"Oh, I think it's a perfect anecdote for my next cocktail party." Upon realizing he didn't get the irony, I added, "Actually, I find it repulsive."

His smile withered, and his tone changed abruptly. "Murder is repulsive, Pauline. And you want to know somethin'? I think if you really want to find your friend, forget about her family, forget about da phone records. You'd do better looking in trash cans."

With that he proceeded to finish off his lunch.

9
Great Expectations

My mind was riveted on Jerry Malloy's words the entire cab ride back to my co-op for the afternoon progress check. With each curbside trash can we passed, I couldn't help but think of Whitney. Up until this point, it had never occurred to me that Jack might have had something to do with her disappearance. After all, he'd been out of town the night she left, so how could he have possibly done it?

Then a disturbing notion occurred to me in a twelve-carat flash of canary-yellow diamond. Whitney's Harry Winston ring. It could be quite irritating the way she would rest her left hand on a table or gesture just a little too long in front of a waiter to be certain everyone saw it. Knowing how much she adored that ring, and how much it was worth, it made no sense that she would leave it behind. Maybe it had been left behind for her. The notion began to congeal like aspic on duck confit. Maybe Jack had been so generous in offering me five million dollars to find Whitney because it was money he knew he would never have to pay.

The taxi pulled under the porte cochere, and Tony Papanapoulous sauntered out to greet it. Tony was my least favorite of the co-op's doormen, a huge creature whose thick head of black hair covered a thicker mind beneath it. In fact, the man was so obtuse it made one question the entire legacy of the Greeks. Though entirely well-meaning, he had a knack for frequently doing or saying the inappropriate. At the moment, his gaffe was holding the taxi door wide open in the mach-three gale with a double-digit below-zero wind chill while the driver rummaged through his pockets in search of change for my twenty-dollar bill. I nearly snapped at him to shut the door until I was ready, but then I remembered how difficult it had been for the board to find him in the first place, doormen in general being in short supply. I didn't want to be the one to cause his leave-taking, no matter how miserable the service.

"Thank you, Tony," I managed through clenched teeth after the driver unearthed an envelope packed with dollar bills from somewhere deep within the glovebox, and counted out fourteen of them one by one. I got out of the cab and he rushed ahead of me to open the door. I blew into the lobby and was headed straight to the elevator when I remembered the call from Air France. "Tony, I'm expecting a delivery of luggage from Air France sometime in the near future. When it arrives, please have it sent to the Drake."

"Yes, Mrs. C.," he said. "I'll be sure to take care of it."

He followed me to the elevator and pushed the penthouse button. I was feeling optimistic that I would disembark to magical happenings of the sort that would see me happily ensconced in my home before Christmas. By then Fleur would be back with me, curled in my lap on the chenille sofa in front of my glistening tree, purring while I sipped a glass of wine and listened to "Greensleeves."

The door opened into the private foyer, and my ears were met with a most unwelcome silence. No saws. No hammers. Not even any mildly irritating Eastern European music. I checked my Cartier. It was past two o'clock. Was it possible the workers were still on their lunch break?

I walked through the apartment. The wires still hung from the ceiling in the same colorful twists as before, and the ladders stood vacant. A length of crown molding came to an abrupt end like an uncompleted span of bridge. Nothing had been touched since Saturday.

A bang from down the hall indicated some life within. I walked back to the master bedroom suite and found Mr. McKay once again on the bathroom floor, fussing with the same cabinet he had been working on the day of our first encounter.

I cleared my throat loudly.

"Oh, hi," he said simply, glancing up for a fraction of a second before turning his attention back to the cabinet.

"Mr. McKay, what's going on here? Where are all the workers you promised? I expected to see some progress."

He didn't answer, but continued banging at the cabinet door with his fist until it swung shut. "Ah, got it," he cried victoriously, opening and closing the door several times. "These European hinges can be a bitch." He wiped his sawdust-covered hands on his pants and stood up to face me. Once again, I found myself staring down at him. "I'm afraid there's been a little setback, Pauline."

"Setback?"

He coughed into his hand. "Uh, yeah. I've lost my subs."

"I don't understand."

"The subs. The guys who were doing the tile work and the electric and the carpentry. They got hired off to another job. Son of a bitch, O'Hallaran, bribed 'em to help him meet a deadline. There was nothing I could do."

"But don't they work for you?"

"No. They're subs. Subcontractors. They work for whoever they feel like."

"So where are the people who work for you?"

"You're looking at them. For now. But don't worry, I'm working on getting some more subs in here soon. Things are always changing in this business."

I was overwhelmed with disbelief. In our last conversation, Tag McKay had promised to bring in as many warm bodies as humanly possible and they were going to hammer this job out. Instead I was looking at one man with a screwdriver who had just spent fifteen minutes getting a cabinet door to close.

"All I know is that you promised you would get this job done for me as quickly as possible. I told you money is no object, now go hire some people," I commanded. I huffed back down the hall, past the idle tools, past the taped walls, through the hanging plastic sheet, and into my library. I sat down at my desk and placed a call to my decorator. It was answered by Raoul Simone, Bharrie's partner in both business and life. Tall and square-jawed, with a dimpled smile and blue-eyed charm, Raoul was a divinely gorgeous Argentine who reduced women to tears when they learned he was gay. Decorator or no, loss of him from the dating pool was a definite travesty. Raoul was not only the masculine side of the partnership, he also happened to be the business half. Under normal circumstances I would have exchanged pleasantries with Raoul, but my mood was far from pleasant. I asked to speak to Bharrie immediately.

"He's not here, Pauline," oozed the smooth Spanish-accented voice, "but you can reach him on his mobile."

"Thank you," I said, preparing to hang up.

"Wait, Pauline . . . I'm glad you called. We've got several outstanding invoices here that need to be taken care of. They're quite substantial."

"Just send them to me," I said, hanging up before he could say anything more. I called Bharrie on his cell phone.

"*Pronto!*" he answered as if he was in the heart of Tuscany and not the frigid American Midwest.

"Bharrie, that man has got to go. Do you realize he is working on my apartment all alone? Alone! He's lost all his subordinates."

Bharrie's jaunty tone changed significantly. "Pauline, calm down. I've already spoken to him. He's working on getting some new ones. The word is subcontractors, by the way."

"I don't care if it's submarines. I can't stand the man. He's arrogant and offensive and I'm going to fire him."

"DON'T FIRE HIM," Bharrie commanded in a voice so contrary to his usual obsequious self, it even took me by surprise. "We don't have anyone else. Look, I'll come over and we can talk about it. Just don't fire him."

My blood was boiling. "I refuse to stay here in this mess. Meet me in the Drake lobby at the Palm Court."

"Even better," he said. "I'll be there in ten minutes."

Afraid of what I might do should I see Mr. McKay again before talking with Bharrie, I left the apartment without saying good-bye. Down in the lobby, Tony was engaged in deep conversation with a deliveryman. He greeted me once again jovially. "Mrs. C., you going so soon?" I was never quite certain if he called me Mrs. C. as an attempt to sound friendly or because he wasn't quite certain of my last name.

"Not soon enough, unfortunately." I crossed the room in anger-fueled haste and banged through the door. Tony followed me outside. The bag lady was back on the parkway, hunkered down beneath her tent of clothing, a puff of steam emitting from her mouth with each breath so that she appeared to be smoking. I stopped in my tracks. "That woman is back."

"I know. I've told her a bunch of times to move, but she just won't go."

"Well, call the police or the fire department or something. Just move her along." As I started to walk away, an idea occurred to me. I reached into my wallet and took out a five-dollar bill. Then I changed it for a ten. "Here, give her this and tell her to get a cup of coffee."

Then I left the building, throwing myself at the mercy of the wind, which practically carried me down the street to the Drake.

The calming influence of palm trees in the dead of winter should never be overlooked. I would suggest that therapists in northern climes install several of the plants in their offices if they haven't already. And a harp player while they're at it. Between the gardenlike atmosphere of the room and the strains of Vivaldi's *Spring*, by the time Bharrie arrived I was feeling far more human. And humane. Humane enough to listen to Bharrie tell me why I shouldn't fire my inept contractor. The sad fact was there were no other contractors available at present. I agreed we could retain him for the time being.

With that issue settled, my mind circled back to my larger mission. Though Jack had asked me to be discreet, I had to start somewhere, and I knew Bharrie could be a good source of information. Plus he was known for keeping his mouth shut. He had decorated many a Gold Coast home, and I'd never heard him mention word one about any of his clients—a trait that Elsa found maddening since he probably had collected a treasure trove of intelligentsia.

Bharrie had decorated the Armstrong mansion, and his relationship with Whitney ran deeper than that of decorator/client. He was often seen in tow when Whitney went off on her shopping excursions, acting as her personal style arbiter. He was the one responsible for steering her from skin-revealing Jean Paul Gaultier toward elegant Mainbocher. She had even treated him with buying trips to Milan and Paris. I often wondered if Bharrie had any idea how much the two of them had in common. Or used to have.

"What do you hear from Whitney lately?" I tossed out lightly, sipping a fragrant cup of chamomile from a fragile china teacup.

Bharrie's eyes bugged out in their trademark manner, and he coughed after swallowing his espresso too quickly. He recovered and made an irritated face. "I'd like to hear anything from Whitney, thank you ever so much. Do you happen to know where she is?"

"You mean you don't?"

A master at the art of expressing indignation through body language, Bharrie shook his head, crossing and recrossing his legs petulantly. "All I know is she stood me up last week and hasn't even called to apologize. She was supposed to meet me at the Mart to look at period pieces—we've been working on the Palm Beach house remodel. We were envisioning a sort of Florida empire look. Anyhow, she never showed and she never called to cancel or anything. I'm still getting over it. There I was standing in Holly Hunt looking like the girl being stood up for the prom. And in front of John Scaparetti on top of it, who had come into town especially to show us his fabrics. When I called her house Surrendra told me she was out of town and that he'd have her call me when she got back."

"And you've heard nothing from her since?"

"Not a peep," he huffed. "I don't know if I'll ever forgive her for making me look like the village idiot. I was embarrassed as hell. Imagine, my client doesn't even tell me she's going out of town after I go to all this trouble. I mean, can't you pick up a cell phone?" He took a final swig of his espresso.

"Bharrie, I'm going to tell you something, but this has to remain between us."

He crossed his chest in an exaggerated X and said, "I've already forgotten it."

"Whitney's missing. She's left Jack. I know you two are close. I thought you might have some idea where she's gone."

"Whitney's missing?"

"Let me put it this way. She and Jack fought and she left. She took those damn Yorkies, and my Fleur, and disappeared into the night. Jack hasn't heard a word from her since."

"My God," he exclaimed, sitting back in his chair. "I had no idea. Here I thought she'd run off to some spa. Or blown me off for some other decorator and didn't have the nerve to tell me. That sort of thing has happened before." His eyes drifted to the right momentarily as he revisited some past slight. He turned them back toward me. "I can't believe she'd just up and leave Jack. I've never seen anyone so dedicated to a man."

"So you don't think there could be someone else?" I asked him.

"Pauline, if Whitney has someone on the side, then she is without doubt the best actress I've ever seen. The woman dotes on Jack. I've been with her in Milan with the most gorgeous Italian stallions just drooling all over her, and she could be in a nunnery for the attention she pays them. I'd love to just pick up on her leftovers . . . don't ever tell Raoul I said that."

"So what do you suppose happened to her?"

Bharrie sat back in his chair and crossed his arms in thought. Then the look on his face changed to one of enlightenment. He pursed his lips and his head bobbed up and down on his spindly neck.

"The week before she stood me up we had a meeting and she was totally moody, really unlike herself. She was distracted. I showed her some things she would usually go ga-ga over, and it was as if she didn't even see them. Like it didn't matter that she could get her hands on a couple of vases that had originally been in Vizcaya. She even told me she thought they were frivolous. A waste of money. She was so weird, I just thought it might be her time of the month, if you know what I mean."

Of course, I knew Whitney didn't have a time of the month, but evidently Bharrie didn't. The very thought of Whitney finding something expensive frivolous struck me as odd. This was a woman who bought entire lines of shoes in every color with each new season, and then threw them out at the end of the season to make way for more. Who bought diamond-studded leashes for her Yorkies. Who had at least two appointments a day concerning her personal appearance. She told me once she calculated she spent over ten thousand dollars a month on maintenance. And that didn't even begin to touch her clothes.

"And then," he added, "we went to lunch, and when she came back from the bathroom I could tell she had been crying."

"Did you ask her about it?"

"No, and now I wish I had." His eyes grew wide behind the red frames of his glasses. "Pauline, there have been some rumors going around about Verry Lingerie being in financial trouble. Do you think that could have anything to do with it?"

Now this was news to me. I couldn't fathom that Verry Lingerie was in trouble. Not when Verry had outlets in just about every mall in the country, not to mention a highly lucrative catalogue business.

I hoped this didn't mean Jack wouldn't have a spare five million dollars, because when I found Whitney, I intended to collect.

10

The Republic

The next week and a half flew past faster than Doris Duke spent money. Work on the Amici benefit was taking up more of my time than I liked, but it helped fill the void left by Fleur's absence. I asked around about Whitney as discreetly as I could, learning that she had been almost hermitlike in the weeks before her disappearance, canceling all her lunch and dinner engagements and even failing to show up for her standing appointment with Rene, the colorist who kept her blond hair so perfectly platinum. Maybe there was a lover in the picture after all, and that was where she had been spending her time before her departure. Though I hadn't acted on Detective Malloy's suggestion about getting Whitney's phone records, I realized that should probably be the next step. But ever since the germ had been planted in my mind that Jack might have had something to do with Whitney's disappearance, I had shied away from asking him.

I kept my visits to the co-op to a minimum and only when Bharrie accompanied me. Mr. McKay had an uncanny knack for raising my dander, and I couldn't trust myself not to fire him. He had put together another skeletal crew, and the work was plodding along. The bills were coming in, too, rivaling what Louis XIV had spent on Versailles. Unable to avoid Raoul's pesky phone calls, I had written a check for slightly under two hundred thousand dollars to Raoul Bharrie and Associates to cover antiques and cabinetry and their decorating fees thus far. I had yet to see a bill from Mr. McKay.

Air France continued to treat me with utmost civility each time I called to check on my missing luggage. For some reason, now my bags had been diverted to Tahiti, but mademoiselle assured me that things had *finalement* been straightened out and they should be arriving in Chicago *toute suite*. I reminded both Jeffrey and Tony to keep an eye out for them and to alert the other doormen as well.

Though I had sworn off fund-raisers, I broke down and bought a ticket to a Republican fund-raiser taking place at the Drake that week. I have no political affiliation and find politics to be dreadfully boring, not to mention Mr. Bush, the younger, a bit obtuse, but the room would be swarming with men of power and power is always sexy, not to mention frequently accompanied by vast amounts of money. Some of it even made honestly.

When the Wednesday of the fund-raiser arrived and my luggage still had not, I rushed over to Neiman's and picked up something low-cut and black. That evening, after shaking my breasts into my push-up bra to obtain the desired cleavage, I assessed the results in the full-length bathroom mirror. With my hair in an updo and my legs endless in three-inch heels, even the staunchest of Republicans would have trouble resisting me. I headed down to the reception confident that my thousand-dollar investment would turn out to be a good one.

As the elevator light clicked off, floor after floor, I mused how most women balked at attending social events unescorted. While I'm not terribly fond of showing up alone, the very thought of dredging up a date sends me into apoplexy. Besides, it sends out an "attached" message to any single, widowed, divorced, or soon-to-be-divorced men in the crowd who might otherwise be interested. Once in a while I'll borrow a friend from Bharrie, but only if he's flamingly gay. The one thing I refuse to do is bring another woman. Nothing screams desperation louder.

When I got to the reception, the line at the coat check looked like someone had opened every cage in the Lincoln Park Zoo. With so much fur gathered in one place, the days of the Republican cloth coat appeared to be left far behind. I worked my way through the well-dressed crowd and retrieved my table card from the welcome desk. Then I went into the ballroom.

The noise in the room was deafening—as was to be expected where Scotch, vodka, and wine flowed like the headwaters of the Mississippi. Standing by myself, I scanned the room for a familiar face and spotted Suzanne Free Worthington, the former concierge of the Drake and a fellow Amici board member. Slim and blue-eyed, with thick blond hair styled in a blunt cut that tapered down her strong jawline, she hailed from London and had come to this country to work as the concierge at the Drake. Since marrying Dexter Worthington Jr., she was seldom seen in her former place of employ anymore. I imagine it reminded her too much of her earlier plebeian times. Arguably one of the most eligible bachelors in the city before marrying Suzanne, Dexter Jr. had graced the cover of *Chicago Social* as the man most likely to be stalked by twentysomethings. They had met when he stopped at the concierge desk to ask where an event was being held. The rest is history. There is so much to be said for good timing.

Of course, Suzanne would be in attendance this evening. As the city's preeminent Republicans, all Worthingtons showed up on deck when the party called. She looked stunning in violet Valentino, dressed in the manner of one who not only knows how to dress but can afford to. One of the parvenu who could handle money with grace, Suzanne had made the leap from cubic zirconia to marquise diamonds and wasn't looking back.

Not that the Worthington fortune was in any way parvenu. With Dexter Jr., the Worthington money was headed into its fourth generation. The empire had started with a New England textile company, but it had been expanded into a conglomerate that manufactured everything from blue jeans to men's skivvies to women's wear. Dexter Worthington Sr. was a permanent fixture on the Forbes 400 list, and Junior wasn't far behind.

Suzanne saw me looking at her and worked her way across the crowd to speak to me. "Pauline, what a wonderful surprise," she said in her refined British accent. "I didn't know you would be here."

"I only decided to attend the other day. Since this is practically my living room I couldn't pass it up."

"Your living room?"

I explained my construction difficulties, and she was understandably sympathetic. At that point a couple of the GOP leaders walked up, and Suzanne's attention was distracted. I turned to walk away, but she reached through the crowd to catch my sleeve.

"Wait, Pauline. Where are you sitting?"

I took my place card from my purse and glanced at it as if for the first time. "I'm at table forty," I said, which I knew was in the hinterlands. That was all a thousand-dollar last-minute purchase merited.

She grabbed the card from my hand and tore it in two. "You must sit with us. Table three. Dex Sr. bought the entire table, and he wasn't able to come, so we have an extra seat. Please join us."

After acquiescing to take a seat I wouldn't have turned down under any circumstances, I peeled off to mingle. As I rotated in and out of the crowd, the conversations were one-dimensional as nerves remained raw over 9/11 and the position of the United States in our postterrorist world. There was talk of the swift victory in Afghanistan and how the apprehension of Osama bin Laden was guaranteed to be next. There was some grumbling about a possible war in Iraq, which I found laughable. A far more distressing topic that kept coming up was the bankruptcy of Enron, officially declared the week before. The drained corpse had been put to rest.

Dinner was called and I was delighted to see there were two single men seated at the Worthington table. Much to my dismay, Suzanne patted the empty place next to her. "Pauline, please come sit with me. We can catch up." There was another open seat next to her husband, Dexter Jr., who was looking duly Republican with his wire-rimmed glasses and close-cropped dark hair. I would have far preferred to sit there since that would have put me between him and a very handsome man. But, after all, Suzanne had invited me to join them, and jilting her at her own table wouldn't have been sporting. I sat down next to her, rounding my shoulders ever so slightly to add depth to my cleavage for the benefit of the men at the table.

"Who else is missing?" I asked Suzanne, indicating the open seat next to Dexter.

"Oh, that was going to be for Senior's latest. But she's been painted out of the picture, thankfully."

"How so?"

The words out of her mouth were contrary to her white-teethed, even-lipped smile. "Senior caught her in bed with her fitness instructor. He didn't feel he should be paying to have her work those muscles."

"That will do it every time," I agreed.

Dinner was served, an enormous piece of beef (it was a Republican fundraiser, after all), runny mashed potatoes, and overcooked vegetables. I calculated each bite cost me about fifty dollars. I made small talk with the man seated on the other side of me, an investment banker who felt as soon as we finished with Afghanistan we should move on to Iraq and blow them all to their final reward. Our conversation was interrupted when the speeches started. They were frighteningly xenophobic, and even more insufferably tough than the beef. The country had changed indeed. Personally, my political strategy is to vote against whoever is in power. That was what Henry had always believed to be the wisest strategy, saying it was best to keep the two parties at each other's throats and away from ours. I tuned out the unpleasantness and sipped at the wine. When there was a break for dessert service, Suzanne and I had a chance to talk.

"Are you coming to the Amici gala on New Year's?" she asked.

"I bought two tickets, though I'm not sure who I'm bringing. I'm helping out with decorating, you know."

"That's right. Sunny told me Whitney's taken a powder," she said.

Feeling that Whitney's absence was no longer a big secret, I said, "Yes, and unfortunately she took it with my cat."

Suzanne looked astonished. "Do tell."

"There's really nothing to tell. She and Jack had a tiff. But she was watching Fleur for me while I was overseas, so she took her along when she left. I'm trying to find her, if for no other reason than to find Fleur," I said, making no mention of Jack's offer of money. "I'm terribly lonely without her."

"I'd forgotten you're solo these days," she said, as if that was any news in our circles. Suzanne was pensive for a minute, and then she said, "I've just had the grandest idea. Pauline, do you have plans for this weekend?"

"Nothing firm," I fibbed. Though I had accepted for a couple of parties, it never hurts to hear the other offers.

"Then you must come to Aspen with us. The holiday season is just getting under way and the skiing is fabulous." She turned to her husband, who was speaking to the woman beside him, and tapped at his arm. He brushed her off with a raised index finger, and she turned back to me unruffled. "Oh, please think about it, Pauline. It will be such good fun."

"Well, I don't know. This is really last-minute." I thought about all the reasons not to go. My vow not to leave town until the co-op was finished. The help I'd promised Sunny with the Amici. My ongoing search for Whitney and Fleur. "Getting a flight would probably be a nightmare."

"Oh, you don't need to get a flight. You'll come with us on the Worthington plane. See, there's nothing for you to worry about."

The lure of Aspen was tempting. I hadn't been to the mountain paradise in ages, which was a shame, since half of Chicago's moneyed people keep a second home there. There was so much money floating around that mountain town that it was a wonder the snow wasn't green.

"I don't know, Suzanne. I'm terribly busy and I haven't skied since Henry died. Besides, I don't have any ski wear," I said, still unsure. Then Suzanne uttered the magic words that solidified my decision.

"Dexter Sr. is coming, of course. That's why I think this is such a smashing idea. As I just told you, he's single at the moment."

That was the clincher. I would have to be out of my mind to pass up a long weekend in the same house as Dexter Worthington Sr. "Well, I suppose I could rent skis . . ."

"It's settled then," said Suzanne, smiling broadly. "We leave from Palwaukee on Friday."

An hour later, I climbed into bed thinking that my thousand dollars had indeed turned out to be money well spent. As I made up a mental list of what would be needed for a winter weekend in the mountains, the revelation hit me like the needles of an icy cold shower. Maria's prediction, the one I had discounted completely.

I see travel. Sometime soon. Someplace cold.

It was coming true. I was traveling to someplace cold. Maybe there was something to the psychic after all. I lay beneath the sheets and tried not to get too excited to sleep as I thought about another one of her predictions. That I would find my soul mate and he would come from great means. And that I would look up to him.

Dexter Sr. was six foot five.

11

Sonnet Number Seventy-Three

With only a couple of days to prepare for the trip to Aspen, there was much to do. I had to buy appropriate clothes for both skiing and social engagements, and luggage to pack them in since mine was still missing. There were a myriad of personal maintenance issues to be attended to as well. I made back-to-back appointments for a manicure, pedicure, facial, and the all-important facial wax. It's the oddest thing about facial hair—how one moment one's face can be smooth as silk and the next something sprouts from God-only-knows-where and grows an inch before being detected. There could be no risk of such an occurrence while skiing with Dexter Sr. in unforgiving bright light reflecting off pure white snow.

Before leaving on Friday afternoon, I decided to brave a visit to my penthouse sans Bharrie. When I got there, I headed directly to the master suite where I assumed Mr. McKay would be working. The room was empty. Assuming he had left for the day, I took the opportunity to have a leisurely look around. Things were finally taking shape. The crown molding had been installed to perfection, the walls were sealed and the wiring hidden, and my new alabaster light fixtures cast the room in a soft golden glow. I went into the bathroom and flicked the switch. Here the quality of the construction really shined. The onyx countertops glowed beneath the recessed lighting. The modern touch of the brushed-nickel fixtures that Bharrie had insisted upon now made perfect sense instead of the gold plate I had once preferred. A freestanding Jacuzzi tub built into walnut cabinetry stood in the center of the room, and a clear glass shower wall behind it gave the room an open feel. Though I would never say it within earshot of Mr. McKay or Bharrie, the project was beginning to feel worth every penny, even if I hadn't quite figured out how to pay for it.

But perhaps money problems would become a moot issue if all went well this weekend.

I was exuberant as I headed back down the hall. Upon reaching the library, I noticed that the French doors were ajar behind the protective plastic sheeting. From the hall, I could hear the sound of Mr. McKay's voice. Irritated that he would violate my private domain, I swept the plastic aside and burst into the room ready to give him a piece of my mind. He was standing behind my desk talking on my telephone. Though he wore his usual paint-splattered overalls, he was shirtless beneath them and his smooth muscles glowed with a light sweat. His turquoise eyes swept toward me from his lined face, and he held up a finger in a nonverbal communication that said "patience."

"Right. So I'll see you tonight," he said in a voice that told me he was speaking to a woman. For some reason, this bothered me. I crossed my arms and waited. Hanging up a moment later, he discounted my folded arms and gave me a warm smile. "Sorry, I had to use your phone. My cell battery is dead."

Caught off guard by his smile, my anger over his invasion of my private sanctuary would have been diffused had I not noticed the open book lying on the desk in front of him. He traced the path of my eyes to the rare edition of Shakespeare's sonnets that Henry had obtained at a Notting Hill bookstore.

"Do you like the sonnets?" he asked, and without waiting for an answer, he picked up the book and began to read aloud. His voice caressed Shakespeare's words with familiarity.

That time of year thou mayst in me behold
when yellow leaves, or none, or few, do hang
Upon those boughs which shake against the cold,
Bare ruin'd choirs where late the sweet birds sang.
In me thou see'st the twilight of such day
As after sunset fadeth in the west,
Which by and by black night doth take away,
Death's second self, that seals up all in rest.
In me thou see'st the glowing of such fire
That on the ashes of his youth doth lie,
As the death-bed whereon it must expire,
Consumed with that which it was nourish'd by,
This thou perceiv'st, which makes thy love more strong,
To love that well which thou must leave ere long.

"That's always been one of my favorites," he said, flicking the book closed and placing it reverently back into its gap on the shelf. "Sorry. I just happened to notice the book and had to take a look at it."

I stared at him slack-jawed. It came as a complete surprise to me that a man who wore a tool belt could be so familiar with the bard. Was it possible there was some intellectual activity lurking behind the tough veneer of his face? I recalled my English Lit class at Foxcroft and this particular sonnet about aging being one that our spinster teacher, Miss Shingleheart, chose to tortuously analyze. As a teenager I found the theme depressing. I found it even more so now.

And then, for reasons that escape me, I said, "Every time I hear that sonnet, it puts me in fear of ending up gray and shriveled."

He smiled more broadly than before, and I realized it was the first time I had actually seen his teeth. They were slightly crooked in a charming way and natural-looking. No caps. No veneers.

"Pauline," he said with disarming familiarity. "Nowhere in my radar screen do I ever see you as gray and shriveled." For a woman in the throes of middle age there is no compliment beyond accepting, and no source of compliment to be discounted. Fighting back a blush, I was actually ready to thank him for his words when he went on to finish his statement. "I'm sure you'll find someone to fix you up before that happens."

Nothing puts one more off balance than rapid ego deflation. All bonhomie gone, I fought back ire and snapped, "I'm leaving for Aspen tomorrow and I'm not certain how long I'll be gone, but I hope you're planning on working over the weekend. I'd really like to have you out of here as soon as possible."

"Believe me, Pauline. I'd like to be out of here as soon as possible myself."

We locked eyes in a nonverbal standoff. Then he walked past me wordlessly and went out the door.

12

The Worst Journey in the World

If there was any silver lining to be found in the tragedy of 9/11, it came in the increased usage of private jets. People who never would have considered going to the expense of purchasing and maintaining a private aircraft, not to mention absorb the cost of a crew and their ancillary benefit package, were now snapping up Gulfstreams like nobody's business. The lines at the airports had become so atrocious, the government so impotent at making any effective move to expedite things, that a situation had been created where those who were used to getting from point A to point B at will had simply come up with an alternative. It seemed everyone I knew was either buying a jet, or sharing a jet, or at the very least borrowing someone else's. I, for one, was going to do my best to avoid flying commercially whenever possible. To be quite frank, even before the terrorist threat, air travel had become tedious as more and more of the proletariat accessed it. It was tiring to watch people come onboard a plane wearing clothing that one might wear to a beach and trying to cram what appeared to be all their worldly possessions into the bin overhead. Though I was generally protected from this situation in first class, the parade still passed through, and it was a slovenly one, to be sure.

Thus it was sublime pleasure to be waiting on a leather sofa in the private airport lounge at Palwaukee Airport, sipping coffee and reading a copy of *Bel Canto* that Elsa had passed along to me while waiting for *la famille* Worthington to arrive. I was wearing sport jeans and a cropped Escada jacket I had purchased on a whirlwind shopping trip the day before. A visit to the Bogner store on Oak Street had yielded the outerwear I would need for skiing, and it was all snugly packed in three newly purchased Louis Vuitton bags from the luggage department at Neiman Marcus.

I wondered if drinking coffee had been a wise choice, however, as I was already somewhat nervous at the thought of seeing Dexter Worthington Sr. An accomplished industrialist, it was he who had turned a successful family business into a global enterprise. He had married young and remained married to the same woman until she died several years ago. So not only was he extremely good-looking, wealthy, and cultured, he was available. Seldom do all four stars align in such a manner. He could be quite a catch.

And frankly, I could use a catch. The stress of the past weeks and the loss of Fleur, not to mention Whitney, had left me lonely, hammering home a need for some companionship in my life. It had been thirteen years since Henry's death, and though I had enjoyed my independence, not to mention more than a few affairs, I was tired of thrashing things out on my own. It was time to find someone to lean on in those worst of times as well as someone with whom to celebrate when the sun broke through the clouds. I was ready to show up with a companion at social events instead of showing up in search of one.

I didn't have too terribly long to be nervous. The very instant I drained the last sip from my cup, the door opened and the waiting area was filled with the larger-than-life presence of Dexter Worthington Sr. I smoothed my hair with my hand and reassured myself I was looking my best as I noted that he was far more handsome than memory had served me. Not only did he have a full head of hair, its admirable silver color gave him the distinguished air of a Southern planter. His face was lean and serious with a pair of riveting dark eyes staring out from beneath a thick and still dark brow.

Junior followed behind him. Though he physically resembled his father in many ways, he simply didn't command the same presence. Rumor had it he wasn't the brightest either. Though with what their empire was worth, he didn't really need smarts. He just needed good hiring skills. He started to introduce me to his father, whom I hadn't seen in years, but Dexter Sr. interrupted him before he could finish.

"You need not introduce me to this elegant woman," Senior said, taking my hand. "I first met Pauline when she was Henry's child bride."

"How good of you to remember, Dexter," I offered, none too subtle in my flirting. "Thank you for including me on this trip."

"Thank Susie," he said, and right on cue, Suzanne swept through the door wrapped in a silver fox hat and coat. The only thing missing was Dr. Zhivago. She gave me a warm hug and kissed my cheek.

"We're so glad you're joining us, Pauline. Father Worthington was the first to say that it gets tedious being around all those young, unsophisticated women in Aspen. He said it would be such a nice change to be around someone more mature, someone he could hold an intelligent conversation with."

"Did I say that? I guess I did," said Senior. I faked a smile and reminded myself to drop a payback on Suzanne at first opportunity. And what was with the Father Worthington? Suzanne may have been younger, but she wasn't that much younger. My train of thought circled back to my host as I listened to his next words. "Now if I could find a mature woman who could ski Walsh's, well, that would be the end of me." He laughed.

I filed Walsh's in the front of my brain for easy retrieval.

When we stepped onto the plane I was reminded of the benefits of being one of the ultra-rich. The cabin was the size of a small apartment, finished in shining leather and zebrawood, and decorated better than many a living room. There were deep, comfortable chairs for lounging, tables for playing cards or dining, a desk for working. The only thing missing was a piano, but there was certainly ample room for one.

A clean, scrubbed young woman named Stacey greeted us with a toothy smile and took our coats. She was dressed in a black spandex uniform that not too subtly enhanced her assets, which were round and high in the front and round and high in the back, as yet untouched by gravity. We buckled in to await takeoff while Stacey arranged for the comfort of all. I couldn't help but notice she was just a bit warmer in her treatment of Dexter Sr., stretching her body so that her breasts were in his face as she tucked a pillow behind his neck, a gesture he seemed not to mind.

We were swiftly airborne, the plane skipping from the earth and into the air like a soaring eagle. Stacey offered us chilled Taittinger from stemmed glasses while Dexter Sr. and I revisited our many mutual acquaintances. I was greatly encouraged when he wondered aloud how it was we hadn't crossed paths in the years since his wife had passed away.

"I'm afraid I've kept to myself more than I should," I suggested, hoping to make it clear that I was available but not desperate. Over his shoulder, I noticed Suzanne working hard to suppress a smile. We made some small talk, and after a while Dexter Sr. picked up some work he had brought along. Junior and Suzanne played gin, and I retreated to *Bel Canto*. Being an inveterate opera patron, I found the story of an opera singer being held hostage in a Latin American country riveting, though I was dubious about Roxanne's attraction to the Japanese businessman. I seldom find Asian men attractive. They're so terribly hairless.

Though the book was engaging, the champagne, combined with the hypnotic hum of the engines, lulled me to sleep. Soon I was dreaming of carving beautiful turns down the powder-covered slopes of Aspen Mountain with Dexter Worthington skiing beside me. Every time I stopped to catch my breath he would stop and try to kiss me, at which point I would laugh teasingly and ski away. Then, as he followed me in chase, the trail suddenly disappeared beneath me and I fell off an edge into space.

I awoke with a jolt to realize that the falling sensation was not exclusive to my dream. The Gulfstream was losing altitude, as if it too had gone off an edge. My wakefulness was immediately followed by the sound of the captain's voice telling us to be sure that we were buckled in. After checking my seat belt, I leaned over to look out the window, hoping to spy the snow-covered pistes beneath us. Instead, we were immersed in solid gray, neither ground nor mountain anywhere in sight. The plane took another dip, this one so extreme it caused me to gasp aloud. I sought the eyes of my fellow passengers. Dexter Sr. continued working as if nothing was wrong, while both Junior and Suzanne, trying to look nonchalant, had taken a firmer grip on their armrests.

Suzanne noticed me looking at her and must have read the fear in my face. "Sometimes it gets a bit bumpy going in," she said, her words missing their reassuring mark as the plane lurched violently to the right. Then it lurched left in what appeared to be an overcorrection on the part of the pilot. My stomach began to churn and I hoped the plane was equipped with the small white bags I had come to rely on during some of my more challenging flights with Henry. He was quite the adventurer, and during our marriage, we had survived everything from African bush pilots in Kenya who brushed the very tops of the trees before landing on rutted dirt runways to lumbering float planes that barely seemed capable of leaving the water in the outer reaches of Alaska. Surely, the risk of landing in Aspen during a blinding snowstorm hardly compared. Unfortunately, either my memory was short or time had veiled the worst, but I could not recall ever being in an aircraft that felt so out of place in the sky.

The plane took another frightening thump and then shuddered to and fro as if it were being spun on a turntable. My stomach churned again.

Dexter Jr. looked rattled by this one. "Jesus Christ, it feels like we're going down Walsh's without skis." Before he could say another word, the engines screamed and the plane roared upward at an angle that pressed me back into my seat. My grip on the armrests grew ever more firm as I appealed to an entity from my earliest days attending the Episcopalian church with Grandmother. After an eternity packed into thirty seconds, the plane leveled out and the phone on the console next to Dexter Sr. rang. He picked it up and barked into it.

"What the hell is going on up there?"

I was all ears.

"Uh huh. Uh huh," he said. I strained to read his face, but it was an impenetrable wall. "Well, if we don't make curfew we'll have to go to Grand Junction, and I sure as hell don't want to do that. Go around and give it another shot." He hung up the phone and turned to the rest of us. "The weather in

Aspen has deteriorated and at the moment we don't have the visibility the FAA requires for landing. So Jason's going to circle around a couple of times and hope things get better, so we can give it another try before curfew."

Suzanne groaned aloud and Dexter Jr. said, "Damn these people with their ridiculous curfew. Don't they know how dangerous it can be to make us rush? Well, let's hope for that hole." He turned his attention back to his magazine while I swiveled my chair toward Suzanne. She was twirling a lock of blond hair around a manicured finger while putting on an Academy Award–winning version of nonchalance. I tried to return to the opera singer, but the words swam on the page as we lurched to and fro in the airspace over Aspen. Dexter Sr.'s words reverberated in my brain. "Give it another shot?"

The plane took another sudden dip, and my book flew from my lap. Even Dexter Sr.'s papers became airborne. The face-hollowing centrifugal force that followed made me feel like my cheeks had joined my neck. I don't ever recall a Tilt-o-Whirl having the same erratic behavior. The copilot's voice came over the intercom.

"Do not leave your seats," he commanded curtly. He certainly didn't have to worry about me going anywhere. From my seat, I could see young Stacey strapped in near the galley, swaying to and fro as she tried to catch hold of a couple of rolling champagne glasses. The plane bucked up and down like a sailboat in rough seas. Except that there was neither water beneath us nor lifeboats to board in the eventuality of the worst. Fear's trenchant hold grew tighter and my mouth grew so dry, my tongue stuck to my palate. I abandoned all thoughts of a small white bag, my greater concern being having to handwash my Courtnay lingerie upon arrival. Everyone looked beyond nervous, with the exception of Senior, who merely looked irritated.

The phone rang again. "No, we're fine back here," he barked. "What are they saying at the tower?" A pause. "Well, you can do it on instruments, can't you? Just tell them you have a visual."

My heart literally lurched in my chest and I closed my eyes, hiding behind my lids and praying to any god who might be available. The engines whined louder and the bumping grew worse. We were actually descending again. Had I been capable of speech, I would have suggested that a night in Grand Junction, wherever that might be, could be fun. But something told me that any such suggestion would never overrule Senior. I also had a sense that the pilot knew Dexter Sr.'s determination and that if he wanted to keep his job he had to "give it a shot."

I managed to peel one eye slightly open and peer out the window in search of anything other than the shroud of dark gray. Knowing we would be landing on one of the shortest runways with one of the steepest descents in the United States, I was acutely aware that we were surrounded on all sides by mountains I couldn't see. Neither, I assumed, could Jason.

The bumping stopped, and we continued in a smooth downward glide. I kept looking outside for signs of life and saw nothing. Nothing. My breath caught in my throat and everyone was silent, even Senior now, who was either the coolest creature on the earth or the stupidest. I hoped I might live to have an answer to that question.

And then a highway appeared below us, and I could see the headlights of cars passing in opposite directions. Not a second later, the earth came up to meet us as the plane set down on the runway—a highly uneventful landing in light of the approach. The plane rolled to a stop amidst the sound of the reverse thrust of the engines. Jason's comforting voice came over the intercom.

"Got lucky there, sir. Beat curfew by one minute," he said.

A phrase one wishes never to hear from one's pilot, "Got lucky."

As we taxied to the private terminal, and my heart gradually regained its normal rhythm, a look out the window told me too much time had passed between visits to Aspen. The tarmac resembled the parking lot of a car dealership, and a very elite car dealership at that. Private aircraft were parked three-deep, and not the same sort of aircraft as when the Learjet was considered state-of-the-art. This tarmac was weighty with heavy iron. Gulfstream threes, fours, and fives made the Citations parked beside them look like Volkswagens, and the prop planes farther down the pavement looked like the minuscule Fiats the Italians had once crowded entire families into. Caught up in the euphoria of still being alive, I resolved that if things on this trip did not go well with Senior, then it would be wise to start visiting Aspen on a regular basis.

13

Adventures in Wonderland

The Worthingtons' caretaker waited outside the private terminal in a Range Rover to take us to the Worthington compound. The storm had lifted and everything was covered in white as we drove through the former mining town, its streets aglitter with Christmas lights. There had been some changes since my last visit with Henry. But although there were more stoplights on Main Street than before, and many of the quaint old buildings had been replaced with larger ones, the town still retained its charm. It was a true gem.

The driver turned off Main Street at the Hotel Jerome, a landmark of luxury built during the mining boom, and headed toward Red Mountain. This was where the biggest changes appeared to have taken place. The hills that I remembered as being dark were now filled with brightly lit mansions and glowed like the Pacific Palisades. We drove halfway up the mountain, taking several hairpin turns, before finally pulling into a hidden driveway and coming to a stop in front of a stone manor that stretched to the sky.

"Welcome to Casa W.," said Senior.

I got out of the car and paused in the crisp cold to look at Aspen Mountain, glowing in the moonlight across the valley. The air was filled with the scent of pine and I found myself temporarily transported back to the Christmases Mother and I spent in Vermont in the years after my father left us. She claimed it was to get away from the chaos of the city, but even at my young age I knew better. She was escaping the memories of Christmas with my father, when their marriage was fresh and strong, before he squandered all his money and the better part of hers, before he abandoned us for the woman Mother referred to as "Medea." I suspect my mother never got over my father, rascal and libertine that he was. And though I pretended not to care about his existence after his departure, I missed him, too. He brought a certain vivacity and vitality to life, a capriciousness and carelessness that was at the same time exhilarating and frightening. And thus, rather than face the loneliness of the holidays without him, Mother spirited us away to Vermont, where we stayed in a family-run chalet. While she drank wine around the fireplace, I played in the snow with the housekeeper's children, who showed me how to build snowmen and pilot a sled down treacherous slopes with little care for safety. For a child used to the insulation of city life, it was an eye-opening experience, not only the discovery of the great outdoors but being permitted to play with the children of the help, something forbidden at Grandmother's home.

We went into Casa W. through a pair of twelve-foot-high doors with massive lion's-head knockers. The view from the inside, unobstructed through two-story-high glass windows, actually topped the view from the driveway. In the great room a fire roared in the stone fireplace, and Senior made a point of telling me it was one of the few wood-burning fireplaces left on Red Mountain as new codes had made wood burning illegal. Tree huggers worried about pollution, he explained. Rosa, the maid, came in with a tray of drinks and snacks, and we curled up in front of the fireplace and sipped another glass of champagne before Suzanne declared we should dress for the evening. We were invited to Samuel Seawell's Christmas party, the official kick-off of the holiday season in Aspen. The developer's party was the party to be topped by other hostesses, who watched this initial foray and then scrambled to outdo it.

I was escorted to my quarters, a substantial suite with yet another outstanding view of the mountain. It was decorated with heavy log furniture, deep leather chairs littered with cashmere throws, and a good measure of Western paraphernalia. There was a vast en suite bathroom with heated floors and a pool-sized Jacuzzi tub, as well as a walk-in closet the size of two Paris hotel rooms combined. I quickly unpacked and took a cat nap, not wanting to sleep long enough for my eyes to puff up. I had trained myself long ago to sleep on my back so as to keep my face out of the pillow, yet another wrinkle accelerator. Feeling refreshed, I stood in the middle of the closet and carefully sorted through the wardrobe I had brought with me, searching for the appropriate wear for the evening's party. Mountain wear was always tricky. One wanted to look appropriately chic, but in no way "city." Low-cut only worked if it was a sweater, tight was for jeans, skirts were out unless they were mid-calf and accompanied by boots. Aspen was not the place for my Chanel or Féraud suits. I settled on butter-soft, mint-colored suede slacks, which I topped with an angora sweater in the same shade, a pair of mint-colored ostrich boots, a Ferragamo belt, and a few trinkets from Bulgari. I stood in front of the full-length mirror and nodded with approval. The monochromatic effect of the boots, slacks, and sweater made me appear even taller and slimmer than usual.

I returned to the great room, where the others were waiting for me. Suzanne had traded in Siberia for Carson City, dressed in leather like a cowgirl sans horse. The men wore jeans and casual sweaters. Availing myself once again of my vantage point, I looked across the valley toward the slopes of Aspen Mountain and found myself filled with a sense of well-being that had escaped me since my return from Europe.

Though he'd already had a few drinks, Dexter Jr. decided to drive since we were only going a short distance, calculating that the odds of the local gendarmerie being this far up the hill were remote. As we stepped out onto the driveway, the stars overhead twinkled with an intensity I'd never seen before, not even in the remote reaches of the Mediterranean sea. They appeared to be almost within reach, shining down upon us like so many good wishes. Junior drove up the winding, snow-covered road until we reached a Spanish-style edifice that put the Worthington domicile to shame. Lit up like Boston Harbor on the Fourth of July, it resembled a three-story spaceship protruding from the mountain.

A scurrying valet took the car and we went into the party. We were greeted at the door by a sweet-looking young thing wearing a sliplike garment that looked like a gold nightie. She handed us each a glass of champagne. In light of the Arctic air coming through the open door, I wondered how she managed to keep warm in the flimsy dress, and whispered as much to Suzanne. "I hope they're paying her enough to freeze like that."

"Oh, she's well-paid," Suzanne replied. "That's Virginia Seawell, Samuel's latest. She used to be his caterer. Seems she can't break the habit."

Introductions were made and we moved into the fracas. I almost immediately became separated from the Worthingtons who flowed into the party like molten copper into bronze. Working my way across the vast entry hall, beneath an antler chandelier whose progeny had to be in the Guinness Book of World Records, I politely refused girls dressed like elves passing trays heaped with blini and caviar. Left to my own devices, I wandered into a room dedicated entirely to food, filled with numerous stations and massive ice sculptures. At one position an islander wearing a sarong shucked oysters at an enormous raw bar; at another a Japanese chef prepared handmade sushi; at a third a French chef flambéed crepes. I passed into another room where a band that looked suspiciously like the Beatles was playing so loudly I had to move on. Everywhere I looked the people were beautiful, and though I am no expert on celebrities, I was fairly certain that I saw Melanie Griffith and Joe Cocker in the crowd, as well as several supermodels. Not since I'd attended a party at the Playboy Mansion in Chicago in the seventies had I seen so many young, nubile, and smooth-faced girls under one roof. Although these girls were wearing more clothing than those at Mr. Hefner's party, there were glaring similarities. Short skirts gave way to long legs and deep-cut clinging sweaters gave way to proportionately inappropriate breasts.

Thankfully, as I moved farther into the house, the party yielded up some women who were middle-aged. At least I think they were middle-aged. One can never be certain when it's a good face-lift. The bad ones are easily recognizable; their owners sport the combined look of mannequin, Barbie doll, and recovering burn victim. But the good ones? Always a challenge. While breast sizes remained competitive in the older group, hip sizes were as narrow, if not more so, than their younger counterparts. These women were slim with a vengeance. An athletic vengeance, one might point out, their arms, waists, and legs whittled into tight sinewy cords of muscle. One could certainly say there was not a lot of fat in Aspen.

I climbed up a winding stone staircase and found myself in another large room, this one dominated by two things: an enormous bar layered with shelves of crystal glasses and decanters of premium cognacs, and an art collection to rival the Louvre. Or on a smaller scale the Musée d'Orsay. Even my semi-trained eye immediately recognized a Signac, a de Kooning, a couple of Mirós, and a de Chirico. But the true pièce de resistance was in the center of the room in a larger-than-life aquarium.

"My god, is that a Damien Hirst?" I asked the man standing beside me. He was tall and tanned with long thinning hair and an athletically lean frame. Perhaps in his mid-forties. He turned to me and smiled the easy smile of one who is totally comfortable within his own frame.

"Looks like a dead sheep to me," he replied evenly. His dark eyes danced in well-placed laugh lines that extended in a semicircle down his rugged face. He held out a hand and introduced himself. "Dusty Craw."

"Pauline Cook," I countered. "Quite a crowd here. I don't know that I've ever seen anything quite like it."

"This is nothing compared to some of Sam's parties. His attitude is when you've got it, you've got to spend it. Or spread it like manure like what's-his-face said."

"I believe it was Thornton Wilder, though Brooke Astor has said it, too," I informed him, and then feeling a bit pedantic, quickly added, "He seems to be doing a fine job at spreading it. I take it you're friends."

"I've been Sam's ski instructor for over twenty years. I've taken him from a snow plow on Little Nell to flying down Walsh's," he said with pride. "He's so determined, he'd outski me if he ever had the chance to put in a hundred days. Too bad he's got to work so hard to keep all this up."

The word "Walsh's" sounded an alarm in my brain where I had filed it away. Dexter Sr. had said his heart would go out to the mature woman who could ski Walsh's. It had been a long time since I'd been on skis, and though I had been a competent skier at the time, I was no Ivana Trump. The last thing

I wanted to do after hearing Dexter Sr.'s words was make a fool out of myself in front of him. Not when the stakes were so high.

"Did you say you're a ski instructor?"

"And a realtor. Are you in the market for a place here in Aspen?"

"No, but I am in the market for a ski instructor. Would you be available tomorrow?"

"Your timing is golden, Pauline Cook. Just so happens my private for tomorrow cancelled. She's down with a cold. Otherwise, with the holidays and all, I'm booked out the rest of the month."

"Then I guess I have to thank my lucky stars," I said. "Can you get me down Walsh's?"

"Walsh's?" He paused. "It depends. What kind of skier are you?"

"I haven't been on skis in over thirteen years."

He paused again. "Walsh's can be challenging."

"That's not what I'm asking. I'm asking you if you can get me down Walsh's."

He stared me boldly in the eye. "Sure. If you want to ski it, I can get you down it."

"Then you're hired," I announced.

We made arrangements to meet the next morning at the gondola and he drifted off to talk to a group of identically endowed young women wearing identical ribbed turtlenecks in different shades. I continued down the hall and into a large media area where a huge screen was showing music videos. This party was a far cry from the subdued and elegant Christmas parties in Chicago or back east. Parties where we sipped traditional Christmas punch, nibbled at tenderloin sandwiches, and gathered around a roaring fire to sing Christmas carols. Those celebrations were a bit stuffier, I might add, but somehow reminiscent of the holiday. Here, there wasn't even any Christmas music playing.

I rotated out of the room and back into the wide stone hall where I finally saw someone from Chicago, Meredith Levin. Her husband was one of the largest real estate barons on the North Shore. She was at least thirty years younger than Jerry (who was pushing eighty, by my best guestimate) and not only his third wife, but his trophy gentile. The story goes that Meredith had promised to convert, but after starting the classes she decided it was far too much work. She and Jerry finally settled on her attending temple on the high holidays and sitting shiva when called upon. Rumor had it that he could be none-too-kind to his younger wife, and that she was greatly disappointed when he was snatched from the jaws of death years ago when a matching liver donor miraculously appeared. He subsequently donated a wing to the hospital.

"Pauline, come join us," Meredith called, waving me over. She looked fabulous, rail-thin in red velvet pants and a red beaded sweater. She was speaking with a dark-haired woman who was wearing a diamond ring so large it looked like a piece of glass. If I had been anyplace other than Aspen I would have doubted it was real.

Meredith kissed my cheek. "Pauline, meet Renee Ryan. Lucky Renee gets to live here all year 'round. How fabulous is that?"

"Except when we're in our homes in Cabo and Cannes," Renee volunteered with a capped smile.

I smiled back and asked Renee how she enjoyed life in the mountains. "It's paradise," she replied. "True paradise. The only problem is the locals, but once you get past them, there's not a better place on earth."

I raised an eyebrow. "Are the locals dangerous? I just engaged one as a ski instructor."

She laughed aloud. "They're only dangerous if you want to develop something. Honestly, I've never met such obtuse people. There is an entirely absurd communist mindset among them that since they've been hiking over a piece of land for decades, somehow it belongs to the public. They have no concept of private property. We've got hundreds of acres we're just waiting to improve with luxury houses and they've got us so bogged down in court we may have to sell it to pay the taxes."

Meredith chimed in. "Thank God we got our twenty-thousand square feet built before they started changing all the rules. Frankly, I just think they're jealous when they see these big, beautiful houses beyond their means."

I thought of the little miner's cottages and Victorian houses and ski lodges that had been the mainstay of the town in the 1970s. I must admit to thinking there was a certain charm to them at the time. But certainly there was no room for antler chandeliers in the entry of an 1880 Victorian, much less a video room and lap pool. And as for the miner's shacks, those humble buildings now served as little more than entry closets for the houses that had sprung up behind them. I nodded in implied agreement as to the short-sightedness of the working class while some small demon in me, birthed I have no idea where, rooted slightly for the values they fought for.

Having no interest in pursuing this particular conversation further, I made my excuses and continued down the hall, past men in alligator cowboy boots and ultrasuede shirts and women in fur-trimmed cashmere and heavy glittering jewelry. Spotting what appeared to be an empty room, I slipped into it and found myself in the library. My admiration for Samuel Seawell grew immensely as I scanned the unbroken rows of books, noting among them several first and rare editions. I took a deep breath of rarefied air, and thought about how all this new money felt alien to me. Old money didn't develop the land. They kept if for themselves.

Across the room, a roaring fire blazed in a great stone fireplace. Two wide, high-backed leather chairs faced it, and I could see the crown of a male head peeking over the top of one. The other chair appeared to be empty. I tiptoed over in pretense of admiring the fire, but I was more interested in seeing the man who chose the tranquillity of the library over the madding crowd.

It wasn't until I had reached the fireplace that I realized the seated man was not alone. There was actually a second person sharing his chair, a petite blonde nestled in his lap. Under normal circumstances, I would have politely backed away unnoticed. I would have left the room and let myself be reabsorbed into the crowd. But these were not normal circumstances in that I recognized the man whose tortoiseshell glasses were making an imprint upon the flesh of the woman's neck. It was Jack Armstrong.

"Hello, Jack," I said crisply, dispensing with the polite throat-clearing that usually precedes such an intimate interruption. "What a surprise to see you in Aspen."

His eyes flicked upward, the same indifferent hazel eyes I had watched flood with tears only weeks before. I could hear his voice over endless hours on the phone, imploring me to help him find his missing wife. Was this possibly the same man?

"Pauline," he said, sitting up so straight that the blonde slid from his lap. He reached out almost absentmindedly to help her up. "How do you know Sam Seawell?"

"I don't know that that is relevant, Jack. I do find it a bit peculiar to see you here when you claim to be in such deep mourning over Whitney."

We stared each other down, the blonde on her feet now, marking her newfound territory. Jack didn't bother with introductions. "Pauline, this is neither the time nor the place to discuss this. We can talk later."

"As if we haven't talked enough already. My ear is swollen with your words, Jack, though I now believe them to be empty ones. And what about your offer, Jack? Does that still hold?"

I did not wait for him to answer, but turned and walked from the room. Heading straight for the closest bar, my mind swirled with thoughts that raised goose bumps upon my flesh. Jack's behavior was hardly that of a man in pain. Putting aside the scene I had just witnessed, how could he think of leaving Chicago if the possibility loomed that Whitney might return? She hadn't been gone a month. Much like a child who does not want to accept that there is no Santa Claus, the thought I had pushed to the back of my mind surfaced strongly. The one that Detective Malloy had suggested and I hadn't taken seriously. For the first time my belief was stronger than not that Jack Armstrong could be behind his wife's disappearance. And that of Fleur.

I was standing at the bar waiting for a glass of Taittinger when there was a firm tug at my arm. Certain it was Jack, I turned defensively and was surprised to see Dexter Worthington Sr. standing beside me. His face glowed with the effect of too much good drink.

"Well, now, where have you been all evening, Mrs. Cook?"

All my concerns about Whitney and Jack ebbed from my mind as I stared at the possible goal of all desire. He was alone, no fresh-faced firm body anywhere in sight. Maybe this opportunity did stand a chance.

"I've been wandering around," I said, returning his smile. "This is quite a party. They certainly know how to do things here in Aspen."

"We certainly do," he echoed, and without pausing, he added, "And now it's time to get going. Early wake-up call for skiing."

"Actually, I've arranged for an instructor tomorrow. It's been awhile since I've been on skis, and I just want a little help until I'm back on my feet."

"Don't worry, Pauline," he said lightly, taking me by the elbow and guiding me toward the front door. "It'll come back. It's just like riding a bike."

I hadn't been on a bicycle in years either.

Junior and Suzanne were waiting out front for the car. The air was even crisper than before, almost insulating in its coldness. Beneath the full moon, the ski runs of Aspen Mountain gleamed like great white arteries flowing from a star-studded sky. The champagne served to make the world both sharper and more romantic, and I was all too aware of the warm presence of Dexter Sr. at my side.

My mind was engaged with the endless possibilities stretching before me when Jack Armstrong stumbled out the front door. He was drunk, and he was alone. Our eyes locked for a brief moment before I jerked my head back toward my hosts. Though my back was to him, I could sense him drawing up behind me.

"Jack," I heard Senior say. "I didn't know you were in Aspen."

The tone in Jack's voice was that of one who isn't often questioned. "It was a last-minute thing. Samuel invited me." Then he said loudly, "I need to talk to Pauline about a business arrangement." His bizarre behavior drew the attention of everyone waiting for their cars, and people either stared at him like he was a freak or didn't for the same reason. Seeing no other option, I turned toward him to listen. "What you witnessed in there was the desperation of a lonely man. I miss my wife more than you could ever know. You asked if the offer I made before still holds. Yes, it does, except I'm upping the ante to ten million dollars. Do you hear that, Pauline? Ten million dollars. Just find out where Whitney is."

Now he had everyone's attention. One of the valets pulled up with a Lexus SUV, and the couple it belonged to were clearly devastated at having to leave the scene prematurely. Another valet arrived in the Range Rover, and Senior took a firm grip on me and led me calmly toward the car while the others gathered stared in stunned silence. Just before getting into the car I turned back to Jack and said, "I assume that means dead or alive."

14

The Magic Mountain

I appeared at the breakfast table the next morning ready to go in a new gold turtleneck and ski pants topped off with the latest in designer fleece. Suzanne and Dexter Jr. were helping themselves to the buffet laid out on the table, fresh fruit and freshly squeezed orange juice, a variety of pastries, crispy fried bacon, and feathery light scrambled eggs. I was slightly disappointed that Senior wasn't there after spending the last hour trying to make my hair look appealing in my new gold headband. I sat down and helped myself to some cantaloupe and a mouth-watering croissant. Rosa emerged from the kitchen and delivered a steaming cappuccino before I could even ask. I sipped at the hot drink and stared outside. The view in the daylight was even more stunning than by moonlight, with a sky as blue as lapis and stark white mountains standing out against it like veins of marble.

It goes without saying that the trip back home in the car last night had been an interesting one. Suzanne and Dexter Jr. had peppered me with questions, while Dexter Sr. had remained quiet. One never inquired about another's business. I had been as evasive as I could, but finally realizing it made little difference after Jack's performance, I told them about his offer of money to find his wife. Now in the light of the morning, it felt like it hadn't even happened, that the night before was some kind of bizarre dream.

"So, Pauline," Suzanne gibed in her smooth British accent. "Will you be leaving us now to take Jack Armstrong up on his offer?"

Little did she realize the irony in her jest, that Jack's offer was a tempting fallback position should things not work out with Senior. I wondered if Jack's announcement in front of so many people made it legally binding. I studied Suzanne's glowing face, perched over her raised coffee cup. Three years ago she had been a concierge, wearing the same black Ginny suit for days on end, changing blouses and accessories in hopes of creating a fresh enough look so no one would notice she was wearing the same suit. Her vanilla-skinned face and melodious accent had carried her far from those days, and even though she had signed one of the most iron-clad of prenuptials, it was pretty well guaranteed that no matter what course her marriage ever took, Suzanne Worthington would be set for life. Unlike *moi* who, surrounded by so much easy wealth, had no idea where her next penny lay.

"Well," I said. "Whitney's disappearance is a bit disturbing. I wouldn't mind getting to the bottom of it."

I looked up to see Dexter Sr. standing in the doorway listening to us. "I have a feeling it's Whitney's bottom that's responsible for her disappearance," he said. Suzanne and Dexter Jr. laughed aloud while I forced a tolerant smile. He was, after all, a billionaire. He dropped the subject and clapped his hands together forcefully.

"Enough of that. Let's go skiing."

The driver dropped us off at the Gondola Plaza. The red brick square in the shadow of Aspen Mountain was adjacent to the five-star Little Nell Hotel and lined with tony, expensive shops that made for a shopper's paradise. Skiers and nonskiers alike milled about people-watching, the skiers dressed in the latest ski fashions, the nonskiers in stylish cowboy hats and voluminous furs. Dusty Craw was already waiting, dressed in the gray and red uniform of an Aspen Skiing Company employee. He was flirting with a couple of blondes wearing identical fur headbands, but when he saw us he quickly cut the conversation short and came over to greet me. It was obvious he already knew the Worthingtons, because Senior gave the tall, lean instructor a firm handshake and a familiar pat on the back, and Junior followed suit. Suzanne settled for a kiss on the cheek.

"Dustin," Dexter Sr. said. "So you're the sly fox teaching Pauline today. I know you'll take special care of her."

"I'll do my best, sir," he replied.

"That's what we like to hear. Meet us at the club for lunch at, say, twelve o'clock?"

"Yes, sir," Dusty Craw snapped, nearly clicking his heels together.

"And don't be too hard on her," Dexter Jr. added, reminding me of a child mimicking his father in an attempt to show his own importance.

"Don't worry, I'll take good care of Pauline," Dusty replied, wrapping his arm around my shoulder as if we were old acquaintances. Never comfortable with those who act overly familiar, I shrugged my way out from under his arm. The three Worthingtons rushed off to hit the slopes, and Dusty took me to rent equipment at a nearby store. I was surprised to see that skis had become much shorter since I had last skied.

"You'll be glad they're so short once you're on them. I guarantee it," he said, countering my protests that I should be skiing on something longer. I acquiesced to the new length, but drew the line when he suggested I rent a helmet. Every woman I saw wearing one looked ridiculous, and besides, I hadn't spent all that time coaxing my hair into the gold headband to see it crushed by a plastic bowling ball with vents.

Dusty and I bypassed the long queue waiting for the gondola and took the line reserved for private lessons. Since there were only two of us, we were joined in the six-person cabin by four sweaty young men from the regular line. They had already been skiing, and as soon as the cabin door closed, they started noisily loosening snaps and opening zippers in order to cool down. Once they had finished getting comfortable, they leaned back in their seats and engaged in conversation as if Dusty and I weren't even there.

"Dude! You nearly bought it on that rock."

"I know, dude. Didn't see it with all this freshie. That would'a been a real bone grinder."

They laughed collectively as the heat of their bodies fogged the windows of the lift.

Dusty started to give me a refresher in skiing, explaining that the engineering of the new skis would make skiing infinitely easier than before. But I was having difficulty paying attention to my instructor in light of the other conversation taking place in the gondola, one that seemed to have a language of its own.

"Dude, how was the action at the boo last night?" the head behind me asked.

"It was full of trim, but the ones that cream my panties only want a dude with a private jet," Dude responded.

"Guys," Dusty said protectively. "You're not the only ones in here."

Their heads turned toward us as if they were just now noticing there were six of us in the car. "Sorry," one of them grunted. They fell into silence, adjusting boots and buckles, and zipping and unzipping jackets for the rest of the fifteen-minute ride to the top. When the door opened and we climbed out to retrieve our gear, one of them turned to Dusty and said, "Nice-looking cougar you got there, dude." Then they were gone.

Dusty carried our skis from the gondola terminal and laid them out on the ground. After clicking into my bindings, I lowered my sunglasses and asked, "What on earth is a cougar?"

He coughed into his gloved hand and smiled a wry smile. "You really want to know?"

"I do."

"A cougar is an older woman who preys on younger men."

I wasn't sure whether to be complimented that I had been considered a good-looking cougar or insulted that they thought I was older than Dusty Craw.

Dexter Sr. was right. It was like riding a bicycle. In my previous life with Henry, we had skied in the Alps and, while not an expert, I was a capable skier. With the benefit of new technology and the capable teaching skills of Dusty Craw, I soon found myself sailing down the slopes as if I'd never been away. I reveled in the euphoria of gliding along the surface of smoothly groomed snow, letting gravity do most of the work while taking in the breathtaking beauty of the rough-hewn Rockies wearing true winter white.

Twelve o'clock found us hanging our skis on the racks outside the entrance to the Aspen Mountain Club, a private enclave where members paid over a hundred thousand dollars for the privilege of having lunch away from the hoi polloi in the adjacent Sundeck Restaurant. We slipped into the cloakroom next to the entrance, hung up our jackets, and changed out our ski boots for warm slippers. Not wanting to jeopardize my chances with Senior, I ducked into the ladies lounge to check my appearance. Satisfied that all was well, I joined Dusty Craw in the entry where a bright, blue-eyed woman named Luky greeted me by name, her persona ringing as large as she was small. "You must be Pauline. The others are waiting for you," she said.

She led us into the dining room, a tastefully decorated room of subtle yellows and blues with one of the most spectacular views I've ever seen. Mountain ranges stretched in all directions with a massive smooth bowl of white directly in the center opposite us. The atmosphere was quiet and subdued, reminding me of the old clubs back east where people spoke in polite whispers and the scent of money virtually hung in the air. As we crossed the room, I did a quick inventory of the people we passed along the way and realized that an explosion in that room would shorten the current Forbes 400 by a page.

Luky took us to a table in the window where the three Worthingtons and another woman I didn't know were seated. The other woman was speaking animatedly to Dexter Sr. as if they were alone at the table. She was a pert, raven-haired beauty with azure eyes and a nauseatingly charming pair of dimples that were revealed each time she smiled at him. Which was about every three or four seconds. The pair of dimples was introduced as Lizzie Bodine who, I was informed, had climbed everything from Mount McKinley to Everest, competed in several Ironmen—which consists of a quarter-mile ocean swim, a one-hundred-ten-mile bicycle ride, and a twenty-six-mile marathon—and sailed solo from California to Hawaii. Did I also mention that her father had been one of the inventors of the pacemaker?

"And you haven't swum the English Channel?" I asked her.

"I would love to, but I can't. I don't weigh enough, so the currents would sweep me away."

"You should really give it a try," I couldn't resist saying.

Suzanne deftly changed the subject. "How was your morning, Pauline?" she asked.

"It was amazing," I said. "I'd forgotten how good it feels to be on skis."

Dusty took the opportunity to ensure a good tip at the end of the day. "You should see Pauline ski. She's really grace on the snow." I blushed in acknowledgment of the compliment.

"Well then, you'll just have to ski with us after lunch," said Dexter Sr., to my great delight.

"Yes, Pauline," the world's most spritely Amazon chimed in as if she were the one extending the invitation. "You have to ski with us after lunch." I graced her with a withering smile.

We dined on the buffet, an energy-replenishing mix of soups, stews, seafood, and salads. I had a glass of wine, and feeling remarkably relaxed after one glass at eleven thousand feet, I ordered a second. Conversation centered on skiing as each person revisited the pleasures of the morning, the perfect weather, and the condition of the snow. Comparisons to St. Moritz and Val d'Isère were made, with everyone agreeing that the skiing in Aspen was far superior. Much to the dismay of Ms. Bodine, Senior was paying me a great deal of attention, and I hadn't seen her dimples for practically a minute. I could tell she was greatly relieved when Junior made the move to break things up.

"Look at the time," he said, checking his watch. "It's nearly one-thirty. We'd better get going before the day is gone."

Feeling more like taking a siesta than strapping the skis on again, I knew that to leave Senior alone with Lizzie Bodine for the rest of the day would be an error tantamount to buying Enron. Dexter Sr. signed the check, and we traded our nice warm slippers in for ski boots. By the time we assembled outside, a patch of thin clouds had pulled in front of the winter sun and the light had turned flat. While Lizzie and the Worthingtons debated what to ski, Dusty took the opportunity to suggest that it might not be such a great idea if we skied with the group.

"They're talking about some pretty difficult runs," he whispered to me. "We did groomers all morning."

"Ridiculous, I'll be fine," I insisted, shutting him off. Dexter Sr.'s words about a woman who could ski Walsh's rang in my mind, and I had no intention of letting that honor go to Lizzie Bodine alone.

"I'm not sure that Pauline . . ." Suzanne started to say, but Lizzie finished for her.

"Pauline, we're skiing a double black diamond. Is that OK with you?" she asked, dripping with false sweetness. When I didn't answer right away she turned to Dusty. "Can she handle Walsh's?"

Dusty opened his mouth to speak, but I silenced him with a glare.

"I've always maintained that two diamonds are far better than one," I said.

"Pauline, I've got to love your spunk," Dexter Sr. said, flashing a dashing smile. "Then it's settled. Walsh's it is."

Humiliation can take many forms. The occasional faux pas. A spilled drink at the cotillion. Underdressing for Ascot. Overdressing for a picnic. Being the poorest in one's class at Foxcroft. But I'm afraid nothing equals making a fool of oneself on skis.

Hubris may have had something to do with it, but I prefer to place the blame on Dusty Craw. He should have known better than to let me do as I wished. After a rather innocuous start down a relatively innocuous incline, we came around a bend to find ourselves at the top of a hill one might liken to a sea squall turned on its side and then frozen. I screeched to a halt beside a sign that warned CAUTION CLIFFS. My faithful servant Dusty skied up beside me. One look over the edge and the legs that had been so confident all morning turned to putty. Recalling Dexter Sr.'s coolness when the Gulfstream threatened to come apart in the sky, I realized it would have been wise to take his recklessness into consideration before allowing myself to come to the place where I now stood.

I turned to Dusty, who actually looked more frightened than I. "Don't say I didn't warn you," he said. "We can take the skis off and walk back up if you want."

I peered down the run—if one so much as dared to call it that. It was more like a plunge. The three Worthingtons and Madam Edmund Hillary had gone ahead and now stood halfway down, looking up at me expectantly. If one thing can be said about me, I am determined, and I was determined not to let that wiry little woman take my desired position. If Dexter Sr. wanted a woman who could ski Walsh's, then ski Walsh's I would. Maybe it had to do with the second glass of wine, but fear wrestled blind ambition and the latter won out.

"Mr. Craw," I croaked from a mouth dryer than one might think possible in anyone with a pulse. "You will get me down this in one piece and without me making an ass out of myself. Do you understand?"

He nodded, and in a voice filled with forced calm, he said, "OK, Pauline, now listen to me. It's really far easier than it looks. I want you to forget about looking down the hill. Just look ahead to your next turn. That should help lessen the intimidation factor."

Intimidation factor? The wine may have motivated me, but it was doing little to take the edge off the terror. The city equivalent of my situation would be standing in a dead-end alley faced down by four rather large men with knives. While I tried to rise above my fear, Junior and Suzanne stared impatiently back up the hill. It was then I noticed that Senior and Ms. Bodine were so engrossed in conversation they weren't even looking at me anymore.

I took a deep breath and dropped onto the run.

My skis took off like a horse racing back to the barn, carrying my unwilling body along with them. Hanging on for dear life, I careened sideways across the mountain, bouncing from bump to bump while fighting to stay upright. As I accelerated toward the trees at the edge of the run, I realized if I didn't turn I would end up crashing into them. Employing every hint Dusty had given me that morning, not to mention a huge dose of courage, I shifted my weight enough to tip the skis over and turn them in the other direction. This was all well and good, except that now I was in the same situation as before, only barreling in the opposite direction. Appealing to a higher power, I miraculously managed to bring the skis around again, and then again, and then several more times until I ended up bouncing to a breathless stop in front of the others. Dusty Craw came up behind me, the second most relieved person on the mountain.

While Junior, Suzanne, and Ms. Bodine stared at me gape-jawed, Dexter

Sr. reached out and gave me a spirited pat on the derriere. "My God, Pauline. I've never seen anything quite like that. Sort of a combination of the Ballet Russe and a demolition derby."

"It's been awhile since I've done moguls," I panted.

"Well, you sure showed those moguls a thing or two." He turned to the other three skiers. "Let's cut through the trees here and finish up on Christie's."

I gave my instructor a guarded glance, and he grimaced slightly. "The worst is over," he encouraged.

Buoyed by the knowledge that my ordeal was nearly finished, I followed the other skiers across a small path through the woods. The track was narrow, but level, and feeling triumphant at having survived thus far, I wasn't paying attention when the path wound around to reveal a low hanging branch.

In retrospect, it would have been better to duck. But the branch took me so by surprise that I tried to stop instead and was catapulted off the trail into the woods below. Both of my skis came off, and I continued to travel downhill for some distance before coming to a stop in the waist-deep snow. After managing to extricate my face, I looked uphill to see Dusty Craw stopped on the trail above me. The look on his face did little to instill confidence.

"Pauline," he called out. "I don't want to frighten you, but don't go any lower. You're on the edge of a drop-off."

"What do you mean a drop-off?" I cried out, a combination of outraged paying client and frightened child. Pushing back panic, I asked, "How do I get out of here?"

"You'll have to climb out."

"I don't think I can," I yelled back up the steep snow-covered terrain. Forgetting all about humiliation, all I wanted now was to get out alive. And I knew just how to do it. "I think I've injured something."

"Oh no!" he said, the voice of doom coming from above. "Where are you hurt?"

I gave it some thought. "It's my knee. I've done something to my knee."

"All right, Pauline. I'm going to have to go for the ski patrol. Sit tight. I'll get them here as quickly as I can."

Sit tight? Did he think I had any intention of moving one fraction of an inch after just being informed that my battered body rested on the edge of an unseen precipice? He skied off and I spent the next fifteen minutes shivering in the snow while working to repress visions of falling to my death. Finally, I looked up to see two incredibly handsome men wearing red jackets with white crosses climbing down through the snow. They asked me which knee was injured, and after some consideration, I told them it was the right one. They put it in a splint and attached me to some ropes. Then they lowered me over the drop-off onto the road below, where I was met by two more capable and attractive ski patrollers. They strapped me into a toboggan and covered me with a yellow tarp, leaving it open over my face so I could see.

As my chariot headed down the catwalk, one of the most excruciatingly embarrassing moments of my life occurred as we came around a bend and passed the Worthingtons and Lizzie Bodine. They must have been waiting there the entire time. When they saw the toboggan, they called out my name. I quickly pulled the tarp over my face and held it shut with my hand, so no one could see in, and I couldn't see out.

When we got to the bottom of the mountain, I was loaded into an ambulance and taken to Aspen Valley Hospital, where an annoyingly assured orthopedic doctor did some probing and announced that he didn't think there was anything wrong with my knee. After my insistence that it was truly injured, he suggested I may have possibly torn my anterior cruciate ligament, a body part I'd never heard of in my life. That sounded perfectly acceptable to me. He put the knee in a brace and told me to get an MRI upon my return to Chicago. He also told me not to ski for the rest of my visit. Those were the words I wanted to hear.

As I hobbled out of the emergency room, the earlier humiliation suddenly seemed worth it. Dexter Sr. was sitting in the waiting room. Alone. He took one look at the brace and apologized for allowing me to attempt such a ski run. I told him to put his mind to rest, and that I would be fine. Then I hobbled alongside him to the Range Rover where he helped me into the backseat, and we drove together back up Red Mountain to Casa W.

Suzanne told me later that Senior told her a woman with spunk such as mine was exactly what he was looking for.

15

Dangerous Liaisons

There was an intimate sit-down dinner at the Worthingtons' that evening. The brace severely restricted my wardrobe selection, and after numerous attempts involving skirts and fashion boots, I finally settled for velcroing it over a pair of jeans, which I topped with a cashmere sweater. As I hobbled into the room, Senior rushed up to greet me. I was happy to see that Lizzie Bodine was nowhere in sight. He took me around to meet the other guests, among them a couple who owned a basketball team, a famous television actor I had never heard of since I rarely turn on a television except to watch MacNeil/Lehrer, and a software developer and his wife who had an art collection valued at over one hundred million dollars. The actor's girlfriend was a starstruck young woman named Becky whose last literary undertaking was most likely *Seventeen* magazine. She hung on the actor's arm throughout the evening, nodding as if she understood what was being discussed, though I'm certain much of it passed through her airy little head. When the wife of the software developer lamented they had lost their house curator, Becky asked her if she had called a plumber.

Seated beside me at dinner, Senior was beyond attentive, at times resting his hand upon mine to indicate he found something I said to be exceptional.

I found myself laughing a little louder than usual, smiling a little wider, and tipping my head in the most coquettish manner a woman has ever practiced before a mirror. I drank quite a bit of wine, as did he. And after the guests had gone home to rest up for the next ski day, and a yawning Suzanne and Junior retired to their quarters, I found myself alone with Dexter Sr. I was sitting in a deep chair in front of the fire, my right leg in the brace propped up on an ottoman, when he came over and sat on the arm. He handed me a brandy.

I took the glass from him and our eyes locked in a way that told me this opportunity was an actual possibility. He moved his face closer to mine, and I could smell the pleasing scent of brandy on his breath. He tipped my face up toward his, and I closed my eyes. Then, to my absolute horror, a vision of Tag McKay popped into my brain.

I opened my eyes to assure my wine-befuddled self who I was getting ready to kiss. Thank God, what greeted me was the aristocratic face of Dexter Sr. and not some dusty blue-collar worker. He stroked my cheek with his long, silky fingers and took the snifter from me.

"Come," he said, tugging at my hand. "We'll be far more comfortable in my room."

So things were moving along according to plan, though complicated somewhat by the knee brace velcroed to the outside of my jeans. I stood rather awkwardly—not exactly the way I had envisioned my seduction—and let Dexter lead me down the long stone hall to the master suite. The room was cavernous with cascades of silk drapes and beautiful, yet masculine, furniture clearly selected by a decorator who was sensitive to the needs of a single male. Animal skins were strewn across the floor, and a wet bar lined one entire wall. A free-standing marble-wrapped Jacuzzi stood in clear sight through the open bathroom door. Dexter led me to the enormous bed where he seated me on the edge. Then he sat down beside me and kissed me with a wet, open-mouthed kiss.

I found myself wanting to recoil. He kissed me again, the sensation of his rubbery, damp lips calling to mind a blowfish seeking oxygen. This felt more like artificial respiration than *amour*. Once again, an uninvited vision of Tag McKay popped into my brain. What was wrong with me? I wondered.

Here I was in the bedroom of a billionaire, and I couldn't shake unwelcome thoughts about a common laborer? But my drunken mind fixated on his eyes, those turquoise eyes I first saw blink from beneath a coating of dust. I could see the rough-hewn contours of his face and the cleft in his chin. His compact muscular body and the ruggedness of his strong hands. I thought of him reading from Shakespeare's *Sonnets*.

While my mind wrestled with these inappropriate thoughts, Dexter Sr. was forging onward, gently lifting my legs onto his bed. Though I give him credit for being mindful of the brace, what happened next reigns high in the annals of unbelievable sexual behavior on the part of the rich and powerful. After gracing me with a few more wet, slobbery kisses, he slid open his nightstand drawer and took out a jar of Vaseline. I stared in curious wonder as he took off the lid and placed the jar in my hand.

"Here," he actually cooed. "Rub it on your palm." He started unbuckling his turquoise-studded belt buckle without any further effort to romance me. Looking down into the Vaseline jar in my hand, I was overcome with a wave of nausea to see it was half-empty. Need it be said that Pauline Cook never performs any act against her wishes, no matter what the reward? Suddenly, I had no interest in this man whatsoever, no matter how many planes, homes, and connections he had. All I knew was that I wanted out of that room and I wanted out now. I dropped the Vaseline onto the floor as though it were a scorpion that had just bitten me.

"I'm afraid I have to be going," I said.

He stared at me as though I had just challenged him to a duel. I was certain he was used to getting his way. Money can do that for a man. Well, for anyone, I suppose. But his money wasn't going to work with me. I may have been a middle-aged woman teetering on the rim of poverty's canyon and treading water in a sea of young flesh, but I had no intention of performing a sex act that originated in the backseats of cars in high school.

Though I was severely hampered by the knee brace, I tried to crawl over him. He raised a leg to stop me.

"Is something wrong?" he asked. For the first time, I could tell he was really drunk. He tried to grab me, but I moved out of reach and swung myself off the other side of the enormous bed.

"I'd just really rather be alone this evening," I said, marching to the door as quickly as the brace would permit. Once outside his room, I took off the brace and ran back to my suite, locking the door behind me. Then I called the airlines and booked myself the first flight I could get back to Chicago the next day, which was at three in the afternoon.

I sat in bed in the dark with my eyes wide open, staring at the white mountains outside the window, thinking about how much there was to be done once I got home. With Dexter Worthington Sr. no longer in the picture, it was more important than ever that I get that ten million dollars.

Suzanne came to my room the next morning to find out why I hadn't shown up for breakfast. I told her I had a terrible headache, and that since I wasn't able to ski I would be leaving. After all, there was really no reason to stay.

"But, Pauline, you can't leave. The parties are just beginning."

"I'm just not feeling right about this knee injury. I think I'd best get back to Chicago and have a doctor see to it."

She seemed genuinely saddened that I would be leaving. I wondered if she had any idea how lecherous her father-in-law was.

The Worthingtons went skiing, and I finished reading *Bel Canto* while taking a long, luxurious bath. Then I packed and had the caretaker drive me into town, where I left my bags with the bell captain at the Little Nell while I lunched in their gourmet restaurant, Montagna. The room was filled, but I sat peacefully alone, nodding to the occasional Chicago person I knew. (Let them wonder what I was doing there all by myself for all I cared.) I had a steely glass of premier Cru Chablis, a lovely piece of salmon, and finished up with a cup of herbal tea, trying not to think about the bills that awaited me upon my return to Chicago.

It was then I noticed Jack Armstrong sitting at a table in the back of the restaurant with two women, both of whom were fairly draped over him. I wondered why they hadn't taken a room in the hotel. He didn't notice me, and so I turned back to my tea and thought about the plan I had come up with the night before. I was going to find Whitney, and he was going to pay me the ten million dollars. And he would have to. I had plenty of witnesses.

I checked my watch. It was time to head to the airport. I was preparing to ask for the check when the hostess seated a party of four at the table beside me. One of the foursome, a bald-headed man with a kindly face, looked somehow familiar. He returned my glance with a sheepish smile. And then slowly, like an ice cube thawing in an abandoned glass of scotch, it dawned on me who was sitting beside me. My spine stiffened in anger, and I had to struggle to place my cup back into the saucer without chipping it. I told myself it was unkind to hate the man, that he had lost a lot more money than I. In fact, it was my understanding that his wife had been forced to take some kind of a job in a furniture store.

But if he was so down-and-out, what was he doing here in Aspen?

I gathered up my purse and went to the reception desk, where I turned in my coat check. While I was waiting for the hostess to come back with my coat, my waiter came running up.

"I'm sorry, ma'am, but you've forgotten to pay your check."

Pushing the leather sleeve back at him, I gestured into the dining room. "I didn't forget. Give it to that man over there."

"Who?" the waiter asked, perplexed.

"The man sitting right over there. Mr. Kenneth Lay. Tell him it's the least he can do for one of his former investors."

16
Gulliver's Travels

The first thing I did when I got to the airport was hobble up to the check-in desk where my knee brace secured me a bulkhead seat from the sympathetic agent. The next thing I did was dump the now-useless brace in the trash. Then I sat down to wait, immersing myself in a Donna Leon mystery that transported me from wintery Aspen to the sunny Piazza San Marco in Venice.

It was just beginning to snow as my flight was called to board. I was connecting through Denver, and if all went on schedule, I would be back in Chicago just in time for a late dinner in the Cape Cod room. But, as my recent run of luck would have it, things didn't go on schedule. Twenty minutes into the flight, the pilot announced that the Denver airport had been closed due to bad weather, so we would have to return to Aspen. Another twenty minutes later, he announced that the ceiling in Aspen had also become too low for a landing. Evidently this pilot took the FAA regulations far more seriously than the Worthingtons' pilot did. So, as things turned out, I ended up seeing Grand Junction after all. After a bad meal and a night in a cheap motel in the outpost of civilization, I understood why Dexter Worthington had not wanted to divert there.

What's worse, the following morning my fellow passengers and I were loaded onto a bus to Denver. We drove through a harrowing storm, so blinding it felt like being encapsulated in a snow globe. On the lighter side, at least I couldn't see the mountain passes we threatened to plunge off. We arrived in Denver six and a half hours later, where I was informed that although I had booked a first-class ticket, for the hefty last-minute price of fifteen hundred dollars, for some reason I was seated in coach. My insistence that I be seated in first class only seemed to aggravate the already stressed gate agent who, claiming overbooked flights due to weather, not only kept me in coach but put me in a middle seat. As I sat wedged between a woman who was a prime candidate for a surgical staple in the stomach and a teenager wearing headphones turned up so loudly it was a wonder he had any gray matter left between his ears, I vowed to treat airline employees more kindly in the future.

Having finished *Aqua Alta* on the bus, I rooted through the seat pocket in front of me for something to read, finding little more than the airline magazine and a crushed Starbucks cup from the previous passenger. Noticing the torn masthead of a *Wall Street Journal* poking out from the seat pocket in front of the soon-to-be-deaf teenager, I reached over and took it, feeling secure that the paper did not belong to him.

Though it was Monday, the paper was dated the previous Friday, more evidence of the abysmal disregard for cleanliness on the part of commercial carriers. I skimmed the news items on the front page. There were recaps of our success in liberating the Afghan women of their dreadful burkas and warnings of a stagnant economy. My eye traveled to the right-hand column, where a sketch of Jack Armstrong caused me to jolt upright in my seat. Jack was the focus of an article profiling the success of Verry Lingerie, and how he had built it up from a manufacturer of basic cotton panties to the style giant it was today. In direct contrast to what Bharrie had heard about Verry being in trouble, the article detailed Jack's financial success with the company. It quoted him saying that his business remained steady, and due to his judicial management of costs, his bottom line stayed high. No pun intended, he added.

"After all," he said, "women want to feel confident, and where better to start than underneath it all. The same goes for a business. Confidence begins with what lies beneath the surface."

I wondered what lay beneath Jack's surface.

Twenty-four hours after leaving Aspen, my three suitcases and I arrived back at the Drake. Of course, the airlines didn't lose these bags, filled with now useless casual winter wear and ski clothes. I wondered if there was any possible way to return the ridiculously expensive Bogner ski outfit worn only once, but that idea was put to rest upon seeing a snag I must have picked up from the tree branch before being thrown into the abyss.

The thought of luggage inspired me to put in another call to Air France. This time Madame Duchamp was overjoyed to inform me that all seven Louis Vuitton bags had been delivered to my co-op last Friday afternoon. Finally, something had gone right. Rejoicing that my new clothes had arrived in time for the holidays, I rushed down the block to my building. The bag lady had taken up residence on the parkway again with her head bowed beneath a filthy scarf. Though I was taking Maria's words more seriously since visiting a "cold place," her prediction of a man I would "look up to" certainly hadn't panned out, so I decided to overlook this stranger in rags for the time being. I rushed into the lobby where Louis, who is usually the night doorman, was on duty. A tall, distinguished-looking African American with prominent sideburns and better posture than Lady Astor, he was in the process of sorting through the mail.

"Good afternoon, Mrs. Cook," he said, snapping to attention upon seeing me.

"Good afternoon, Louis. I'm surprised to see you here in the afternoon."

"Tony's on vacation for the holidays, ma'am, so I'll be covering his shifts until he gets back."

"How nice," I said, thinking that only Tony would be so dense as to take time off during the holidays when generosity is running high. "Louis, I understand that Air France has delivered some luggage for me."

"Luggage?" he said. "I don't know anything about any luggage, but let me check." He disappeared into the storage closet behind him and came back scratching his cap. "I don't have anything here from Air France."

"But Madame Duchamp has assured me that my luggage was delivered on Friday."

"It's not here, Mrs. Cook. Are you sure they delivered it to the right building?"

My blood hummed in exasperation at this ongoing nightmare. My clothes. My shoes. My gown. It was simply too much to bear. I had a claim check and the phone number for Air France's luggage department in my wallet. I handed them over to Louis.

"Be a darling, would you, and see if you can straighten this out. They insist the bags were delivered here."

"I'll take care of it, Mrs. Cook."

I thanked him and walked to the elevator, where the gilded doors stood open awaiting a passenger. He trailed behind me. "Oh, Mrs. Cook, before you go up, there's something you need to know—"

I broke in without giving him an opportunity to finish. "Louis," I commanded, pushing the button for my penthouse. "Air France. Now. Please." As the doors closed upon him, the look on his dark face reminded me of a child who has waited too long to ask permission to use the facilities.

On the way up in the elevator, my thoughts turned to Tag McKay, and the image of him that had flashed before me during the ill-executed seduction attempt by Dexter Worthington Sr. Telling myself the vision was an aberration, I hoped that the cold, harsh reality of seeing Mr. McKay in his paint-splattered work gear would put any inappropriate thoughts about him to rest. But before I could give the notion any more thought, I got out of the elevator and stepped into my apartment to see my downstairs neighbors, Joan and Reed Armitage, standing in the middle of my living room alongside Tag McKay and a mousy little man I had never seen before. Hailing from Philadelphia, Joan is a former debutante and DAR, while Reed is one of the lock-jawed landed gentry actually brave enough to eat asparagus with his fingers. Mystified by their presence in my home, I walked toward them only to realize the floor was undulating beneath my feet. I looked down to see what resembled the bed of a dried lake. A strange odor in the air smelled like the dampness of the forest. The look on Louis's face began to take on meaning.

I turned to Tag McKay and demanded, "What is going on here?"

It was Joan who replied. "It seems a water pipe has burst and leaked into our apartment," she said. "There's been damage to some of our art. Mr. Reynaud here is from Chusett, and he wanted to come up and take a look."

I recognized the name of Chusett, the insurer to the wealthy, a company that specialized in underwriting priceless objects of art and irreplaceable jewelry. Though the premiums were stratospherically high, I used them myself for my Pissarro and a few other items. Knowing the Armitages to be collectors of museum-quality art, I cringed to think what damage a flood might wreak in their house.

"Well, that's all I need for now," Mr. Reynaud said as he made a couple of notes on a pad of paper. "I'll get back to you when we determine who is liable." He nodded to me and walked out.

"We have to be going, too, Pauline. Reed's got a plane to catch, and I've got book group at Sunny's," Joan said, as if the loss of valuable works of art was an everyday occurrence. With one of the mildest dispositions I had ever encountered, Joan was the sort of person who generally faced disaster unruffled. Unlike Reed, who was the polar opposite. His voice seethed with pent-up frustration. "I just pray the humidity hasn't ruined the Dubuffet."

Joan looked down at her feet. "It's a shame about your floors," she said, and then they were gone in a flurry, leaving me alone with Tag McKay. The band of patience that had been drawing ever more taut snapped. Any romantic notions I harbored involving the short, ill-mannered, incompetent standing in front of me had to be a result of my subconscious playing a practical joke.

"How on earth did you manage this?" I spewed, spinning about as I took in the damage. The surface of my floors looked like Lake Michigan on a windy day. "Look at this mess. Do you realize that because of your incompetence, the Armitages may lose some valuable pieces of art? Have you any idea what their art collection is worth? I just hope your insurance is paid up, because I refuse to pay for anything. How can anyone do something so stupid?"

He took my insults without flinching, staring at me with unblinking turquoise eyes. Though I would have expected to see anger rise in them at my insults, frighteningly enough, all they revealed was pity.

"Have you finished?" he asked with measured calm.

"For the moment." I found myself working hard to keep my façade from crumbling under his gaze.

"Then perhaps you might wanna take a minute and listen for a change and maybe you'll learn exactly what happened here. The main hot-water supply feed to this floor had rusted through, and it blew on Sunday. It's a building issue and had nothing to do with this construction. It's damn lucky I stopped here on Sunday and saw the steam coming up through the floor. If I hadn't been here, the water would have traveled a lot farther, and there would have been a hell of a lot more damage."

I tried to speak, but it's rather difficult when one has a crow stuck in one's throat. And a rather large crow at that. I wished fruitlessly that I could breathe back the unkind words I had said, suck them back the way a vacuum cleaner recovers dust. But they had been spewed, mean and malicious, and I stood reduced in their wake. My face turned red with embarrassment and shame. That is, until Mr. Tag McKay pointed a finger at me and said, "Pauline Cook, I know you couldn't help being a spoiled brat as a child, but it's truly a shame you can't stop behaving like one as a grown woman. What you really need is a politically incorrect spanking. You might actually turn out to be likable."

My face grew even redder as his insult settled on me like an oil slick on marine life. I gasped in anger like a fish searching for oxygen. How dare he upbraid me! It was time to put the societal order back into balance.

"You're fired," I spouted. "Gather your things, and don't be here the next time I return."

I crossed my arms and waited for an argument, some plea for leniency. Instead he smirked wordlessly and started picking up his tools. I turned and took measured strides across the wobbly floor to the elevator and descended to the lobby where I found Louis deep in conversation with Air France. I held up a hand indicating he need not help me, and stormed out the door, ready to personally displace the homeless woman myself. But even those intentions were met with frustration. The homeless woman was gone.

17

Pride and Prejudice

The Palm Court at the Drake might be considered one of the last bastions of civilization. Subdued and refined, with potted palms and coffered ceilings, with some imagination it transports me to the finest hotels of Europe, which is where I would have preferred to be at the moment. I sat sullenly drinking a vodka martini—desperate times call for desperate measures—wondering whether it was a wise move or a foolhardy one to shed myself of the insolent Tag McKay.

A well-dressed woman carrying a shopping bag walked into the crowded room and looked around in search of a seat. She appeared to be about my age; rivulets of gray flowed through her chestnut hair and the permanent lines of previous laughter splayed from her wide-set brown eyes. She was slim, though her narrow body thickened as the eye moved lower, the result of flesh following gravity as one ages. Her eyes fell upon the vacant table next to me and she walked toward it, her pointed chin held high and shoulders squared, bringing to mind my mother's words about proper posture. *Think of a string coming out the top of your head.*

"Is this table taken?" she asked, looking at a couple of empty glasses left from the people beforehand.

"It's free. It hasn't been cleared yet."

She placed her bag on the banquette and sat down. "They make a good martini here?" she asked, the question at odds with her prim appearance.

"Ample," I replied. "That's all that matters."

"Anchovy olives?"

"Is there any other kind?"

A waiter approached and she ordered a vodka martini, straight up, with two anchovy olives. Then she relaxed in her chair and turned toward me. "This weather is truly wicked. I don't know how people can stand living here."

"I've been asking myself the same question ever since moving here to marry my husband twenty-six years ago. Now that he's gone, I'm not quite sure why I stay."

"You're divorced?" she asked, not impolitely, as my tone had implied we were no longer together.

"I'm a widow," I confided. "Henry died thirteen years ago."

"I'm sorry to hear that," she apologized. "My husband is dead, too—to me. Unfortunately, he's still breathing."

"Sounds like a nasty divorce."

"Is there a good one?"

"Not that I've ever heard of." I held out a hand. "I'm Pauline Cook."

"Emily Rossetti." She shook my hand and continued as if we were already in the middle of a conversation. "Unfortunately, my husband tired of me. You know the story. Young mistress. He came to me one day and told me he was looking for something more in life, neglecting to tell me he'd already found it. I was devastated. We've only just ironed out the last of the financial details. Or battered them out, I should say." She sighed. "Sometimes I wonder if we had had children if that would have kept us together."

I took the last sip of my drink, and generally would have stopped there. But struck with the desire for conversation, I signaled the waiter for a refill. "We didn't have children either. But we loved each other until the day he died. A brain tumor," I added without prompting. And then, not wishing to elaborate on Henry's death, I said, "I hope at least you did well."

"Nothing near what I should have. He kept the bulk of our assets, not to mention the bulk of our friends. Of our social life. The club memberships.

And Houston is such a closed society, I decided I wasn't going to stay there and fight it, that I was going to relocate altogether. I looked at the map and settled on Chicago. My reasoning was that New York is too big, Los Angeles too strange. And I don't know a soul here, so I don't have any history to live up or live down. I just closed on a condominium on LaSalle Street, but it won't be ready for a couple of weeks. Now that I'm getting a taste of the weather, I'm beginning to second-guess my decision."

"Houston?" My ears perked up at the sound. "A lot of unhappy people down there these days."

"Ah, the Enron debacle. The local economy is suffering."

So is this local economy, I thought, taking another steely sip.

"Are you staying at the Drake too?" she asked.

"I'm living here while my co-op is under construction. Which may be forever. I just fired my contractor."

"Oh, my," she said. "That sounds dire."

"It is," I concurred, and then told her my Job's tale of a construction project. When I finished, she placed a compassionate hand on my arm.

"Is your contractor any good?"

I sighed. "His work is beautiful. It's his arrogance that put me over the edge."

"Well, honey, maybe you should forget about his arrogance. A good contractor is harder to find than a husband. You might think about going back and eating some humble pie."

I thought about what she had said. She had just put into words what I had been thinking of doing all along. I took a last bracing sip of vodka, and signed my check. "Emily," I said, "you were a godsend."

I reentered my lobby riding on the momentum of the two martinis. Louis tried to tell me something, but I held up my hand to silence him, afraid to lose my momentum. After all, humble is a word infrequently employed in my vernacular and only when referring to others. Humble, think humble, was my mantra the entire way up the elevator. For some reason my hands were shaking. The truth was, I would have preferred to be standing at the top of Walsh's again than beg Tag McKay not to desert me.

The elevator doors opened onto a foyer stacked high with construction equipment. He certainly wasn't losing any time in evacuating. I tiptoed around it and down the hall, the soggy hardwood floor giving way beneath my feet like the marshy undergrowth of a forest. I located Mr. McKay in the same place I had first laid eyes on him, my master bathroom. But the room no longer resembled the aftermath of a pillaged town. It was flawless. He was standing in the center of it, and I could tell he was admiring his own handiwork. Fighting back a last-minute impulse to turn and run, I cleared my throat. He started and turned around.

"What is it now?" he asked, sounding irritated. "Don't worry. I'm on my way out. I just wanted to come and take a last look. You have to admit it turned out pretty good."

"It certainly did," I admitted. I took a deep breath to bolster my courage and let the words float out on the exhaled air. "There's something I'd like to discuss with you."

"Pauline, no disrespect intended, but we have nothing to discuss. I'm not your whipping boy anymore. I'll pick up my stuff tomorrow and leave the bill on the way out. You're right. This relationship is much better severed."

My pride told me to let him go. Though Emily Rossetti had said a good contractor is harder to find than a good husband, maybe I was willing to take that chance. Then again, keeping him had become a challenge, too, and I hated to lose.

"I'm not so sure about that," I said.

"Not so sure about what?"

"I'm not so sure that this relationship is better severed."

"Really?" He raised a brow. If his goal was to make me squirm, it was working.

"I've given it some consideration, and though we don't exactly get along, I must admit the quality of your work is outstanding. So taking that in mind, I'd like to retract my earlier request."

"You mean the request that I take my incompetent sorry ass and get out of here?"

How it can sting one's ears to hear one's words repeated to one. Then again, I had never used the words "sorry ass" in my life. "I never said that."

"Never said what? Pauline, quit talking in riddles. Spit it out already."

"I'm willing to give you another opportunity." There, I had said it. All he had to do was agree, and he could get back to work in the morning. Unfortunately, his response to my fairness was not what I had expected. Not even close. He made a sound that carried with it such a total lack of respect that the notion occurred to me that I might not win this battle after all.

"Ha!"

I waited for him to elaborate on the "ha." He did not do me the honor. I toed something nonexistent on the imported marble tile of the bathroom floor as I tried another tack. "I'm serious about this. I feel that your work is of such high quality that despite any differences we may have, I would like to keep you in my employ."

Another "ha" was followed by, "You are something else, Pauline. Working with you has been only slightly less harrowing than the Viet Cong. Believe me, I have only barely tolerated this job and you for one reason and one reason only. And let me tell you something. It's not because I need the money. There's plenty of work out there. It's love for the work. I love putting my hands to something and watching it change, watching something new emerge because of my efforts. I have the soul of an artist and would have loved to be an artist or a writer, but unfortunately, I don't have the talent. What I do have the talent for is this—transforming something old into something new. And doing it with my own hands."

He held his hands out in front of him and stared at them as if they were alien objects, before dropping them back to his sides.

"I fell in love with this project. Your apartment has been my palette. It's like a child that I'm nurturing and watching grow.

"But dealing with someone as difficult as you takes away from the satisfaction. I ask myself, Why am I creating this masterpiece for this sour unhappy soul to inhabit? The day you cried, I truly felt sorry for you and thought there was some humanity in you. I was wrong. I still feel sorry for you because you should be happy. Instead you work hard at being miserable, and making others miserable along with you."

I wanted to reach out and slap his face. How dare he speak to me that way, a mere workman, an employee, and a fired one at that? I wanted to tell him to forget what I had just said, that he could continue making his way to the door, and not to hold his breath waiting for my check. I wanted to tell him that my overtures to retain him were a huge mistake and there was now no doubt in my mind that my decision to terminate him had been the right one.

That's what I wanted to tell him, but I didn't. I didn't because what he said about my unhappiness was so right. Though I went through every day, from person to person, from event to event, like a whole person, I felt hollow inside, like a chocolate Easter bunny that looks solid until one pushes on the shell and it collapses. I used outside events and desires to keep the shell firm over the hollowness, not allowing anyone near for fear it would collapse. But I was aware of its existence and sometimes feared it might cave in of its own volition. So I was always in search of something that might make the shell thicker. An Italian captain. An art collection. A couture gown.

However, one does not change immediately, if ever, and I wasn't going to give him the satisfaction of knowing he had so accurately pierced my façade. Pretending that what he had said made no impression on me, I toned down my hubris and said quietly, "I would like you to finish this project. What would it take for you to stay?"

Though some of the anger still lingered on his face, it had softened. Taking his chin in his hand, he pursed his lips and gave me a sidelong glance, narrowing his eyes as if in deep thought. "An apology," he said.

His words caught me off guard. I'd already admitted I was wrong. What more did he want? "I believe I've already done that."

"No, Pauline. You've talked around it. But you haven't come out and apologized for treating me as less than an equal. Here's something you'd do well to learn, Pauline. No one is better than anyone else. And no one is lesser."

"Thank you for the lesson," I said. "So you'll stay on?"

"As soon as you apologize."

"I said I already have."

"No, you haven't. I haven't heard you say, 'I'm sorry, Tag. I'm sorry if I said something that may have been hurtful to you.' I want to hear those words. Then I'll stay."

It was a standoff. If I didn't perform as he asked he would walk away.

I tried to wrap my lips around the words and found myself balking, like a horse at a jump when the gate is set too high. Instead of apologizing I heard myself say, "This is nonsense. Now do you want to stay or not?"

"I gave you my condition."

I tried again to say it, but the apology lodged in my throat, like trying to say "I love you" when one doesn't. The words "I'm sorry" carry with them a great deal of power, but also a great deal of submission, and they did not want to issue forth from my mouth.

He recognized my dilemma, but was not going to give me any slack. "How can you hurt another person's feelings and not care?" he asked. "Forget it, I'm outta here." He grabbed a few odd tools from the bathroom counter and brushed past me into the hall.

A new light was suddenly shed on the situation. Since first meeting him I had viewed him as stubborn and obtuse. The notion that he had feelings to hurt had never occurred to me.

"Wait," I called out.

He stopped in his tracks.

"I'm sorry," I said to his back. "I'm sorry I hurt your feelings."

He stood like a statue for a minute and then continued down the hall without turning back. I stood in defeat, feeling for all the world like a warrior who has not only lost the battle but has painful wounds to deal with as well. I had made a fool of myself and lost. The only thing missing was a sword to fall upon.

Then I saw his compact, sturdy form come back into the hall. He was carrying a toolbox. He walked up to me and put it down on the floor, his face inches from mine. "OK, I'll finish the job," he said.

"Thank you," I whispered. Avoiding his eyes, as if we were two strangers in the hall of an office building, I moved away from him. "I'll be going now," I whispered even more softly.

I walked around him and down the soggy hall. His footsteps behind me made me nervous until I realized he was just coming back to the foyer to get some more of his equipment. I pushed the call button for the elevator and tried to mentally hurry it up as he puttered around behind me. The moment the elevator doors opened, I practically leaped into the gilded box. Before the doors could close again, he looked toward me and our eyes locked.

"'Had we but world enough, and time, This coyness, lady, were no crime,'" he said smiling.

My cheeks flushed red.

I stopped in the lobby to talk to Louis. He told me that Air France was going to get back to him with the name of the delivery service they used, and he would take it from there. I thanked him and headed back to the Drake, realizing that suddenly I wasn't worried about my bags anymore.

That night I lay restlessly in bed, my thoughts dominated by Tag McKay. I recognized the words he had said as the elevator doors were closing. They were from yet another poem studied in Miss Shingleheart's English Lit class, Andrew Marvell's "To His Coy Mistress." I remembered laughing with Rebecca Leach and Drusilla Butler as we tried to imagine why dried-out old Miss Shingleheart so loved this poem. Part of the poem came back to me.

Had we but world enough, and time,
This coyness, Lady, were no crime.
We would sit down, and think which way
To walk, and pass our long love's day.

And then I recalled Miss Shingleheart standing in front of the class after we had dissected the poem, and her exact words rang in my brain. *In Andrew Marvell's poems we learn that deepest passion rises from frustration.*

I stared into the darkness of my empty room trying to understand my inappropriate feelings toward Tag McKay. It had to be menopause, the genetic drive so hard-wired it will settle for anything in the last surges of fertility.

I wondered if hormone therapy might help to fight off this rash behavior.

18

Portrait of a Lady

Tuesday was filled with the mundane, a hair appointment, lunch with Sunny and the rest of the Amici of the Literati team, an evening cocktail party. Christmas was a mere week away, but it didn't make a huge difference to me since there was no one special to shop for anyway. I tried to think of Christmas outside my home, with no tree and no Fleur trying to knock it over. My heart was heavy.

My obsession with Jack's offer became even greater. Who was this chameleon Jack Armstrong anyway? With Whitney he had been the attentive and loving husband. When she disappeared, he played the inconsolable, wronged spouse. In Aspen, he acted as a libertine. I had come to the conclusion that last night in Aspen that the key to finding Whitney might lie with Jack himself. I needed to know what made him tick. And who better to tell me than someone who had known him long before Whitney. Someone who had probably seen all those sides and more. Someone who had no reason to hold back.

That someone would be his first wife.

Theresa Armstrong and I had been close at one time, but we fell out of touch after she and Jack got divorced. I didn't even have a phone number for her anymore, but when I looked in the phone book, there was a Theresa Armstrong listed on West Fullerton, so I called it and was surprised when she picked up. I hadn't expected it to be that easy to find her.

She seemed very pleased to hear from me. After all, we had been close at one time. Not wanting to reveal my true motive for contacting her, I fibbed and told her she had been on my mind lately, and that I wondered if she would like to get together for lunch. She said she had a job and that breaking away for lunch was difficult for her. She suggested I come to her apartment for coffee the next morning, and we could catch up then.

I accepted the invitation and hung up in total shock that Jack Armstrong's ex-wife worked.

The next morning I retrieved my car from the nearby garage where it was housed. My landmark building was constructed in the twenties when most people had drivers and no need for garages. The attendant pulled the car around and the usual twang of melancholy struck me at the sight of it. The 1972 limited-edition Jaguar XKE in opalescent metallic bronze had been one of Henry's prized possessions and always drew admiring looks when I drove it. Which was seldom these days. I didn't like subjecting it to the rudeness and unpredictability of present-day drivers, especially ones on cell phones. And honestly, would it be so difficult to employ an occasional turn signal?

I drove west on Fullerton in the early morning traffic until I reached Theresa Armstrong's building, a dreadfully bland high-rise with a sign out front advertising available space. At first I thought I had the wrong address. It was bad enough that Theresa had a job, but was it truly possible she lived in a rental? What was worse, there was no place to park. The metered spots in front of the building were filled and there was no underground parking, which I couldn't understand. This was hardly a landmark building. I circled the block a few times before finally finding a parking space on a side street where I locked the Jaguar and prayed no one would disturb it. Honestly. If one doesn't have parking, there should at least be a valet.

Once inside the entry I dialed in the code beside T. ARMSTRONG, and she picked up on the second ring. "I'll buzz you in," she said. As I rode the elevator to her floor, I thought how sad it was that Jack Armstrong's first wife was not only living in a rental building with no valet, but there wasn't even a doorman.

Theresa met me at the door wearing some kind of a uniform that reminded me of a nurse. She gave me a tired smile upon seeing me. Five years older than I, she looked good for her age. Well, perhaps dignified is a better word. She had let her hair go gray and her upper eyelids were practically parked on her eyelashes. The minimal makeup she wore didn't even cover her age spots. But there was still evidence of the beauty she had been in her youth and her high cheekbones and strong jawline kept her face from sliding too far south. Though I respected her choice to go *au naturel*, a good plastic surgeon could have easily restored much of her original glory.

"Theresa, it's been far too long. You look fabulous," I lied, as we hugged each other.

"Pauline, I swear you don't change. You just don't age," she responded, hopefully telling the truth.

I went into the apartment. It was charming in an odd sort of way despite the wall-to-wall carpeting and impossibly low ceilings. She had decorated it in a modern and inexpensive fashion—about as far as one could get from the antique-filled mansion she and Jack had once inhabited together. There were framed prints of Léger and Matisse, a poster announcing the opening of some exhibit at the Museum of Contemporary Art, and knockoff Barcelona chairs. The western exposure looked out on Chicago's grittier side as opposed to the lake. Just as in Emily Rossetti's case, it served to underline how the first wife truly does get the shaft. But considering all Jack's money, Theresa should have had more—a lot more. I decided she must have had the world's most inept divorce attorney.

She led me into a nook of a kitchen where a tray was laid with rolls and pastry. We sat down and she poured us a cup of coffee. How times had changed. There was a time when Theresa merely rang a little bell and coffee appeared before us. I nibbled at a crusty Danish and she devoured a couple of pastries while we made polite chitchat about people who had once been her close friends, but had been inherited by Jack in the divorce. The cold, hard truth is loyalty usually goes with the money. I knew Theresa had gotten a raw deal, but I hadn't known how raw.

"So tell me how you've been, Pauline," she prompted.

"Busy. Aside from the normal holiday insanity, I've been drafted to help out with the Amici of the Literati gala on New Year's Eve. Maybe you'd like to attend. There's a private showing of *A Midsummer Night's Dream*," I said, knowing from years ago she was a devotee of Shakespeare. For a moment I thought maybe she'd even like to be on the board, get out of this wretched apartment and see some people, but board dues alone were forty thousand dollars. From what I saw around me, I didn't think that was in her budget.

"*A Midsummer Night's Dream* in the dead of Chicago winter," she said, not answering my question. "What a stunning idea." She stopped in reflection, and I could all but see her drifting back to a previous time and place. Then a snap back to the present day, and her eyes focused back on me, their dark grayness veiled by folds of flesh, but their intensity clearer than ever. "Unfortunately my philanthropic plate is fully invested these days. Both financially and timewise. All my charitable donations and time go to the Women and Children First Foundation. It's a wonderful organization right here in Chicago. Very hands-on. We take care of battered and abused women, help them to get financially on their feet. We also help with their legal fees, get them safe homes, medical care for the children. I can't even begin to tell you all the good things we do. That's where I work, and the days just aren't long enough."

I feigned interest as she went on, trying to think of how to turn the conversation around to her ex-husband. As it turned out I needn't have troubled myself, because Theresa did it for me. "You know, when Jack left me, I was devastated. I didn't think I'd ever have a life again. You know how it is, Pauline. What man wants anything to do with someone our age?" I blinked stoically, not terribly pleased with her statement. "But it turns out that by leaving me, Jack actually liberated me. He liberated me from that catty, competitive life and the materialism of all those ridiculous people."

Another stoic blink as I wondered if I came under the umbrella of catty, ridiculous people as well. I took the opportunity to put in my probe. "I can't believe how terribly he treated you. With all his money, I would have thought he would have provided better for you."

The smile that crept across her face could be described in no other way than ironic. "Pauline, do you remember the good times we had together when Henry was alive and the four of us would go to dinner and the theater?"

"Of course I do. They're among my fondest memories."

"Well, while you and Henry were so in love and so happy together, Jack, who is so competitive he has to make everyone think that he is not only richer, but happier than anyone else, would come home after an evening like that and drink half a bottle of scotch. Then he would proceed to berate me for reasons I still haven't figured out. For not being clever enough. For not being beautiful enough. For getting older. There were times he actually hit me in his drunken stupors. And forced me to have sex while cursing at me the entire time. In fact, it wasn't sex, it was more like rape.

"When he quit drinking, I thought things would get better. That the alcohol was responsible for his behavior. But his abuse of me didn't stop. In fact, it actually got worse. I can't begin to tell you the mental and physical torment I went through. And I put up with it for one reason and one reason only—the money. When Jack divorced me, he not only liberated me from him, he liberated me from money."

Liberated from money? The two of us certainly had different outlooks. To my way of thinking, money was the great liberator.

"I'm telling you all this because I don't want you to feel sorry for me," she continued. "He did give me a substantial settlement. I've given most of it away."

I was appalled. In all the years that Henry and I had known Jack and Theresa as a couple I had never seen any indication that anything was amiss in their private lives. Thesesa had always led me to believe that they were one of the better-suited couples in our circle. It had always been my impression that Whitney had stolen Jack away. Was the truth that Theresa had allowed him to be stolen?

Then she added, "I almost feel like getting down on my knees and kissing Whitney's feet for saving me from that horrible life. I only hope Jack's not treating that poor woman the same way he treated me."

That poor woman? That poor woman had the finest designer clothes I had ever seen. That poor woman had three houses, her own Bentley, jewelry to make the Queen cry out in envy, and an unlimited allowance for her upkeep. It was hard to believe such words were coming from someone living under such mundane living conditions.

The sound of steps behind me told me we were not alone. Theresa looked up from her coffee cup and a sunny smile came to her face. "Good morning," she chimed to the yawning young man who had come in the room. His hair was dyed an unnatural voltage of orange, his eyebrows had multiple piercings, and a thorny tattoo snaked up his forearm. His dirty T-shirt was torn, and I would bet my co-op that the military pants he wore were not procured by any form of service to his country. It took me a minute to realize the creature was Jack Jr. The last time I had seen him was over ten years ago, and then he was a clean-cut teenager attending Latin School and wearing polo shirts. This creature neither resembled that boy nor any offspring I could imagine Jack Armstrong laying claim to.

He grunted something unintelligible about too much noise to which Theresa prompted, "Mind your manners, J.J. Do you remember Mrs. Cook?"

"Yeah, hey," he said, giving me all of one second's attention. He turned back to his mother. "I heard you talking about that bitch who took my father away."

The venom in his voice was lethal. Evidently, there was no love lost between Jack Jr. and his stepmother. Theresa gave him a leveling look. "J.J., don't speak that way about anyone and especially in front of a guest."

"Yeah, well if not for that whore, I'd be driving a Lexus instead of a fuckin' piece of shit Suburu."

"J.J. Your language!"

He ignored her and went into the refrigerator, taking out a carton of orange juice and drinking directly from it, before carrying it with him from the room. Her eyes followed his pierced, tattooed, dyed personage with a motherly love-is-blind kind of look.

"You must pardon my son. He tends to get emotional sometimes. He wanted to live with his father after the divorce, but he thinks Whitney didn't want him there. In truth it was Jack who didn't want him there, but I never wanted to tell J.J. that. So he blames her that he isn't living a high lifestyle, and I let him. He's a good boy overall."

"I'm sure he is," I said, thinking maybe it wasn't so bad that I hadn't had children after all.

Theresa looked at her watch. "Oh, look at the time," she said. "I really have to be going."

After stacking the plates in the single sink, she grabbed a down coat that made her look like the Michelin man, and we rode the elevator down together. Before we said our good-byes, there was one last question I needed an answer to, and I hoped she wouldn't think it odd.

"Theresa, can I just ask you one more thing?"

"Of course, Pauline. What is it?"

"Do you think your ex-husband is a man of his word?"

She didn't even have to think about the question. "He may have been an abusive pig and an utter ass, but there is one thing I can say about Jack Armstrong. He is a man of his word."

That was exactly what I wanted to hear.

19
My Life as an Explorer

Later that day, I sat in my hotel room thinking about my next move. There was no question about it. I had to get Whitney's cell phone records, just as Detective Malloy had suggested over lunch a couple of weeks ago. The question was how. Whitney had once told me that Jack paid all their personal bills. Though he let her spend at will, he was a stickler for control and was always double-checking her credit card statements to make sure there were no errors. If my logic was correct, all the paid bills would most likely be in the Armstong mansion in Jack's ground-floor office. But still having no idea if Jack was friend or foe, I wasn't going to ask him for them directly. And after talking to Theresa, the possibility loomed greater that Whitney might not want to be found, in which case I didn't want to give away her whereabouts to Jack until I talked to her first.

So how could I get those records without Jack knowing? The answer came to me in the bowing, obsequious image of Surrendra. He adored Madam, perhaps more than Jack did, and I strongly suspected he would be happy to be of assistance in helping to locate her. I decided go to him personally and ask for his help.

I grabbed the mink coat and hat I had retrieved from storage and headed for the door. I seldom wear fur, but this venture could entail some time spent outdoors, and with a wind like a nor'easter blowing off the lake, I wanted to be warm. I'd basically sworn off fur after my first safari with Henry. After seeing the magnificent animals in the wild, I'd returned home and given all my furs away. But I held onto the mink for emergencies. After all, those animals were long dead, so why should their lives have been completely in vain? And we did live in Chicago.

It was nearly three o'clock when I turned onto Astor Street. It had started to snow hard white pellets that stung my face. I pulled my cap down tightly over my ears and thought about buying a condo in Palm Beach when I got the money. I drew near the graystone mansion and slowed my pace. Staring at the snow-covered driveway, I wondered how I would know if the man of the house was in residence or not, since Jack frequently worked from home. The mansion was dark in front, but Jack's office was around the back next to the solarium. I walked slowly past the house hidden beneath my hat and coat, a solitary walker taking a pleasant stroll on a snowy day. The stone structure with its ornate carving and neoclassical façade yielded no clues. Halfway down the next block, I crossed the street and walked back on the other side, stymied as to how I could know if Jack was home or not. I could call on my cell phone to see if Jack picked up, but with the increasing use of caller ID, if Jack was home he would know it was me. Personally, I still hadn't signed on to the service, preferring to give my callers the courtesy of speaking with me before cutting them off.

Despite my outer trappings, my feet were getting cold and I berated myself for not having any true winter boots. I decided to walk to nearby Division Street and stop in the corner Starbucks to warm up and plan my next move. Though I am generally against any kind of chain store, I found the coffee shop to be an agreeable addition to the neighborhood. The brightly lit shop felt warm and welcoming with the rich scent of coffee in the air and the soothing sounds of Christmas music playing in the background. I ordered an espresso and carried it to a vacant table in the window. I took off my fur hat and smoothed my hair with a frozen hand as I pondered what to do next. I could do as the police do—what do they call it?—a stakeout?

But that might yield nothing, as there was a good possibility that while I stood watching his house, Jack Armstrong could actually return instead of leave. A sense of futility came over me, a sense that was further aggravated by the young man sitting next to me who appeared to have set up his office in the store, clicking nonstop at his computer while talking nonstop into his cell phone as well. After a solid fifteen minutes of this, I took a last, exasperated, sip of my espresso and decided to return to the Drake to give the situation further thought. Then genius set in. I was struck with a plan that would both let me know if Jack Armstrong was in his home and get him out if he was.

"Excuse me," I said to the young man, catching him in the nanosecond between calls. His long, thin body was a bundle of energy that flowed nonstop to his long, thin face. A small wisp of hair meant to pass as a beard formed a honeycomb on his chin. "I wonder if I might ask you a favor."

He shrugged his shoulders and raised his hands palms up, indicating I could certainly ask, but that he didn't guarantee the outcome.

"It's my anniversary and I have a little surprise planned for my husband. I've just come up with the idea that a call from a stranger would add a little more intrigue to my surprise. Would you mind terribly calling him and telling him that Whitney is waiting for him in our regular booth at Milano's?" Whitney had once told me that when the two of them wanted to be alone, this dinosaur of a restaurant was their favorite sneak joint. They had frequented it before Jack had divorced Theresa.

His grin added some depth to his narrow face. "Anything for love. Gimme the number."

And so this perfect stranger obliged me by calling the Armstrong residence and asking for Jack, who was home, as it turned out. He told him that his lovely wife, Whitney, would be waiting for him to make his appearance at Milano's, ad libbing on his own that Jack wouldn't be sorry that he came. I could hear the industry tycoon's voice demanding to know who was on the line as my newfound friend clicked his phone shut with a wry smile.

"He sounded a little angry," he said.

"Oh, he always sounds angry when he's surprised," I said, trying to put myself in Jack's shoes at the moment. He had to be very confused. Then another thought occurred to me. "Oh dear, if he uses caller ID to call you back, will you just stick to the story?"

"No worries there. He won't call back. I blocked the number."

"Blocked the number?" Technology always seemed to be several steps ahead of me.

"Sure," he said. "You just enter star-six-seven before dialing and it blocks the number of the incoming call." The stranger held out his hand. "My name is Marcel," he said.

"Pauline," I replied, and then realizing my mistake, I added, "but my friends call me Whitney."

The tire marks in the snow on Jack's driveway told me that he had taken the bait. I wondered what his frame of mind was now as he drove halfway across snowy Chicagoland. Was he hoping to find his beloved wife, or had he responded to the call for appearance's sake, knowing full well she couldn't possibly be there since he already knew her fate? If it was the former, I sincerely regretted putting him through any pain, but I couldn't risk jeopardizing my mission. Especially if the truth was the latter.

Feeling giddy with myself and my genius, I marched boldly up the walkway and rang the bell. Surrendra answered the door and stared at me quizzically before ushering me in out of the snow.

"Madam," he said, "I'm afraid Mr. Armstrong is not at home."

"I know that, Surrendra. That's why I'm here."

"I'm not sure I understand, Madam."

"Surrendra, you care deeply about Mrs. Armstrong, don't you?"

The anguished look on his face gave me my answer. "Yes, Madam."

"Well, so do I. And I intend to get to the bottom of her disappearance. But I'm going to need your help. I need to get something from Mr. Armstrong's desk."

Surrendra's eyes grew large. "But Mr. Armstrong—"

"Forget about Mr. Armstrong. What I'm doing may either help us find Mrs. Armstrong or prove that Mr. Armstrong had something to do with her going away. Now will you help me?"

He thought, but not too terribly long. "Mrs. Armstrong saved my life."

"I know that, Surrendra, and that's why I'm asking you to help possibly save hers. This is the only way. Are you with me?"

He bowed his shiny black head and stared at his feet. Then he looked back up, his eyes gleaming in his smooth brown face. "I told you they fought."

"Yes, I know that. Now come quickly."

Surrendra followed me down the hall, past a virtual gallery of Chinese art, and into Jack Armstrong's office. In the waning afternoon light, it was set in semidarkness, the two east-facing windows framed in heavy draperies. I flicked the switch and the room came to life beneath the overhead fixture. It was a masculine room, with a ponderous stone fireplace set beneath a heavy wooden mantle and a corner bar sporting crystal decanters filled with whiskey, scotch, and other liquors. Two heavy leather chairs sat in front of a massive mahogany desk.

With no time to waste, I walked around to the front of the desk and sat down. A narrow center drawer was banked by three deeper drawers on either side. I tried each one of the drawers, but they were all locked. I stared at the heavy piece of furniture and cursed to myself. I didn't know what I had expected, but this certainly wasn't it. A movielike scenario of breaking into the desk with a letter opener was little more than absurd as I studied the heavy hardware securing each drawer. It would take something more akin to a sledgehammer. Surrendra stood before me with rounded shoulders, his concave chest barely moving, as if taking too deep a breath might give him away.

"You wouldn't happen to know where Mr. Armstrong keeps the keys, would you?" I asked.

He blinked his long lashes and looked at me guiltily. "It's possible Sir keeps them in his bureau upstairs."

I'd always suspected Surrendra to be something of a snoop, especially with the way he was always appearing from out of the shadows. It had irritated me on previous visits to the Armstrong house, but in this case I found myself pleased.

"Show me," I commanded.

We mounted the winding staircase to the second floor and hurried down a hall of closed doors to the master bedroom at the end. If Jack's office was masculine, this room glowed with femininity. Through the light, airy drapes that hung from the French doors leading to the balcony, I could see the snow collecting on the wrought-iron railing outside. The large canopied bed had a peach silk headboard and matching duvet, and the sides of the room were lined with French antiques ranging from the Sun King to his unlucky descendant. Despite the urgency of my present mission, I had to let out an envious sigh at the sight of a finished master bedroom.

Surrendra went directly to the semainier in the corner of the room and opened the top drawer. He removed a small key ring and handed it to me with an obligatory look of guilt. "I have seen Sir put these keys in this drawer many times," he explained. If I found it odd that Jack Armstrong would go so far as to lock his desk, but leave his keys in plain sight of his manservant, I didn't let it bother me. I was only happy to have them in my possession.

We rushed back downstairs and into the office, where I quickly located the household files in one of the deep bottom drawers. They were neatly alphabetized, with categories ranging from the household help's tax withholding to the gas bill. I located the file marked TELEPHONE, WHITNEY, and neatly laid therein were her cell phone bills dating back a year. I removed the bills from the most recent months and left the rest in the file. I took a quick look at one, hoping that it was itemized, and, hurrah, it was. I relocked the drawer and was preparing to hand the keys back to Surrendra when another thought popped into my mind.

When I had visited Maria nearly three weeks before, she had indicated she might be able to give me some insight into Whitney's whereabouts if I were to bring her a personal item of Whitney's. Though I had yet to find my rich, tall soul mate, the psychic had been right about my visit to a cold place. Why leave any stone unturned? I decided to take advantage of being in Whitney's house.

"There's just one more thing, Surrendra. I must have something of Madam's."

We mounted the grand stairs again and rushed back down the hall into the bedroom. I went directly into Whitney's walk-in closet, a vast emporium of purse- and shoe-weighty shelves, and rod after rod of color-coded clothing, ranging from casual lunch suits to cocktail dresses to floor-length formals. In the center was a stack of built-in drawers, and I started opening them randomly in my search for something appropriate. Passing on a king's ransom of silk lingerie, bustiers, and garter belts, I opted for a far more sensible Hermès scarf. It was copper and olive and depicted the autumn harvest. Whitney had been wearing it knotted elegantly around her slim throat the last time I had seen her, the day I had dropped Fleur off before leaving for Europe. Secreting the scarf in my handbag, I stepped out of the closet and ran smack into a terrified Surrendra, who was holding a finger to his lips. "Mr. Armstrong has returned," he whispered, his eyes wild with excitement. "He is downstairs."

My heart began beating like the percussion section at Orchestra Hall. Surrendra pushed me back into the closet. "I will come for you when it is safe," he said, closing the door. Standing in the middle of Whitney Armstrong's closet, among some of the most beautiful and expensive couture clothing in Chicago, wearing a mink coat and hat, I wondered what possible explanation I could offer Jack Armstrong if he found me there. That I was shopping?

I sat down in the corner of the closet near Whitney's floor-length formals with the thought in mind that crawling behind them could provide a good hiding place if necessary. Fortuitously, the closet had a window, so there was some light, but the December day was quickly waning, and the light was poor. The sound of Jack Armstrong's voice coming down the hall set my heart back into a wild drumroll. He was speaking to Surrendra and he sounded angry. I imagined it had something to do with the wild goose chase he had been on. Unable to make out what he was saying, I started crawling toward the door to listen when the sound of a harsh "hello" in the bedroom sent me flying back into my corner. My heart pounded in my ears as I waited for him to fling the door open, thinking of what Theresa Armstrong had said about his capacity for violence. Cowering in fear, I drew myself farther beneath the wide skirt of a black Valentino gown I had envied at the Lyric's last wine auction. Something hard poked at my bottom, and when I reached around to feel what it was, I knocked over a stack of books.

Hoping the sound had been muffled by satin and organza, I held my breath and waited. Jack was still speaking, but the drone of his voice told me he was on the phone. I relaxed a little and picked up one of the books that had been hidden beneath the gowns, squinting in disbelief at the title. *The Jungle* by Upton Sinclair. What was Whitney doing with a book like that? Someone must have given it to her. I looked at a couple more. Steinbeck's *Grapes of Wrath*. Marx's *The Communist Manifesto*. There were a dozen books with similar themes of politics and humanity. Henry had been an inveterate reader, and I recognized most of the titles from the collection in my library. I'd read a couple of them at most, so to think of Whitney reading them was a real stretch. One thing was for certain. These books assuredly hadn't come from Sunny's book group.

There was one title I didn't recognize at all. *Human Chattel* by Chia Arunasetya. It was published by a small university press. The picture of the author on the back cover showed a middle-aged Asian woman. Though she stood with her arms defiantly crossed, something in her eyes bespoke unresolved fear. I opened the book and read the inscription.

To Whitney. May humanity never suffer again as we have. Chia.

I slipped the book into my bag alongside the Hermès scarf and cell phone bills. This was quite a little scavenger hunt I had going, I thought.

Then I heard the blessed word "good-bye" coming through the closet door, and the seam of light beneath the door disappeared. I was in the dark now, and I sat impatiently waiting for Surrendra to come and tell me the coast was clear. Ten minutes passed and then ten more. An hour ticked away. I was overheated in my fur coat and hat, but had left them on in the event I had to make a rapid escape. Wondering why Surrendra hadn't returned, I quietly cracked the door and looked out into the bedroom. I could see the white snow falling outside the windows. If the blizzard was getting worse, the chances of Jack Armstrong going out again were as slim as a third wife. What if he decided to go to sleep while I was still in the closet? I might be able to make it through the night without food or water, but how was I going to make it without a bathroom?

Knowing that there was a fire escape that dropped from the balcony to the ground floor, I decided to use it to make my escape. Tiptoeing from the closet, I stood in the middle of the room listening for any sound. When I was sure there was no one in the vicinity, I made my way slowly across the floor. When I reached the balcony door, I stood in front of it taking deep breaths to build my courage. The plan was to open the door quickly, slip outside, and shut it quietly behind me. I turned the knob and pulled the door toward me. A loud siren began to wail in a manner that could have roused Marjorie Wilken after her best night. Realizing I had tripped the security system, I rushed out onto the balcony. The fire escape steps were retracted, which meant it would take several minutes to get them to drop down. Spotlights had come on around the perimeter of the mansion and, torn between the panic of getting caught and the panic of a fall to the ground from the second story, I opted for the fall. I had survived Walsh's, after all.

I climbed over the railing and hunkered down as low as I could. Then, with a tight grip on the rails, I dangled my legs from the balcony. I could see the snow-covered bushes below me, and without giving it any more thought, I let go and dropped into them. I looked up and saw the shadow of someone standing over me. My heart clutched until I saw it was Surrendra. He called out loudly, "There is no one here, Sir," and then whispered to me urgently. "The keys. You forgot the keys."

I had indeed. I pulled the keys from my pocket and tossed them at him. Then I took off like a fugitive, my fashion boots slipping and sliding in the snow.

Upon reaching Dearborn Street I stopped running, figuring I had put enough distance between myself and the crime scene. Beads of moisture dotted my forehead, and rivulets of sweat ran beneath my mink coat. The Christmas lights of the brownstones glowed like colorful halos and the falling snow lent a peaceful feeling to the night. I looked up and down the street and with no taxi in sight, I started walking again. A police car came out of an alley and drove slowly alongside me. I kept my eyes forward, as if by ignoring the vehicle's existence, it would go away. It continued to keep pace with me for another excruciating minute before the officer on the passenger side rolled down the window.

"Excuse me, ma'am," a female voice called out.

I turned and looked at the car as if I was surprised to see it there. A young woman peered from the window, her dark hair pulled into a ponytail beneath her uniform cap. My first thought was this seemed an unlikely profession for such a pretty girl. My second thought was that she was eying me suspiciously. My heart was pounding again, and I wondered if she could see the sweat that was now running down my face.

"Are you speaking to me?" I asked in my most incredulous manner.

"Yes, ma'am. Do you live in this area?"

"I live on East Lake Shore," my quivering voice responded. Then thinking I sounded obsequiously cooperative, I pictured myself in a similar circumstance when not squirming under the umbrella of guilt. More in keeping with my usual self, I demanded, "Is this some new service of the Chicago Police Department, stopping pedestrians and demanding their home addresses?"

"No, ma'am. But there's an intruder running at large around here and he may be dangerous. Why don't we give you a ride home?"

I was about to say I would be fine on my own when I saw Jack Armstrong rounding the corner. With my red hair hidden beneath my fur hat he would never recognize me until he got closer. "I would love a ride," I said. The female officer got out of the car and opened the back door for me.

"You're sweating," she said.

"It's this mink. I'm afraid it's awfully warm."

20

A Room of One's Own

My hotel suite felt like a cocoon, insulated and safe, far removed from the dangers of intruders lurking about outside. After a long, steaming-hot bath, I ordered room service. Curled in the comfortable folds of my terrycloth bathrobe, I washed a green salad and a bowl of Bookbinder's soup down with a half bottle of Taittinger. Then, feeling very much the proper thief, I reviewed the phone bills I had lifted from the Armstrong residence.

I studied the numbers that Whitney had called before her disappearance. The list was long. My eyes scanned the pages and I saw many numbers familiar to me. There were multiple calls to Sunny, Bharrie, Suzanne Worthington, and a bevy of other Gold Coasters who were on my own speed dial. There was Emilio's, the tony salon we both frequented, and Dr. Rimsky, the preferred Gold Coast practitioner for Botox and the latest fillers. I crossed off all the numbers I recognized. When I had finished, there were twenty-three numbers left. Five of these were repeated enough times to be of interest. I thought of Detective Malloy asking me if it was possible that Whitney had a boyfriend, and wondered if I had been off the mark when I'd laughed at the suggestion.

Having winnowed down the list, I wondered how to find out who belonged to the unidentified numbers. Then I remembered what young Marcel had shown me at Starbucks earlier. How to block one's phone number by dialing *67. How serendipitous it was to have learned this trick today. I could call every person on the list and no one would know where the call originated. Hidden behind the curtain of *67, I dialed the numbers one by one, hanging up when I heard a familiar voice on the answering machine or, just as often, in person. Some of the calls were to ladies we lunched with the first Friday of every month. Though many of them smiled to Whitney's face and bad-mouthed her the minute she left, there was little reason to think they would have had anything to do with her disappearance. They most certainly would have taken her jewelry if that was the case. There were calls to shops and services, and I ruled them out, too. There was a call to my downstairs neighbor, Philadelphian Joan Armitage, which had me puzzled until I remembered that she was part of Sunny's book group.

Next I turned to the numbers that had been dialed more than once. One turned out to be Jack's offices downtown, another the Gold Coast veterinary clinic where Monet and Amitié received their services. The company had probably gone into receivership since Whitney had disappeared, since a fraction of what Whitney spent on the two Yorkies' pedicures probably could have paid for my new master bath.

That left me with three unexplained numbers that had been called with some regularity in the last months. From the area code, I could tell the first two were located in the near west suburbs. Employing my newly discovered *67 yet again, I dialed the first number and hung up when I heard the soft accent of a black man. I got an answering machine with the second number, two women speaking in unison—Esther and Elaine—telling me what to do when. I hung up without doing it and dialed the third number. My call was answered by a live person speaking a foreign tongue that could have been Chinese or Korean or Vietnamese. I wasn't certain. All I knew was that it sounded like its owner had just swallowed boiling water. Thinking I might have dialed wrong, I redialed and got the same person. Honestly. If they're going to live in this country they should really speak English. After all, we've conquered them all, haven't we? If not with a gun, then with dollars.

Thinking that I had three very interesting leads to track down the next day, I went to bed and slept better than I had in a long time.

After breakfast the next morning, I went back to the Starbucks on Division on a hunch that I might find Marcel there. My hunch proved right. Not only was he there, he had set up office at the same table he had occupied the day before. When he saw me he waved me over. It never fails to amaze me how casual our attitudes have become. Yesterday I was a perfect stranger to him. Now I was a friend. I carried my coffee to his table and listened while he conducted some kind of money transaction on his cell phone. He finished and clicked the phone shut, tapped out something on his computer, and then widened his narrow face with a smile.

"Hey, Whitney, how'd it go yesterday? Was your husband surprised?"

"I guess you could say that," I replied. "I stopped in to thank you for your help."

"Glad to be of service."

"Marcel, I have another little favor to ask you. You seem to be rather computer-savvy, and I wondered if you might help me with one other little project I have. I need to get an address from a phone number. A few of them, as a matter of fact."

He gave me a look containing wisdom far beyond his years. "Worried about the old man, aren't you?"

I hadn't thought to propose it that way, but it seemed as good a way as any. "How did you know?"

"Because I'll bet anything your friends don't call you Whitney. Whitney's the other woman, isn't she?" I looked at my hand and feigned the finest wronged wife look I could muster. "I thought so. So it really is Pauline?"

My hurt but proud look could have gotten me Academy Award recognition.

"Well, Pauline, I'd say he's a real dick to mess around when he's got a hottie like you at home. I suggest you lose him. You'd make the hottest cougar around. You come see me then, hey?"

I wondered how I'd missed out on this cougar thing for so long. "Thank you, Marcel, and I promise to keep you in mind if I end up solo. Now, could you tell me how I might get an address from a phone number?"

"Pauline, it's totally easy as long as the number isn't unlisted. All you have to do is call the phone company's address verification service. But here, give me your numbers and I'll get 'em for you online." He entered the numbers into his computer and then, using a wireless printer that was part of his portable office, he printed off a sheet of paper and handed it to me. Not only did it have the names and addresses of the people Whitney had called, it had directions of how to get there. All three were located in the same general area, two in Oak Park and one on the west side of the city.

"How did you do this?" I asked, impressed.

"The magic of the tech age, Pauline baby. It's called Mapquest."

"Well, you certainly know your way around the computer world," I said.

"I should. I used to have a dot-com company worth millions. I had fifty employees and rented an entire floor in Manhattan. That was before the bubble burst," he said blithely. Using his arms to indicate his surroundings, he added. "This is my office now."

And before I could get to my feet, he was back on the phone conducting business.

21

Emma

My Jaguar does not like winter in the least. It is a sporting vehicle intended for long country drives on smooth, dry roads. And thus, I have no fondness for driving it in bad weather, especially in the lake-effect storm that had started up in the last hour, leaving huge white flakes on top of those from the night before.

Had I been sane, I would have stayed in my suite reading—I had just picked up a copy of *The Hours*—but I believe sanity is better served in one's youth when there's so much more to look forward to. Being on the downward slope of the half-century peak, I'm more willing to act on impulse. Which explains why I found myself on the Eisenhower Expressway in a snowstorm that reduced traffic to a speed only marginally faster than the lines at airport security. After spending nearly an hour to go ten miles, I exited the expressway at Austin Avenue and drove through a somewhat rundown urban area before coming into a nicer residential section where the barren trees held promise of lush green summers. Thanks to Marcel's miracle map, I located the Mitchell residence in no time at all. As I sat in front of the solid redbrick structure with a black Mercedes parked in the driveway, I wondered what business Whitney could have there.

The front door opened and a man and two little girls stepped out. The man was tall and slim with a dark chocolate complexion and was wearing pressed blue jeans beneath a fitted camel-hair overcoat. The girls were dressed in matching pink parkas, their hair sticking sideways from their head in curly dark pigtails with pink bows on the end. Seeing the scene as nonthreatening, I cinched my coat tightly about my waist and got out of the car.

"Good day," I called out as I walked up the drive. The threesome eyed me with natural curiosity. I looked down at the girls. They had gleaming dark eyes fringed with heavy black eyelashes any woman would die for.

"Can I help you with something?" the man asked. Now that I was closer I could see that he was quite handsome. Was it possible that Whitney had been having an affair with him? I looked down at the girls again. They were no more than five years old. I decided to proceed cautiously.

"My name is Pauline Cook, and I believe we have a mutual friend. Whitney Armstrong?"

His face was a total blank and he pursed his lips, shaking his head subtly. If he was an actor, he was a darn good one. "I don't know a Whitney Armstrong."

"Oh. Well, she knows someone here. She's called here quite a bit. Perhaps your wife?"

He stiffened visibly and let go of his daughters' hands. "Go on, girls. Get in the car. I'll be there in one second. And strap your seatbelts," he ordered. The girls obediently walked to the car and opened the door. Once they had climbed inside, he turned to me and held out a hand. "Wilbur Mitchell," he said. I shook his hand and he held mine a moment longer than would be customary, looking me straight in the eye. "Maybe Annie did know your friend, but unfortunately, she is no longer with us. She was struck and killed by a hit-and-run driver a couple of weeks ago. The girls are now without a mother and I have lost the best friend and companion a man could ever wish for."

I was stunned and looked at the car where two little faces peered out the frosty window. I recalled the times my mother left me to go off on some adventure and how much I missed her while she was gone. And then how exciting it was when she returned. These two little girls would only know the heartbreak.

"I'm so sorry," I whispered.

He nodded to let me know that it was all right, that he didn't expect the entire world to have been informed of his loss. "The world lost a fine woman. Beautiful. Selfless. The world's greatest mother. A loyal and loving wife. An attorney who did more charity work than paid." Tears pooled in his eyes, and he raised a gloved hand to wipe them away. "Excuse me. It's still so fresh. Anyhow, is there something I can do for you, Pauline?"

"No," I said, lost for words at stumbling into such a tragic situation. I made something up. "I'd just hoped to meet your wife. Whitney said such wonderful things about her."

"Everyone did." He paused and looked like he was going to say something more, but stopped. "Well, I've got to go. I'm taking the girls to their grandmother's. She's going to mind them while I go out of town on business."

"Of course," I said, feeling foolish the moment the words left my mouth. I had no idea what they meant. I walked back down the drive to my car and brushed the snow from the windshield. After fishing the keys from my purse, I got in the car and watched in the rearview mirror as the sad trio in the Mercedes disappeared into the blowing flakes.

And then I realized why I said "of course." Of course it was the grandmother taking care of the children. That was how it had always been for me.

22

A Vindication of the Rights of Woman

The next person I was looking for was an E. Kidder who lived less than a mile from the Mitchell home. Once again I found myself in a residential neighborhood, the streets lined with sturdy stone houses built back in the twenties. This particular residence actually turned out to be in an apartment building set between the homes, which I considered a setback. That meant having to explain my purpose over an intercom instead of face-to-face. The message on the answering machine had said Esther and Elaine. I wondered which E. was E. Kidder.

I parked my car in the lot, directly beneath a sign that warned that all unauthorized cars would be towed to someplace on the other side of the moon. I ignored the advisory and went into the lobby, an unremarkable area with an industrial-looking sofa and some obligatory potted plants. A camera lens stared at me from above a directory. After locating E. McLean and E. Kidder on the directory, I pushed the buzzer and waited, staring up at the camera and trying to look harmless.

"Yeah, what can I do for you?" came a harsh-sounding female voice with a less than subtle trace of Brooklyn clinging to her tongue.

"I'm sorry to disturb you but my name is Pauline Cook, and I'm here on behalf of Whitney Armstrong," I said, hoping the conversation would propel itself from that point. Which it did.

"Whitney? Did you say Whitney?"

"Yes, I did. I wondered if I might come up and talk to you about her."

I heard a clicking sound. "Five B," the voice said.

I took the elevator to the fifth floor, where a woman stood waiting for me in the open door of an apartment. She was large, but not fat, with broad shoulders and the torso of a Roman discus thrower. She wore a white chef's jacket streaked with chocolate atop a pair of loose black and white checked pants. Her wildly cropped hair sprung in all directions, and bright purple glasses perched on the bridge of her ample nose.

"I'm Elaine," she bellowed. "C'mon down. Excuse the mess. I'm working." She welcomed me into the apartment where the rich smell of cocoa practically emanated from the walls. We passed through a smartly decorated living room into the kitchen where a woman as petite as Elaine was large was placing chocolate truffles into paper forms. Dozens of empty boxes lined the counters. "This is Esther," Elaine said.

The smaller woman studied me with a pair of violet eyes so intense, Elizabeth Taylor would have been envious. Her impossibly curly hair roamed wildly across her head, and she wore a white jacket, too, except hers was actually still white. She graced me with a sweet smile and then turned it toward Elaine. It dawned on me that they were lesbians.

"So you're Pauline," said Esther, the words coming as a surprise. "I feel I already know you. Whitney says some very interesting things about you."

"She does?" I queried excitedly. "Does that mean you've spoken to her lately?" I took her words to mean that she had been in contact with Whitney, and at that moment I wasn't sure which pleased me more: the thought of hugging Fleur to my lonely chest or the seven zeros preceded by the number one that Jack would be inking onto a rectangular piece of paper.

"No, we haven't seen her in a while. She used to stop over practically every week. We thought maybe she sent you here to pick up some chocolates," Esther explained. Elaine nodded in the background. I watched the zeros roll off my imaginary check.

"No, she didn't send me. She's been missing. I was hoping you might have some idea where she could be." The two women exchanged glances but said nothing. Taking in my surroundings—the chocolate-laden counters and the two lesbians—I wondered where they fit into Whitney's world. "May I ask how you know Whitney in the first place?"

"It's sort of a long story, but I guess the short answer is she's in our book group," said Elaine.

"Your book group?" The answer floored me. I knew that Whitney had joined Sunny's book group at Jack's behest, but this second book group was news to me.

"Yes, we met her in Barbara's bookstore. Elaine was signing her book on chocolates, and here this femme fatale stops to talk to us. We kind of felt sorry for her," said Esther, arranging the chocolates in the boxes as if she was working a jigsaw puzzle.

Elaine jumped in. "All that makeup and those spiked heels. Look at what she'd done to her body—the boobs and all. I've never seen anyone more victimized by this male-dominated culture. We felt sorry for her." I doubted they had any clue how much she had really done to her body, how she had physically changed herself from one of the repressors into one of the repressed.

"We felt so bad we invited her to join our radical women's book group," Esther piped in.

Elaine continued. "We wanted to take her on as a project—introduce her to a more enlightened way of thinking. It was pretty clear she was looking for something deeper than what she had. I mean, I know about all that money and how seductive it is. I sell my chocolates to those people." She pointed at the kitchen counter and all the beribboned boxes. "I mean, who else but the rich would pay over fifty bucks for a box of chocolates?" She chuckled to herself and continued. "But as far as our book group is concerned, she had a hard time fitting in and sometimes the conversation went over her sweet blond head. And some of the women didn't like her."

"We have a few PETAs in the group," Esther chimed in. "They weren't big on her fur coats."

"But I give her credit for sticking to it," her significant other added. "She bought all the books on our recommended list."

"Would that include books like *The Jungle*?"

"Exactly," said Elaine. "We're very socially conscious."

"What about a book called *Human Chattel*?"

"By Chia Arunasetya. That book should be mandatory reading in our schools. It exposes the underbelly of capitalism and its exploitive nature. Chia actually spoke at the last meeting that Whitney attended. I know Whitney was totally absorbed by what she had to say."

"When was that?" I asked, trying to put a time frame together.

Esther stopped packing her chocolates to think. "It was our November meeting, a couple of weeks before Thanksgiving. Remember, Elaine, how Chia said that while we were eating turkey and mashed pototoes, the women she wrote about would be happy for some extra rice."

"I sure do," Elaine concurred. "Yeah, now that I think of it, the night that Chia was here was the last time we saw Whitney."

My mind drifted back to the Mitchell household, not a mile away, and the two little girls who would never see their mother again. I wondered if there could be a connection "Did you know Annie Mitchell?" I ventured.

They took a simultaneous deep breath and then shook their heads. "No," said Elaine.

"Name rings a bell for some reason," Esther volunteered, "but I can't place her."

"She was killed in a hit-and-run accident," I said.

"That's how I know the name," Esther said. "I read about it in the paper. I guess she did a lot of pro bono work. Especially for immigration cases. I'm sorry we never met her."

I stared out the window where the snow was coming down harder than ever. There was still one last stop to make before darkness fell. Feeling there wasn't more that they could tell me, I thanked the women for their time and hospitality, and left their apartment carrying a box of deluxe chocolates that cost one hundred dollars.

For a couple with such disdain for capitalism, they certainly didn't suffer any shame from profiting by it.

23

The Maltese Falcon

My last stop was on the west side of the city in one of the rapidly gentrifying neighborhoods. New construction buildings of clean white concrete proming Eurokitchens and thousands of square feet of living space were being built alongside decaying three-flats with sagging front porches and false brick façades. The Madison Street address I sought turned out to be a Cambodian restaurant called Khmer Time. That explained the accent. I was surprised to see a Cambodian restaurant since I was unaware of any Cambodian presence in Chicago. I was all too familiar with the huge influx of Vietnamese who had practically taken over the entire manicure and pedicure business. I wondered what area the Cambodians would end up dominating. The Koreans already had the dry cleaning business.

There was no parking on Madison, so I turned onto a side street and drove around in search of a space. Every spot appeared to be taken, with the exception of one space that was marked by a pair of green-striped lawn chairs. I double-parked beside the lawn chairs and got out to move them onto the sidewalk. Then I pulled the Jaguar into the open spot.

I was adjusting the rear-view mirror to put on my lipstick when I heard a tapping on my window. A grizzled gray face with several days of speckled growth sprouting from its chins was staring at me. Beside him, a brown van idled on the street.

"Yo," he said. "Ya gotta move the car."

I rolled down the automatic window. "Pardon me?"

"I said ya gotta move the car."

"Really. And who is mandating this move?"

His face went blank as he struggled to translate my words. And apparently met with little success. "This man. This date. This spot's mine." I leaned forward and looked through the windshield for any sign indicating the spot in which my car was parked was reserved. Seeing nothing, I said, "I don't believe so."

"Lady, I live here and this spot is mine." Choosing to ignore him, I rolled the window back up and got out of the car. He came rushing toward me, bringing his hulking frame well within inches of my personal space. "Lady, I ain't kidding. If you don't move this car, I can't be responsible for what might happen to it."

"Is that a threat?"

"Yeah."

I looked at the bungalow behind us. There were two green-striped lawn chairs on the front porch identical to the pair I had placed on the sidewalk. Though I had no intention of moving my car, neither did I want to return and find it had been damaged. Thrashing about in my brain for a way to win this standoff, I was struck with a brilliant inspiration. I would employ the "who you know" tactic.

"I don't imagine you are familiar with Detective Malloy of the Chicago Police Department?" I asked. He did not merit me with an answer. "Well, he happens to be a close friend. I also happen to know that that is your house there, and if I return and anything has happened to my car, you will have Detective Malloy to contend with. And to be quite frank, the man can be quite unethical when necessary."

The grizzled face stared at me with barely contained anger. Before he had another chance to interject, I simply said, "I will be back within the hour and my car had best be intact."

As I turned to walk away, he called out to my back, "I ain't shittin' you, lady. Get back here and move this car." I ignored him and kept walking.

Though the sign said Khmer Time didn't open until five, the door was open, so I went inside. The storefront restaurant was packed with formica tables, and the walls were covered with erratically hung pictures that could have come from Chinatown as easily as Cambodia. Had Whitney cultivated a taste for Cambodian food while I was gone, I wondered? Or was a place this unremarkable the perfect location for an illicit rendezvous?

There was an Asian couple seated in the back rolling chopsticks into napkins. The man got up to greet me. He carried the look of one who has seen far too much, his face pulled downward by deep lines that ran from his eyes to the corners of his mouth, making it appear that a smile would take great effort.

"I sorry. We no open half hour."

"That's fine. I haven't come here to eat. I just want to ask a couple of questions." The man stared at me with his hangdog expression, the flaps of his close-set eyes nearly obscuring his pupils. His wife continued rolling napkins as if he were still sitting across from her, but the bend of her head told me she was hanging on every word that passed between us. "I have a friend who appears to be a regular customer. I wonder if you might know anything about her?"

"Friend?" he echoed. He stood bent slightly at the waist, one hand tucked tightly into the other.

"Yes, a friend. Whitney Armstrong?" I asked, looking to see if her name had evoked any kind of response. "Do you know her?"

He gathered his eyebrows into a tight frown. "Ritney. No Ritney."

"But she called here often. Maybe she bought carry-out food. Would you remember a customer's name? Armstrong? Whitney Armstrong?"

Again he frowned in concentration and then shook his head definitively, saying, "No Ritney. No Almstlong."

I was ready to give this up as another dead end when the woman started speaking rapid-fire Cambodian to her husband. An annoyed look came over his face, and he fired back at her. The woman went back to rolling her napkins, and the man stared at me blankly. "Solly, I don't know her." But there

WELL READ AND DEAD

had been a climate change. His wife glanced at me briefly, and I thought I read fright in her face. They were hiding something, but I didn't know how to press them for whatever it was. As I looked from one to the other, they returned my gaze in mute silence.

"You come back later, we open," the man finally said.

I left the restaurant and stood outside on the sidewalk with bits of snow peppering my eyes, trying to shake off the sense that something was terribly wrong. My gaze drifted upward toward the window of the residence directly over the restaurant, and my heart caught in my throat at the sight that greeted me. Sitting on the windowsill, with her mouth opened in a silent meow, was Fleur.

I charged directly back into the restaurant, where the two were engaged in heated discussion again.

"My cat," I said. "You have my cat." They once again honored me with the silent treatment. This time my way of dealing with them was far more concrete. "My cat is in the window of the upstairs apartment. I want her back now or I'm calling the police."

The word "police" drew a response. The couple rushed toward me and my anger turned to fright. I pulled out my cell phone and brandished it in front of them. "It's set for speed dial to my detective friend."

To my surprise the woman began speaking in fluent English. "Please, do not call the police. We can explain. Your friend left the cat with us."

I lowered my cell phone. "Whitney left the cat with you?"

The woman nodded. "Yes, she left the animals with us. Please, come with me and I will reunite you with your cat. We will have tea and I will explain."

The woman, who I learned was named Sou, led me through the kitchen at the back of the restaurant and up the wooden steps to an apartment on the second floor. The moment she opened the door, we were accosted by Whitney's two Yorkies, their incessant yapping a shrill reminder of why cats are preferable to dogs. We passed through the apartment's fluorescent-lit kitchen with its tired linoleum floors and formica countertops into the adjacent living room, the dogs yapping excitedly at our heels the entire time. On the windowsill behind a brown velour loveseat sat Fleur, her cream-colored tail flicking rhythmically. She gave me a sly, revenge-exacting glare before jumping down and burrowing out of reach beneath the loveseat. My heart leaped with happiness. There was no question: this was my cat.

Sou fixed some green tea and brought it into the living room on a tray. Amitié and Monet started yapping again, but Sou fixed them with a severe scowl, and they retreated obediently into a corner. She poured our tea into china cups and took an exasperated sip, placing her cup back in the saucer.

"Your friend left the animals with us one month ago for safekeeping. On Thanksgiving holiday. She did not trust her husband to give them good care. She came with Chia and asked that we watch them."

"Chia, the author of *Human Chattel*?" I didn't attempt to say the last name.

"Yes, Chia Arunasetya. She is cousin of dead friend from Phnom Penh. She was staying with us while she was in Chicago."

"And you're telling me she and Whitney left together, and Chia told you nothing of her plans?" I asked, not believing the woman didn't know more.

"We are from Cambodia. We have seen much bad. We do not ask too many questions anymore. I do know she was losing her visa and had to leave country." She sipped her tea, and I saw how her skin had the same downward pull that cloaked her husband's face. Then she surprised me with a slight smile. "You will be taking the animals now? They have been very exhausting. Especially the dogs. My husband and I had spoken of getting rid of them if the blond woman did not return soon."

Although I wasn't leaving without Fleur, there was no way in creation Amitié and Monet were coming with me, too. As good a friend as Whitney was to me, I could never tolerate her two dust magnets.

"I will take the cat, but I'm afraid I can't take the dogs."

She gave me a look bordering on desperate. "Please, they bark and they bark. And they are very expensive. They will only eat certain food."

What did one expect when they had been weaned from their mother's milk on foie gras and lamb shank? I imagined that Whitney had probably left a king's ransom for their care, and for Fleur's albacore tuna as well. Now Sou was trying to unload them on me. Well, I didn't want the dogs, but I didn't want them ending up in the daily special either. I reached into my wallet and took out two hundred dollars I kept in my emergency fund.

"This is all the money I have on me, but I promise to come back with more if you will keep the dogs." She eyed the bills and slowly picked them up one by one. "This is only good for one week."

"One week!" I thundered. "Are you trying to tell me two hundred dollars will only feed these two for one week?"

"Maybe less. They only eat very best."

Bandit! I thought, wondering how much money Whitney had left to keep her little darlings fed. But since there was no way I wanted to be responsible for their care, she had me by the financial thumbscrew. "I'll bring more money soon," I promised.

I won't recap the entire next couple of hours, but suffice it to say I made a bit of an error. After finally coaxing Fleur out from under the sofa, I left Sou's hugging my beloved pet to my chest and walked to where I had parked the car. To my great surprise, there was a battered brown van sitting in the place where my metallic gold limited-edition Jaguar XKE had been. Despite my squirming cat clawing to break my grip, I managed to call the police on my cell phone to report its theft. A squad car showed up within minutes, and I related the story of the cretin claiming he could save a parking spot for himself by placing a couple of lawn chairs on the street. I pointed out that I paid far more taxes than he did, and then I pointed out the culprit's house. The police rang the bell while I sat in the nice warm back of the squad car stroking Fleur. A woman answered their ring and I could see her shake her head and raise her palms in denial. Leaving Fleur in the car, I went up to the door. She was a rather large, lumpy woman with a sad, battered-looking face.

"Pardon me, but a little over an hour ago your husband and I were having words over the ownership of a parking spot. And now you claim he doesn't live here."

"Lady, I don't know what your problem is, but I ain't seen no Jaguar parked in front of my house. Believe me, I would notice it if I did. And besides, my husband has been dead for five years."

With that two children appeared behind her, one of them crying that the other had broken something. I couldn't be certain through the tears whether the broken object was a toy or a body part, but I had a sudden urge to quit the premises. The two policemen did, too, and so the three of us walked back to the squad car.

"We'll put in a report, Mrs. Cook. That's the best we can do right now. But we can give you a ride home if you want."

"Thank you," I huffed, understandably. "But I would look into her story about being a widow. I'm certain she's just protecting her husband." The police car drove to the end of the block and circled back down the next street. It was then I realized my mistake as I spied the unmistakable silhouette of the Jaguar peeking out from beneath a dusting of snow. On the sidewalk behind it stood two green-striped lawn chairs.

I pointed out the car and apologized to the police, explaining somewhat sheepishly that I must have had the wrong street. Could I help it if all these bungalows looked the same to me?

Back at the Drake, the first thing I did was contact Silvio DeLuca. The general manager of the hotel assured me that he would throw out the rule book on Fleur's behalf and permit me to keep her in my suite until my apartment was finished. Of course there would be a small fee for cleaning the room when I left—allergy sufferers, he explained—but I was all too happy to agree to anything now that I had Fleur back. With my beloved cat with me, the world didn't feel as cold a place as it had that morning.

24
The Awakening

The day dawned bright and sunny and I luxuriated over breakfast in my room with Fleur purring contentedly in my lap. I called Maria and got her answering machine, her message proof that even clairvoyants are not beyond humor. "This is Maria. I knew you'd call. But leave a message at the beep anyway." I left a message asking for her earliest appointment, so I could take the Hermès scarf to her and see if it might give her some insight as to Whitney's whereabouts. I also knew I could be considered certifiable for believing in any of this hocus-pocus, but what the hell, the police use psychics to help locate bodies all the time. I only hoped the body I was looking for was alive.

The phone rang not a minute later. I picked up, certain that it would be Maria, but it was Bharrie. He was at the co-op, and he wanted me to come over to approve the placement of the Venetian glass chandelier in the dining room. Telling him I would be there shortly, I finished my coffee and got dressed, fixing Whitney's copper and olive scarf around my neck. Then I headed out the door for the short walk to my building. It was a mild day—the sun had actually poked through the clouds—and when I got there I was happy to see the bag lady was nowhere in sight.

Louis was on duty, his posture straighter than ever, his cap tipped ever so slightly upon his stately head. "Good morning, Mrs. Cook," he said. "I'm afraid I have some bad news."

I steeled for the worst. "What is it, Louis?"

"Air France finally got back to me with the number of the delivery company they use here in Chicago. It's one of them Russian companies. According to the guy I talked to, their driver quit last Friday and took off with all the records. So there's no proof where your bags were delivered."

"Wonderful, just wonderful," I said. Now the KGB had possession of my clothes. I could just see my Dior gown dancing in the new year in Red Square. It was time to turn the whole thing over to the insurance company.

When I got to my penthouse, a team of men was hard at work replacing the buckled hardwood in the living room. I stepped over them and went into the dining room where Bharrie stood at the foot of a ladder. Tag McKay was atop the ladder marking the ceiling with a pencil.

"We thought we'd better ask you about the placement first, Pauline," Bharrie said. "This fixture is so heavy we're going to have to reinforce the ceiling before hanging it, and we don't want to make any expensive mistakes."

"We certainly don't," I concurred, looking up at Tag McKay. His face was speckled with its usual coat of dust. "I think a little to the left."

"Here?" he asked, moving his arm ever so slightly to the left and marking the space with an X. He looked down at me for approval.

"That's perfect," I said, and as the words left my mouth, my eyes locked with those of the contractor. Our eyes had locked many times before, usually in battle, but this time there was something more, something that made it difficult for me to look away. My stomach fluttered in a most disconcerting manner.

"Well, Pauline, I have good news for you," he said from his perch. "We're going to get you in for Christmas after all."

"What do you mean?" I asked, not sure I understood what he was saying.

He put the pencil into a side pocket and climbed down the ladder. Bharrie was smiling with a self-satisfied air. "That's right. After Tag hangs this chandelier, he's finished. The flooring men will finish repairing the floor today, I have a team of painters lined up for the weekend, we'll move your furniture in on Monday. Voilà, you're home on Christmas Eve."

There is no logical explanation for my reaction. I felt like the wind had been knocked from my lungs, depleting the flow of oxygen to my brain. The blood drained from my face and I started to swoon. Tag reached out and caught me by the arm. "Are you all right?" he asked with genuine concern.

"I don't know. I just got dizzy."

He dragged up a stool and seated me on it. The look on his face was far more than that of an employee worried about his paycheck. I found myself basking in it. "Take a couple of deep breaths," he said.

I closed my eyes and did as I was told. After the second breath, I knew what had to be done. I opened my eyes and turned to Bharrie. "I'm afraid this job is not finished yet," I said, mustering my best imperiousness. "I've been thinking, and I'm not happy with the wainscoting. I want it changed to cherry. And now that I think of it, the granite in the guest bathroom isn't quite right either. I want it torn out and replaced with a tumbled marble." I went on to list several other things that simply had to be changed. Bharrie stared at me slack-jawed while Tag looked on bemused.

These changes would all have to be done at great expense, of course. But I didn't have the money to pay for the first part of the project anyway, so what difference would it make? I couldn't have Tag McKay going away. Not just yet.

Now I was more determined than ever to find Whitney. Maria returned my call shortly after I left Bharrie and Tag scratching their heads in my apartment, and told me she could see me anytime. I practically floated down the street and up the dark stairwell to her apartment. I recalled my dark frame of mind the last time I'd been there, and how life hadn't felt worth living. Something had changed since that day. Suddenly, the world was bursting with promise.

Maria met me at the door. She was wearing jeans and a T-shirt again, her hair pulled back into its shiny ponytail. She led me back across the red carpeted room, past her husband who sat in the kitchen smoking, past the sleeping cat on the cat bed. We stepped into her private cubicle with its myriad of holy statues. I took the same chair I had occupied before.

She sat down opposite me and cocked her head curiously. Then she smiled. "So it's just as I predicted."

"What's just as you predicted?" I asked.

"You have found your soul mate."

"I don't believe so," I denied. The very moment the words left my lips, the image of Tag McKay leapt into my mind. He was staring down at me from the ladder. And I was looking up at him. Maria had predicted that my soul mate would be someone I looked up to. Was that what she meant? But this was wrong—all wrong. I was meant to be with men of power. Not men with power tools. And where was the great means he came from?

"This appointment isn't about me," I said. "Besides, if I haven't given you anything of mine to hold, how can you do a reading?"

"I don't need to do a psychic reading for this. It is written all over your face."

I'm certain I was trembling. Not wishing to explore the issue of the soul mate any further, I quickly changed the subject. "You said you might be able to tell me something about Whitney's whereabouts if I had a personal object of hers."

Maria's face turned all business. I took off the Hermès scarf and handed it to her. She ran the imported silk through her fingers, the tips of them passing back and forth over the images of the French peasantry at the harvest. Closing her eyes, she appeared to go into a trance. "She is far, far away. Across much water. She sleeps to escape the pain." And then her eyes burst open like one startled by a crashing sound in the midst of deepest sleep. "She must be found quickly if she is to be saved."

"But can you tell me where she is? Can you tell me the country? Is she in the United States?"

She rubbed the scarf and shook her head. "That is it," she declared. She handed the scarf back to me, and I stared down at the swirl of olive and copper silk, and the peasants forever woven into their tasks. Or at least until some irresponsible dry cleaner ruined them. I knotted the scarf back around my neck and took out my credit card.

"What do I owe you?" I asked, holding out the card.

"The usual. One hundred and twenty-five dollars." As she reached out to take my credit card, our fingers touched. Her expression changed greatly and, just as before, she appeared to be staring into the furthest reaches of hell. "Pauline," she intoned in a dark voice. "I warned you before about danger from those in rags. One in rags will take him from you."

I walked home thinking it was ridiculous to put any more stock into this voodoo. Maria was no more an oracle than I was a high priestess. She'd hit on a couple of things—the cold weather vacation and possibly the man I looked up to being my soul mate. But even if that was right, there certainly weren't any great means. As for Whitney being far away with lots of water between us, that remained to be seen.

I told myself, next time I wanted to waste a hundred twenty-five dollars, there were far better ways to do it. Like buying a Prada keychain. So why was it that as I turned onto Oak Street and saw the bag lady coming in my direction, her body draped in filthy rags, my blood ran cold?

Though her hood covered her face, I was certain she was staring at me.

25

Brave New World

I called Detective Malloy to let him know I had found Fleur, and that, contrary to his belief that she had been done in, it looked like my friend had run off voluntarily. A clucking sound from his end told me he was flicking his lower lip with his tongue, a habit he engaged in when he wasn't able to smoke a cigarette.

"Damn, I would have given you twenty to one that the husband offed her. I would've thought dem pets were six feet under too."

"Are you unhappy that they're alive?"

"Nah. I'm a cop. I'm glad dere alive. I just hate being wrong."

"Well, as in the past, Detective, thank you for your great sensitivity. But now I wonder if I might implore some more advice from you?"

"Do I get another lunch?"

"I'll have to owe you," I promised. "I need to know how I can find out where someone went if they flew. Is there any way of obtaining airline records for a certain time period?"

"Not without a warrant."

"I don't suppose you'd . . . ?"

"No, Pauline. For one it's an invasion of privacy. For two, you just said there's been no crime committed."

I thought of my ten million dollars incubating while the clock ticked away. "Detective, I really need to find this person. What would you suggest I do?"

"You want my real answer. Here it is—and it's off the record. Find yourself a computer hacker. And a good one at that."

He wished me luck and hung up, rushing out to smoke a cigarette, no doubt. Struck with inspiration from what he had told me, I gave the mewing Fleur a quick kiss on the back of her head and rushed out the door to my local Starbucks.

Marcel was in his regular seat in the window, his bowed head practically impaled on his computer keyboard. I bought him a double espresso and carried it over. He remained oblivious to my presence until I put the coffee down in front of him. Then he lifted his head like a rodent sniffing cheese.

"Pauline, my favorite cougar. Please take a seat."

"Marcel, I am not a cougar."

"But I want you to be," he said. "What brings you into my office?"

"I have another favor to ask," I said, getting straight to the point. "Would your computer be able to find out if someone flew out of here last month?"

"Still checking up on the old man, huh?"

"Something along those lines," I answered, humoring him.

"You happen to know what day this person flew?"

"If she did fly, I believe it would have been Thanksgiving Day."

"Hmmm. Find out where someone flew on Thanksgiving Day. That's a pretty broad request," he said, scratching at his sparse goatee. I studied his frayed coat and his tired scarf. His boots were soggy from the street. It was evident his dot-com fortune had not only been short-lived, but poorly invested. I imagined a bit of financial remuneration might help sweeten the pot.

"I'd be willing to pay you."

His eyes lit up like the Eiffel Tower at the millennium, little flickers of light rotating around as they moved back and forth in thought. "Any idea what part of the world this person might want to visit?"

I had harbored a certain suspicion since learning that Whitney had left with Chia. "Maybe someplace in the Far East."

"And a name this person would be traveling under?"

"Whitney Armstrong."

He gave me one of those all-knowing looks. "Hmmph," he muttered aloud, and then he added, "This will take awhile, Pauline. And it's going to take some coin."

I thought of what could be gained if he was successful. "All right. Whatever it takes," I agreed, hoping I wouldn't regret giving him a blank check. I stood up and put on my coat. Then I went back up to the counter and bought him another double espresso, hoping it would help him work faster. I put the coffee down on his table, and he lifted a momentary finger from his keyboard, his left ear already glued to his cell phone. I didn't even bother to say good-bye. I sensed we would be speaking again soon.

26

Ship of Fools

I had rushed out without my cell phone, so when I returned to the Drake, the red message light was blinking. There were three messages. Sunny had called and wanted me to call her immediately regarding the Amici of the Literati. Elsa had called to ask if I wanted to have dinner since her husband was out of town. And Suzanne Worthington called to say they were back from Aspen and she wondered how my knee was. I called Elsa first and told her I was dining with Emily Rossetti that evening, but she was welcome to join us. I called Sunny next who informed me in a tizzy that her silent auction committee chair had resigned due to a sick grandchild in San Diego.

"Oh my God, Pauline. I only have ten days. With Christmas falling in between I don't know what I'm going to do."

Despite appearances to the contrary, Sunny wasn't a complete dummy. She knew when one wanted things done right to go to the pros, and she was well aware of my expertise in the thankless chore of chairing a benefit. I had chaired nearly a dozen in my life until I got smart and opted to be a worker bee instead of the queen. Sometimes I wondered what drove us to the madness anyway, assembling several hundred people in one room, feeding and entertaining them, and then trying to pry copious amounts of money from them for causes ranging from animals to art to disease. At this point in life, I preferred a quiet night at home to a benefit of any flavor, and wondered why we couldn't just send a check and save all that money on food and flowers. But having been in Sunny's shoes numerous times before, I relented and promised to help her out with the silent auction, too.

Next I dialed Suzanne Worthington. We hadn't spoken since I had jumped ship on Red Mountain.

"Pauline," she said graciously, her English accent a bit more pronounced than usual. "I've been thinking about you since you left Aspen. How are you getting on?"

"I'm fine, actually. Uh, the orthopedic specialist here said it was just a bad bruise. It's already better," I lied.

"A bruised knee. I'm so glad to hear it wasn't anything worse. And Senior will be too. He's been worried sick that he was responsible for your accident. He's quite attracted to you, you know?"

"He told you that?" I said, an unattractive picture of him unfastening his turquoise belt buckle coming to mind. He hadn't appeared too concerned about my accident then.

"Yes, and he was devastated that you left."

Dexter Worthington Sr. devastated over me? Simply because I took umbrage at his wanting me to lubricate his rather aged appendage. Perhaps he found me unique because I balked at what some young gold digger might consider an opportunity. I happen to come from a school where at the early stage of the game the man is generally trying to romance the woman, not drag her into his employ. Then again, he was very, very rich. I thought about my unhealthy attraction to Tag McKay and how troubling it was. Maybe it was worth giving Dexter Worthington Sr. another chance.

"Well, Suzanne, you can pass along to Dexter that I might consider another engagement with him."

"That's terrific, Pauline." She sounded more excited about it than I was. She certainly was a dedicated matchmaker. "We're having a little reception here tomorrow night for the Contessa Visconti. She's staying with us through Christmas. Just close friends and family. Would you be available to join us?"

"I'd love to," I said.

I was reviewing the silent auction items for the Amici gala that Sunny had dropped off, thinking I might bid on the first-class trip to Florence with a private viewing of the Uffizi, when the phone rang. The slightly arrogant and overly familiar voice of Marcel came over the line.

"Pauline, baby, I got good news for you. But first I gotta confirm price. This is going to cost five hundo."

I swallowed hard. "All right, five hundred dollars," I agreed.

"Sweet," he said. "Bangkok."

"Come again?"

"Bangkok. Your girl flew to New York and then Thai Airways to Bangkok on November 22. First class, by the way. And she paid cash."

"Marcel, you are a miracle worker," I told him, pondering what he had told me. Though I didn't want to give Maria too much credit, Bangkok certainly was far away, and there was a lot of water between us. "How on earth did you find that out?"

"You can thank the computer age, Pauline. And the gaping holes that creatives such as myself can pierce right through."

I decided to never handle my finances online.

My travel agent sounded glad to hear my voice. She had probably put her two children through college on the commissions she had gotten off my trips. I told her I wanted to go to Bangkok the next day. "That puts you in Bangkok two days before Christmas, Mrs. Cook. Are you sure that's what you want to do?"

I thought about my plans—or rather lack of them—for the holiday. Why not? Christmas was the same as any other day of the year, only worse. It was the day that truly affirmed one's solitary status. The options were always the same. Join a friend's celebration with their extended family, children, and grandchildren, where one recognizes how truly alone one is. Or spend the day with one's cat. The warmth of the Far East beckoned. That and the warmth of ten million dollars.

"I'm certain. Book me out of New York on Thai. First class."

"Of course, Mrs. Cook."

That night Elsa, Emily Rossetti, and I had dinner in River North at one of the new trendy, highly overpriced restaurants that absolutely everyone had to try. This being the weekend before Christmas, the restaurant was past overflowing, and being far too trendy to consider Christmas music, some obnoxious current style was playing too loudly. Being a well-known columnist, Elsa had gotten us a table, but as I fought to speak over the noise that bounced back at us from the ceiling, I wondered what the draw was. The clamor was especially troublesome to me, because I felt a need to talk. So much had happened in such a short period of time that my head was awhirl. Whitney's disappearance, losing and finding Fleur, Dexter Worthington's attraction to me and, worst of all, my attraction to Tag McKay. Well, not worst of all. Worst of all was my fortune dwindling to a fraction of its former value, but Tag McKay came in a strong second.

I have very few good friends in this world, but I count Elsa Tower among them. It is a dangerous friendship—just about anything one says to Elsa can be considered fair game. But when I employ my caveat of "this is between us," she honors my wishes. Which is what I did that evening. As for Emily Rossetti, I wasn't worried she would repeat anything. She didn't know enough people yet to be dangerous.

"I'm going to Thailand tomorrow," I announced over the din as a waiter, wearing the tightest-fitting slacks I'd ever seen, placed our drinks in front of us—scotch for Elsa, a vodka martini with anchovy olives for Emily, a bubbly flute of Taittinger for me. Though the trip wasn't really what I wanted to talk about, it was a safe start. Both my old friend and my new friend gawked at my announcement, Elsa's jaw actually falling ever so slightly open before she caught herself and clapped it shut. I raised my champagne to my lips and took a contented sip.

"You are going where?" Elsa finally intoned.

"Bangkok," I repeated, though I knew she had heard me perfectly well the first time.

"Are you out of your mind? It's Christmas. Besides, Sunny needs your help with the Amici benefit. You can't disappear right now."

"She's going to have to survive without me. Besides, I should be back in time for the gala," I said, adding a dreaded call to Sunny to my list of things to do first thing in the morning.

"Who's traveling with you?" Elsa pressed, taking a huge gulp of her scotch. I could tell she was agitated.

"I'm traveling alone."

"Pauline, have you lost your mind? Why on earth are you going to Thailand?" She stopped her tirade for a second and a knowing look came over her face. "There's a man involved, isn't there?"

I wanted to say yes and not have to answer any more of Elsa's prying questions. After all, in a way, Whitney qualified as a man if anyone ever scraped her cheek for DNA. But there was another man I was thinking of, and I wanted to come clean about it with someone. If Elsa couldn't knock some sense into me then no one could. But I couldn't bring myself to say it.

"No. No man."

"Pauline, that's a dangerous place for a single woman," she said.

"Tish," Emily Rossetti broke in. "It's no more dangerous than any of our big cities. Less dangerous in fact." She turned toward me. "Good for you, Pauline. I think it's wonderful that you can take a trip so spontaneously." She drank her martini while Elsa stared at me from under the brim of her hat, a wide-brimmed black felt with a rhinestone band. We went on to debate the wisdom of a woman traveling alone in the Far East. The waiter came, and we ordered some dreadfully expensive dishes containing at least four components I had never heard of. Emily went on to complain about how shabbily her husband had treated her in the divorce and that in her naïvety she had permitted it to happen. "Of course, I didn't care about losing the Bayou Club, since I planned on moving anyway, but it's the principle, don't you agree?"

I did, and I said so. Clearly, Elsa's train of thought was elsewhere, that is, until she abruptly blurted out in a knowing manner, "It's Edwin Von Rosman, isn't it? I know he just separated from his wife and I saw the two of you talking at the Night at the Races. I thought he might have a thing for you."

"Elsa, there's no man." And then I turned toward Emily, because it felt safer to direct it toward her than drop the bomb directly on Elsa. "Not in Thailand, anyhow."

That was all Elsa needed. "Not in Thailand, but there's a man! Pauline, who is it? Come clean with me."

I looked at both the women and thought how ridiculous my next statement was going to sound. But if one can't tell one's friends one's darkest secrets, who can one tell?

"Between us, Elsa?" I reminded her, not wanting to read:

What socialite widow thinks she may have found love in the trenches. Though she is dating outside her class, there is a bright side to it. At least if anything breaks in her home, she'll always have someone to fix it.

Elsa's face wore a perturbed look that told me she hated being muzzled. But her curiosity won out and she swore secrecy. As did Emily Rossetti, whom I made cross her heart with her fingers.

"I have this horrid attraction to the man working on my co-op." Elsa nearly choked on her scotch while Emily stared at me wide-eyed. "I know it sounds ridiculous, but I feel like a teenager when I'm around him. He does something to me that I can't explain."

"Have you taken leave of your senses?" Elsa demanded. "He'll take you for every dime."

Emily piped in. "Pauline, I know it's none of my business, but you know there is the rule of similarities. The more common interests you have, the better the chances you'll get along."

"My mother lectured me on that, too," I said, cutting her short. "I know it's ridiculous. I can't imagine bringing him to any of the clubs or the opera or the Amici gala. I don't even know if he owns a suit, much less a tuxedo."

"Have yourself checked for rabies!" Elsa berated me. "This reminds me of when Evan Appleton dropped his wife for the coat-check girl he met at Gibson's. Do you remember how embarrassing it was for the poor girl? Every time she opened her mouth, people laughed at her."

"That didn't stop him from marrying her," I interjected.

"It only lasted two months, if you recall."

I did recall. The buxom young thing had the number-one attorney in Chicago so under her spell, he actually married her without a prenup. No dummy that one, no matter what Elsa thought. I also recalled another instance of a person marrying beneath what everyone thought to be his financial and intellectual station. Jack Armstrong. But Jack had kept enough of his wits about him to make Whitney sign a prenup. I knew this for certain since Whitney had been the one to tell me.

"Elsa, I know you're right, and I know I can talk myself out of this," I said, hoping I was speaking the truth. "I just needed to get it off my chest."

"Darling, I'm glad that you've come to your senses. Aren't you, Emily?"

Emily nodded and added, "I would just hate to see you get hurt."

"Me get hurt?" I asked incredulously. "I would think it might be him in the end who would suffer when I lost interest."

Elsa shrugged. "One never knows in affairs of the heart."

27

A Christmas Carol

The next morning I woke up with a full plate of matters to be attended to before my departure for the Far East. First I called Sunny, who was traumatized beyond description when I explained I was leaving and told me it would be my fault if she had a stroke in the upcoming week. Then I called Suzanne Worthington to inform her that I wouldn't be joining them for the Contessa's reception that evening because I was going to Bangkok. She was surprised at my spontaneity.

"I envy you being able to just get up and go like that," she said. "Be sure and get the full body massage while you're there. It's beyond pampering, trust me. You're staying at the Oriental, I gather."

"Is there anyplace else?" I replied.

Having paid an emergency visit to the cruise wear department at Neiman Marcus the day before, I began hurriedly packing. One of the Vuitton bags I had purchased for the Aspen trip was lying open on the bed when Fleur jumped into it and began to mew loudly. My pulse surged at my oversight. It was no wonder God had protected me from having children. In my rush to take this trip, I had completely forgotten about my cat. I tried to think who might help me out at this late date. I called Emily's room and got no answer. Elsa was out of the question. She had several poodles who would like nothing better than to chase Fleur under a bed and keep her there. With the holidays looming, who could I possibly ask without it being a great imposition? And then it came to me in an inspirational flash.

I gave Fleur a quick rub on the head, threw on my coat, and practically ran the block to my apartment. Though it was Saturday, he was there as I knew he would be, atop his ladder, working on the crown molding I had decided to change. He didn't hear me come in, so I watched him work in silence, his hammer reminding me of a sculptor chipping away at marble. An enormous lump lodged in my throat, and I cursed the fates at the reaction this man invoked in me. I gave a little cough to alert him to my presence, and he turned and looked down at me, surprised that he had company.

"Hi, I have a favor to ask," I said, preparing to grovel if necessary. "I know this is very last-minute, but I'm going away over Christmas and I wonder if you might keep an eye on my cat if I brought her here. She's very little trouble, and I don't want to leave her alone in unfamiliar surroundings." He looked perturbed, so I quickly added, "I'll pay you extra, of course."

The perturbed look changed to one of insult. "You don't have to pay me extra to look after your cat. I'll do it."

"Thank you. I really appreciate this. I'll bring her things over and leave a note of how to care for her. I should be back within the week."

"Where're you going, anyhow?" he asked, turning back to his work and pounding in a nail.

"Bangkok."

"Long way to go for such a short time."

"I have some business there."

"Who are you going with?"

"I'm traveling alone."

He stopped his hammering and turned to stare at me. Then he climbed down the ladder and stood in front of me. As usual, I towered over him in my high-heeled boots. "Let me get this straight. You're going alone?"

I nodded.

"Bangkok is no city for a woman to be running around alone. There's a lot there you might find, well, distasteful."

"Thank you for the pearls of wisdom, Mr. McKay, but I am a grown woman and can take care of myself."

"Look, can you quit with the Mr. McKay? My name is Tag."

He waited for my reaction. "All right. Tag."

"It just so happens I have a good friend in Bangkok," he continued. "I'm going to give you my friend's number and you should call her if you have any kind of trouble. Lienne is very well-connected. She knows everyone." Taking his pencil from behind his ear, he scribbled out a name and phone number on the notepad where he kept a running list of my requests. He tore off the page and handed it to me. I tucked it into my wallet, telling myself that it did not bother me in the least that he had this woman's multiple-digit phone number committed to memory.

Then he came up with a most unwelcome request. "What are the odds of getting a check from you before you take off?" he asked.

"I'd like to see the finished product first," I said, turning on my narrow heels and walking from the room.

28
The Tell-Tale Heart

The porter came to my room and picked up my bags, and I stopped at the Drake's front desk to advise the staff I would be gone for several days. The desk clerk reached into a box behind him and pulled out an envelope for me.

"This was left for you, Mrs. Cook."

"Thank you, Roy," I said, taking the envelope from him. With three days left until Christmas, it most likely was a Christmas card.

"Happy holidays," he said, exercising contemporary political correctness.

"Merry Christmas, Roy," I said, exercising some political incorrectness back. I tucked the envelope into my purse and, with Fleur's carrier firmly in hand, followed the bell captain out to my waiting limousine. Tag had gone when I stopped off at my apartment with Fleur. I took her into the master bedroom, which I had outfitted with a new cat bed as well as a kitty box, water, and a dry food feeder. Tins of albacore tuna were stacked in the kitchen, to be served to her by Tag in the morning and evening. Knowing that my leaving so soon after being reunited would be traumatizing for her, I hoped that at least being in familiar surroundings would make it easier. Even though there was no furniture, at least she could perch in her favorite window. I stroked her lovingly and put her on the windowsill. Then I slipped out the door. The moment I closed it behind me, she started to mew. I covered my ears and ran to the elevator.

The ride to O'Hare was excruciating as I wallowed in guilt. How could I leave my cat so soon after all she had recently been through? I told myself it was for good reason, that when I found Whitney and collected the money from Jack, Fleur would be in diamond collars and albacore tuna for the rest of her days. But the guilt stayed with me my entire flight to New York, and was still bothering me as I boarded the Thai Airways flight at Kennedy and settled into my first-class seat. Finally I could take it no more. I took out my cell phone and called Tag McKay on his.

"It's Pauline," I said, as a stunningly beautiful flight attendant with flawless skin and a subtle cant to her dark eyes handed me a chilled glass of champagne. My mind flicked to Tag's friend, Lienne, and I felt an uncomfortable tinge of jealousy. "I'm in New York waiting for my flight to Bangkok to depart and I have an enormous favor to ask. Could you possibly stop over and check on Fleur? She was really crying when I left, and now I don't know how I'm going to get through this flight without being worried sick. I realize it's a great imposition, but—" The sound of a familiar mew in the background caused me to stop short. "Where are you?" I asked.

"I'm at your place. I was in the neighborhood, so I came up to check on her. How does someone like you manage to have such a nice cat?"

Normally such a comment might have elicited an angry response from me, but I was so relieved that Fleur wasn't alone that I let it go, saying instead, "You know how they say personality skips a generation."

"Is that it?"

"I can't think of any other reason." I suddenly felt the desire to talk with him more, to thank him for being so kind to my cat. But the purser was announcing that in preparation for departure it was time to turn all cell phones off. Before hanging up, some words did slip from my mouth that caused my face to glow red as a Christmas ornament. "I'll see you when I get back. I'll miss you."

"Did you say you'd miss me?"

"Sorry, I meant Fleur." I clicked the phone shut. Both of you, I thought.

It wasn't until we were airborne that I remembered the envelope the desk clerk had handed me before leaving. I reached into my purse and took it out. It was of high-quality paper, but bore several greasy fingerprints. Sipping from my champagne flute, I eyed it curiously before finally tearing it open and pulling out a sheet of cream-colored linen stock, the sort used for good stationery. The solitary phrase printed in the center of the page was one of the strangest Christmas greetings I'd ever read.

*And what rough beast, its hour come round at last,
slouches towards Bethlehem to be born?*

I crumpled up the sheet of paper and stuffed it into my seat pocket alongside the airline magazine and requisite aircraft evacuation details. If the excerpt from "The Second Coming" was in some way meant to disturb me, the sender fell short of the mark. I had no idea who had sent me the poem and, for that matter, didn't care. Obviously, the sender had no clue that the poem reflected Yeats's rather dire view of the world on the eve of the First World War, and his reference to Bethlehem had nothing to do with the holiday season.

The cabin lights dimmed, and the flight attendants began meal service. Sitting at my solo seat in the window, I was grateful that there would be no need to engage in conversation with anyone other than the flight attendants during the flight. After dining on what was possibly the best airline food I had ever eaten, I stretched out and tried to make some headway in the copy of *Moby-Dick* I had brought to read. The book had been unfinished business with me ever since Radcliffe, where I bluffed my way through a great books class by watching the movie several times. One of my life's goals was to finish the book at some time, and what better place to reacquaint myself with the leviathan than trapped aboard a plane for seventeen hours? But even as Ishmael was crawling into bed with the cannibal, my mind refused to stay focused on the page, so I put the book aside and stared at my reflection in the blackened window.

Catherine O'Connell

Was Elsa right? Had I taken leave of my senses? For the first time, I admitted to myself the true reason I was on this flight, ill-prepared and with no idea what awaited me at the other end. Certainly, my initial quest to find Whitney had also been fueled by my strong desire to find my cat. Now Fleur was safely back with me, and I was reasonably sure that Jack had not cut up Whitney and disposed of her in some trash bin. Whitney had left him of her own accord. Who knew? Maybe Whitney had decided too late that she liked women after all. So what was driving me in the pursuit to find her? Why wasn't I doing the rational thing, pursuing real wealth and security in the form of Dexter Worthington Sr., instead of heading on this wild-goose chase?

The true reason could no longer be denied. Tag McKay had gotten under my skin. So much so I felt like a blithering idiot in his presence. Truth was I would sit and fantasize about him for hours: his manliness, his quiet intelligence, his surprising familiarity with literature, even the smell that emanated from his work clothes, the scent of sweat brought about by physical labor. Dexter Worthington Sr., with his smooth hands and arced ski turns, paled in comparison to him. Tag was a man proud of his creations and not of his bank account. He was my Michelangelo, and my apartment was his Sistine Chapel.

I was on this flight because I needed to collect that money from Jack Armstrong. But it wasn't to keep my own head above water. It was so that I could afford a life for Tag and me.

The flight attendant returned with a hot towel and I wiped my face, taking off the day's grime. Could a mixed marriage work? Our culture had changed so much since my coming out as a young woman over—well, never mind—let's just say many years ago. The long-desired clubs had lowered their standards; the exclusive private schools that enrolled generation after generation of the same names until the boards of directors looked like a grand case of incest were now taking students on merit alone and having a legacy was no guarantee of admission. Money was still important, but it seemed to matter naught where it originated, be it inheritance, entrepreneurship, or lottery. It didn't matter, as long as you could afford that Lincoln Park townhouse and Mercedes, that Hatteras in Palm Beach or that lakefront cottage in Lake Geneva. The new money came from pimply boys like Bill Gates and ill-dressed characters like Steven Case. It was a brave new world, on the brink of large changes as we drew near the liberation of Afghanistan. But one thing remained the same. Money always wrote its own ticket.

Another flight attendant came around offering cognac. As I took a snifter and sipped from it, I pictured Tag McKay seated beside me in the center section of first class. He would luxuriate in the excesses he had never been privy to, and I would share them with him happily. It would be my gift to him. It never occurred to me that he might want otherwise.

29

Remembrance of Things Past

It was four in the afternoon when my plane touched down at Suvarnabhumi. I picked up my luggage and passed through immigration and then customs, marching confidently through the "nothing to declare" lane. A uniformed driver from the Oriental met me with a cheerful "*Sawadee*" and a deep *wah* from the waist, his hands joined together and pointed toward the heavens. He was a square-faced man, his brown skin mottled like a pineapple. I acknowledged his welcome with a slight bow myself. He took charge of my luggage and we exited the terminal into the late afternoon heat. Though the temperature hovered near ninety and the humidity was high, it was a welcome change from the Chicago cold. The hotel's Mercedes was parked curbside and after a quick handout of some Baht to a nearby official, we pulled away in air-conditioned comfort. Things could not have been going smoother until we hit the highway, where we came to a dead halt in a traffic jam that resembled Los Angeles on its worst day.

"My apologies, Madam," my driver said. "It is Bangkok rush hour. I'm afraid this may take some time."

I leaned back against the smooth leather seat and stared out the window. The palm trees waved languidly in the mild afternoon breeze, and the sun was a bright red ball in the sky. We inched along in traffic, the only movement coming from the motorbikes that roared past us every ten seconds or so in between the lanes. I recalled my only other visit to Thailand with Henry on our honeymoon. I had been mesmerized from the moment I set foot in the Orient with its myriad of religions and multitude of foods and smells so unlike those of the Occident. I was especially struck by the politeness of the people and their gentle, smiling nature. The Thais had more words for "smile" than the Eskimos did for "snow," and with good reason. A smile was never far from the face of a Thai.

But that had been long ago and there had been many changes since. The first thing that struck me was the proliferation of modern high-rises. Large billboards with modern-day ads dominated the landscape along the highway, and when I cracked the window open, the scent of diesel fumes made me quickly close it. The East had met the West and surpassed it. I leaned back against the headrest and shut my eyes. Having slept soundly on the plane, stretched out beneath a down comforter on a seat transformed into a bed, I wasn't particularly tired. What I needed was to contemplate. Back on terra firma, I realized it might have been smart to have some plan in place before arriving, but my best inspirations come once I'm embroiled in a situation.

As one did now. Though I had no idea where Whitney might have stayed, why not start with the Oriental? I tapped on the driver's glass window, and he lowered it.

"What is your name, please?"

"I am Arun, Mrs. Cook."

"Arun, do you often pick up the guests for the Oriental?"

"Every day, Madam. Except Buddhist holiday."

"Do you remember most of your clientele?"

He was silent as his brain cells sorted through company policy for an appropriate answer. "I remember those who wish to be remembered, Madam."

"Yes, I see. I had a very dear friend visit Bangkok last month. A Mrs. Armstrong. Might you remember her?"

"I'm sorry, Madam. I pick up many customers."

"You would remember this one. She's quite tall with a most remarkable figure and platinum blond hair." I shoved a photo of Whitney in front of his face. She was at her most improper, wearing low-cut Gaultier at last summer's Arts Club benefit. He glanced at the picture and looked away far too quickly for my liking.

"I have not seen her," he said.

Now, I have to say that Whitney makes an impression on people. It may be good or it may be bad, but it is always indelible. And though a photo doesn't do her attributes justice, they still stand out all the same. I'm referring to her remarkable implanted breasts, and the way she nearly always wore something that either showed off their silhouette or the canyonlike cleavage that ran between them. They were unavoidable and any male, gay or straight, or any person for that matter, would spend more than a millisecond regarding those breasts. Arun's quick dismissal of them told me he was familiar with them.

Having no idea why he didn't want to acknowledge he'd seen Whitney, I was confident that she had stayed at the hotel. I decided to let the matter rest for the time being and pursue it further once I got there.

After crawling along city streets choked with cars and bicycles and tuk-tuks, a three-wheeled contraption that served the same function as a taxi, we finally arrived at the Oriental on the banks of the Chao Phraya River. As we drove past an armed guard and up the palm tree–lined drive, I could see there had been many changes to the colonial-era hotel since my last visit. But the service remained the same. The moment the car pulled to a stop in front of the entrance, the doorman met me with orchids and escorted me through the tall glass doors into the high-ceilinged lobby. My eyes danced around the bright room, taking in the flowers and the palm trees and the relaxed elegance of well-dressed guests sipping cocktails or iced tea and speaking in hushed tones. There was not a pair of shorts to be seen, and no one was wearing a duck-billed cap, not to mention wearing one backward. The environment spoke to me of more mannered, graceful times.

At the reception desk, a clerk in a Spartan-white uniform *wahed* deeply before checking me in. I requested a room in the Authors' Residence, the older part of the hotel, where the rooms are named after the authors who have frequented the hotel over the years dating back to the 1880s. He was able to put me in the same suite that Henry and I had stayed in, the Somerset Maugham suite. As the bellman unlocked the door and ushered me into the elegant room, I was overcome with nostalgia. Little had changed in over a quarter century, from the heavy colonial furnishings to the sweeping ceiling fan.

I unpacked and took a brief nap, setting the clock so as not to sleep too long. It has always been my opinion that the best way to adapt when traveling internationally is to get onto local time as quickly as possible. After awakening, I treated my travel-weary body with a bath, luxuriating in jasmine-perfumed bath salts. The silky water drained my tension away as I contemplated the job before me. My first thought was of Arun, the limousine driver, and his denial of Whitney's existence when it was clear that he had seen her before. If he was familiar with her, then someone else in the hotel must be. Which meant my work could start amid these pleasant surroundings. After drying off with thick terry towels, I donned a silk sundress and headed to the Authors' Lounge to begin my queries.

As with the Authors' Residence, the Authors' Lounge is named in honor of the many famous authors who have graced the Oriental's halls, from Joseph Conrad to Noël Coward to that grand dame of grand dames, the overly made-up Barbara Cartland, whose mother once said, "Poor I may be, but common I am not." Those were words I certainly took to heart.

I took a seat in the white-shuttered room, among the potted palms and bamboo trees, and thought it fitting that the lions of literature would have found themselves at home in such tranquil surroundings. A beautiful young Thai woman wearing a spotless white silk blouse and long black silk skirt brought me a pot of Ceylon tea along with a lovely plate of finger sandwiches, scones, and clotted cream. As out of place as such fare may have seemed in a gastronomical paradise such as Bangkok, the pull of the afternoon tea ritual was far too appealing to resist. The face of the young woman serving me was so open and friendly, I decided to show her Whitney's picture and see if I got any response. As soon as she had laid the delicate china plates before me and began the obligatory *wah*, I took Whitney's photo out and laid it on the table.

"I wonder if this person looks at all familiar to you?" I ventured, watching her face for the same kind of telltale sign Arun had given in the limousine. She politely examined the photograph and handed it back to me, head bowed. "You must excuse me, but I cannot help you. Perhaps someone else can be of help," she said, *wah*ing deeply before disappearing back into the sea of palms.

Enjoying the peace, I took a bite of my cucumber sandwich and wondered what she meant. Suddenly, my bit of paradise was rocked by the sound of my name.

"Pauline Cook, as I live and breathe, is that you?" I turned to see Eve Longacre sitting across the room with two other women. Eve was a fixture in Chicago social circles, an honor earned by serving on just about every board in the city, including the Lyric Opera and the Chicago Symphony. Sunny would have given her right breast to have Eve Longacre on the Amici board and was lying in wait for the day Eve rolled off one of the others so she could sweep her up. Her husband, Dillon, had a hugely philanthropic bent, but he could afford to be generous. His family's real estate holdings in northern Indiana were second to none, and he had given so much to the University of Notre Dame there was discussion of naming a building after him. Though she was worth a fortune and had no need to put on airs, she had a fondness for expressions from the deep South.

"Eve, darling, whatever are you doing here?" I asked, having no choice but to go over and visit her table. Looking impeccable as always, she was dressed for the tropics in a white linen shift that I recognized as a Chanel. Oddly enough the two other women looked as if they had gone shopping together sometime in the late fifties. Eve introduced me to Helen Abbott and Eunice Berman from Fort Wayne, women on the late edge of middle-age with short, sensible haircuts. Dressed in inexpensive flowered pantsuits that might have come from Walmart, they were clearly old school midwesterners who put their money in the bank and not on their backs. That Warren Buffett sort of mentality. I mean, honestly, to have all that money and live in the same modest house their entire lives. What could his wife be thinking?

"The same thing as tout le monde," Eve answered. "Visiting the colonies. Everyone's in the Far East this year. Just seems a lot safer, you know. The Buddhists and Hindus don't have a lot of grudges against us. At least not yet. We're going to Vietnam next. Hard to believe, isn't it, that it feels safer to visit our last war than Europe? What about you, darling? You're not travelling alone?"

"Yes, I am," I said, not bothering to mention that Thailand had never been anyone's colony. "I'm here for a bit of business," I added, already working up an excuse to duck a dinner invitation. "How are you finding Bangkok?"

"Well, it's nice and warm, but it's so dirty."

Helen Abbott agreed, adding, "We've eaten in the hotel nearly every night. We tried one local restaurant and they nearly had to take Bernard to the hospital, his heartburn was so bad. I thought he was going to have a heart attack. He refuses to eat anyplace else now. At least here they understand what mild is."

Her cohort concurred. "Our husbands are anxious to get home. They have no sense of adventure."

Of course they didn't. They were anxious to get back to their redbrick colonials and the country clubs probably within a mile of their residence where one ate safe food like steak and potatoes. Adventure was forgoing the club on a Saturday night and heading into downtown Fort Wayne to a noisy Italian restaurant. I could never lead such a vanilla life, no matter how much money was involved.

As feared, Eve asked me if I would like to join them for dinner. Reprieve came in the form of the waitress, accompanied by a Thai man dressed in the most perfectly fitted tropical-weight suit I'd ever seen. He was tall and slim, his golden face the ultimate meld of East meets West. His eyes surveyed the room from behind a pair of black glasses, telling me he missed little that happened under his watch. He *wah*ed the waitress, who *wah*ed him back deeper.

"Ladies," he greeted us, as he *wah*ed us all around. "I am Waen Sanitawatra, the general manager of the hotel. I trust everything at the Oriental is meeting with your approval." Uplifted chins followed by subtle nods indicated that everything was in order. He turned his all-knowing eyes directly toward me, and said, "Mrs. Cook. I understand there may be some question as to your accommodation. If you could follow me, please, it would be my pleasure to be of assistance."

Grateful for an escape, I told Eve I would call her later and followed Mr. Sanitawatra from the Authors' Lounge. He escorted me down a hallway adorned with gold-framed photos of generations of Thai royalty. Just like the British, whom they had managed to thwart as conquerors, the Thais held onto their monarchy. Unlike the British, no Thai resented the vast amounts of capital that went into keeping their king and queen in silk and palaces.

The general manager stopped in front of a door marked EXECUTIVE OFFICES and swept a card through a slot on the door. The door clicked open, and he led me to an office at the end of the hall. The room held a large desk in its center and was adorned with showcases filled with Thai art. A large window looked out upon a flower-filled garden.

"Please take a seat, Mrs. Cook." He seated himself behind the desk and lit a cigarette with a slim gold lighter. Flicking the lighter closed with a flourish, he took a deep puff and let the smoke out in a steady stream. I couldn't help but think the scene had the elements of a spy movie, the only thing missing being Peter Lorre.

"It has been brought to my attention that you are looking for someone?"

"That is correct. I have reason to believe my friend may have stayed here in November. Her name is Whitney Armstrong. Mrs. Jack Armstrong." I reached into my purse to get the photo, but he waved me aside.

"I'm familiar with Mrs. Armstrong," he said.

Though I've never played the game in my life, the word "bingo" came to mind. How serendipitous to strike gold on the first try. My intuition that Whitney would always stay in the finest place had been right.

"Is she still here?"

"She stayed here for several days in November. Then she had the concierge obtain plane tickets for her to Phnom Penh and asked us to keep her room until she returned. Of course, we are accommodating her, but she has not returned."

"And she has not contacted you?"

"No."

"Was she traveling alone?"

"To the best of my knowledge."

I wondered what had happened to Chia. "And have you contacted the authorities about this?"

"No. She said she couldn't be certain how long she might be. But when I learned you were making inquiries, I thought it best to inform you."

Knowing that Whitney had paid cash for her first-class flight to Bangkok, I assumed she would have done the same thing at the hotel, thereby giving Jack no trace on a credit card. I asked Mr. Sanitawatra, and he confirmed my assumption. "Yes, she paid for everything in dollars." The thought that Whitney was paying in greenbacks in third-world countries alarmed me. She was likely enough to draw attention just by her appearance. Throwing money around could be dangerous.

"Do you think that could have made Mrs. Armstrong some kind of target?"

He blew a stream of smoke and stubbed the cigarette out in an enamel dish. "Anything is possible, Mrs. Cook. My job here is to accommodate our guests' requests. To be quite frank, I did warn her to be discreet in her use of money, but that is all I can do. I certainly cannot tell one of my honored guests how to behave."

No, he couldn't. And I sincerely doubted anyone could have told Whitney how to behave at that point. I had no idea what she was doing, but I did know one thing. I had had phenomenal luck in stumbling onto her on the first try. And if she stuck out in Bangkok, she would certainly stick out more in Cambodia. So my course was set.

Next stop: Phnom Penh.

30

Les Misérables

The good fortune I'd enjoyed thus far came to a screeching halt when I tried to book a flight to Phnom Penh for the next day. Mr. Luang, the hotel concierge, shook his head in a tsking manner and informed me that it would be impossible since the Cambodian airline, Royal Air Cambodge, had the poor timing to have gone out of business in October. Now the only carrier servicing Cambodia was Bangkok Airways and those flights were all overbooked. At first I refused to take Mr. Luang at his word and insisted he make a few calls, that he could certainly find me a flight. He gave me a condescending smile and dialed away. But true to his word, the new popularity of Cambodia among Westerners had put a strain on the existing airline. The best he could do was put me on a standby list for a flight at the end of the week.

I found it ironic that people avoiding the newfound danger in the Western world would flock to the land of the killing fields where Pol Pot had systematically eliminated anyone displaying a smidgen of intellect in his quest for the ultimate agrarian society. But the despot was now dead, and evidently twenty years was long enough to soften that memory for Westerners. "Is there some other way for me to get to Phnom Penh?"

"Overland, Madam, by car. But of course that will take longer than a flight."

"It won't take a week, will it?"

"No, Madam. But it is a considerable drive."

"How far?" I asked.

"In the area of two hundred fifty kilometers."

I did the math. A kilometer being basically two thirds of a mile, I took one third off two fifty and came up with something in the area of one hundred seventy miles. That would make it a three-or four-hour drive, depending on how fast one drove.

"Can I get a driver to take me there?"

"I can get a hotel driver to take you to Aranyaprathet near the border, but from there you must go to Poipet and pass through on your own. Once in Cambodia you must hire a driver to take you into Siem Reap. In Siem Reap you can find a boat to Phnom Penh. But I must warn you, the journey from Poipet to Siem Reap may not be of the sort of travel conditions that Madam is accustomed to."

"But you say there are plenty of vehicles for transport," I confirmed.

"Yes, Madam." He looked me up and down as if seeing me for the first time, taking in my Versace sundress and strappy Gucci sandals. "But I worry that you would not be terribly comfortable."

I thought of my pressing need to pick up Whitney's trail as soon as possible, before it went cold—if it hadn't already. A bit of discomfort in the pursuit of a comfortable ten million dollars was manageable. Besides, only last week I had run into Regan Cunning Swift who had visited Siem Reap recently, and she told me the service at the Hotel d'Angkor was among the best she had experienced in her life. Surely transportation to the city existed in the same category.

"I'll be just fine," I countered him. "So if I leave tomorrow morning for Siem Reap, I can be there by afternoon?"

Mr. Luang stared up at the white ceiling and appeared to be counting the rotations of the fan swirling lazily above us. "With good luck, Madam."

"Do I need any documents?" I asked him.

"You can buy a visa at the border for twenty dollars."

Twenty dollars was certainly in the budget. "Please arrange for a driver to take me to the border in the morning." Then thinking better of trying to make it all the way to Phnom Penh in one day, I added, "And please book me into the Hotel d'Angkor tomorrow evening."

"As you wish, Madam." He smiled and *wahed*.

In retrospect, if I have to sleep in the Bangkok airport for a week next time, I will. But I was determined to be on my way, so shortly after sunrise the next morning, I embarked in a hired car for the Cambodian border. I had given some careful consideration as to what would be best to wear for travel, and I had settled on sensible silk slacks, a linen blouse, and a pair of flat sandals in the event I might have to do any walking. And although I'd applied several layers of sunblock, I carried a wide-brimmed straw hat as well to ensure protection from the sun.

We departed early enough to beat the morning traffic and sailed smoothly out of the city in air-conditioned comfort, arriving in the border town of Aranyaprathet two hours later. As we pulled into a crowded, dirt parking lot filled with vendors selling everything from cold drinks to trinkets, I had my first taste of what was to come. Half a dozen men descended upon us speaking rapid-fire Thai and pointing to an equal number of tuktuks parked nearby. My driver engaged in what appeared to be negotiations until all the men walked away except for one.

"This man take you six kilometers to Poipet in tuk-tuk. There you go through customs. Be careful on other side. Keep your things close." He pantomimed holding a makeshift purse close to his side. "Look out for children."

My new driver took my bag—for once I'd had the prescience to travel light and had but one large Vuitton tote—which he carried to his tuk-tuk, an egglike contraption pulled by a motorcycle. Though the vehicles were ubiquitous throughout the Far East in various shapes and sizes, I had yet to ride in one. I climbed in and he placed the tote beside me on the seat. Then he went back to my original driver and handed him something that looked suspiciously like money.

As we drove off, I peered out from my seat inside the plastic shell and felt rather taken with myself for being so adventurous, superior to those of my class who traveled on arranged tours, isolated from the very cultures they had come to see.

That was certainly not going to be the case on this trip.

The short hop from Aranyaprathet to Poipet should have been my first indication that perhaps things wouldn't be quite as smooth as anticipated. As we drove along the unpaved road, my first thought was that I was at the outskirts of civilization. The garbage-strewn streets were lined with ramshackle buildings, and filthy children in rags stood beside equally dirty locals. Clutching my purse tightly for fear it would fly free of me, I bounced along in the back of the tuk-tuk like the ball on a roulette wheel, choking on the thick scent of diesel fuel. Though I shouted for the driver to slow down, the high-pitched buzz of the motorcycle engine made it impossible for him to hear me.

After fifteen minutes and a case of whiplash, we arrived in Poipet. There was blessed silence as the driver pulled up to a block of concrete buildings and turned off his engine. He jumped from the tuk-tuk and grabbed my tote, holding it in one hand while holding his other hand out for payment. Realizing too late that I had forgotten to ask my first driver what price he had negotiated, I took out a hundred-baht note and placed it in his hand. He stared at it as if it were an insect to be flicked off. I put down another hundred baht. Still the hand did not move. Finally the driver said, "Dollar. You pay in dollar."

Although a dollar certainly didn't seem an unreasonable charge, I suspected the trip should have cost less. But anxious to be on my way, I reached back into my wallet and pulled out a U.S. dollar and laid it on top of the baht. The hand did not waver, and my Vuitton bag remained firmly in his clasp. "Not one dollar. Five dollar," he said firmly.

Now I knew he was taking advantage of me. I looked about for someone with authority to help, but all I saw about me were the lines of people waiting to enter immigration. There were precious few Westerners, and they were young people carrying backpacks. Then I spied a man wearing an official-looking uniform and raised my hand to get his attention. When the official started walking toward me, the tuk-tuk driver quickly folded his hand around the dollar and relinquished my bag. A second later he was back on his vehicle making a hasty departure, leaving a cloud of diesel fumes in his wake.

Proud of myself for not allowing him to take advantage of me, I prepared to take my place in line when the official indicated that I come with him. Thinking he had singled me out for some special treatment, I followed him into the building, where he deposited me in front of a stern-faced officer with a long scar down the right side of his face and his right earlobe missing.

Without saying a word, the immigration official held out his hand for my passport. He studied my picture for an inordinate amount of time and then looked at me in my washable silk and linen. His eyes traveled pruriently to my Gucci purse and Vuitton tote, resting on them long enough to make me uncomfortable.

"Visa?" he inquired.

"I was told I could get one here at the border," I answered.

He shook his head and flipped through the pages of my passport. "Health document. Cholera. Yellow fever. You have shots, no?"

"I wasn't told I needed shots."

"Twenty dollars, visa. Twenty dollars penalty, no cholera vaccine."

"Forty dollars, that's absurd. I was told twenty for the visa, but nothing about inoculations. I would like to speak to your superior."

He stared at me with the eyes of a ferret, dark and treacherous and connected only to that section of the brain stem that controlled survival. I knew I could refuse and turn back. I could take another one-dollar tuk-tuk ride back to Aranyaprathet where I could seek transportation back to the Oriental. Or I could pay and be on with it. I took two crisp twenty-dollar bills from my bag.

The sun was well overhead by the time I emerged onto the Cambodian side of the border and found myself in yet another dusty parking lot. Before I had time to catch my breath, sweating men came running from all directions, calling out offers of rides. Siem Reap. You come me. You come my truck. Good price. Dressed in dirty T-shirts or cotton button-downs atop baggy pants, they swarmed about me like bees, their closeness making me uneasy.

Maria's words came back to me, to beware around those in rags. Could this be the oracle's vision coming true?

The circle closed in tighter as one driver vied harder than the next for my business. Since I towered over them, I searched beyond the sea of heads for the place where the Mercedes or BMWs or some other manner of luxury transport awaited. Something tugged at my handbag, and I looked down to see several children had joined in the fray. Keeping a tight grip on my tote as well as my purse, I tried to shoo them away.

"That's enough, get away," I commanded forcefully. The swarm of humanity pressed ever closer, like the pull of gravity to the center of the earth. I began to panic, fearing they might pull me down and devour me like locusts do grain. And then my ears picked up the welcome sound of English coming from behind me. I turned my head and saw a stocky young woman pushing her way through the crowd, her hair the color of carrots, her freckled face burnt to a beet red. She was flanked on either side by two scruffy-looking men, both of them large enough to squash the natives under their heels. One of the men sported a head of wild black hair and a week's growth of beard; the other's head was shaved, his only hair a silky brown goatee fringing his chin.

"Out of the way, you buggers," the young woman shouted. "Out of the way. Leave her be." With the two men to give weight to her words, the crowd parted. She reached me and grabbed my arm, pulling me out of the circle. The two men followed vigilantly behind us.

"You 'right?" she asked when we had distanced ourselves from the fray, who were still calling out offers of rides, although at a distance now.

Checking to see that all my possessions were still in hand, I nodded.

"Good God, that lot's obnoxious. Don't know who's worse, the touts or the ankle biters," she said in about as thick an Australian accent as I'd ever heard. She stared back at the great unwashed and nodded. "We saw you from over there and could tell you'd gotten yourself into a bit of a fix."

"Thank you for coming to my rescue," I said, with a newfound empathy for those who suffer from claustrophobia.

"No worries." She stuck out a freckled hand. "Victoria Kelly. These are me mates. Wassau Blake and Cameron Kearney."

"G'day," said Wassau Blake. "G'day," echoed Cameron Kearney.

"And I am Pauline Cook," I said, looking back at the crowd. An occasional offer was still called out in our direction. "Are they always like that?"

"Yeah. The Khmer are basically harmless, but they can be a bit overwhelming at first, especially if you don't know what you're doing. Mostly they're good-hearted people. Just hungry and you stand out like shag on a rock."

"Like shag on a . . . ?"

"Yea're. Look at yourself. You don't mike a trip like this wearing that sort of clothes," she admonished me, sizing up my silk and linen. Her eyes rested on my sandals, and she made a face but said nothing. I thought they would be perfect for travel. Both she and the two men were wearing jeans that were in dire need of a washing, T-shirts, and closed-toe shoes. She looked down at my purse and tote, still firmly in my grasp, my fingers practically fused to them. "Or carrying bags like that. You might as well be wearing a sign that says 'separate me from my money.'" She continued on in her loquacious manner. "You're headed for Siem Reap, I take it."

"Actually, Phnom Penh is my final destination, but I'm staying in Siem Reap tonight. I was hoping to find some decent transportation here. Where does one find the private cars?"

This drew a loud chortle from both Wassau and Cameron. Victoria actually rolled her eyes and jerked her head toward a sad-looking collection of pickup trucks and beaten-up vans parked on a patch of dirt that served as the parking lot. The vehicles' proximity to each other reminded me of the junks that once inhabited Hong Kong bay. "There're your private cars."

Then she pointed out a filthy white pickup truck with at least a dozen people milling about it. "We're taking that one. Should be room for one more. Do you want to come with us?"

I looked at the ragtag group in disbelief. It was comprised of half men and half women, the men dressed in shirtsleeves and pants with drawstring waists, the women in colorful skirts with scarves wrapped around their heads. Several of them carried chickens. "You can't possibly tell me all those people are going in that one truck?"

"That's nothing," she said. "I've seen 'em take twice that many."

"Couldn't we just hire one truck just for ourselves?" I asked hopefully.

Victoria gave me a motherly look. "Pauline, you better learn the ropes around here. First, they're going to fill that truck no matter what. Space is money. You think you're buying the whole truck and you'll turn around and the back'll be full up just the same."

"That's absurd. If one pays for an entire truck, one should get an entire truck."

She stared at me as if I had just fallen from the moon. "Are you coming or not?" she asked. I decided not to press my luck. At least I was with people who spoke my language. Sort of. I promised myself to listen to people like Mr. Luang more carefully in the future.

Victoria negotiated a place for me inside the truck's cab for five U.S. dollars. She told me it normally would have cost four dollars, but seeing the way I was dressed, the driver had upped the fare. Before I knew it, I was one of four people wedged across the front seat of the dirty white pickup truck. Victoria was seated next to our driver, Mr. Eng, a thin, nervous man with the whisper of a moustache tracing his lip. I was next to her with Cam at the window. The driver had tried to give me Victoria's seat first, but I balked at taking a seat that demanded having the gearshift between one's legs, even though Victoria assured me it was the safest place in the truck since there were no seat belts. Wassau had volunteered to ride in the back of the truck with the Cambodians, thereby saving himself two dollars. As I looked out the dusty back window at the gigantic hairy Australian wedged in the flatbed with the peasants, a mild pang of guilt struck me, knowing he had given up his seat on my behalf.

"Don't worry, he'll do baiter back there anyhow. He was off his face last night and the fraish air'll do 'im good," said Cam. Then he rested his shaved head against the back of the seat and fell asleep. With my tote tucked beneath the seat away from prying hands, my purse resting on my lap, and my new friends either side of me, I felt secure for the time being. As we bounced along the rutted and garbage-filled streets, leaving the beggars and touts of the border town behind, Victoria was quick to point out that Poipet rhymed with toilet.

The road smoothed out once we left town, an ongoing stretch of orange dirt bordered on either side by rice paddies. The day was getting ever warmer and

I was grateful for the cool stream of air-conditioning blowing from the vent onto my now gritty face. I found myself starting to nod off, too, and it wasn't long before my head fell against the back of the seat. I had just started to dream when the sharp sound of Victoria's voice brought me back to present day.

"Watch out," she shouted.

I opened my eyes just in time to brace myself as the driver slammed on the brakes. There was a sickening thud behind me, and I turned around to see a collage of faces and a couple of chickens pressed up against the window. Turning forward again, my heart nearly breached my chest at the sight before me. We teetered on the edge of a hole that could only have been made by a meteor or a land mine.

"My god, did the Khmer Rouge do this?" I asked, thinking of the limbless I had been seeing with some regularity since crossing into Cambodia.

"Nope, the rainy season is responsible for this." Victoria yelped excitedly as Mr. Eng eased the truck into the crater. The back end came down with a thump. Beside me, Cam blinked his eyes momentarily open, assessed the situation, and finding it to be of no great importance, closed them again. Had I been a nail biter, mine would have been down to the quick.

Mr. Eng nosed the truck out of what was possibly the world's largest pot-hole and accelerated only to have to stop again and repeat the entire process a hundred yards down the road. The people in the flatbed seemed better prepared this time, and only a couple of them slammed into the window when he applied the brakes.

"My God, one would think the Cambodians would build a new road," I said to Victoria.

She laughed aloud. "Build a new road! This is the new road. You should have seen the old one. Welcome to the infamous Route Six."

"Well, I hope I can take this for a couple more hours," I said as we arrived at yet another crater.

"A couple of hours? What d'yer mean a couple of hours?"

"A couple of hours to Siem Reap."

"Lord, I knew you Seppos could be dodgy, but . . . It's at least a couple of hours to Sisophone, which is nearly halfway, and *thait's* only because this is the dry season. In the rainy season it can tike *eight* hours—if you're lucky."

✳   ✳   ✳

For the next couple of hours, it seemed that Mr. Eng would just get up a head of steam when he would have to hit the brakes before the truck lurched through another hole. The air-conditioning had stopped working after the third pothole, and the dust and dirt that floated in the open windows formed a crust around my eyes and lips.

"My god, it's dusty," I said to Victoria as I loosened a ball of dirt from the corner of my eye.

"Drier than a Pommie's towel," she agreed.

I had long since stopped cursing the driver every time he clunked into a hole, and turned to praying that he had some idea of what he was doing. Remarkably enough, Cam slept through most of it, waking only when his head banged against the door frame on some particularly difficult lurch. In an effort to distract myself from the tooth-jarring ride, I closed my eyes and tried to liken the motion to a sailboat. I imagined I was back onboard the *Herakles* with the boat rocking at the will of the sea. It was a time before my money had evaporated and my world had gone to hell, before my cat and friend disappeared, when remodeling brought desired results and one's heart didn't actually go out to a laborer. I was traipsing across the ruined columns of temples to Apollo with Gianfranco, naïvely unaware of his marital status. Or was I naïvely unaware, I asked myself? Had I known his marital status all along and been in denial? Regardless, my picture of him was not as fulfilling as it had once been. My amorous sailor had been replaced by a man with calloused hands.

A collective gasp from within the cab and a howl from without drew me from my reverie. This time I opened my eyes to a situation that demanded far more attention than a mere pothole. We were stopped on what appeared to be a bridge. I say "appeared" because it served the elemental purpose of a bridge—that is, it connected the land on one side of a body of water to the land on the opposite side. However, the bridge had given way under the truck, all four tires having penetrated the rotted wood, so that it rested on its chassis over the running water below.

This made the near-death experience on the Gulfstream look like a mild roller-coaster ride.

31
The Red Badge of Courage

The trials of the Joad family paled in comparison to our present situation. Though the vehicle's chassis was firmly resting on what remained of our lane, we were no better off than a cow with four legs dangling. Those in the back of the truck quickly got a handle on the situation and climbed over its tailgate. Cam opened the passenger door and announced that it wouldn't be a good idea to get out on his side since it dropped off directly into the river. Mr. Eng opened the driver's-side door and rattled off something in Cambodian. Then he jumped from the cab and stepped into the oncoming traffic, which consisted of an ox-drawn cart with two men perched high upon a bindle of wood. He waved a skinny arm to the rest of us to follow him.

Victoria eased herself out onto the bridge, and I started crawling around the gear shift behind her when I remembered my Vuitton bag tucked beneath the seat. I grabbed it and followed her out. The ox-drawn cart lumbered past, the two men atop it not so much as turning their heads at our predicament as the bridge trembled in a threatening manner.

Victoria and I and the rest of the women followed the oxcart back to the shore, careful to leave enough distance between us in case the ox opted to attend to its business, while Cam and Wassau stayed back with the rest of the men, who appeared to be debating what to do about our predicament. Now, I have no degree in engineering or physics, but I could inform them definitively that the dirty white pickup was going nowhere. Unless Mr. Eng kept a helicopter rotor under its hood. When we reached the river's edge, Victoria sat down on the dirt while I made myself comfortable by sitting on the tote. Off in the distance, we could see the peasants working the rice paddies, indifferent to our dilemma, as if this sort of thing happened every day.

The men on the bridge started to argue, their arms gesticulating wildly and their voices growing louder. Then suddenly all grew quiet. What happened next defies all rational thought. The group split in half, took positions at opposite ends of the truck, and began rocking it back and forth. At first I thought they were trying to rock the vehicle out of the impossible situation, but then it dawned on me what they were actually doing. They were trying to break through the dilapidated wooden structure. As I watched with great appreciation for their insanity, they rocked the vehicle first one way, then the other. Suddenly, there was a loud crack as a supporting beam of the bridge fell into the water. The men started running in opposite directions as if the truck was a stick of dynamite about to explode. As the last bits of rotted wood gave way, the bridge came apart. The truck dropped into the river, miraculously landing squarely on all four wheels like some kind of vehicular cat, the water just brushing the bottom of the truck's doors.

Without hesitating, Mr. Eng got down on his hands and knees and crawled back along the thread of wood that was left of the bridge. When he was directly over the truck, he swung his legs over the edge and dropped about twenty feet onto its hood. From there it was easy for him to climb in the open window, and a moment later there was the sound of an engine starting. He put the truck into reverse and backed it up to the river's edge, where Victoria and I sat with the peasant women and their chickens and the half of the men who had run in our direction as the bridge was coming down. Mr. Eng stopped the truck and gestured that we come down.

I gave Victoria a concerned look. "Are you sure this is safe?" I queried.

She shrugged and got up. "Just be glad it's not the rainy season."

We filed down the bank, and the peasants took their places, back in the flatbed of the truck. It had gotten soaked with river water and what had once been dust was now a sea of mud. I stood at the back of the truck with orange-brown slime slipping over the soles of my sandals. Since the front of the truck was in the water, we were going to have to wade through it to get to the door. I started to take my sandals off when Victoria said, "Keep an eye out for water snakes."

"Snakes!" I shrieked loudly, taking refuge back on the shore. It is rare for me to make such a scene, but the image of one snake, never mind the plural form, was enough to reduce me to tears. An undaunted Victoria shrugged and slogged through the mud, resuming her position in the front seat. I looked down at my sandals, swearing off ever again wearing an open-toed shoe in a third-world country.

"C'mon, Pauline," she called, holding the door open. Mr. Eng began screaming and the other passengers joined in. Though I would like to think they were offering encouragement I don't believe that was the case. Holding my bag tightly, I tested the water with my toe, my eyes glued to the surface for any sign of a movement. I had just stepped into the river when I picked up the shadow of a long, dark figure darting toward me. I jumped for the first safe place available, which happened to be over the tailgate and into the muddy back of the pickup. As I felt the mud soak through to my thighs, I realized my clothes would be a total write-off.

"I'll ride here until we get across," I called to Victoria, looking around at my fellow passengers. Most of them returned my gaze blankly. Some smiled weakly, but their smiles were not the same as the Thais'. The Khmer smiles came from faces that had seen too much. For the first time I noticed some of them were missing limbs.

Mr. Eng put the truck into drive and as he inched forward, I could feel the tires sinking into the riverbed. I looked over the side at the river. It wasn't terribly deep, but it could still swamp us. I looked at my fellow passengers again, this time for some reassurance. Most of them seemed to be in a world of their own, except for one man who was staring at me in a most unnerving manner. He had a full head of shiny black hair and a face that tapered from his forehead to his chin in a way that made him look triangular. A yellow and orange scarf was draped around his neck so that it could be pulled up to keep the dust out of his mouth and nose. When I caught his eye, he looked away. The woman next to him was holding a chicken, and she gave me a semitoothed, hollow smile, which I returned as best I could under the circumstances. Then she held out the fowl for me to take. I didn't know if she wanted to trade it for my Vuitton bag or my Gucci purse, both of which were now covered in mud, or was offering it as a gift. I passed on the opportunity and turned my eyes back to the brown water.

Somehow we made it across the river and up the riverbank on the other side amid an ear-shattering screeching of tires and engine grinding that made me fear the truck would explode. Mr. Eng stopped so that the rest of the men could get back in, and I climbed out to reclaim my seat in the cab between Victoria and Cam. The door was slammed, and soon we were bumping along Route 6 again.

One could call the rest of the journey uneventful if one considers being stopped and asked to pay a toll by a stone-faced teenager armed with a rather intimidating weapon as uneventful. While Mr. Eng argued price with the boy soldier, Victoria informed me that the gun was called an AK-47 and was capable of killing every one of us, including the chickens, without its owner having to reload. Even I was inclined to dig in my purse and chip in after hearing that. But Mr. Eng's argument must have been convincing because after shooting several ear-shattering bullets into the air, the log in the road that had been used to stop us was rolled aside, and we were waved through without any money changing hands.

Three hours later, after striking and killing an unfortunate dog who had dared venture in our way, we pulled into Siem Reap. In comparison to the pig-filled hamlets we had passed through that day, the town felt like a modern metropolis. It showed signs of a boom with construction everywhere, the streets lined with hotels, restaurants, and bars. The Cambodians climbed out and without being asked, Mr. Eng drove the three Australians and me to a guesthouse called Happy Sleep.

"Very nice place. You sleep good," he said, pointing to the small inn.

"Sleep good or happy?" Victoria asked. She went on to explain that everyone in Cambodia worked on the commission system. Hotels, restaurants, and shops all paid small sums for referrals. It was a way for the cash-poor Khmer to bolster their incomes. Cam chimed in that they had stayed at this particular guesthouse before and found it quite comfortable.

"Join us, Pauline?" Victoria asked.

"Thank you, but I've already reserved at the Grand Hotel d'Angkor."

"This very good. You like much better," said Mr. Eng, the first words of English I'd heard him speak. But despite his recommendation, I stuck to my guns, and after saying good-bye to the Australians, I had him deliver me to the Grand Hotel d'Angkor.

Though Mr. Eng was greatly disappointed that I wouldn't be staying at Happy Sleep, the disappointment was his alone. The very moment we pulled up the white gravel driveway in front of the old colonial beauty, I wanted to get down and kiss the earth. It was an oasis after a long desert trek. To show my appreciation that I had succeeded in arriving in one piece, I tipped him an extra dollar over the agreed-upon five-dollar fare.

The doorman took my bag, paying no heed to my appearance, as if guests arrived caked in mud every day. I checked in and took the opportunity to show my picture of Whitney to the reception clerk, who did not recognize her. A porter took me up in an iron-cage elevator to a large room with a bamboo floor and shutters and a large four-poster bed centered beneath a sweeping ceiling fan. Certain that Odysseus had not encountered travails equal to those I had endured that day, I drew a bath and had a long soak. When I found myself starting to nod off in the bathtub, I got out and toweled myself dry with plush terry towels, and gratefully crawled between the cool, white sheets.

It was only as I was falling asleep that I realized it was Christmas Eve.

32

Wuthering Heights

On Christmas morning I woke up ravenous, having gone to sleep without any dinner. I dressed and went down to the dining room, giving thanks to God for French colonization, as a crusty baguette arrived with my breakfast. Though my original plan was to go directly to Phnom Penh, after some consideration, I decided to put that plan on hold. My bruised posterior needed a day's rest. Besides, I had never visited Siem Reap before, and it would be a travesty to leave without seeing Angkor Wat, the temple believed to be the largest religious structure in the world. So after dining I stopped at the concierge desk and arranged for a tour. Then I went back to my room, put on a quart of sunblock, my now battered straw hat, and a pair of closed-toe shoes. When I returned to the lobby, my guide was waiting.

She was an accommodating young woman who informed me her name was Saran. She had a unique beauty, her face sharp and angular and set upon a long neck that called to mind the Egyptian goddess Nefertiti. Saran had arranged for a tuk-tuk to take us to Angkor and en route to the temple, she gave me a brief history of the region. She explained that the name Siem Reap meant Siamese defeated, a point of great pride with the Khmer people, and that at its peak the Angkorian empire was the largest in Indochina.

"At the time your Western city of London had only fifty thousand people," she said, "Angkor was home to over a thousand temples and nearly a million people. Each ruler wanted to do better than the last to show his reverence to the gods, so each ruler built a bigger, more elaborate temple. Largest of these temples is the most famous, Angkor Wat, built in the twelfth century to the Hindu god Vishnu."

The words had barely left her mouth when the temple loomed into sight, its five towers rising from the horizon like colossal gray pinecones, which Saran explained represented lotus flowers. I was completely overwhelmed. Nothing had prepared me for its breathtaking beauty or immense size. I have been fortunate enough in my life to see many monuments to man's ingenuity: the Great Pyramids at Giza, Machu Picchu, the Forbidden City, the Taj Mahal. Not to mention the classical ruins of the Greeks and Romans. These works of architecture and engineering still remain mind-boggling by current standards. But the magnificence of Angkor Wat nearly put the others to shame.

We drove up a great sandstone causeway and across a vast moat. Early-morning tourists had already begun flowing through the entrance past vendors selling fruits or cold drinks. We climbed out of the tuk-tuk and children ran around our legs pushing postcards, flutes, and miniature Buddhas. Orange-robed monks sang chants, and beggars, most of them missing limbs, held out empty bowls. I asked Saran if there were so many amputees because of the war.

"Yes, many Khmer people were victims of land mines. Many animals, too, lost their legs," she said sadly. She told me that no Cambodian family had escaped the war and the long reach of Pol Pot unscathed. She had never known her parents, as they were educators and some of the first to be singled out by the Khmer Rouge for death. The wounds ran deep among the people, and they were only now starting to smile and trust. Some would never trust again.

The subject of the war was dropped and for the rest of the morning Saran guided me through the Wat, an intricate maze of buildings that ranged from places of worship to libraries. She led me from one bas-relief to another, intricate stone carvings that embellished nearly every inch of every façade, and told stories of armies and battles and demons and gods. One ceiling that depicted the rewards of heaven and the chilling punishments of hell was unsettling in its similarity to medieval thinking in Christianity. And then she took me to what was perhaps the most remarkable carving of all, the Churning of the Ocean of Milk. "This most famous work of art represents the center of the Hindu universe. Here Vishnu stirs the milk, helped by both deities and demons as they battle over the elixir for immortality," she said.

I reflected on how little mankind had changed.

From there we walked back to the grand plaza where Saran pointed up a long flight of steep steps. "This takes us to the mountain of the five towers. The most beautiful view. We can go up if you want. Are you afraid of heights?"

"Absolutely not," I said, always willing to take a challenge. The stories always come in handy at lunch conversations. "If this is the best view, I can't miss it."

Saran nodded and smiled, and we started the long ascent up an ancient staircase that would have challenged the nimblest of monkeys. The steps were tiny, barely able to hold the ball of my foot, and Saran explained that the staircase was literally meant as a stairway to heaven. Therefore the builders fifteen hundred years ago had intentionally made it challenging. I wondered how a large man could make the ascent, but then again, as I looked around, I didn't see many of them.

We reached the plaza at the top, and as I raised a last foot upward, I breathed a sigh of relief. The three-hundred-sixty-degree view of the Cambodian countryside made the climb seem worth the effort. The countryside opened up into a green tropical lushness visible for miles, worlds away from the hardscrabble landscape I had suffered through the day before. I wondered how a person would have felt standing there one and a half millennia before me. A feeling of contentment came upon me and I was thankful that a sore derriere had kept me in Siem Reap an extra day.

The contentment quickly left me when it was time to go down. We returned to the steps we had ascended earlier, and as I put my foot out to step down, the most horrible thing happened. I froze.

All of a sudden I was back on Walsh's with Dusty Craw. Only this time instead of a snow-covered tempest in front of me, there was a washboard of stone. One false step could mean falling the entire length of this Mount Olympus. My heart pounded with the insistence of a harpsichord in a piece of Baroque music as I stepped back from this bête noir. As black a sense of dread came over me as any I had ever experienced. How was I going to get down those steps? Was there a Cambodian equivalent of the ski patrol?

"Mrs. Cook, are you all right?" Saran asked, noticing the change in my demeanor.

"At this precise moment, no. I don't think I can walk down these steps. We'll have to go some other way," I said hopefully. Her face told me all hope was false.

"This is only way down. Not so bad. I do it every day. You follow me."

I ventured a tentative foot, but found myself unable to even stretch it over the step without falling into a trembling frenzy. Drawing back from the edge, I found myself overcome with vertigo. Saran walked me to a bench where I sat down and waited for my pulse to return to normal. But it was futile to expect my pulse to slow as long as my mind knew we had those steps to descend.

It was then I heard the sound of a most welcome voice.

"Ah, here you go now. Wha' happened, Pauline? You make it here from Poipet to lose it at the top of a pile of rocks?" It was Victoria with her two attachments, Wassau and Cam.

"What are you doing up here?" I managed to gasp.

"Same's you. Havin' a look 'round," she replied and then she pulled her face closer to mine. "You don't look so well."

"It seems I have a bit of vertigo and I'm not certain if I can make it down."

"Vertigo," she said, all seriousness. "Me mum used to suffer from it. Let me help you." She came around to my side and took one of my arms. "Now, don't be embarrassed. I've seen some of the bravest of them go to putty when it comes to 'ights."

"I don't suppose *you* know some other way down aside from those steps?" I ventured.

She laughed. "Yair, there's the fire exit around back." But when she noticed the pained look upon my face, her own became serious with the same sympathy she had shown in the parking lot at Poipet. "Sorry, Pauline, this is the only way down. But I've got an idear. If the boys'll walk in front of you, they block out the scenery, so you can't see down. I'll walk beside you and you'll never even know you're anything but one or two steps off the ground. It's all psychological."

Saran stood there looking appropriately sober, probably wishing she didn't have to do this for a living, thinking that she would rather be off somewhere selling Cambodian real estate than dealing with a middle-aged woman who has just had a panic attack. Knowing there was no other way, I bucked up and nodded to the assembled group. Wassau and Cam took the steps in front of me and started down with me inching along behind them. With Victoria at my side and the two huge men in front of me, the descent didn't feel as intimidating. It was as if the massive wall moving before me protected me from harm. And so we moved down in the little cocoon, step by step. By the time I set foot on the paved earth of the terrace, I was my usual collected self.

To show my gratefulness, I insisted on buying my Australian friends a drink. We found a drinks stall nearby and they had Coca-Colas while I had a mineral water. Saran did not want anything. Taking a seat in the shade, I took off my hat and began to fan myself. Out of the corner of my eye, I caught the flash of a yellow and orange scarf. I looked toward it and saw a familiar triangular face.

"That's odd," I said.

"What's odd?" Victoria asked.

"That man over there. He was on the truck yesterday."

Wassau, who was usually quiet, spoke up. "He's been following us."

"What do you mean following us?" Victoria demanded.

"I mean the wog was up on the platform before. I think he's got a thing for Pauline. He keeps watching her."

"Watching me? Is he watching me now?" I asked, unwilling to look in the man's direction.

"No, he's gone," said Wassau. I looked back to where the man had been standing. The spot was now occupied by an overweight American couple looking at a map. I could tell they were American by their gleaming white tennis shoes. Americans who have any fear of being attacked by terrorists would be well served to know that by wearing those shoes they might just as well be wearing the flag.

"Well, he's only human," I said, only half-joking. Just the same, the thought that he might have been following me made me only slightly less nervous than the stairs had.

33
Heart of Darkness

The next morning, after a five-o'clock wake-up call, the hotel driver delivered me dockside at Tonle Sap Lake just in time to make the seven o'clock longboat ride to Phnom Penh. Though the term "longboat" referred to the length of the vessel, the moniker could appropriately refer to the time spent onboard as well. I had been advised the bus was quicker, but after my previous experience with the Cambodian interstate system, I had opted for a mode of transportation that didn't involve crater-sized potholes, broken-down bridges, or stray dogs.

Having taken a bit longer with my sunblock than anticipated, we arrived at the dock with only minutes to spare. The driver indicated I should hurry and pointed me toward a crowd of people boarding a long, flat vessel that looked questionably seaworthy. As I drew nearer the boat, it occurred to me that this was not going to be the pleasant excursion I had envisioned. The only covered seating was inside its long, low wooden bow, and that appeared to be filled with locals. The alternative was to take a place on the flat deck up top in the open air, which was what the tourists appeared to be doing. Open air, however, meant being exposed to the brutal tropical sun for hours, and since I would rather take a bullet than put my skin through that travail, I managed to secure a window seat inside after bribing the ticket taker with an American five-dollar bill.

Once the boat was dangerously full, we pulled away from the dock. Plying across the smooth brown waters of the lake, we passed a floating village where locals were fishing in the murky waters and children waved excitedly at us. As we moved farther into the lake, there was not much of interest to look at, so I took out my tattered copy of *Moby-Dick* and tried to read. But it soon became difficult to concentrate as the air in the cabin began to turn stagnant and the scent of perspiring bodies permeated it. Though I realized too late that I should have brought some food and water, I politely declined partaking in any of the gray, unidentifiable mass my seat mate was eating.

Six hours later, after a brief stop to put out an engine fire, I arrived in Phnom Penh, hungry, thirsty, and in desperate need of a ladies room, as the facilities onboard had raised my capacity for continence to a new level. As to be expected, a phalanx of tuk-tuk drivers swarmed toward me as I got off the boat. Knowing they would continue to hound me until I selected one, I stared into the mélange of humanity and spotted a man wearing freshly pressed khaki pants and a bow tie. His broad face held a nose so flat it was a wonder he could breathe, and his thick black hair stuck up from his forehead like a horsetail. He appealed to me for two reasons. He was well-dressed and he wasn't smiling a solicitous smile. Since I had tipped the hotel driver my last single, I knew that all I had was a twenty.

"You there. Can you make change?" He nodded. "All right then. Take me to Hotel le Royal."

There was a collective gasp as the other drivers recognized the value of the passenger they had lost, but they parted the way for us as my newly hired driver carried my bag to his tuk-tuk, the most colorful version of the vehicle I had encountered thus far. The carriage had two bench seats that faced each other beneath a fire-engine red canopy with great yellow flames painted on the sides. Bells and whistles dangled from its periphery. It looked better suited for the Barnum and Bailey circus museum than a city street.

"My name Sokhom," said my driver, placing my bag on the seat beside me. He mounted the motorbike that pulled the carriage and revved the engine. At that moment, I just happened to glance back at the dock and saw a lonely last passenger sliding from the top of the longboat. The sight of him struck a chord in me that reverberated to the ends of my nervous system. Though he had traded in the yellow and orange scarf for a red one, there was no mistaking the triangular shape of his face. When he saw me looking at him, he turned abruptly and faced the river. This time it was too much to be a coincidence.

34

The Importance of Being Earnest

Another Asian city and another crumbling example of French colonial glory. Mr. Sokhom sped along the boulevards of Phnom Penh at death-defying speed, barely avoiding a cat, several bicyclists, and a couple of oblivious tourists, *barang loblobs*, he called them. Having decided to cast my lot to the fates, I sat back and took in the passing sights. The city was a combination of old and new, neoclassical buildings with Corinthian columns and wrought-iron balconies juxtaposed with stucco structures whose sunny yellow and flamingo pink façades were streaked with black sweating mold as the tropical heat staked its claim. Saffron-robed monks rode on the backs of motorcycles while beggars without legs held up bowls at street corners. As with other cities of the east, it was a combination of chaos and vitality.

When we reached Hotel le Royal, a grand edifice that had been constructed in the twenties when the world was awash in money, I took out a twenty-dollar bill and handed it to Mr. Sokhom. He shook his head and handed it back to me.

"I thought you had change," I said. I turned to the doorman, who spoke English. "Will you tell him I will go inside and get some change?" There was a brief exchange of conversation, and the doorman said, "This man says your ride is free and if you want an expert driver for a tour tomorrow, he will come back."

I studied the odd-looking man with the khakis and bow tie. Though I couldn't put my finger on it, there was something endearing about him. And his open tuk-tuk was the most comfortable transportation I had ridden in so far. "OK, then. Tell him to be here tomorrow morning at nine-thirty," I said.

I walked into Hotel le Royal to the strains of a string quartet. Though it had fallen into disrepair under the Khmer Rouge, the Raffles chain had bought it since and restored it to its former glory. The lobby was a dramatic room with high arches, a gleaming marble floor, and Western-style furniture mixed with Eastern. There were numerous elephant statues, enormous vases holding flower arrangements, palm trees, and the obligatory sweeping overhead fan. At the reception desk I was again graced with the deferential service of the Orient—something I could certainly get used to. Service in the West has become so appalling that I had forgotten what good service could be, which only goes to show what happens when the proletariat becomes elevated. Exclusivity goes to hell and one can't find proper service at any price. Happily that aspect of democracy had not found its way to the Far East yet. The help still treated customers as patrons and not as acquaintances.

I showed the desk clerk my picture of Whitney, Jean Paul Gaultier and all. He passed it around, and while the entire staff stared at it curiously, no one had seen her. This was actually a surprise to me. I was certain that if she had stayed at the Oriental in Bangkok, it only stood to reason that Le Royal would be her choice in Phnom Penh.

My room was located off the pool, an oasis from the noise, dirt, and dust of the city. After taking a cool bath in a tub one could practically swim laps in, I dressed for dinner and headed down to the Elephant Bar. The crowd in the bar was well-heeled, though not as elegant as that at the Oriental. The slim, smiling waitress brought me a chilled French chablis, and as I sipped it, a French couple came in and seated themselves at the table beside me. We struck up a conversation, and I learned they had come from Siem Reap today as well.

"*Vous êtes venus par bateau?*" I asked in my best French.

"We took ze bus," the woman replied in English. Since the French would rather have their eyebrows plucked out one by one than stray from their own language, I hoped this wasn't a reflection on my accent. "It seemed a bettair choice zan sitting on top of ze boat in zis sun," she explained, her pink face dewy in the evening heat.

Her husband took out a handkerchief and wiped along the top of his receding hairline. "It took us four hours," he said. "And you? Your trip was OK?"

"I'm here," was all I could opine, wondering why I invariably chose the wrong route. "I don't suppose you had air-conditioning?" When they informed me that it had been spotty, I felt somewhat better with my decision. They introduced themselves as Jacqueline and Michel Portet, archaeologists from the Sorbonne who had spent the last two months in Cambodia doing research at Siem Reap. They intended on staying in Phnom Penh for the next couple of days before returning to France for New Year's.

"And you? Will you be here for ze Nouvelle Année?"

"I hope to be home by then," I said. I thought of the Amici gala and realized that I didn't have a date for that evening. I thought of the stroke of midnight and being alone amid well-dressed revelers giving one another kisses. My mind flashed to Tag McKay, and I found myself wondering what he was doing that evening. Not that I could ever present him at the gala—I just wondered.

Jacqueline and Michel must have sensed my loneliness, because they invited me to join them for dinner. That night as we dined in the old quarter of the city, Michel relayed the story of the killing fields, now a popular tourist attraction, something everyone must see, he insisted, adding that the inhumanity was heartbreaking. Then the conversation shifted to the holidays again, and they said how their children were angry with them for missing Christmas with the grandchildren, but that the opportunity for this sabbatical was simply too much for them to pass up. "And to sink zat until 1953, zis was part of the French empire." We spoke of the other French colonies, the most obvious one Vietnam, and the civil war taking place in Sierra Leone over diamonds. "I sink it is a tragedy for some of zese third-world countries to have natural resources. Zis costs them dearly, pits brother against brother," Michel lamented. "But now it is you Americans who are under attack. Like ze French, like ze English, I fear you are in your waning days."

I thought of our president, the not-too-bright son of friends of friends, and I sincerely hoped he was capable of handling the challenges before him. I had lived through the Vietnam era and student rebellion, and although I was fairly sheltered from unrest at Radcliffe, the ripples through the culture had dramatically changed the life I had been brought up to live. Fraternities and sororities fell into disfavor, fashion took a backseat to tattered blue jeans—white gloves all but going the way of bloomers—and no one had wanted to display any sign of material wealth, except in the clubs, of course. And while the quest for material wealth had swung back, we had never recovered the gentility of earlier days.

The French love their politics and after covering everything from our stock market bubble to the war in Afghanistan to the cost of health care in America, we made our way down a dimly lit Phnom Penh street back to the hotel. Michel was the one to sum it up before we parted ways in the lobby. "Tourism. Tourism is the natural resource of this country. It will bring wealth to them. But zere is an advantage in that, unlike oil or diamonds, it cannot be exported. Zis country may become Disneyland, but at least it will be zeres."

I didn't think it worth mentioning that we were staying at a hotel owned by Europeans.

35
The Lost World

The next morning Mr. Sokhom and his circus wagon, cum tuk-tuk, were waiting for me outside the hotel after breakfast. I had a sense he had probably been there since dawn. Upon seeing me he smiled for the first time, and I saw he was missing his front teeth. With the help of the concierge, I had compiled a list of local hotels and guesthouses in Phnom Penh and my goal was to visit them all and show my picture of Whitney in hopes someone had seen her. I had the doorman explain to my driver that I would not be taking a tour but that I wanted him to drive me to all these locations.

"No killing field?" Mr. Sokhol asked incredulously.

"No killing field," I said, having no desire to set foot upon a place of such misery. I climbed into the circus wagon, and we were off. However, there was one flaw in my plan as he immediately veered from the itinerary and drove me to an immense dark yellow art deco building. "Psar Thmei," he said, smiling and nodding. "Central Market." Since shopping was nowhere in the day's plan, I shook my head and asked to move on. His response to my gesture was to get off the motorbike and point toward the entry. "Hotel after. Market now. Special. You see."

He wouldn't budge despite my repeated commands and the use of words like "I insist" and even "I refuse to pay you if you do not take me where I want to go." In frustration, I decided to humor him and visit the market so that we could get back on track.

I climbed down from my seat, and a moment later a small doll-like child was standing before me, her ebony hair braided into two plaits that ran down her back. I waited for the smile which naturally spread across her face a moment later. Sokhom smiled his tooth-missing smile, and nodded that I should follow the child. I rolled my eyes toward the heavens and followed her.

Like all Asian markets, this one was filled with foods and spices entirely alien to a Westerner, unidentifiable plants and fruits, including durian, a fruit that smells so foul it was banned from most hotels. Turning periodically to make sure I was still in her wake, the little girl led me past long rows of vendors selling dried fish or bags of herbs, their heads wrapped in bright scarves or covered by straw hats.

We turned a corner onto an entirely new row of vendors, whose wares were held in waist-high wicker baskets. It was here the little girl stopped. My skin crawled when I looked into one of the baskets and saw that it was filled with dead bugs. There were baskets of crickets and beetles, and the worst of the lot, enormous spiders that may have been tarantulas for all I knew. They were so large that had they been living, they could have been saddled and ridden into town. As I watched in nauseated horror, the little girl reached into the basket of spiders and popped one into her mouth, eating the head and legs first, finishing with the bulblike posterior. When she had finished, she opened her mouth wide as proof that she had really consumed the beast.

She offered me one, which I rather vehemently declined. With the show finished she took me back to the tuk-tuk where Mr. Sokhom looked to me for approval. I graced him with a tolerant smile, climbed back into the tuk-tuk, and was summarily delivered to a silk shop. This time I held my ground and refused to go in the shop despite the shop's owner coming out to greet me. When I made my point by getting out of the tuk-tuk and walking away from it, Mr. Sokhom finally realized I meant business. From then on, he was the best of chauffers.

As I called off the name of one hotel after another, he drove me tirelessly across the city, from the riverfront to the outskirts near the airport. At each hotel or guesthouse, Sokhom waited faithfully beside the tuk-tuk while I went into the establishment to show Whitney's picture. At the larger hotels, I spoke with at least a dozen employees, hoping that was a wide enough net to cast. The guesthouses rarely had more than one person on duty, but from their small size I knew if she had been there, she most certainly would have been remembered. And while my picture of Whitney nearly always drew some sort of response, not one person claimed to have seen her.

It was nearing lunchtime as I walked dejectedly from the last guesthouse on my list. I was still holding Whitney's picture in my hand as I climbed back into my seat. Sokhom's face took on a look as if he finally understood what this wild-goose chase was about. He held out his hand for the picture.

With nothing to lose I handed it over to him. He studied it for less than ten seconds before nodding his head vigorously. "She here Phnom Penh."

I was flabbergasted that after all the morning's work, it was my driver who claimed to have seen Whitney. Then again, maybe this was some ploy for money. "Where is she?"

"No now. Long time. Maybe one month. She hire my brother drive her. She pay *beaucoup*."

Yes, that would be Whitney. She would pay beaucoup. "Where did she stay?"

He raised his hands toward the heavens. "No know."

"Who would know?"

"My brother. He know."

"Then let's find your brother."

He started the motorcycle and my life passed before my eyes as he made one of the most daring U-turns I have ever experienced in my life, turning in front of a crowded minibus and a motorcycle piled high with caged chickens. Then he shifted into a fast gear, and we sped through the streets of Phnom Penh like an ambulance carrying a politician.

In my haste to find Whitney, I hadn't given my safety much thought and now as we headed into the outskirts of town, I was beginning to question the wisdom of this move. With my hands knotted into two nervous fists,

I bumped along in my carriage as Mr. Sokhom drove down roads in such disrepair that the jungle threatened to reclaim them. It occurred to me that I was now so removed from civilization that if Mr. Sokhom had ulterior motives, it could be decades before anyone found my body.

My fears were not put to rest when we drove through a rusted iron gate and pulled into a courtyard lush with fruit trees gone wild and sidewalks broken up by weeds. Off the courtyard was an abandoned colonial mansion, its wide verandas lined with stone balustrades. The windows were completely broken out and the once-white façade was mottled with the ubiquitous black mold. The only sign of habitation was a Citroën parked beneath a tree, one of the more roadworthy-looking vehicles I had seen since my arrival in Cambodia.

Mr. Sokhom shut off the motorcycle and signaled me to come with him up the crumbling walkway. I climbed out of the carriage and started following him on tentative legs when a low moo caught my attention. I looked to my left to see a three-legged cow chewing on the grass beneath a palm tree. The rest of the way, I was careful to walk in his steps. That is, until we reached the house and a menagerie of animals burst from the open—or missing—door of the old mansion. The collection of chickens and pigs headed straight toward me, and weak with fear I started running back toward the tuk-tuk, saw the three-legged cow, and ran back toward Mr. Sokhom, where I sought refuge behind him. He shooed the animals and they ran away, with the exception of one pig who circled behind me and pushed his damp snout against my leg. Not knowing whether or not pigs bite, I shrieked, first in fear, then at the animal, then at Mr. Sokhom himself. "Get this thing away from me."

At that point, a rail-thin man appeared in one of the open windows on the ground floor, popping up from the floor as if he had been sleeping. He was clad in a dingy gray robe similar in style to the type the the monks wore. He took one look at me and a conversation ensued between him and Mr. Sokhom. I have never been able to tell if a conversation in an Eastern tongue is amiable or heated, and so I couldn't tell if the man was angry or asking Mr. Sokhom how they would dispose of my body. After exchanging more words than there are in a college dictionary, the noise stopped, and Mr. Sokhom held out his hand.

"Picture, please."

I handed him my picture of Whitney, and he in turn handed it over to the monk, or whatever he was. The monk took one look and the conversation between the two men resumed, only this time, even from my limited perspective, there was anger involved. I watched in anxious anticipation, aware that the pig had begun sniffing its way back in my direction. Finally, after much nodding of heads, Mr. Sokhom turned back to me with his hand extended again. He wanted a picture, but one of a very different sort.

"My brother say he need money to help remember. Very difficult memory. He say he want one American president Benjamin Franklin to help him think."

I thought it over. In a land where a person could travel from the border of Thailand to Siem Reap for five dollars, albeit under grueling circumstances, a hundred dollars was highway robbery. Then again, it didn't compare to the banditry of a Neapolitan cab driver, but this was Cambodia, not Italy, and a hundred dollars went a lot further here. What would this man do with one hundred dollars anyway? Redecorate? "His demand is too high. I will give him twenty dollars. No more."

This time Sokhom's brother spoke for himself in the king's English. "This remembering can be very dangerous."

Pursing my lips to convey seriousness, I glared at him. Behind the impassive look he had drawn on his face, I recognized fear. We were in a land where people had been marched to fields and summarily shot not so long ago. Was it something like that he feared? Maria's words came back to me. *Beware of those in rags.* Maybe it was I who should fear him. I reached into my wallet and fished out five pictures of Andrew Jackson. "Here is one hundred dollars. And for your information, Benjamin Franklin was never a president. Now, where did you take Mrs. Armstrong that was so damn secret?"

The money had helped clear his mind. "I take her from airport to 14 Banteay Park. I wait and when she is finished I take her back to airport."

"What did she do in this park?"

He shrugged.

"And then you took her back to the airport on the same day?"

"Yes, Madam."

"Was she alone?"

"Yes."

I wondered why she was no longer with Chia. I turned to Sokhom. "Can you take me to this park?"

"Yes, Madam."

"Let's go then."

Mr. Sokhom stared defiantly at the gray-robed man. "Yes, Madam."

I turned and nearly tripped over the pig, who had quietly snuck up during the negotiations. Sokhom's brother clapped his hands, and the grunting animal waddled away. Sokhom walked back to the tuk-tuk with me close on his heels, gingerly placing each foot in the shadow of his steps. After all, there was a reason that cow was three-legged.

36

The Jungle

The park turned out not to be a park at all, but a large industrial complex on the outskirts of the city. Number 14 was a large factory building, cold and austere, but something that had been built in recent history. There was no trace of colonialism here. I wondered what could have possibly drawn Whitney to this place. And then as I walked up to the entrance and stared at the glass doors, I saw it. A feather reclining on a chaise longue. The Verry Lingerie logo.

I tried the doors, but they were locked. There was a buzzer beside the door and I pushed it hard. It wasn't long before a woman appeared on the other side of the glass. She took one look at us and disappeared. A moment later, she returned followed by a stern-looking man wearing a suit. He gave Mr. Sokhom a dismissive look, but when he saw me his expression changed and he opened the door. While he was Asian, his facial features differed from the Khmer. His skin was lighter and of a yellow hue, the fold to his eyes more pronounced, in fact so much so that when he blinked, his eyes appeared as mere slits in his face. He had a rather unsightly mole beside his left ear, and he addressed me through protruding teeth from a severe overbite.

"May I help you?" he asked in perfect English, looking me up and down as he did. Something told me he was taking in my clothes with a practiced eye. I wasn't exactly sure what I would do, but encouraged by the fact that he spoke English, I decided to take a big chance. "I was sent here by a friend."

"A friend, Madam? Here, Madam?"

"Yes, here. Perhaps you know my friend? Mrs. Armstrong. Mrs. Jack Armstrong?"

Stiffening visibly at the mention of the name, he opened the door the rest of the way for me to enter, letting it fall shut on Mr. Sokhom. Then he turned the lock again. He bowed slightly from the waist and said, "You are a friend of Mrs. Armstrong?"

"Yes, my name is Pauline Cook."

He bowed. "My pleasure, Mrs. Cook. I am Mr. Kwan. Welcome to the Sunshine Factory. Please follow me."

He took me down a hall and up some stairs into a Spartan, but modern, office area where women dressed in Western garb pecked away at computers. At the end of the room was a private office, and he ushered me inside, closing the door behind us. This room was better appointed than the one we had just passed through. Behind a large cherry desk, a set of of bookcases that displayed numerous pictures of Mr. Kwan standing with various men who appeared to be dignitaries of some sort. My eyes singled out Jack Armstrong shaking his hand in one of them. There were several plaques in Khmer and one in English commending the great productivity of the facility.

On three of the walls, large windows with Venetian blinds monitored three different scenes. One window looked out onto the parking lot where I could see the tuk-tuk and Mr. Sokhom squatting on the ground beside it. The second window looked back into the office area we had just passed through. And the third overlooked a cavernous factory with hundreds of women bent over sewing machines. He pointed to two plastic chairs in front of the desk and indicated I take one.

"I am sorry the seating is not more comfortable. We do not get many visitors here. Now how may I be of help?"

"Mrs. Armstrong has gone missing, and I am retracing her steps before she disappeared. I already know she came here, but I would like to know why."

A look of ingenuous concern crossed his face, although I could have no way of knowing whether it was for Whitney or for some other reason. "Why, this is the primary manufacturing facility for Verry Lingerie, Mrs. Cook. Mrs. Armstrong is a great humanitarian, and she came here to see the facility after reading some most unfavorable articles about our labor practices in the United States. She was very impressed by our facility after seeing it." Then he added, "It is most distressing that she is missing."

"It is," I said, oversimplifying. I looked out the office window onto the crowded room of workers. "Might I have a look around?"

"It is most unusual, Mrs. Cook. We do not normally give tours to lay people."

"And I feel these are not normal circumstances," I pressed. "I do this with Mr. Armstrong's complete approval."

Mentioning Jack Armstrong seemed to be the ticket, spurring a soldier like Mr. Kwan to his feet. "Then we shall take a tour, but it must be quick. I am expecting some visitors within the hour."

Not wanting to mention that he had just informed me he had few visitors, I followed him out the office door and into the bowels of the factory. Under the hue of fluorescent lighting, the sea of tables stretched endlessly, rows and rows of women with their heads wrapped in scarves, bent over whirring sewing machines that lent the room the sound of an insect's nest. There was little interaction between the women as they worked. Each appeared totally absorbed in the job before her. Even as Mr. Kwan led me up and down the aisles, our presence drew little more than a quick glance from any of them, and when it did, the woman would return quickly to her work. In fact, one might say the woman worked even more diligently after seeing us.

His impatience with me barely masked, Mr. Kwan took me from one end of the factory to the other, starting with the area where large bolts of cloth were rolled from huge spools, to the place where the materials were cut. In one section I watched a woman sew a Verry Lingerie tag into the elastic of a thong so small that the tag was more substantial than the garment. I stood in front of each woman's station, looking for signs of abuse, of starvation, of illness. But everyone appeared healthy and well-fed and there were no Dickensian boils or hacking coughs. No one fell from her chair weak with hunger. Still, something disturbed me about the way these women performed their jobs. It was as if they were automatons.

When Mr. Kwan had concluded the tour, he led me back to his office and offered to answer any questions I may have. I asked about the hours his workforce put in and he told me that his employees worked twelve-hour shifts, six days a week. That Sunday was a free day. Having noticed the smooth unlined faces of the workers, I asked him if any of them was under-age. He assured me they did not hire children, that every worker in his plant was sixteen or older. He insisted that everything that took place at the plant was in strict compliance with international labor standards.

"This is most important," he said, "because our compliance means we will receive a fourteen percent increase in our U.S. import quota."

"And what does the average worker make, Mr. Kwan?" I asked.

His answer appeared forced as he looked me in the eye without blinking and said, "Forty-five dollars a month."

Forty-five dollars a month? The bras these women were affixing labels to sold for over forty-five dollars apiece. I was appalled. And twelve-hour days, six days a week? I felt proud of myself that my couture clothes came from France and Italy. Surely they weren't manufactured under such conditions.

As if he was reading my thoughts, he went on to say, "Mrs. Armstrong came here because she was concerned about the workers' well-being. There are some of what you Americans call sweatshops active in Cambodia, but this is certainly not one of them. What you see as long hours and low pay is an economic opportunity for these women. This is what Mrs. Armstrong and I discussed."

Twelve hours in front of a sewing machine didn't seem to be much of an opportunity to me. Then again, this wasn't my homeland, and maybe this sort of job was preferable to working in the rice paddies, bent from the waist the entire day. I looked around the room and noticed for the first time what appeared to be a cot against the far wall. Mr. Kwan followed my eyes. "I work long hours, too," he said. "Sometimes, it is necessary to sleep here."

"It seems everyone here works hard," I said, rising. "I want to thank you for your time."

"It is my pleasure, Mrs. Cook." He escorted me from the room and back to the factory entrance where Sokhom waited, squatting on his heels like a loyal dog. Mr. Kwan unlocked the door to let me out. As Sokhom rose up from the ground and graced me with his toothless smile, Mr. Kwan barked something at him in Khmer that quickly banished the smile from his face. The plant manager continued speaking to my driver in a harsh fashion until the little man's face turned ashen. He bowed and nodded his head in a way that couldn't have been clearer if he had taken a position lying prostrate on the ground. As if no conversation had taken place at all, Mr. Kwan turned coolly back to me and extended his hand in the Western manner. "Good day to you, Mrs. Cook. Enjoy the rest of your stay in Cambodia."

"What was that about, Mr. Sokhom?" I asked before he started the motorcycle.

"Not important," he replied. But I had a sense it was.

By the time Sokhom delivered me to Hotel le Royal, he was back in normal spirits despite the tongue-lashing that Mr. Kwan had given him. Since I now knew that Whitney had not stayed in Phnom Penh, I was eager to get back to Bangkok as soon as possible to see if I could pick up her trail again. But unwilling to travel overland again, I decided to book myself on the first possible flight back to Bangkok. However, knowing that it could be days before a flight was available, I finally caved in to Mr. Sokhom's tireless overtures to escort me the next day to the killing fields and Tuol Sleng Genocide Museum, the high school that Pol Pot had turned into a torture chamber. If I was going to subject myself to such visions of man's inhumanity, it might as well be with Mr. Sokhom, to whom I had grown rather accustomed. It was like having my own servant.

Besides, I could think of no more appropriate way to spend December 28 than in the shadow of death and destruction. It was, after all, my fifty-second birthday.

When we pulled up in front of the hotel, I reached in my purse to pay him for the day's services. He waved the money off. "You pay tomorrow. Or next day. When we all finish."

We arranged to meet the next morning, and I went into the lobby, where the sound of the string quartet was like a salve on a wound. I stopped at the concierge's desk and asked him to book me on the first possible flight to

Bangkok. When the concierge told me it would be a week I sighed aloud and asked if there wasn't any sort of special arrangement that might be made. He told me that sometimes exceptions were made at the airport for special circumstances.

"What kind of circumstances?" I asked him.

He stared at my purse and the message came through loud and clear. I asked the concierge to order transportation to the airport for me in the morning.

With no way to contact Mr. Sokhom to tell him that I wouldn't be taking his tour, I left an envelope for him at the desk with a picture of Benjamin Franklin in it, knowing I had greatly overpaid. Somehow the insanity of the East was turning me soft.

Early the next morning, as I rode in the clean, cool comfort of a closed vehicle, I gazed out the window at the panorama of a country rapidly undergoing change. I didn't regret not visiting the killing fields or the prison where so many had been tortured, but I knew they were there. These are the sorts of things a world should not forget, I thought.

Traffic came to a grinding halt just as the driver was preparing to turn on to the main highway to the airport. As we slowly started crawling, it became evident that the slowdown was due to an accident. One lane was blocked, and a Khmer police officer was directing traffic around it. As we came upon the scene, I looked out the window to see what had happened and felt the morning's breakfast tug at the base of my throat.

Shattered into hundreds of wooden pieces on the ground was a bright red and yellow carriage. A twisted motorcycle lay on the ground beside it.

37

The Turn of the Screw

The scene at Pochentong Airport was one of pandemonium, with frustrated tourists trying to obtain seats on the already oversold flight to Bangkok. Fortuitously, the concierge had given me good advice. A Benjamin Franklin discreetly dropped on the desk of the ticket agent got me a seat on the plane. In fact, the agent was so accommodating I decided to ask if he could verify that Whitney flew back to Bangkok when she left Phnom Penh. This, he said, would be more difficult. It became easier for him, however, when I put my last U.S. dollars into play. Though they didn't quite equal Mr. Franklin, four Andrew Jacksons, an Alexander Hamilton, and two George Washingtons did the trick. After checking his computer, he informed me that Whitney had, indeed, flown round-trip from Bangkok all on the same day in November.

I went to the gate and waited. Though rumor had it a new airport was to be built soon, the current one reminded me of the aftermath of a bombing in a World War II movie. Much of it was open-air, and it would be no surprise if at any minute a pig appeared and began sniffing at my legs. My mind kept circling back to the broken tuk-tuk and Mr. Sokhom. Was the little man a victim of his own erratic driving, or did his accident have something to do with Mr. Kwan's anger yesterday? I also couldn't stop thinking about the stranger in the colorful scarves who kept turning up every place I did. I carefully scrutinized all the passengers in the waiting area to make sure he wasn't among them. Still, it wasn't until we were taxiing down the runway, past the rusted remnants of old Chinese warplanes, that I was able to sigh with relief that he would remain in Cambodia.

The wheels lifted from the ground, and from the sky I could see the brown Mekong snaking through the lush green countryside on its way toward Vietnam. The plane banked and flew in the opposite direction, and my thoughts finally turned to Whitney. If she had gone to the Sunshine Factory on some quest for justice, and she had left satisfied, as Mr. Kwan had claimed, what happened to her when she got back to Bangkok? Why hadn't she gone back to the Oriental? And then another possibility occurred to me. Perhaps she had only passed through the airport in Bangkok that day. Maybe her final destination was someplace else. That was the only thing that made any sense.

We touched down in Bangkok just over an hour later. Mr. Franklin had certainly saved me a lot of time and aggravation, I thought, revisiting my steeplechase to Phnom Penh. As I passed through customs and emerged into the pandemonium of the Bangkok Airport, the usual crush of drivers and touts were lined up looking for passengers. Since I had spent my last dollar in Cambodia and didn't have any baht either, I was wondering how I was going to get to the hotel. But before I had a chance to give it much thought, I saw Arun, the driver who had picked me up that first day. He was wearing his crisp white uniform with the Oriental logo stitched on the right breast. He came up to me and *wah*ed deeply.

"Welcome back, Mrs. Cook," he greeted me.

"Now this is service," I said, relinquishing my bag to his outstretched hand. "How did you know I was coming in?"

"There is always a driver from the hotel waiting at the airport, Madam," he said. I followed him across the terminal, past faces from every corner of the earth all mixed up like some great stew of humanity. We had just reached the exit when our exodus was cut short by a pair of loud voices calling out over the crowd.

"Yo. Oriental! Wait. Oriental!" I turned to see a couple rushing toward us, their arms waving as they rolled huge square bags on wheels behind them. They were both overweight, with bands of sweat circling the armpits of their polo shirts and beads of sweat collecting on their foreheads. Arun appeared not to hear them and picked up the pace.

"I believe you're being called," I pointed out.

He turned slightly so that the couple was in his peripheral vision. "Not enough room. I'll have hotel send another car."

Much as I would have liked to ride alone, since it was my birthday my more charitable side came forward. "Nonsense. There's plenty of room. I have only the one bag."

Arun continued to ignore the couple, but I stood my ground until they reached us, huffing and puffing so hard I feared they might be better served by an ambulance. "Thank God we caught you. Our travel agent gave us the wrong meeting spot. Are you going to the Oriental?" the man asked me.

Arun put my bag down in a resigned manner. He *wah*ed deeply and said, "Welcome to Bangkok."

On the way into the city, the couple turned out to be so chatty, I revisited my act of good will in sharing this ride. As luck would have it, traffic was beyond horrendous. By the time we pulled into the hotel driveway, I knew more about Bob and Betty Miller than any person not related by blood should have to, from the particulars of his dentistry practice to the ages of their four grandchildren, all of whom were natural geniuses, to this trip being their thirty-fifth wedding-anniversary gift from their kids. They had thought of canceling after the terrorist attacks but decided that if your number's up, your number's up.

In the lobby, after extricating myself from the Millers, I ran into a British couple that Henry and I had befriended in Biarritz over twenty years before when it was still fashionable. The Bedford-Hills were upper-crust British, he being of the third generation of a gin-distilling family, she the daughter of a member of Parliament. They were pleased to see me and invited me to join them for dinner. I accepted the invitation and we arranged to meet in the lobby for cocktails that evening.

I returned to my room and called Marcel. Though it was late at night in Chicago, he answered right away. The sound of chatter around him told me he was in his Starbucks office.

"Hey, how's my favorite cougar?" he asked.

"I am not a cougar, but for the record I'm in Bangkok."

"Bangkok?" he effused. "That means this call is costing me boo-coo. I don't have international in my package."

"I will reimburse you for your expenses. I need your help again. You remember the information you provided me before about Whitney Armstrong's flight to Bangkok? Now I need to know if she was on any flight on any airline out of Bangkok the last week in November."

"Whew, that's a big one, Pauline. It'll cost you big-time coin."

"Yes, I've already factored 'coin' into the equation."

"Smokin'. I'll get on this right away and get back to you as soon as I hear something."

I hung up and for a birthday treat went to the spa for a facial to rinse the orange dust of Cambodia from my pores. I followed it with a Thai foot massage, a procedure that comes as close to sex as anything I've ever done with my clothes on. When I got back to my room, hours later, the red message light on the telephone was flashing. Marcel had called to tell me that he had checked every airline that flew out of Bangkok, from Singapore Airlines to Mongolian Air, and Whitney Armstrong had not taken any other flight out of Bangkok after her arrival from Phnom Penh. And that I owed him seven hundred dollars.

I put the receiver back in the cradle. Well, that answered that. Whitney had not gone anyplace after Bangkok—not by air anyhow. So had she disappeared into thin air? I don't know if it was because it was my birthday and I was feeling old, or if the Far East had finally worn me down, but frustrated tears set in. What was I doing, running around armed with a photo of someone who clearly didn't want to be found? And spending a fortune while doing it, I might add. Maybe it was time to give up on the dream of collecting money from Jack Armstrong and just go home.

Then I realized there was someone whose voice might make my birthday more tolerable. I put in another call to the States, to Tag McKay's cell phone. When he answered with a sleep-choked hello after the third ring, I nearly hung up. But I didn't.

"It's Pauline," I said.

There was a pause and then, "Do you know it's three in the morning?"

"Is it? I must've gotten my timetable backwards. I thought it was more like ten. I just wanted to check on Fleur and on how the work's progressing in my penthouse."

I heard him whisper something to a third party and my heart fell as I realized he wasn't alone. I was going to hang up and pretend we were disconnected when he said, "The changes are almost finished and Fleur is fine. In fact, she's right here." I was astonished, but before I could ask for an explanation, he went on to add, "I didn't like leaving her alone all night, so I've been bringing her home with me. She's curled up next to me right now."

"Oh, well, thank you." I was completely tongue-tied, like a silly young girl. "I'll let you get back to sleep, then."

"Pauline?" he said. "Is everything all right? Because if it isn't, call Lienne. You still have her number, don't you?"

"I still have it, but everything is fine. I'll be home in a day or so."

I hung up the phone and stared at it for some time, trying to put a finger on what was bothering me. Then it dawned on me. I was jealous of my cat.

That night the Bedford-Hills selected a restaurant with the spiciest food I have ever consumed in my life. While I spent most of the meal with my tongue immersed in a glass of ice water, they chatted blithely away, eating copious amounts of food so hot it threatened to self-ignite. How the British can consume such hot food like it was orange Jell-O, especially in light of their bland diets, is beyond me.

When we got back to the hotel, the Bedford-Hills headed straight up to bed, and I decided to end my least favorite day of the year with a nightcap in the Authors' Lounge. I had just started across the lobby when my eyes fell upon a man staring at me from across the room. My heart nearly stopped. Though he was better dressed than he had been the previous times I had seen him, wearing a silk tunic and pressed slacks, there was no mistaking the triangular face. He saw me and stood up. My body went limp with fear, and I spun around to make my retreat only to smack into one of the security guards who had obviously been keeping an eye on the situation.

"Mrs. Cook. That man has been waiting to see you all evening. He insists he has something you are looking for. Of course, if you do not wish to speak to him, I can send him away."

My legs regained some of their stability, and my blood resumed some of its usual flow. Emboldened by the small army of security floating through the lobby, I decided this would be a good opportunity to find out why this man had been shadowing me like a commissioned salesperson in a fur salon. "I will talk to him," I told the guard. The guard made a gesture and the man approached. When he reached me he *wahed* deeply at the waist. I ignored the gesture and demanded, "Why have you been following me?"

His lips parted in a half-smile. I noticed that his teeth were long and narrow, practically coming to points at the ends. "You are looking for someone," he said.

"It's no secret that I'm looking for Whitney Armstrong. I've been showing her photograph from here to Timbuktu."

"I know where you can find your friend."

"Yes? Well then, where is she?"

"It will cost money."

Knowing one must always have ready cash in this land of the extended hand, I had replenished my cash supply with baht drawn from an ATM. But that didn't mean I was going to allow this stranger to separate me from baht one without some kind of proof. "How can I believe that you know where to find Mrs. Armstrong? How do I know that you're not just making it up so you can take my money?"

"I know where she is," he repeated. His face was solemn and his next words were whispered, but he may as well have shouted them for the clarity with which they struck me. "Or maybe better I say I know where the he/she is."

38

The Age of Innocence

A neon sign above the dimly lit entrance read SEXY.

I took a deep breath and followed the wiry little man, whom I now knew as Chamrat, up a dark, narrow staircase. He had brought me into the heart of Pad Pong, a notorious bar district, and although the area was what one would mildly call sleazy, it was so crowded that up until this point I had felt safety in numbers. Now, alone with Chamrat in the dark stairwell, I began to question the wisdom of agreeing to accompany him. But my fears were quickly allayed as we emerged from the stairs into a crowded, smoke-filled room with canned music playing over a cheap sound system. The predominantly male clientele was an international mix, ranging from moon-faced Japanese to boisterous Australians, packed around small tables laden with beer bottles and smoking ashtrays.

Feeling conspicuous in my paisley sundress and strappy sandals, I wondered if my presence would draw undue attention. But the few heads that did turn my way merely gave me a bored once-over. This crowd had little interest in a tall middle-aged redhead. Especially one wearing clothes. Not when one took into consideration what was taking place on the stage up front. All eyes faced forward while a naked woman on the stage dropped

Ping-Pong balls from between her legs into a water glass beneath her. With great accuracy, I might add. While not quite the sort of act one might find at the Folies Bergère, the crowd appreciated it nonetheless.

When the woman had exhausted her supply of Ping-Pong balls, she bowed to great applause and disappeared into the wings. There was a change of music and some scantily clad women charged into the room holding helium balloons on strings. I'm not quite sure how it happened, but somehow I ended up in possession of one.

"What is this all about?" I demanded.

"You watch, you see," he said, giving me a ferrety smile.

The music turned to a drumroll as another naked woman emerged from behind the curtain and stood defiantly before the sweating crowd. Her long, gleaming black hair hung to the middle of her back, her smooth olive-skinned face was an emotionless mask, and her full lips were a lonely pout beneath her straight nose. Despite her indelicate line of work, there was a certain dignity about her. In another life, she might have merited first place in a beauty pageant. I wondered what had driven her to exploit herself so in this one.

As the drumroll increased in intensity, the woman got down on the stage and extended her legs in front of her. Leaning back on her elbows, she scanned the crowd from between her bent knees until her searching eyes locked on me. Her lips curled ever so slightly, and the next thing I knew, my balloon burst, causing me to nearly jump out of my sandals. The crowd broke into raucous cheers. The woman adjusted her position, and a moment later, another loud pop was heard as another balloon was rendered into shreds.

"She's not shooting darts?" I gasped in disbelief.

Chamrat nodded gleefully.

"Good God, get me out of here," I commanded. The last thing in the world I wanted was to end up in a Thai eye clinic. "This was not what we discussed. Now take me to my friend. Immediately."

He suppressed a superior squeak and led me through the crowd to an unmarked door beside the stage where an enormous bald African with bulging muscles stood guard. Chamrat jerked his head and the dark giant allowed us to pass. The door closed behind us, reducing the howling crowd and tinny music to a muffled roar. We were standing in a long, dim hallway that was painted a deep red and illuminated by an occasional overhead bulb. Chamrat led me down the hall past a series of closed doors with sounds coming through them that could only be produced by one act, although which form I would not venture to imagine. We walked some distance as the hall twisted and turned upon itself in a maze worthy of Icarus. Finally, he stopped and pointed to a door that looked no different from any of the others.

"Here?" I asked nervously. "You're saying she's here?" He nodded and grinned his pointy-toothed grin. I turned the knob and pushed the door open onto a cubicle with a narrow mattress in the center of the room. A red bulb burned in the solitary lamp, washing the scene in eerie rose light. A woman was lying on her stomach beneath a dirty sheet, her hair a matted blond rat's nest. An elaborate pipe with a cord extending from it rested on the floor next to the bed.

"Is this supposed to be some kind of a joke?" I asked.

"Friend," he replied, waving both hands to sweep me into the claustrophobic space. "Man-woman you look for. You see."

"I can assure you I don't know this person," I insisted, hoping my own denial would make my words ring true. But at the sound of my voice the creature stirred and its legs poked out from under the filthy sheet, a pair of enviably fabulous legs, even longer and better-shaped than mine. It rolled onto its back and took a deep breath, the silhouette of generous implants visible in the dim light. And then I recognized the rags she wore to be tattered remnants of last summer's Yves St. Laurent collection. Treading gingerly on my strappy sandals, I moved into the room and stood over the pallid face. Though my brain resonated with disbelief, there was no denying who it was.

"Oh my God, Whitney. What have you done to yourself?" I whispered.

Three heavy seconds passed before she cracked her eyes open. Deep brown irises set in reddened whites wavered from behind her barely parted lids. "Pauline, is that you?" came the wispy voice. "How did you find me here?"

Chamrat was dancing around the bed like he had just won a prize. "You pay, Madam. You pay now."

"Leave us alone, you rodent. I'll pay you soon enough," I exploded, turning back to Whitney. I knelt down and drew myself closer to this shell of my dear friend.

"You pay, Madam," Chamrat insisted, more firmly this time.

I reached into my bag and pulled out a handful of baht. I had no idea how much money it represented, but I threw the entire lot at him.

"Take this and leave us alone, you cretin," I commanded. "Wait in the hall. We'll need you to take us out of this place."

He collected the last of the baht and thrust it deep into his tunic. My back was to him as the door clicked shut behind me. "Oh, Whitney, why?" I asked, studying her disheveled form. I was fearful to touch her, she looked so frail. And so filthy.

She lifted her head from the pillow, her platinum hair rampant with the black roots of negligence. Her arm flopped beside her until it located the pipe, and she pulled the cord to her mouth, taking a deep drag. Through my revulsion, I wasn't sure whether to be appalled or relieved that at least she wasn't onstage. She had once shared the story of her drug-addled youth with me, and it wasn't pretty. The pipe's cord fell from her hand and clattered onto the bare floor. She stared at me with eyes from another solar system. "Pauline, you're really here."

"Yes, I am, Whitney, and we're going to get you out of here. But why, Whitney? Why?"

She shook her head. "It's all about the pictures, Pauline. You have to find the pictures. They're hidden."

"Pictures? What pictures?"

Her eyes rolled back in her head as she spoke. "The Khmer want them."

"The Khmer? What are you talking about?"

"Jack," she whispered.

"Jack did this to you?"

"No. Jack." In her stupor it sounded almost as if she were praying. And then, as I watched in stunned horror, she gasped noisily and stopped breathing.

"Whitney!" I cried aloud, jumping to my feet. I had to find help. I turned and saw that Chamrat had never left the room. "Quickly, find a doctor. She needs medical attention."

The gnome made no effort to move as his dark eyes traveled from the figure on the bed to me. "Hurry," I insisted, wondering if it was ridiculous to hope the establishment kept a physician on hand. I indicated the money he had secreted in his tunic. "I'll give you twice what you have there."

But instead of going out the door, he charged toward me and pushed me onto the bed beside Whitney. Then, in the ensuing millisecond, he jumped down onto me and knelt on my chest, pinning my arms to my sides with his knees. I tried to break away, but he was amazingly strong for one of such small stature. The gravity of my situation began to sink in. I was trapped in the bowels of a sex club, thousands of miles from my home, and no one save Chamrat knew it. I tried to buck and kick myself free, but he squeezed all the tighter. He stared down at me with a face fixed in a lecherous pointy-toothed smile. I wondered if there was a Thai word for such an ominous smile.

"What do you think you are doing?" I demanded, summoning my last bit of courage in an attempt to appear forceful. I leveled my most venomous gaze at him, to no effect. In fact, the eyes that stared back at me were so devoid of emotion, they rendered me speechless.

He picked up the hose of the discarded pipe from the floor and pushed it toward my face, saying, "Now, *farang* woman, you show me how superior you are."

39

Through the Looking-Glass

I have never smoked opium before. Now, while that statement may seem odd in and of itself, there are more members of my social strata who have dabbled in the drug than one might guess. Call it risk-seeking or a way to alleviate the boredom of a life with no obligations, but I've attended parties in both New York and California where the drug was offered. This was in the front of my mind as the pipe was forced closer to my mouth—that Helen and Pug McWithers had smoked opium and survived, no worse for the wear. Except for their divorce, but that had nothing to do with the opium. It was more precipitated by Pug's penchant for underage women.

This knowledge still didn't prevent me from turning away as Chamrat pushed the pipe toward my mouth. But my captor was fiercely strong and his grip on me relentless, his knees practically cutting off the flow of blood to my arms. Still perched upon me, he reached into his tunic, where the baht had disappeared, and a knife appeared. It was ornately decorated, the handle inlaid with mother-of-pearl. He held it to my nose and issued a non-negotiable command. "You smoke or I will slit your face."

This was a threat of substance. I'd spent far too much time and money preserving this face to have it carved up. The fear was overwhelming, so strong it hummed in my ears, obliterating all the other senses. I reluctantly opened my mouth, and he forced the metal tip of the hose between my lips. "Now, smoke. Smoke."

I inhaled, doing my best to take a shallow breath. The warm smoke traveled down my throat and into my lungs, expanding as it did so. I coughed it out and took a breath of clean air.

"Again," he demanded.

At his behest I took another puff and then another. The world began to soften, and I had a sensation of floating. This may have been the most dangerous situation of my life, but it didn't seem so bad after all. I could feel the residual warmth of Whitney's body beside me and was thinking that she was going to be all right. The pipe fell from my mouth, and this time Chamrat did not bother to retrieve it. Rather, he raised his tunic and began to loosen his trousers.

Now, I may have been stoned, but not stoned enough that his action didn't raise a red flag. He tore at the front of my dress, and I hissed at him through tight-clenched teeth, groping in my consciousness for some threat that could reach into the depths of his mentality to alert him to what his violation of me would cost him.

"I have powerful friends here in Thailand, they will hunt you down if you do this," I bluffed.

"Let them hunt you down first, *farang* whore," he said, bending over me so that his face came within inches of mine. The stink of his breath made me want to vomit and I shut my eyes to block out reality. "What is left of you."

Those were the last words he would say to me, because at that very instant, the door crashed open. Chamrat released me and spun around. I lifted my groggy head to see the African bouncer standing beside one of the most beautiful Thai women I have ever seen. She was exquisitely slim, her long shiny hair a sheet of black silk, her golden skin enhanced by dark eyes that outwardly suggested modesty but behind which lay great intelligence. The woman said something in Thai and Chamrat fired back twice as many syllables. Then all three of them looked from me to Whitney's lifeless body.

More Thai was uttered and then Chamrat picked up the knife and flicked it in their direction. The African flicked his sleeve, revealing a knife three times the size of the one Chamrat held. The two stood motionless, holding each other at bay like the United States and Russia during the cold war. And then, in a move that seemed to slice time, the Thai woman twirled around and jabbed her fist into Chamrat's Adam's apple. The puny man crumpled wordlessly to the floor.

Losing no time, the Thai woman stepped to the foot of the bed and said, "Come with me. Quickly."

As if in a dream, I slid to the edge of the bed. The woman tried to take my arm, but I pulled away from her grasp. With all due appreciation for what she had just done, there was some healthy skepticism on my part. For all I knew she had come to collect me for a white slavery ring. "Who are you?"

"I am Lienne," she replied, *wah*ing. Lienne. The name hastily scrawled on a piece of paper by Tag. The number he had known by heart. I had not thought she would be this beautiful. Was it possible to be feeling a pang of jealousy at a moment like this? "Tag called me tonight and asked to me look out for you. He was right to be worried."

I looked down at Whitney's unmoving form. "I can't leave her here like this."

"That is for later. Now come. We must go quickly." Spurred by the urgency in her voice, I followed her into the hall, turning back at the last instant to take what I thought would be my last look at Whitney. Lienne headed in the opposite direction from which Chamrat and I had come, away from the noise and the hooting and the closed doors emitting guttural sounds. At the end of the hall was an exit door with a metal bar across it. She lifted the bar, and we stepped outside into a dirt alley. I felt something cross my bare toes and then scurry away. I screamed and Lienne silenced me with a fierce look. Revisiting my vow to never wear open-toed shoes in a third-world country, I was seized with a gut fear almost worse than when Chamrat was seated upon my chest. The Thai woman grabbed my arm and dragged my uncooperative feet down the dark passageway until we emerged into the lights and frenetic activity of Pad Pong. We made our way down the streets of the nightclub district, past girls in taffeta dresses who looked barely old enough for the prom, sitting outside dimly lit doors hawking their wares, and touts handing out free drink cards for the ubiquitous sex shows.

Lienne flagged down a taxi and shoved me inside. The next thing I knew, we were weaving through Bangkok traffic like we were qualifying for Le Mans. My head swam in a drugged stupor, and the lights of the city melted into a photolike blur. I nodded out, and when I awoke the Oriental's doorman was holding the taxi door open for me. Lienne was with me, and she walked me through the lobby, holding my arm as I nodded to the army of security guards, hoping they wouldn't notice my indelicate condition.

She got me to my room where I made straight for the turned-down bed, planting my face in the evening's chocolates. With eyelids heavier than Sunny Livermore's engagement ring, the only thing in the world that mattered to me at that moment was sleep. As I started to lose consciousness, I could hear the door shutting as Lienne took her leave. Then I slept like the dead.

40

The Sun Also Rises

The seams of bright light at the shuttered windows told me it was a new day. My head felt as though it was in a vise and my mouth was dry as . . . How did the Australians put it . . . "As dry as a Pommie's towel?" The memory of the night before came flooding back, along with the bleak reality that I had abandoned Whitney's body. Dragging my weary body into the bathroom to splash some cold water on my face, what greeted me in the mirror could have passed for a self-portrait of Damien Hirst. My hair was disheveled, my skin gray, and my eyes had huge dark rings beneath them.

I called for room service and some coffee to help me think. I opened the shutters and then thought better of it, closing them again. There was a knock at the door and I looked through the peephole to see a room service waiter pushing a cart. He set up the coffee along with a vase of orchids, and I got my wallet to tip him. I opened the wallet and stared blankly into its folds. It had been emptied. I recalled throwing the money at Chamrat and paying the taxi, but there still should have been a substantial amount of baht left. It had to have been Lienne. I found it ironic that the only thing left in my wallet was her phone number, and I took it out and held it in front of me, studying the confident, masculine strokes of Tag's cursive. I wondered if he knew that his friend was a thief.

"I'm sorry, I don't have any change," I said to the waiter. He acted as if this made no difference, and his smile remained pasted on his face as he *wahed* his way from the room. I double-locked the door behind him and put on the chain. On top of the opium hangover, I was frightened. Or perhaps paranoid would be the more appropriate word. Whitney was dead, I had nearly been raped, and now I had been robbed by my savior. A stranger in a strange land. Was there no one to be trusted?

The telephone rang, nearly causing me to jump from my skin. It was Waen Sanitawatra, the hotel's general manager. He asked me if I might come and see him in his office immediately. That it concerned a matter of utmost urgency.

Donning my straw hat and a pair of dark sunglasses, I ventured from my room and went to the executive offices, checking over my shoulder every third step. Mr. Sanitawatra's secretary escorted me into his inner sanctum, where the general manager sat at his desk smoking a cigarette. Upon seeing me he extinguished it and rose to his feet.

"Good day, Mrs. Cook," he said, extending a hand indicating that I should sit, waiting until I was seated before sitting back down himself. And it was a good thing I was sitting, because had I been standing his next words would have sent me tumbling to the ground. "I thought you would like to know that Mrs. Armstrong returned to the hotel last night."

"Mrs. Armstrong *what*?" I cried out in disbelief. Before I could tell him that was impossible, he informed me that she had returned from her travels late last night and that she complained she hadn't been feeling well. The hotel had called for a doctor, but, unfortunately, when the doctor arrived she was found to be in dire straits. It was his regrettable task to inform me that my friend had passed away sometime during the night.

He delivered this entire speech with a straight face.

"Is the body still here?" I asked.

"Yes, Mrs. Cook. We must wait for the proper authorities before we move her."

"I would like to see her," I said.

Mr. Sanitawatra led me to a suite in the newer part of the hotel where two Thai policemen were stationed at the door. The first thing I noticed was that Whitney's suite was even more magnificent than mine. The second thing was Whitney's body laid out in the center of the king-sized bed. I could scarcely believe what I was seeing. Her face was glowing clean, her hair fresh and combed, and she was wearing one of the fluffy terrycloth bathrobes provided by the hotel. All in all, she looked angelic. Like a doubting Thomas, I reached out and touched her icy hand. It was lifeless human flesh, all right. This was no illusion. I had no idea how, but somehow between last night and this minute Whitney had been brought back to the hotel.

"The doctors did everything they could. Of course, she was in such trauma we could not move her," Mr. Sanitawatra elaborated.

"I'm sure you did your very best," I said.

"Would you like me to contact next of kin?" he asked quietly.

"No, I'll take care of that myself."

When I got back to my room, I was more spooked than ever. How had Whitney's body gotten to the hotel? And while it was disturbing, there was relief involved, too. Whitney's name would not be dragged through the mud. Her legacy would not be that she died of an overdose in a seedy sex club. I would take her home and Jack could stand at her funeral with dignity instead of Gold Coast society reading in Elsa's column that her common upbringing had brought her to an appropriately common end. Or an uncommon one.

Which brought to mind Jack and the reward. I realized it could be considered crass to think of money at a time like this, but Whitney was dead and nothing could change that. Mourning my friend didn't mean I had to remain poor.

I put in a call to the Armstrong residence. It would be the middle of the night, but bad news doesn't adhere to a time schedule. I woke Surrendra, who woke his master when I told him it was urgent. Then I broke the news to Jack as gently as I could, telling him that Whitney was dead, but remaining vague about the actual circumstances. For the time being he could think that she had succumbed to some mysterious Eastern disease. I would tell him the truth later. Or maybe I wouldn't.

Then I got on the phone with the American consulate and started making arrangements to bring Whitney home.

41

The Sound and the Fury

Lienne called later that afternoon. I was resting on the bed with a cold compress on my head when the phone rang. "You have your nerve," I said at the sound of her voice. "Did you think I wouldn't notice that my pocket had been picked?"

"You have my very deepest apologies, Pauline. It was necessary. I needed some money to make arrangements. Most unfortunately, you were sleeping."

I started to ask what she meant by arrangements when a large gong sounded in my head. Arrangements. Like relocating an already dead body. Lienne had been the one to spirit Whitney back to the Oriental. And gotten her cleaned up. And somehow gotten a death certificate issued that read CAUSE OF DEATH: BACTERIAL MENINGITIS, instead of acute narcotic poisoning. Tag had said she was well-connected, but this was off the charts. In the United States she'd make a great public servant.

"It was you? How did you do it?" I asked.

"I have good friends in high places. Unfortunately they do not come free. But now I need to see you again about something very important. Can we meet for dinner?"

"Yes, of course. We can eat here at my hotel."

"No," she replied too quickly. "I have chosen a local restaurant. It will be far better there."

"To be quite frank, Lienne, I'm a bit skittish after last night. I'd prefer to stay here with all the security. After all, I'm not sure what happened to Chamrat."

"Do not worry about him," she said. "He has been detained."

"Detained? You mean arrested?"

"I mean detained. I told you, I have many friends in high places. He will not bother you again. Now please, you will meet me at nine o'clock?"

She gave me the address of a restaurant and told me to take a cab and not the hotel car. Her surreptitious instructions did little to bolster my confidence about leaving the safety of the Oriental, but since she had done so much to help me, I didn't feel I could deny her this mysterious meeting.

At the appointed hour, I took a taxi across Bangkok to a neighborhood of modest-looking homes with vehicles parked bumper to bumper the entire length of the street. The restaurant was at the end of the *soi*, a small riverfront building with a thatched roof.

Lienne was waiting for me in the entrance. "So good to see you again, Pauline," she said as if we were two college chums having a reunion and the dangers of the night before had merely been an initiation prank. I scanned the restaurant and did not see one person of European descent. She had meant it when she said a local restaurant. She gestured toward the busy room. "Please, come. Our table is waiting."

We sat at a table for two right on the water. She took the seat that faced the room, leaving me facing the river. A waiter brought menus but she waved them off. "You like Thai food?" she asked.

"If it's not too spicy," I said, my tongue throbbing in memory of my incendiary meal with the Bedford-Hills.

"OK. Medium spicy." She ordered in Thai and the waiter disappeared, reappearing a minute later with two bowls of tom yum soup and two bottles of beer. One taste of the soup and I was glad she had ordered the beer. If this was medium spicy, hot spicy must melt human flesh.

"It is very regrettable about your friend," Lienne said, her eyes fluttering around the room like butterflies looking for some place to alight.

"I'll never understand how Whitney ended up there in that seedy place anyhow," I said.

"I ask my friend at Sexy Club and I learn that this man, Chamrat, and another man brought her one month ago. They paid for her to take room, to smoke opium. She stay and smoke more. Since she is a he/she they think maybe she is a drug addict, too."

I was surprised that everyone seemed to know Whitney's sex. "How did they know she was a transsexual?"

"This is Thailand. People know. Many things here are different from the United States."

"Last night's show, for one," I said. "How tragic that those women have to exploit themselves like that."

She actually laughed aloud, two perfect dimples forming on either side of her golden face. "You see exploitation. They see job better than twelve hours bent over in rice paddy all day, every day. Better to make money on back than to break back to make money. What you see as exploitation many women here see as economic opportunity."

Strange, I thought. Those were Mr. Kwan's words at the Sunshine Factory.

The waiter arrived and replaced our soup bowls with plates heaped high with noodles and vegetables, chicken, and prawns. There was also an entire fish. "Is this all for us?" I asked. She nodded and began to take food from the plates, indicating I should do so, too. I tried the fish, which, thankfully, was relatively mild.

"So how do you happen to know Tag McKay?" I asked between bites, doing my best to sound casual.

"I met him when he served in Vietnam. Many American servicemen came here on furlough." Lienne went on to tell me that Tag had lent her money to help support her son while she was building her clientele and that she could never forget his generosity. Her face beaming, she told me that her son was now grown and had a child of his own. I listened with mixed emotions, wondering just what their relationship had been, and in disbelief that she was a grandmother.

Lienne ate with rapture, consuming food with a fervor that belied her slim figure. I, in turn, picked at my food, fanning myself with my hand as

I alternated between beer and water in an attempt to put out the fire. The entire time we ate, Lienne's eyes never stopped their restlessness. The waiter returned again, took away what was left of the incendiary dishes, and replaced them with sweet sticky rice and mangoes, the first thing besides the fish I was able to tolerate without pain. After the waiter left, her eyes stopped their fickle dance and she leaned in toward me with a seriousness on her face equal to that of the night before.

"Now, there is something very important we must discuss. When I left you last night I returned to Sexy Club, to see about making arrangements for your friend."

"Weren't you frightened to go back in there?"

She shook her head. "No, they very happy to be rid of *farang* body. They do not want trouble with Thai police. It is very expensive.

"But, in the process of cleaning your friend, it was necessary to remove her clothes. Filthy. But I am a woman who admires style and though her skirt is very dirty, it is very nice. So I look inside skirt band for label. Yves St. Laurent. Very expensive. But something strange, the sewing on the label is loose on one side. I put my finger inside and find this."

She held out her hand and in her palm was a small piece of paper the size of a matchbook cover rolled into a tiny tube. She unrolled it to reveal a series of numbers. "Cell phone number," she said.

The obvious question was why Whitney would hide a cell phone number in the waistband of her skirt. And I wanted an answer. "Well, let's call it."

"I hope you will pardon my boldness, but I have already taken the liberty. The woman who answered was most upset to learn of Mrs. Armstrong's death. When I explain you are her friend, she asks to meet you. She says she has some very important information, but that it is dangerous for her and could be dangerous for you."

"Did she give you a name?"

"Chia Arunasetya."

The author of *Human Chattel*. Whitney had been with her when she left Fleur and the Yorkies with the Cambodian couple in Chicago. What possible interest could she have in me?

"I'll meet her," I said. Lienne tucked a lock of hair behind her ear and a moment later I felt the shadow of another person pass behind me. And a wisp of a shadow it was. The woman was so tiny she couldn't have worn size zero. She was dressed in blue cotton pants that ended below her calf and a loose blue silk top that barely disguised her skeletal figure. Her dark hair was cropped even with her chin, and her cheeks had a hollowed-out look to them for all their roundness. She looked at me from eyes set above dark half moons. She was carrying a plastic bag in her hand. Lienne bade her sit, and she pulled up a chair from an adjacent table.

"You are Mrs. Cook, a friend of Whitney Armstrong's, yes?"

"I was."

"I am Chia. Because of what I have told her, Whitney traveled to Phnom Penh to see the Sunshine Factory, one of the most abusive facilities in all of Cambodia. I could not go, because I am too well known and there would be much danger for both of us."

"And what, may I ask, would put you in such danger?"

She reached into the bag and pulled out a white envelope. "What do you say? A picture tells a thousand words."

I opened the flap and slid out the top photo. It was of an abysmal barracks-style room crammed with unsmiling young women. There were several more pictures along the same lines, with women working elbow to elbow in what appeared to be inhumane conditions. I went one photo further and recognized Mr. Kwan's office. The venetian blinds were closed, and he was putting the cot to use. But he wasn't taking a nap. He appeared to be having sex with a young girl, and the look on her face made it clear the act was not consensual. I slid the photographs back into the sleeve. I had seen enough.

"These pictures were secretly taken at the Sunshine Factory and then smuggled to Whitney during her visit," Chia continued. "The management there is very cruel. Girls are lured to work. They come from the country, they do not know how to take care of themselves, they are told they will be given place to live. When they arrive, they are put into these slave conditions."

"But when I visited I saw no sign of worker abuse."

"That is because you did not see the entire facility. This is the annex.

The basement sweatshop with inadequate fire exits. The dormitories with subhuman conditions."

"Why doesn't someone notify the authorities?"

"For the Khmer the genocide is still very fresh. Wounds still run deep. Fear still runs deep. No one talks for fear their families will be harmed. The only help can come from the manufacturers who buy goods from such places. Sunshine is not the only one. You must take these pictures back to your country. You must put them in the proper hands so these practices can be stopped."

I thought of the shell-shocked looks many of the Khmer still wore, or worse, the vacant ones. They were a people ripe to be exploited.

Chia continued. "The Cambodian government will be very unhappy if these pictures surface. It would prevent them from getting an increase in their import quota to the United States. A scandal like this could be deadly to the process and could cost them very much money."

"So does this have something to do with what happened to Whitney?"

This time Chia shook her head, her black hair swinging sadly. "I do not know. All I know is I met her at the airport to get the photos. The last I saw of her, she was getting in a hotel car. She was supposed to return to the Oriental, but she never did." Chia stood up, leaving the pictures on the table. "I trust you will do the right thing with these. I know Whitney would have."

And then she was gone.

I tucked the envelope into my purse. What I would do with the pictures could be decided later. The check came and I paid it. Lienne and I walked to the door together. There was a taxi waiting, and before getting in I thanked the Thai woman for her help.

"This is a small way to pay Tag back for his help over the years," she said.

42

Pinocchio

The next day both Whitney and I were delivered to Bangkok International for the trip back to the United States, although we arrived at the airport by very different means. Whitney was delivered in a refrigerated vehicle and loaded into the underbelly of the Thai Airways 747. I rode in the Oriental's private car and would be flying two levels above her in the first-class cabin.

At first I was going to take a taxi to the airport. In light of what Chia had told me about Whitney last being seen getting into the hotel car, the chances of my getting into one of the hotel cars alone was as unlikely as me having lunch at McDonald's. I recalled how oddly convenient it was that Arun had been waiting in the Bangkok airport when I returned from Phnom Penh, and the way he had tried to avoid Bob and Betty Miller. My charitable act had paid off. Maybe if they hadn't ridden in the car with me, I would have ended up at Sexy Club, too.

But it just so happened that the Bedford-Hills were leaving at the same time as I, so we arranged to share the hotel vehicle. I felt fairly secure that no one would dare spirit me off with the high-profile British couple in the car. As we moved slowly through the Bangkok traffic, Harriet Bedford-Hill noticed the copy of *Town and Country* I was carrying, pointing out that her good friend Alison Porter-Reid graced the cover with her greyhounds.

"I'd give you my copy," I said, "but there's an article on second homes in the Channel Islands that I really want to read on the plane."

"No worries, darling. I can get my own copy."

A surly Arun unloaded our bags, and I bid the Bedford-Hills adieu and headed to the Thai Airways first-class desk. After checking in, I was escorted to security by a Thai Airways employee and put in the lane that fast-tracked the luxury customers. I was just about to place my carry-on onto the belt when an unsmiling official in a uniform and cap approached.

"You will come with me please, Madam."

My heart leaped into my throat as he motioned for me to follow him. Holding tightly to my belongings, with my copy of *Town and Country* tucked snugly beneath my arm, I was taken down a corridor to a small office with a desk and a metal table. When he shut the door, I was certain my pounding heart could be heard across the room.

He took my carry-on from me, put it down on the metal table, and began methodically sorting through it, unzipping every zipper and checking out my makeup cases. Then he motioned for my purse. He repeated the drill, even looking inside my wallet. To my surprise, he left my money intact. Then he turned his dark, penetrating eyes on me.

"Are you carrying any contraband?" he asked. "Any pictures? Any pornography?"

I held his gaze. "I certainly am not, unless you consider Fire Station Red lipstick to be illegal."

He eyed me up and down. I was wearing a white silk blouse and fitted slacks with a cotton sweater draped over my arm. He took the sweater and gave it a tremendous shake as if he expected something to fall out of it. Then he handed it back to me, zipped up my purse and carry-on, and turned them back over to me as well.

"My apologies, Madam. There has been some high-level smuggling of ancient Thai books. We are taking precautions against this. Please take no insult. We are treating all passengers the same."

He escorted me back to security, where I passed through without further event, although I did notice that no other passenger was taken from the line.

I would say that customs stateside was easier, but *comme d'habitude*, there was a customs agent who felt duty-bound to pull me out of the line. I tapped my foot impatiently as he signaled for my suitcase. For the first time in many travels, I was confident that there was nothing undeclared inside the piece of luggage. My quest to find Whitney had left little time for shopping.

When the customs agent unzipped the bag and opened the top, I gasped aloud. It looked like the Khmer Rouge had marched through it. Not one item of my neatly folded clothing was as it had been when I packed it at the Oriental. Someone had given it a more than thorough search. Even the agent seemed impressed by the mess. Thinking that no one who treated their clothes with such disdain would have anything to declare, he lost interest and returned my bag to me.

If he truly would have wanted to see something of interest, he should have looked in the copy of *Town and Country* I still had clutched beneath my arm. Because therein, taped between two pages about second homes in the Channel Islands, was the envelope with the photos Chia had given me.

43

Women in Love

It had been seven days since I left Chicago, seven days that seemed longer than Creation itself, when Whitney and I finally landed at a snowy O'Hare on the eve of New Year's Eve. Even as I stepped out onto the jetway, the cold penetrated. We were home. Whitney's body was held for the mortuary hearse to pick up, while I was squired back downtown in a different sort of limousine.

As I sat back in leathered luxury, my mind replayed all that had happened. Whitney's death. Chamrat's attack. Lienne. And most puzzling, the pictures I carried with me. What did they mean? Were they really important or were they just a glimpse of the harsh reality of life in another world? In a world where a woman chooses to work in a sex club to earn a living, is working in a sweatshop so terrible? As for the picture of Mr. Kwan and the young girl, could I really be certain the act was not consensual?

And then there was Jack to think about. Since I had found his missing wife, would he make good on his payment? And what would he say about the pictures?

But with all these things to digest, one loomed larger than them all. Tag

McKay. He had stuck his foot in the door of my mind and I couldn't get it shut. He had become the biggest question of all.

I left my bags with the bell captain at the Drake and had the limousine deposit me at the co-op. Jeffrey was on duty and asked me if I'd had a Merry Christmas. I told him the jury was still out. When the doors opened at the penthouse level, all was quiet. Even I didn't expect Tag to be working on a Sunday. I marched directly into the library and peeled the envelope with the pictures from inside the Channel Islands article. Scouring the shelves for the best hiding place, my eyes fell onto the copy of *The Great Gatsby* Henry's grandmother had given him, and he in turn had given to me. Both Scott and Zelda had signed the book with personal notes to his grandmother. Of course, they were probably grateful that she had brought them into her fold. Beatrice Bacon Cook was a patron of the arts akin to Berthe Palmer, and being included in her parties in the twenties was akin to being included in Mrs. Astor's four hundred in the Gilded Age.

I took the book from the shelf and opened it to the title page. A twinge of sweet melancholy struck me as I read words written beneath F. Scott's own, words written by my deceased husband twenty-six years ago on our wedding night. To my Pauline, whose green eyes outshine the light on Daisy's dock. Forever, H. I kissed the cover and tucked the pictures into the book.

A noise behind me told me I was not alone. I turned to see Tag standing in the entry. He was wearing his work clothes and holding a paintbrush in his hand. Fleur trailed behind him and settled at his feet. There was a look in his eyes that frightened me in its intensity. "I was touching up the paint in the bedroom," he said. His words were thick-sounding as though he had trouble getting them out.

"I just got back," I said, saying the first inane thing that came to mind.

"Lienne told me what happened. About Whitney. About the pictures." He was staring at me in an odd way he never had before, and ridiculously enough, the thing that had grabbed my attention was that he'd talked to Lienne. Naturally they would have talked after what had happened, but that didn't stop a nasty green monster from rearing its head over a grandmother who lived halfway around the world.

"Pauline, you could have been killed—or worse."

I made light of his statement. "Sometimes a person just has to do what they have to do."

He stood there with the damned paintbrush in his hand, and I found myself squirming under his gaze. We stood at an impasse, our eyes locked in a paralyzing standoff. Then he smiled at me in a way that made me feel as if I wasn't wearing any clothes and quoted Christopher Marlowe's "The Passionate Shepherd to His Love."

Come live with me and be my Love,
And we will all the pleasures prove
That hills and valleys, dales and fields,
And all the craggy mountain yields.

From somewhere in the depths of my cranium, I dredged up Mrs. Shingleheart's class again, and the words from Raleigh's "The Nymph's Reply to the Shepherd" spilled off my tongue.

If all the world and love were young,
And truth in every shepherd's tongue
These pretty pleasures might me move
To live with thee and be . . .

But my tongue stuck in my mouth and I couldn't finish it. A thread in me still fought to hold out against this folly, but that slender thread was unraveling with each passing second. Tag finished the verse for me. "Thy love?" The words hung in the air, waiting to be plucked from it or left to flutter to the ground. The thread snapped with a vengeance. So what if he was short? I stepped out of my heels and walked to him. We were nose to nose, his turquoise eyes melting into mine.

I took the paintbrush from him and dropped it onto the rug, putting my hand into his. I reveled in the strength I felt coiled there, his coarse masculinity. He raised my other hand to his face and held it before his lips.

"Do you want this?" he asked.

All I could do was nod. He kissed my hand and lifted my chin with his forefinger and kissed it. Then his lips moved to the base of my throat where he kissed me again and again, before moving slowly up my neck until he reached my lips. He hesitated, and said my name. "Pauline." Sometimes there is nothing more sensual than the sound of one's own name coming from another. It flowed from his mouth as if he had given birth to it. A gentle tickle rose from inside my throat. Then he kissed me fully on the lips, and I took his kiss with all the hunger a fiftysomething-year-old woman can have for a fiftysomething-year-old man.

"Tag," I whispered. He lowered me onto the floor, onto the oriental rug, and unbuttoned my blouse, kissing where my cleavage spilled from my Wonderbra. I started to take his shirt off, but he stopped me and did it himself, revealing a lean muscularity that took my breath away. I touched the smooth skin of his biceps and felt a hardness I had never known before.

And that was just above the waist.

And then the coarse, callous, rude man that I once thought I detested proceeded to make selfless love to me. He was sweet, passionate, strong, tireless, and left me begging for more. And as I closed my eyes and went along for the ride, I wondered why I'd never made the leap before.

44
Of Human Bondage

I awoke the next morning feeling better than I had felt in years. Tag was awake beside me staring at the ceiling. We had taken the party over to my suite at the Drake after making love a couple more times on the floor of the library. Even now I could feel the sweet sting of rug burn and I was fairly certain there was some Van Gogh White on my back from rolling on top of the paintbrush.

"Hi," he said, tracing my lips with his finger. "Good morning."

"That was quite a night," I said.

"It was." He kissed me gently, and then there was an awkward silence before he said some words that surprised me. "You know, I was attracted to you the first time I saw you, even though you were reaming me out." I pictured him crawling out from my cabinet. The way his turquoise eyes blinked from behind his dust-covered face. I had felt something then, but it couldn't have been called attraction. Being attracted to him wouldn't have been comprehensible to me. As it was, it was just now barely within my realm of understanding. Why does cold morning have to spoil hot night?

He continued to speak. "But I couldn't have ever been with you before, because you just represent so much that I'm against. It wasn't until I talked to Lienne that I saw the real you shine through. Before that I just thought of you as another spoiled rich bitch."

This was not the sort of first-morning-after-lovemaking romantic line I was hoping to hear. I sat up straight in the bed. "Yes, I'm sure Lienne spoke highly of me," I said, trying to remember that she probably saved my life. "She's a very beautiful woman."

He talked to me with a familiarity that told me he already knew me too well. "Stop it, Pauline. What Lienne and I had was when I was a kid. A soldier strung out on war and blood and mud. She was a port in a time of disaster. We're good friends now and nothing more."

When I said nothing he continued, "If Lienne hadn't told me about you and the pictures, I couldn't have done this." And then he kissed me softly on the lips. And the chin. And the neck. And then . . . well, suffice it to say, the morning was as good as, if not better than, the night.

Afterward, as I lay on my back trying to catch my breath, a new mindset occurred to me. Was it possible that he thought he was sleeping down? Putting that aside, until this very moment I had been so immersed in a physical state of sheer bliss, I had forgotten all about the pictures. Now the question begged of what to do with them. When I first got them from Chia, they seemed important. Now, half a world away, what they represented didn't seemed as urgent anymore. I thought about Jack, and the reward, and wondered if he would still tender it if I revealed those pictures.

"What are you thinking?" Tag asked.

"That I'm going to see Jack Armstrong, and see what he has to say about Sunshine Factory."

"Be careful of him, Pauline. Don't underestimate what people will do when their money is involved. Those pictures will be quite damaging to him."

I didn't like where this conversation was going. Barely half a day after recognizing true passion and love, I was already finding out where we might not be a fit. Which led to another unwelcome thought. It was New Year's Eve and I had two thousand-dollar tickets to the Amici of the Literati Gala, but no date.

I stared at the face across from me, a face that was suddenly so dear, and

I didn't want to think about ringing in the New Year without him. Dare I invite him? Maybe I could skip the gala and we could ring out the old year and ring in the new right here with a bottle of Taittinger.

"Happy New Year," I said.

A sly smile graced his face. "It's tonight, isn't it?"

"I've made plans, but I could come up with a terrible cold," I said, wondering why I couldn't bring myself to invite him.

He touched my nose with his fingers. "That's all right. I've got plans, too. I promised to tend bar at a friend's party. I can't let them down."

I tried not to think how his New Year's plans only highlighted the differences between us. If I were to change my New Year's plans, I would be passing up an A-list gala with gourmet food and wine and all the right people. He would be passing up a bartending job. I cringed internally, but it passed as he pulled me close and his desire for me made itself clear yet again. "So let's do our celebrating now," he said with a grin. All thoughts of bartenders and galas, Shakespeare and gowns, became meaningless as he drew me to him and made love to me, his lips and his hands taking me into that realm where thoughts become nothing more than exquisite nerve endings.

Afterward he showered and came back into the room wearing his work clothes from the day before. I lay in bed, depleted from either jet lag or lovemaking. He sat on the bed and pulled on his boots.

"I've got to go," he said.

"You don't have to work today," I said. "I'm giving you the day off."

A strange look crossed his face, but it swiftly passed. "I hate to tell you, but I hadn't planned on working today. I still have to go. I have some things to take care of before tonight."

I put on my robe and followed him to the door. We kissed deeply before he stepped out into the hall. And as I watched him walk away wearing his heavy boots and paint-splattered pants, I shamed myself by hoping that no one would recognize he was coming from my room.

45

The Man in the Iron Mask

Jack Armstrong awaited me in the solarium, the same room where he had first informed me that Whitney and Fleur had disappeared. His jaw was squared and his steely eyes peered at me from behind his tortoiseshell frames. Surrendra poured coffee from a sterling coffee service before performing his usual vanishing act. I took a sip of the piping hot coffee, my sensitive lips reminding me momentarily of the bruising kisses of the night before.

"Whitney did not die of meningitis," I said, diving in right away. "That was a cover-up I arranged for. She died of an opium overdose. I'm sorry, but I just didn't want to tell you over the phone. I wanted to deliver the information in person."

His cup was halfway to his mouth, but he stopped and placed it back on its saucer. He sighed deeply and slouched forward. "Tell me everything," he said.

So I told him the entire story—leaving out that my journey was prompted by phone records pilfered from his desk. I thought it best to leave that part alone. But I told him I had learned from a friend of Whitney's that she had gone to the Far East and to the place where his lingerie was manufactured in Cambodia. I told him about the manufacturing facility I saw and the very different one in the photos.

"Jack," I said, "Whitney wanted you to know of the abuse the Cambodians were permitting in their factories. That's why she went there. But the Cambodians couldn't have her taking this information back, so they saw to it that she was kidnapped and drugged."

He was understandably silent as he thought, his eyes focused on something outside the glass, something in the winter yard I had stumbled through not so long ago. My tracks had long since been covered by fresh snow, and the trees glistened in the rare winter sun. A tear coursed down his face, and he stared outside for a long time before turning back to me.

"Where are the pictures, Pauline?" he asked coldly.

"They are hidden in my apartment."

"Thank God," he said. "In the wrong hands, they could be a disaster. People just don't understand the way business works. The tree huggers. The bleeding hearts. They get all weepy and can't see the opportunities we are giving these people."

This was the third time I had heard of indentured servitude as an opportunity. "I don't know if I see it that way, Jack. Whitney certainly didn't. She may have died because she didn't."

"Pauline, you're not thinking of doing anything with them other than throwing them out, are you?"

I don't like people telling me what to do. By trying to manipulate me, he brought out the rebel in me. "I'm not sure what I'm going to do with them."

He stood up in a manner that told me he was angry. But the voice that emanated from his throat was calm and measured. He was practicing a self-control I knew had to be difficult for him after what I had learned from his first wife.

"Pauline, there's more involved here than you can ever know. Those pictures could be hugely destructive. I think you remember that I offered you a reward for finding Whitney. Five million, wasn't it?"

"Ten," I was quick to correct.

"Well, you've found Whitney, and as devastated as I am, at least I can find peace knowing where she is. So now if you'll just bring me those pictures, I'll write you the check."

It was my turn to stand. "I believe that's called extortion, Jack. Or is it a bribe?" I was outraged. If I hadn't been certain what I was going to do with the pictures before, he had just convinced me. "Those pictures are the reason that Whitney is dead, Jack. She couldn't stand it. Her heart was too big. Now they are mine, and I'll do with them as I wish." I picked up my purse and headed toward the door.

"Pauline, stop. You don't understand. You have no idea what you are doing."

"Yes, I do, Jack," I said, turning back to him. "And you still owe me ten million dollars. You can put my check in the mail anytime. Happy New Year."

With that I stormed from the room and past Surrendra, who, as I had suspected, was lurking in the hall. Evidently, Jack had not told him about Whitney's death yet. He looked at me, his dark eyes welling with tears. "Madam is dead?" he asked with disbelief.

"I'm afraid so," I said curtly, realizing too late that he was the victim of my anger with his master.

He closed his eyes, and tears streamed down his face.

46

A Midsummer Night's Dream

Emilio's was a madhouse, as it always is on New Year's Eve. There were women in tears holding hundred-dollar bills trying to bribe their way in after Richard of Rizzoli's had suffered an early-morning heart attack on the eve of the busiest day in the hair business. To make matters worse, his lover was the other top stylist at Rizzoli's and refused to quit Richard's side, leaving nearly two dozen women without anyone to do their hair on the biggest night of the year. Luckily Emilio knew better than to dare get sick. Part of his job was to take good care of himself.

I knew half of the women in the place and would be seeing them later in the evening. As I waited beside Honey Rosenblatt, her hand as encrusted with diamonds as her husband's face was with age spots, I wondered if she regretted marrying a man thirty years older just for his money. How much happier I was feeling at this moment thinking of a man my own age! In fact I realized I didn't care about what I was going to wear to the gala. Even the loss of my Dior gown seemed to have diminished in importance.

Emilio performed his magic, sweeping my hair into a flattering updo with a few shining auburn tendrils to camouflage the softness of the skin along my jaw. Then he cemented it with enough spray to withstand a nuclear attack.

Back at the Drake, I was still dealing with attending the gala solo. I wondered if it was too late to call Bharrie and see if one of his walker friends might want to attend. They were always attractive, attentive, and they loved dressing up. But I was in such good spirits that the thought of going alone wasn't troublesome at all. Not when I knew what would be waiting for me the next day. I was crossing the festively decorated lobby with its huge tree when I spied Emily Rossetti drinking a lonely cup of coffee in the Palm Court. A sting of sadness passed over me, and I went over and took a seat beside her.

"Your hair looks divine," she said. "You must be going somewhere special tonight."

"The Amici of the Literati gala, but I'm going solo, I'm afraid."

"That's a shame," she commiserated. "At least you have plans."

"You don't?" I admired her honesty. Who would ever admit to having no plans on New Year's Eve?

She shook her head. And then, in a moment of weakness, I did something I truly abhor. I invited another woman to be my date. But in my love-euphoric state, I didn't really care.

"Since I have an empty seat, would you like to join me tonight?"

"Oh, that's so nice of you, Pauline. But I really don't have anything to wear. Besides, isn't there someone else you'd rather invite?"

"There is," I said, smiling inwardly. "I have to tell someone this. Remember how I said I had some disturbing feelings toward the man remodeling my co-op? Well, I decided to move past the disturbing part. This is so frightening, but I may be in love."

"Then why don't you invite him?"

"He's already got plans. Besides, I can be fairly certain he doesn't own a tuxedo." I sighed. A man without a tuxedo. Was I out of my mind?

Emily was pensive for a minute, and then she said, "I think I'll join you after all." She signaled for the check. "But I'd better hurry, because I've got to get something to wear."

The Shakespeare troupe was masterful in their performance of *A Midsummer Night's Dream*. I sat beside Emily Rossetti, wearing an ancient black St. John's knit I'd unearthed, wishing that it was Tag McKay beside me instead of her. But as I watched the comedic interpretation of the doomed lovers Pyramus and Thisbe, I was reminded of another of Maria's predictions. That one in rags would take my soul mate from me. Of course, she had also said he would come from great means and that wasn't true, so should I fear the other prediction might be? I pushed it to the back of my mind.

The play drew to an end, and after giving the actors a standing applause, we adjourned to the reception area where hors d'oeuvres and drinks were being served. Sunny had outdone herself; the grand hall was festooned with garlands of summer flowers amid the holiday glitter, no thanks to me, I was reminded. My date excused herself to visit the ladies' room, and I stood alone surveying the crowd. The women were wearing Harry Winston jewels and couture gowns, their hair coiffed to within an inch of perfection, their nails smooth with fresh manicures. The men shone, too, all dressed in their penguin suits, as my grandfather used to call his. I don't know what it is about the tuxedo, but it can make the most vile-looking of men attractive. Fat, thin, old, young, the black jacket and cummerbund does something magical for them all.

Everyone was invigorated and animated, and it seemed a good evening to forget terrorist threats and the search for bin Laden and plummeted stocks. The backbiting and envy that permeated my world seemed to have taken the night off.

Sunny Livermore shone in a beaded dress that minimized her bulbous figure; Elsa in a black mink hat and black mink-trimmed gown; Marjorie Wilken, sober and slim in Elsa Peretti. Though I had decided to quit lamenting the Dior gown, it stung to think that it would have made everyone else appeared modestly dressed.

I took a glass of Taittinger from a passed tray and a blini topped with Osetra from another. Across the room I saw the Worthingtons—Suzanne, Junior, and Senior—with a very young woman, talking to the mayor and his wife. There was a tap on my shoulder, and I turned to see Jack Armstrong, the pillar of power that he was, his presence made even larger by the tuxedo.

"How are you this evening, Pauline?" he said as if no ill words had ever passed between us earlier that day.

"I'm fine, Jack," I replied, looking around in the hope someone might come up and join us.

"Listen, I know we have a difference of opinion about those pictures, but until we solve it I wonder if you could do me a favor. It would be a favor to Whitney, too. I want people to know that she was doing some charity work in Southeast Asia when she took ill and died. That's not too much to ask, is it?"

So that was going to be the line. Whitney had died in pursuit of a good cause. Even I liked that better than the truth. And so I agreed to go along with his story. Little did I know how helpful that would be.

Emily finally reappeared wearing a fresh coat of lipstick, and Jack peeled off to talk with those who didn't know his secrets. As word about Whitney's death spread around the room, heads began turning in his direction, and women began plotting how they might introduce him to their newly divorced friends. The room grew noisier with talk of yachts and polo ponies and the upcoming Sotheby's auction of Twombly's work and who would be in Klosters this winter and Monaco next summer. I looked around at all the makeup and surgically enhanced faces, the posing and the forced smiles, the owners of expensive jewels and more expensive old masters, and realized this was my world. I watched Jack Armstrong hold court as if he had not a care in the world. If I went public with those pictures it would definitely alienate me from Jack. Alienation from Jack could mean alienating myself from this world, which was all that I knew. I asked myself how important it was to me and decided I shouldn't be too hasty in my decision.

Elsa and Max were at my table as well as Joan and Reed Armitage, who had moved back into their apartment after Reed paid a fortune for the world's swiftest home repair. The table was rounded out by Sharon and Elmer Iverson from Barrington. Elmer owned a thermos company that had been in his family for decades. It had been rumored to be going under until he got one of the Chicago Bears to endorse it with the expression "How does it know?" I had met the sports figure at a party at the Iversons' one night, and it was my sincere opinion the sports figure didn't have the vaguest idea himself.

Elsa cornered me just as we were sitting for dinner. She was convinced that Whitney had left town for plastic surgery and wouldn't hear otherwise. "Died doing charity work? That's a bit of a stretch."

"I would hope that's how you're going to report it," I said.

"Pauline, who do you think you're talking to here? What was she really doing?"

"Looking after orphans. She was very involved with the orphans in Bangkok."

"Ha! I don't believe you for a New York minute, Pauline Cook. My bet would be she went to get some work done, they botched it, and she died of an infection. That's what I think. The only question is, since Jack can afford the best here, why would she go there?"

I shrugged and Sunny came up and starting feeding Elsa the propaganda she hoped to see in the next edition of *Pipeline*. Taking advantage of the situation, I squirmed out of Elsa's verbal grasp and found my seat, which thankfully happened to be on the far side of the table from her.

The evening dragged on longer than life support for a billionaire. Sharon Iverson seemed to have picked up where Marjorie Wilken had left off, embarrassingly drunk before the second course was served. She insisted on retelling the same story over and over, reaching across Max Tower to grab my hand and make sure I was paying attention. I left before midnight, begging off with a headache. Emily was thick in conversation with Joan Armitage when I told her I was going to go home. Though Emily offered to leave with me, I insisted she stay.

I walked out into breath-robbing cold, the frigid air encircling me like a gang of thieves ripping at my coat. As I stood there shivering, waiting for a taxi to make an appearance, I was seriously revisiting my stance on fur. Maybe I did need to buy a couple of new ones. My thoughts turned back to Tag and I wondered if he was missing me the way I was missing him. I imagined him sitting next to me at the gala, wearing a tuxedo. He would have looked better than any man in the room.

By the time a taxi appeared I was nearly frozen. The driver told me I was lucky to find a cab at all, that he was on his way home because he didn't like dealing with the amateur drunks on this night of nights, and that he had taken pity on me when he saw a single woman, and such a beautiful one, standing all alone. Feeling generous, I overtipped him and walked into the lobby, which was filled with drunken suburbanites who had taken advantage of the hotel's New Year's Eve special. I let myself back into my room where Fleur greeted me with her customary evasion, giving me a bored stare before retreating to the bedroom. She hadn't quite forgiven me yet for abandoning her last night at the co-op while I brought my new lover back to my room.

It was then I noticed an envelope lying on the ground with my name printed on it. I picked it up and examined it. There was something familiar about the hand, but I couldn't quite place it. I tore it open. Inside was a single sheet of cream linen paper with the most peculiar line written on it in all capital letters.

I AM LAZARUS COME FROM THE DEAD.

It occurred to me why the handwriting looked familiar. It was the same writing that had been on the other odd note I had received, the exerpt from the Yeats poem.

I decided to call Detective Malloy in the morning and tell him about it. Then I double-locked the door, put the chain on, and climbed into bed. My last thought before dropping off to sleep was of Tag and I wondered who he would be kissing at midnight.

47

The Taming of the Shrew

"Happy New Year."

Tag called just as I was waking up, before I even had a chance to worry that he might not. The sound of his voice sent a thrill along my spine as I lay in bed with Fleur purring at my side. As if she knew I was talking to her rival, she got up and jumped from the bed.

"Happy New Year to you, too. How was your night?"

"Busy. A lot of crazy people drinking too much. And yours?"

"Expensive. A gala by any other name is still a fund-raiser."

"Hmmm. Listen, what's on your schedule today?"

"You mean after I get out of bed?" I questioned in reply, stretching my leg from beneath the sheets to study my painted toes. Yesterday's pedicure was still fresh, my feet mercilessly pumiced to a silky smoothness. It occurred to me how enjoyable it would be to run my feet along the crests and crevices of his taut, lean body. "In fact, I was thinking maybe you'd like to join me for some breakfast in bed."

"Man, that is a tempting offer. But I have some other breakfast plans. In fact, I was hoping you would join me."

"Breakfast?" I queried. "Where?"

"It's a surprise. I'll pick you up in an hour. But, Pauline, dress casual. And I mean casual." He paused. "And we can take care of that other appetite after breakfast."

After showering and doing my hair, I put on a pair of Escada jeans that cost two hundred and fifty dollars and a cashmere pullover at four times the price, and hoped he wasn't in tune with the cost of women's clothes. I pulled my hair back into a sleek ponytail, applied light makeup, and stood back to assess myself. It is undeniable that love does something to a person. My face glowed in a way it hadn't for years. I donned a pair of lizard boots and then, realizing they had a three-inch heel, changed them out for a pair of flats.

"Happy New Year, Mrs. Cook," the doorman greeted me as I walked out the Drake's Walden Street entrance. "Your chariot is over there." The street was so deserted it gave the city the feel of having been evacuated overnight. It took a minute to realize that the beat-up red pickup truck idling at the curb was my chariot. Though Tag's vehicle would have fit quite nicely on Cambodia's Route 6, it fell well beneath Gold Coast standards. I thought of my sleek Jaguar and the admiring looks it drew from others on the road. Telling myself to be more open-minded, I walked to the truck and Tag jumped out to greet me. He pulled me close with a lust-inspiring kiss that carried all the way to the soles of my flat-heeled boots. So maybe the truck didn't matter so much anyhow.

Though the outside of the truck was filthy and covered with winter slush, I was reassured to see that the interior was immaculate. There were no dirty floor mats or leftover fast food containers. We rode in comfortable silence along Lake Shore Drive as I nestled in the crook of his arm. To our east, the lake was a series of frozen blue-white crests, the waves arrested by the cold before they could make it to the shore. A dusting of lake-effect snow glistened in the weak winter sun, and steam emanated from the building tops in great white clouds, testifying to the frigid temperatures outside.

Tag took the Irving Park exit and after driving another ten minutes through the working-class neighborhood, we pulled up in front of a ramshackle brick building that looked ready to be condemned. Its windows were covered with grime, with steel bars assuring that no one would break them. "Here we are," Tag said, shutting off the engine. The truck gave a little grumble and then quit.

"What is this place?" I queried in all seriousness. If this ramshackle building had anything to do with our breakfast plans, I was glad I wasn't much of a breakfast eater.

"The Northside soup kitchen. I volunteered for the New Year's brunch for the homeless. I thought you'd get a kick out of helping out."

A kick in the derriere was the only kick that came to mind, but I dutifully got out of the truck and followed him into the building. I found myself standing in a large room crowded with people seated at folding tables that stretched wall-to-wall beneath yellow fluorescent lights. I actually recognized several of them as indigents who made pests out of themselves in my neighborhood, hawking a magazine called *Street Time* or something like that. They were people I usually did my best to avoid. As we passed through the room, Tag greeted some of them by name while I stayed in his shadow, trying for all the world to figure out what had brought me here.

We went through a swinging door and into an industrial kitchen where a dozen men and women were frantically working, making pancakes and eggs and pouring steaming coffee from large machines into plastic carafes.

"Oh, good, you're here," called out a harried young woman upon seeing Tag. "And you brought help. Even better. We can use every warm body we can find." She wiped her hand off on her apron and stuck it out. "Kimmy Liebowitz," she said, her toffee-colored eyes meeting mine from beneath a dark thick brow that threatened to unite if it didn't receive some tweezing soon. A wild, untamed nest of black hair framed her heart-shaped face. Though she wasn't a beauty like Lienne, something told me she and Tag had been close at one time. My name was barely out of my mouth when she handed me a platter filled with eggs and told me to start serving. Serving? The only thing I'd ever served was a tennis ball.

"This is the surprise," said Tag, picking up a platter of his own. "Follow me."

I will dispense with a description of the following four hours except that as memory serves me, I passed through those swinging doors more times than Henry VIII visited the altar. There was barely time to speak to Tag as we ladled spoonful after spoonful of scrambled eggs and stacks of pancakes onto paper plates, and filled bottomless styrofoam cups with coffee. Some of the homeless were clean and well-kempt despite their shoddy attire, but more of them reeked of cooled sweat and musky odors and the previous night's alcohol. All of them ate in a manner that bordered on frightening, barely lifting their heads from the plate to take a breath. It was as if they were afraid that someone would take the food from them before they had finished.

I was reminded of the note from the night before, about Lazarus being raised from the dead, and thought it might apply here. But there was something endearing that struck me as I watched men clean their mouths with their sleeves and women eat without even acknowledging the presence of a napkin. They were all grateful. Down to a one, they said, "Thank you, ma'am," with a sincerity seldom heard in my circles.

So, holding my nose at the distasteful parts and accepting the thanks from the not-so-distasteful, before I knew it four hours had passed. As the last of the people had shuffled out into the cold and the last plate was carried in from the tables, I collapsed onto a plastic chair numb with exhaustion. All I could think of was taking off my boots and rubbing my newly pedicured feet. And I was wearing flats. I couldn't imagine how I would be feeling had I worn heels.

Tag sat down beside me and put a hand on my leg, making it almost worth it.

"You did great, Pauline," he said, his turquoise eyes putting me in mind of tranquil tropical waters. "Now, wasn't that better than some champagne brunch?"

I wasn't quite sure how to answer that question. I had to admit it did feel good, but then again, doing anything with him would have made me feel that way.

Once we were back in his truck and driving to the Drake, the subject of the Cambodian pictures came up. "So have you decided what you're going to do with them?" he asked.

"Not exactly," I replied evasively, looking at Lincoln Park where a few runners were keeping their New Year's resolutions despite the cold. There was a crack along the bottom of the windshield that I hadn't noticed before, and it was snaking its way toward the passenger's side. "I still have to give it some more thought."

He turned and stared at me far too long for someone behind the wheel. The car in front of us slowed and he didn't seem to notice. "Watch out," I cried and he swerved to avoid it. But his heart was clearly not in his driving.

"Pauline, you have to turn those pictures over to the media."

"There's more to this than you know, Tag. There's a great deal of money involved. My financial situation isn't quite as healthy as it appears." I turned toward him and touched him on the sleeve. "Tag, if we're serious about being together, we need to have money." There, I'd finally said the thing about our relationship that disturbed me. If he was accepting of it, I could fix him up. Make him presentable. Buy him a new car.

"Pauline, I don't really care about money."

This very concept was inconceivable to me. Everyone cares about money. Even the people we'd just fed cared about money. They just didn't have any. I tried to explain. "Tag, money doesn't have to be bad. It's about freedom. Freedom to make choices. With a lot of money, one can buy food for the food bank instead of serving it." Not to mention luxury goods and hotel rooms and opera seats and charter a yacht to sail in a sea the color of his eyes. "Oh, Tag, you just don't understand what having money can mean."

"Yes, I do understand."

"What is that supposed to mean?"

"It means that I know all about money. I came from a wealthy family. After Vietnam, I saw it for the bullshit it was, so I gave it all up."

"Gave it up? What did you give up?"

"My money. My piece of the family business. Maybe you've heard of McKay Fruit."

McKay Fruit? Of course I'd heard of McKay Fruit. It was just behind Del Monte and Dole in revenues. I believe they supplied all the strawberries in Chicago. "You're one of those McKays?" I asked incredulously.

"Was. My father and I had a difference of opinion over how workers should be treated."

He turned his head forward and his silence spoke volumes. It was a frigid silence, entirely different from the comfortable silence we had enjoyed earlier when we were two people glowing in each other's company. I still couldn't believe what he had just told me. I had spent my entire youth trying to survive when my birthright was taken from me. He had given his away.

When we reached the Drake the doorman rushed up to open the door. I turned pleadingly toward him. "Won't you at least come up so we can talk?" I asked. My heart flattened before he even answered.

"Not right now. I need some time to think." The sound of those words put me right back in adolescence. We're getting older, I thought. There isn't all that much time to think anymore. Can't we just do?

I tugged on the door handle. I wasn't going to plead. Pauline Cook pleads with no man.

He reached out and touched my arm, and my skin tingled at his touch. I turned back hopefully. "I'll call you," he added.

Any woman who doesn't know what "I need some time to think" combined with "I'll call you" means is fooling herself. Each one is bad enough as a stand-alone. It means the telephone won't be ringing, there won't be dinner tomorrow, and the weekend at the summer cottage on Lake Geneva was just a dream. Survival mode kicked in.

"Don't bother," I said, pushing the door open so forcefully, it banged into the doorman who was still standing beside the truck. At that very moment, Madeleine DeForest, doyenne of the Gold Coast, chose to walk past with her black and tan Scotties sporting their winter tartans. She gave me an odd stare as I slammed the truck door and charged past her without saying hello. I stopped inside the lobby doors and stared hopefully back through the glass. Tag was hunched over his steering wheel for what seemed an eternity. Finally, he drove away, taking a piece of my heart with him in that beat-up truck.

Once again, Maria's words rang in my brain. *He comes from great means.* Well, Tag McKay certainly came from great means, even if he didn't have them anymore.

Turned out I'd been fishing in my own pond after all.

48

Paradise Lost

"I'm too old for this," I told myself as I sobbed into my pillow like a girl who has just lost her first love. "I truly am." Be logical, it could never have worked, I tried to convince myself. But logic has no place when it comes to affairs of the heart, and so I cried ever harder. It was so bad that Fleur jumped onto the bed beside me and began mewing in an attempt to get me to stop. But her mews had no effect. I simply wanted to die.

The phone rang and my heart fluttered with the hope it was Tag calling to say he had changed his mind, that he couldn't live without me and he was coming back. He would be up in minutes and we could make sweet love and let all the difficult decisions wait until later. I took a deep sniff and picked up the receiver. Suzanne Worthington's British accent sent my hopes spiraling like a Cessna in a tailspin.

"Pauline, are you all right?" she asked at the sound of my tear-choked hello.

"Just a bit of congestion. Probably last night's champagne." I dabbed at my nose with a handkerchief, not wanting to share my personal sorrow with someone who could never understand.

"My sinuses flare up the day after some wines, too." She went straight on to the reason for her call. "You left so quickly last night, I didn't get a chance to speak to you. Or to tell you we've arranged for a little impromptu dinner tonight. A day-after-the-day thing. I do hope you can join us. Dex Senior specifically asked me to invite you."

I sighed inwardly and weighed my options. I could stay in this suffocating room all night and cry my eyes out, or I could go mix with human beings who lived in the same world as I, not in the world of *Street Time*. Despite my pain, the wisest thing would be to accept the invitation. Maybe even give Dexter Sr. another chance since it seemed that there was no chance for Tag McKay and me. But the thought of making love to any other man after being with Tag was akin to a meal after the degustation at Pierre Gagnaire. There was no more room for food. However, common sense told me the day would come when I'd be hungry again. Why not have someone like Dexter Sr. in the freezer?

"I would love to join you," I said.

"Lovely. Cocktails at seven. See you then."

"Yes, see you then." I hung up the phone and pulled myself together. There could be no more crying if I wanted my eyes unswollen by cocktail hour.

The Worthington Juniors owned the entire two top floors of a new high-rise building several blocks south of me. Suzanne had spared no expense in decorating it, bypassing Bharrie for one of the best decorators in New York. There was no object that was not blatantly pricey, from the light-washed de Kooning in the entry to the Chippendale table and sideboard that graced the enormous dining room.

Foster met me at the door with a tray of champagne. The Worthingtons' white-gloved butler had been imported from England, and since his debut three years ago, he had set off a flurry of demand for British butlers not seen since the twenties. It was my understanding that his compensation package rivaled that of an investment banker.

"Thank you, Foster," I said, taking a flute just as Suzanne swirled into the foyer. She was divinely casual in cream-colored cashmere and a simple gold necklace and earrings, although the Hope diamond on her ring finger could have cut out all the glass windows in the Hancock Building.

"Pauline, I'm so glad you decided to join us," she emoted. She was in a grand dame mode, a very different person from the outdoor enthusiast I'd spent time with in Aspen. Snuggling up close to me so no one else could hear, she whispered. "Senior keeps asking for you. You must have made a good impression on him in Aspen. He said he's finished with brainless young tarts."

He hadn't seem finished with tarts last night, if his date at the gala meant anything. I thought about my go-round with him in Aspen, fleeing his room and his choice of petroleum products, while wearing my extraneous knee brace. Maybe Senior wasn't used to anyone telling him no and this made me attractive to him. I decided not to think about it too much. If things were meant to unfold they would.

Suzanne turned to greet another guest, and I made my way into the living room—a vast expanse of carved ceilings and crown molding, rich tapestries and silk upholstery, and the very finest eighteenth-century paintings one could buy at auction. At the far end of the room the notes of a Brahms piano concerto tinkled on a Steinway concert grand, played by a man wearing a tuxedo. Dexter Sr. was standing near the piano talking to a woman in a red pantsuit, but when he saw me he abruptly turned away from her and left her with the words still spilling from her mouth.

"Pauline," he greeted me warmly as he bent to kiss my cheek. "It's so good to see you here. You left Aspen so quickly."

"Well, I thought I'd done some real damage to my knee, but as it turns out, it was a stretch, not a break," said I, the only stretch here being the truth.

"Well, I'm so relieved to hear that. Come, let me introduce you around," he said, taking my arm and steering me around the room. For the rest of the evening he was glued to my side like Abelard to Heloise. Listening to him engage himself in one conversation after the next about his company and his money, I found myself growing so bored that I kept snatching a glass of champagne every time Foster passed with his tray. By the time Foster rang the dinner bell, the "impromptu" party turning out to be a sit-down dinner for thirty, I was fairly snookered.

We had just finished the main course, and Suzanne was talking about Zaidie Van der Molen's Africa-themed wedding where the bride arrived on an elephant, when I excused myself to visit the powder room. Even though I felt no such urge, I couldn't stand sitting at that table one more second. Having drunk more than my fair share of the '82 Trotanoy served with the

Beef Wellington, I found myself bouncing off the walls as I tried to negotiate the hall. When I finally reached the bedroom-sized bath, I closed the door behind me with a slobbery sigh. Coming to dinner had been a grand mistake. All I wanted was to be out of there. All I wanted was to see Tag.

The tears started to flow. I grabbed a few tissues, but they were as useless as trying to clean up an oil spill with a sponge. Once I'd opened the floodgates, there was no going back. I cried hard and furious, burying my face in my hands so I wouldn't have to see my image in the vanity mirror. And I was really only getting started when there was a knock at the door.

"Pauline," I heard my name whispered from the other side. "It's Suzanne. Are you all right in there?" I cracked the door open. She took one look at my bloated face and said, "Oh, darling, what's the matter?"

Feeling more than slightly ridiculous, I opened the door the rest of the way and invited her into her bathroom. Not since Jonathan Hartigan danced with Cookie Burnside at the cotillion had I felt this kind of misery. Jonathan had been my first boyfriend, and I hadn't been smart enough to know I was jilted until that moment. Now, in my misery and drunkenness, I needed to share my woes with someone.

So just as Patty White had listened to me in our twin-bedded dorm room at Foxcroft, Suzanne Worthington sat quietly at my side in her guest bath as I poured out my woes. I told her that I had fallen for my contractor. An employee, I wailed. I knew that it could never work, but I had these feelings just the same. And I told her about Whitney and the pictures. And how Tag and I had fought because I wasn't sure what I was going to do about them. My wine-fueled words flowed for so long that by the time I finished my story, my tears had practically dried. Suzanne was staring at me with an odd look in her eye. And understandably so.

"I'm going to go home," I said to her. "Please make my excuses. And thank you for listening."

"It's all a friend can do," she said, hugging me with British detachment. "You'll get over this, I'm certain. Think about Senior. He's a far more suitable match. Let that keep you going."

I told her that I would keep Senior in mind. Then I left through the service entrance.

49
The Metamorphosis

The next morning I woke up with a booming headache and new resolve. A resolve that surprised even me. I had dreamed about Tag and we were together and I was wearing T-shirts from the Gap and shoes from Target, and it didn't bother me because I was happy. The happiness stayed with me for the longest time, even though I realized it was a dream. I knew then what I had to do—both for myself and to get Tag back.

Until now I had been battling the eternal struggle between what is right and what we want to be right. Like the adulterer whose excuse is his wife doesn't pay him enough attention or the embezzler who feels he hasn't been properly compensated, I wanted to justify doing what would benefit me most. I had been telling myself that there was no reason to come forward with the pictures, that the Cambodian women were better off with their jobs, just as everyone else had been telling me. That their lot in life was difficult, be it rice paddy, sex show, or sweatshop. But in my heart I knew that was wrong. All wrong. I had nearly allowed my fondness for money to be my moral compass.

Tag had changed all that, and his commitment to what was right had spilled over onto me. I would take the pictures of the Sunshine Factory to a news agency. Of course, Jack would never send me money for finding Whitney and most of my friends would shun me, but what did that matter if Tag and I were together? I would sell the co-op, and we could live off that interest along with whatever he managed to bring in. In fact, the co-op would be worth more now since he had fixed it up. Yes, there would be hardship, but our love could survive anything. I felt a euphoria I thought only money could buy, though I still had to wonder why doing the right thing had to be so expensive.

I didn't doubt that Tag would come back to me when he learned of my decision. There was some chemistry between us that transcended our different worlds, and it was only my moral dilemma that had been standing between us. Now that was resolved, and like Scarlett O'Hara I was going to win him back. Only I wasn't waiting until tomorrow.

I dialed his cell phone to tell him the happy news and went into his voice mail. As much as I wanted to deliver my good news in person, I couldn't wait to tell him, so I left him a message.

"Tag, it's Pauline. I want you to know that I was wrong, terribly wrong for even contemplating giving those pictures to Jack. With your help I'm going to do the right thing. I'm going to be at the apartment later, and maybe we can meet there to decide the best way to do it."

I was certain that he would act on my message, that his principles wouldn't allow him to pass up this opportunity to do good. Then he would see the new me and see that we could make it together. I went into the bathroom and grimaced at the sight of my face. Yesterday's tears and alcohol had taken their toll, leaving me a swollen mess who looked her age. I called for room service and requested they bring up some coffee, toast, and a bucket of ice to bring down the swelling. When there was a knock at the door a short time later, I answered it, expecting the room service waiter. Instead it was Emily Rossetti.

"Hi," she said. "I was wondering if you wanted to get some breakfast."

"I've already ordered," I replied.

She stared at me strangely. "Are you all right? You look tired."

"It's that bad? I had a bit of a crying jag yesterday over unrequited love. But I've resolved it now, and I couldn't be happier. No matter what people think, I'm going to be with Tag."

She smiled weakly and nodded. "True love after fifty. Must be nice."

The elevator doors opened, and the room service waiter came down the hall pushing his trolley of breakfast and ice. Emily turned to leave and stopped suddenly. "Oh, I almost walked away with this. It was leaning against your door."

She handed me a cream-colored envelope. I didn't have to look twice to know what would be in it. I waited until the waiter had gone and then opened it, unfolding the sheet of paper with shaking hands. There it was, in the same odd script as before.

A heap of dust alone remains of thee.
'Tis all thou are and all the proud shall be.

50
As I Lay Dying

Wondering if the wind ever stopped blowing off the lake, I ducked my head into it and walked the block to my building, shivering beneath winter-white wool. The bag lady had resumed her position on the parkway, but a kinder, gentler Pauline decided to let her be. Tony Papanapoulous was on duty in the lobby, finally back from his vacation, his broad face tanned to a deep brown beneath his slicked-back hair. To be frank, I hadn't missed him, and was sorry that Louis would be going back to nights. No matter how well intentioned he was, Tony's lumbering denseness could be irritating. He held the door as the wind carried me and a couple of errant scraps of paper into the lobby.

"Happy New Year, Mrs. C.!" Despite my repeated requests, he seemed unable to address me by my proper name. I imagine I should have been grateful he didn't call me Pauline. But the kinder, gentler me prevailed and I did not dress him down.

"Happy New Year to you, too, Tony. Did you have a good holiday?"

"Went to Florida. It was great. Warm, you know. Sure would like to be there now."

"Wouldn't we both," I said, the frigid air radiating off my clothes. Before he could start in on the particulars of Daytona Beach, I headed toward the elevator.

"Oh, Mrs. C, I meant to tell you. There's some things here for you."

His words stopped me cold. There was a sudden surge in my blood pressure. "Things?"

"Well, some suitcases. They was delivered right before I left. Since your place was all tore up I put them in the basement storage for safekeeping. I meant to tell Jeffrey, but I guess I was so excited about goin' on vacation, I forgot." He looked at me sheepishly, like a dog that has been caught piddling on the floor. I took a slow, deep breath in hopes of keeping my skyrocketing blood pressure within reasonable limits.

"May I see these bags, Tony?" I asked with forced sweetness.

"Sure, follow me."

We left the lobby and went down the stairs into the basement. He unlocked the storage room door, and we stepped inside. In the corner, in a neat orderly row, were seven of Monsieur Vuitton's finest. Filled with my new clothes. And the Dior gown that missed the New Year's gala. The new me worked very hard to rein in her anger.

"Tony, do you have any idea what I have gone through trying to locate these suitcases?"

He shrugged, his large head sinking between his broad shoulders. "I would have put them in the regular storage area, but there were so many of them."

I took a deep breath and counted to ten. And then twenty. And then backward in French, exercising self-control that would have made Gandhi proud. "Tony, would you see to it these bags are delivered to my suite at the Drake?" I said calmly.

"Yes, ma'am," he said. I left him scratching his head and proceeded back through the lobby, where I got into the elevator and rode twenty floors shaking my head in disbelief. But by the time the doors opened, Tony and my newfound clothes had become secondary as all thoughts turned to Tag. I walked into the entry and had a greater appreciation than ever for the transformation of my home at his hands. The perfectly installed crown moldings, the Ionic pillars, the new fixtures, all bespoke a grandeur that could give the Worthington place some competition. In a matter of days, the furniture could be moved in and the job would be complete. It seemed such a shame to think I'd have to sell it.

I went directly to the library to get the pictures out of *Gatsby*, my heels echoing eerily through the empty apartment. Oddly enough, the library doors were open and the hanging plastic sheets that protected it were lying on the ground. The small hairs on the back of my neck were standing on end as I stepped into the room.

"Tag?" I called out. A blur of movement flashed in my periphery, and then darkness closed in on me.

"Mrs. C., Mrs. C., please wake up, Mrs. C." I opened my eyes to see Tony's full head of hair looming over me. It took a minute to recognize my surroundings. I was laid out on the leather sofa in the co-op's lobby, the incessant sound of a fire alarm clanging in my ears. The building's residents trickled into the room from the stairwell wearing fur coats and blankets, and carrying pets and jewelry boxes. I thought of the "Use Stairs in Case of Fire" sign posted in the elevator. It was coming back to me in patches, waking up on the floor of my burning library, going back for *The Great Gatsby* and finding it missing, the locked doors and the umbrella that had been placed through them. "Thank God you're all right," Tony said. "I didn't mean to hit you so hard."

"Are you the one who hit me on the head?"

"No, on the back. I saw you come out of your library with your back on fire. I had to hit you to put it out." He held up his arm, displaying a singed hunter green uniform sleeve as proof.

"Tony, what were you doing in my apartment?"

"I was delivering your suitcases like you asked. I was going to leave them in your foyer, but when I came up and saw all the smoke and then heard glass breaking I ran down the hall. That's when I saw you. Like I said, your back was on fire. You passed out. I had to carry you all the way down the stairs."

"What do you mean, you were delivering my suitcases?"

"You told me to deliver your suitcases."

"To the Drake, Tony. I told you to deliver them to the Drake."

While he stared at me with a stupid look on his face, I was thanking the creator that he was totally incapable of following instructions. Then another thought occurred to me. "Tony, where are the suitcases now?" His eyes traveled upward. Perhaps I was never meant to own a Dior gown.

The wail of sirens out front put an end to any further conversation. Seconds later, the lobby doors burst open, and helmeted firemen in black and yellow rubber suits rushed into the lobby and started clearing residents out. Mimi Van Dorf, birdcage in hand, was arguing that the cold would kill her parakeets. A paramedic appeared at my side and started asking me questions. What was my name? My age?—which I told him was none of his business. Did I know what day it was? Who was the president?

Amid the chaos there was a call for another ambulance.

"George Bush" was on the tip of my tongue, but as I tried to say it my tongue lolled in my mouth. And then my eyelids grew heavy, too, and I was slipping away, back to the Martha's Vineyard cottage where I was making love on the lawn. But this time when I looked into my husband's eyes they were turquoise blue and I realized that it wasn't Henry at all. It was Tag.

51

Jane Eyre

I woke up in Northwestern Hospital with a doctor tapping at my hand and telling me that I must do my best to stay awake as I had suffered a bad concussion. I was less worried about my head and more worried about my face, which felt like I had spent a week in Juan-les-Pins sans sunblock. He told me it looked like I'd suffered first-degree burns, but that he would send a plastic surgeon over to consult with me. Luckily, my wool jacket had prevented the flames from burning my back, but much of my hair had melted. He wanted to keep me overnight for observation because of the concussion, but if all went well I could go home tomorrow.

He left, and a couple of Chicago's finest stepped into my room, a surprisingly young and perky-looking woman and an older, tired-looking man. They apologized for disturbing me, but said they had some questions to ask me since the apartment fire was clearly arson. I told them everything that had happened from the moment I entered the apartment, and then I told them about the strange notes I had been receiving, the last and most ominous being about my remains being a heap of dust.

There was a copious amount of writing on the part of the police, followed by a question that took me totally unawares. "What can you tell us about the other person we found in your apartment?" the older, tired-looking man asked.

"There was someone else in my apartment?"

"There was a man. The doorman says he was doing some work for you."

My heart nearly stopped beating. "Tag! Oh God, please tell me he's all right."

"He's in ICU. The firemen found him facedown in the hallway. Somebody cracked him on the head, too, and he's got some bad burns, but it's the smoke inhalation that's worst."

The police asked me some more questions, and my mouth formed words in response, but my mind was racing, so I couldn't say what they were. The scene took on a surrealistic aura as my entire being surged toward Tag in the Intensive Care Unit. I thought of making love to him, his beautiful body, his wonderful face. If he was badly injured, someone would have to pay. It was then that an image of Jack Armstrong popped into my brain. I had told him I had the pictures in my apartment.

The police were closing up their notebooks and getting up to leave, pulling me back to the present.

"Wait, I think I know who's responsible for the fire."

They stopped in their tracks and stared at me.

"Jack Armstrong," I gulped.

After the police had gone, I lay quietly with the television droning in the background, left on at the insistence of my doctor in order to keep me awake. More than anything I wanted to see Tag, but when I asked my duty nurse if I could get out of bed, she answered with a definite no. I found this to be odd. If I wasn't supposed to sleep, why would they insist I stay in the place where I would be most tempted to do so?

Never one to accept the first no anyhow, I waited until she left and climbed out of bed. There was some kind of tube hooked up to me that dripped into my arm, and upon investigation, I learned that it was on wheels. Good enough. I unplugged it from the wall and dragged it to the bathroom to have a look at my face. Good Lord, I looked like a blanched tomato. Trying to repress what this could mean long-term, I went to the closet next, hoping to find something to wear. It was empty, causing me to realize that the clothes that hadn't burned probably reeked of smoke and had to be disposed of. This left me having to negotiate Northwestern Hospital in a drafty hospital gown, and a pair of blue socks with rubber treads on the bottom. I tied the open back straps of the flimsy gown as tightly as possible and hoped for the best.

Poking my head out the door, I could see a group of nurses talking and laughing at the far end of the hall. With my hanging bag rolling beside me, I left my room and headed in the opposite direction. Before long I came to an elevator bank, where a directory on the wall told me ICU was on the lower level of the building. When the elevator arrived, I just rolled on in, red face, hospital gown, and all. Drawing more than a few glances as the elevator descended, I held my head high and pretended that my presence there was as normal as everyone else's.

I rolled out at the ground floor and over to the ICU. The nurse must have thought I belonged there because she only glanced at me for a second before putting her head back into her paperwork. I went from cubicle to cubicle, peeking inside at sleeping or comatose humans until I found him. At first I barely recognized him. His forehead was bandaged and one ear was covered, but happily the rest of his face seemed relatively unscathed. Both of his hands were wrapped in heavy bandages that resembled swaddling, and wires issued forth from his body toward any number of machines. A fluid drip like mine stood guard at his side.

As I stared at his lonely figure, tears began to run down my cheeks. As if he sensed my presence, his eyes cracked open, revealing a sliver of turquoise. "Pauline?" he asked, staring at me oddly. "What happened to your face?"

I smiled through the tears. "We were in a fire."

He closed his eyes and lifted his chin. I could see him swallow. "A fire." It was a statement, not a question. He looked back at me and I nodded.

"You were right about Jack Armstrong being dangerous," I said. "I went to get the pictures, but I never got a chance."

Though I could tell it hurt him, he smiled. But the smile was short-lived. "I knew all along you'd do the right thing."

"Tag," I choked. "I . . ."

"Stop," he said. "Don't say anything yet. There's something I have to tell you first." He lifted his hands and stared at the bandages, before resting them back on his lean stomach. "I think my wife set the fire."

The blow hit me like a slab of ice sliding off a slanted roof. Though the part about the fire was certainly not to be discounted, there was the one word that stood out above the others. *Wife.* How could I have overlooked the possibility he was married? Hadn't I sworn to never get involved with another man until I was certain of his marital status? Had I thought that since he was a tradesman for some reason he was invulnerable to marriage?

"How could you do this to me?" I managed to rasp.

"It's not what you think," he said weakly. I couldn't tell if he was having difficulty speaking because of his injuries or because of what he had to say. "I haven't been with my wife for years. She's mentally deranged. She walked out of the last facility where she was being treated and I hadn't heard from her since. For all I knew she was dead. And then a couple of weeks ago I thought I saw her in front of your building, but when I approached her she ran off. Then this morning I saw her again, and this time I was sure. She must have been stalking me."

"Your wife was the woman in front of my building this morning?" I asked with true incredulity, thinking of the woman in rags huddled in the parkway. The situation was reaching Felliniesque proportions. Not only was he married, but his wife was . . . a bag lady?

He nodded. "You saw her?"

"I've seen her a lot of times." He closed his eyes and swallowed. Though I could tell this was difficult for him in his condition there was no way I was going to let him off the hook. Not with a story like this one.

"Shantel was a brilliant poet. She comes from a wealthy family, too," he began. "I met her at Stanford when I was in graduate school, studying literature and trying to stay out of the war. But then they lifted the student deferral and I went to Vietnam."

He went on to explain how the war had opened his eyes to the world of suffering, a world he'd never known. He came home and renounced his family wealth, and he and Shantel got married. But over time she started acting erratical and paranoid. He thought it was just her artistic bent, until she started accusing him of seeing other women. She would follow him when he went out with his friends, and then even when he just went to the store. One night he woke up and she was sitting on his chest with an ice pick saying if she couldn't have him no one could.

"That was when I had her institutionalized, and since then she's been in and out of more facilities than I could ever tell you." He took a deep breath and paused. "She must have set the fire in a jealous rage."

"But, Tag, there is no way in creation your wife could have gotten past my doorman." I wanted to add, especially dressed the way she was. That's when I remembered going with Tony to look for my luggage. We must have been downstairs for ten minutes. Plenty of time for a stranger to sashay through the lobby and go upstairs to lie in wait. Even one in rags.

A nurse carrying a clipboard came into the room and looked from Tag to my lobster face to my hanging bag. "What are you doing in here? He's to have no visitors and you should be in your room," she said. Before I could make any argument to the contrary, she was pushing me out the door.

"Good night, Tag. I'll be back as soon as I can," I called over my shoulder. But his eyes had already closed again. As I forlornly dragged my bag of fluid back to the elevator bank, a huge shiver came over me, starting at the top of my throbbing head and ending at my hospital-issue slippers. And it wasn't caused by the drafty hospital gown.

Maria's last prediction resonated in my brain. *There is much danger from the one in rags. The one in rags will take him from you.*

52

The Razor's Edge

The next day dawned bright and sunny. My face was throbbing despite the salve the plastic surgeon had put on it as he assured me that those who suffer first-degree burns usually end up with smoother skin than before. Now there's a silver lining. I wondered what the silver lining was behind the cloud of Tag's deranged wife. Finally, my attending physician appeared and told me I could go home. Since I had nothing to wear, I called Emily at the Drake and made arrangements for her to get some clothes from my room and bring them to me at the hospital.

Then I waited, watching some ridiculous game show on the television set where people were eating insects on a dare. I wondered if they'd ever visited Cambodia. The phone rang and it was Elsa.

"Darling, I just heard about the fire. Are you all right?"

"I'll be fine. I'll fill you in later. I guarantee it will be one of the most interesting lunches you'll ever have," I said, wondering just how much I would share with her. "I've been discharged. I'm just waiting for Emily to show up with something for me to wear."

"It's odd you mention Emily," said Elsa in the confidential tone of voice she always used when she was about to share some juicy information. "Yesterday I had lunch with Lizzie Richards, who's a member of the Bayou Club and knows everybody. I brought up Emily's name, and she'd never heard of her."

"That's odd," I said. "Emily talks about that club all the time."

"To the point of boredom," Elsa concurred.

"Maybe Rossetti was her maiden name and she took it back."

"That could be," said Elsa. "Anyhow, I found it a bit strange."

"I'm sure there's some explanation," I said.

I hung up the phone and before there was a chance to think about Elsa's words, it rang again. It was Tag calling from his hospital bed. All the news was good. It turned out he hadn't suffered as much damage to his lungs as they had first suspected and his burns, while painful, turned out to be only second degree.

"Well, as soon as Emily shows up with some clothes, I'll come down to see you."

"Emily?"

"Emily Rossetti. My divorced friend who's staying at the Drake until she gets settled in." At that instant, I looked up to see Emily standing in the door with a Barney's bag in her hand. "Here she is. I'll see you soon."

"Do you want this closed?" Emily asked, her hand on the door.

"Please. It's going to feel so good to get into something besides this fashion statement." I tucked my thumbs under the short sleeves of my hospital gown for emphasis.

"Who were you talking to?" she asked, putting the Barney's bag on the bed.

"Tag," I said wistfully. "I'm going down to see him as soon as I'm dressed."

"Well, I'm sure he'll like what I've picked out."

I looked into the bag expecting to see a sweater and some slacks. Instead it was filled entirely with lingerie, my lacy bras and teddies, silk panties and bustiers. Treasures chosen with great care from London's Courtenay store. "What's this?" I asked. When I looked up for an answer, her face frightened me. Every attractive aspect of it had completely shifted, moved forward into a penetrating leer. Even her dark eyes appeared to have lost their humanity.

"I'll bet he likes the way you look in these," she said, picking a pair of red panties from the bag and tossing them onto the bed. "Or this." A black push-up bra. "Or these." A white lacy teddy. A satin camisole. She took her fist and smashed it into the bag, sending all its content spilling to the floor.

"Emily, I don't understand." I was shocked at her behavior, but even more so when I looked up from the pile of discarded underwear on the floor to see that she was holding a box cutter. "What are you doing with that?"

"It was good enough for the terrorists," she said, circling around toward me. I backed up, keeping a distance between us as I studied the closed door. Could I open it quickly enough?

"Does he quote poetry to you?" she asked. "Marvell, Marlowe?"

She had to be talking about Tag. I suddenly saw Emily Rossetti through a new lens as a revelation struck me. Emily Rossetti was Tag's wife. And she was the bag lady. The unhinged savant/poet traded back and forth between her warm hotel room and the cold street. Now I understood where the notes had been coming from. "And do you quote poetry, too, Emily? Yeats, Eliot. Perhaps a little Pope?" I asked, trying to buy time until I could get to the door.

She stared at me with unbridled hatred.

"I told you, I'm back from the dead." With those words she lunged at me, the very force of her insanity giving her enough strength to easily overcome me. In an instant, she was standing behind me with the box cutter to my throat. I froze, afraid that any movement might cause the raw blade to slice into my throat. "How about a little plastic surgery?" She teased my jawline with the blade. "I can take care of all those wrinkles for you. He doesn't like wrinkled women."

"Or burned ones," I shot back somehow.

Her hold on me tightened. "If I had burned you, you would be dust." She tipped the blade toward my throat again. "How do you think it felt listening to you talk about him all the time? I saw him, but he didn't see me. Tag thought I was dead, but he was wrong."

"Emily, don't be ridiculous," I said, trying to summon up my normal demeanor. "Of course he saw you. He just told me all about you. That you're his wife."

She eased her hold on my neck. "He did?"

"Yes, he told me all about your life together." It is altogether quite difficult to speak when one's mouth is "drier than a Pommie's towel," but somehow I managed to get the words out. I could sense she was relaxing, and I was looking for the opportunity to twist out from her grasp and run for the door. But before I could, the door crashed open and Tag came rushing in, wires hanging from his body, his bandaged hands held in front of him. He looked pale and weak from the effort of running.

He froze at the scene before him.

"Shantel, don't do it," he cried out.

"You love her, don't you?" she shouted back.

"Yes, I love her, but you're my wife. I will take care of you. I promise. Now put the razor down."

"You love her, but you'll stay with me."

"Yes," he said, looking past me into her eyes. "Yes, I'll stay with you. Now please."

"You for her," she said.

"Fair enough," he replied, and he walked slowly across the room.

"Here," she said, indicating the ground with a nod of her head. "On your knees." He got down in front of her. "Turn around." He turned so that the back of his head was to her, and in one swift movement she pushed me away and had the box cutter at his throat. I looked on in horror, my heart beating in my ears faster than a hummingbird's wings. Shantel stared at her husband humbled below her, the blade to his throat. "You'd do this for her?"

"Yes," he rasped.

"Tag, I don't want to hurt anymore." And with that she took the blade from his neck and with one swift movement put it to her own throat.

"Stop," he called, but it was too late. I covered my eyes and heard her crumple to the floor. When I uncovered them there were people huddled all over her and one of them was saying, "There's nothing we can do." Tag came to me and held me tight. "When you said the name Emily Rossetti I knew it was her. Shantel's two favorite poets were two lovelorn women, Emily Dickinson and Christina Rossetti."

As we held each other tight, I thought of Maria's words again. *One in rags will take him from you.* For once she was wrong. The one in rags couldn't hurt us anymore.

53

Romeo and Juliet

Two days later, I was in my apartment assessing the damage. Tag was going to be released from the hospital later on and I was going to go pick him up. With the mess from the fire and water damage, it looked like his job would go on indefinitely. No need to invent work to keep him around. The library was in a shambles and I didn't dare think of the words that had gone up in flames. No doubt Henry was rolling over in his grave. But the very thought that both Tag and I could have died and neither of us did made all well in the world.

There were a few obstacles left. I'd already received an angry phone call from Jack for telling the police I suspected he had set the fire, and I had been appropriately apologetic. He went on to ask about the pictures and I told him his worries were over. They had burned in the fire. "I think that's probably for the best, Pauline," he said. Then he told me that there would be a service for Whitney later in the week and he hoped I would attend.

The sound of the elevator door opening in the foyer drew my attention. I walked out into the hall and saw Tag coming through the entry doors. His head was still bandaged and his hands, too, but they didn't look so much like swaddling anymore. He had a *Tribune* tucked under his arm.

"Hi," he said.

"I thought they weren't letting you out until later. I was going to come to get you," I said, feeling myself go to putty as he wrapped his arms around me. We walked back along the smoke-damaged halls and looked into the library together. "It's quite a mess," I said.

He shook his head and handed me the newspaper. "I thought you might find this interesting." On the front page was an article about the purchase of Verry Lingerie by Worthington Industries, noting that Dexter Worthington Jr. would be taking the helm. I looked at him with an arched eyebrow.

"Those pictures mean more than ever now," he said.

"Tag, I don't know how to tell you this, but the pictures are gone. I hid them in *The Great Gatsby* and it must have burned in the fire with the other books."

He gave me a wry smile. "I have a confession to make. I saw you hide the pictures in *Gatsby* that first day we made love. When it looked like you might give them to Jack Armstrong, I came back here to get them. But when I heard someone coming into the apartment, I thought it was you, so I hid the book in your bathroom cabinet. When I came back down the hall to look for you, that's when Shantel must have hit me over the head."

"Tag, I still can't believe she did it. How could she be both Emily Rossetti and the bag lady at the same time? Just the wardrobe changes are mind-boggling."

His turquoise eyes narrowed in a way that told me he was confused. "What are you talking about?"

"That Shantel was Emily Rossetti and the bag lady."

"What?" he repeated, looking even more challenged than before. "I have no idea what you are talking about."

"You told me that the day of the fire you saw your wife standing out in front of my building. And that you'd seen her there before."

"Yes, but . . . " And then he started to laugh. "I said I saw her, but I never said she was the bag lady. In fact the last time I saw her in front of your building the bag lady was there, too."

"You're saying Shantel wasn't the bag lady?"

He laughed again, harder, his laugh lines radiating along the contours of his face. I couldn't help but think how dear I found that face to be. "Sorry to disappoint you, but no. Wasn't it enough that she was a deranged poet? You sure have one heck of an imagination."

"I guess I do," I said, blushing with embarrassment, though for once it was hidden beneath the hues of my lobster-colored face.

He stopped laughing and his face turned sober. "Pauline, have you ever looked through all those pictures?" he asked.

"I looked at a few and that was enough. I take no thrill in the prurient."

"I'm going to get them, and I suggest you go through them all the way this time." He went down the hallway to my bedroom; my eyes drank in his swagger as he walked. I couldn't wait until the day there was furniture in that bedroom and we could make love in my canopied bed. As he disappeared into the room, there was the sound of the elevator doors opening in my foyer. Thinking it odd, I went to see who it was, and was surprised to see Suzanne Worthington standing beneath the crystal chandelier.

"Suzanne, what on earth are you doing here?" Tag had unlimited access to the apartment because of the work he was doing, but no other visitors were to come up unannounced. I was furious with Tony for letting a visitor come up without calling. Tony had nearly lost his job for abandoning his post the day of the fire, and if I wasn't so grateful to the half-wit for saving my life, I would have recommended he be fired on the spot.

"Our book group is meeting at Joan's," she said, which explained how she had gotten entry to the building. "But I thought I'd come up here before-hand to have a little discussion with you."

"About what?" I asked, mystified.

"I want those pictures."

"Pictures?" For the moment it didn't even compute what she was talking about. But then I realized she meant the Sunshine Factory pictures, of course. I couldn't fathom how she even knew of their existence, until I remembered pouring my heart out to her in the powder room of the Worthington penthouse. It was then that I saw she was holding a gun. It was a small thing, the type that would fit into a woman's purse, but a gun nonetheless. In fact the size of it made it seem all the more dangerous.

"Whitney called me from Phnom Penh to tell me what was in those pictures. She thought she could use them to make my husband back off the deal. She wanted Jack to keep the company so she could make it nicey-nicey. What a naïve tramp she was. And now you have them and we want them. If you think for one minute we're going to let you do anything to ruin the rag trade, you're out of your head. I told Whitney the same thing, but she wouldn't listen. She had to go and see for herself."

I didn't even see the gun anymore. My focus was on only one thing. Something she had just uttered that jarred me to my very core. About the rag trade. Worthington Industries manufactured textiles and clothes. The rag trade. *One in rags will take him from you.*

"It was you who set that fire, wasn't it?" I said. She didn't answer, but kept the gun pointed at me. My mind was racing when I heard my name called out.

"Pauline? Where are you?" It was Tag. I could hear him coming toward the foyer. I could tell by the look on Suzanne's face that she was surprised that I wasn't alone.

"Tag, go back," I shouted. "Stay where you are."

But my words had no effect and a second later, Suzanne was waving the gun back and forth between Tag and me. His silence frightened me, and I had a sick, sinking feeling he might do something stupid.

"Tag, just put the book on the floor and go back down the hall. Everything will be all right then. Yes, Suzanne?" I pleaded. "You can just take the pictures and everything will be fine, I promise." Tears were running down my cheek and I turned to Tag, who hadn't moved an inch. "Tag, please, the book."

He squatted slowly and placed the book on the floor, sliding it over to Suzanne.

"OK, you can go now," I said, my stomach a boiling cauldron of bile. "Just go."

She cocked the gun. "Sorry, Pauline, but there's no other way."

And then time went into slow motion as Suzanne's finger squeezed the trigger and Tag's taut, muscular body leapt between the two of us. I saw him jolt backward and knew he had been hit. Suzanne was pointing the gun at him on the floor and I was certain she would shoot him again and then me. I recalled the move Lienne had employed to subdue Chamrat in Bangkok. Without ever having done it before, I flattened my hand and hit Suzanne hard in the throat, sending her reeling back through the open door of the elevator. I quickly reached in and pushed the button for the ground floor.

The doors were still closing as I tore through my purse for my cell phone to dial 911. I was holding Tag's hand as I spoke to the operator and begged they send help in a hurry. There was a tremendous amount of blood and I feared something major had been hit. He grew quiet and his face turned frighteningly peaceful. "Please, Tag. Please," I begged. He fixed his turquoise eyes on me.

" 'Sweetest love, I do not go for weariness of thee,' " he said. And then his turquoise eyes fixed on me permanently. I sat cradling his head in my lap for the longest time, recalling the John Donne poem that was yet another staple of Miss Shingleheart's class.

> Sweetest love, I do not go,
> For weariness of thee,
>
> Nor in hope the world can show
> A fitter love for me;
> But since that I
> At last must part, 'tis best,
> Thus to use myself in jest
> By feigned deaths to die.

They closed his eyes before taking his body away. I sat on the hardwood floor in the corner holding onto the copy of *Gatsby*, too numb to cry. Finally, I opened it up and slid out the envelope with the pictures. I leafed through them slowly. The first few were as I recalled them, the horrid living conditions and the tired faces of the women. Then there was the picture of Mr. Kwan with the young girl, where I had stopped the first time. This time I flipped one picture further and my jaw dropped at the pressure of the blood pounding in my ears. Was it possible, what I was seeing? Dexter Worthington Sr. was in the manager's office with two young girls. There were several photos of varying positions, but I could be fairly certain at least one of them was sodomy. I put them down. This time I had really seen enough.

EPILOGUE
Crime and Punishment

Much has happened in the year since Tag's murder. At first, I was so disconsolate I couldn't get out of bed for nearly a month. Elsa would come up to see me and bring me soup, which I barely touched. Fleur refused to leave my side. Then one day a check for ten million dollars arrived in the mail and I stirred. Jack Armstrong may have been unethical, but at least he was a man of his word. I must admit, the money did make me feel better. After all, there were a lot of bills to be paid. And there is no better salve than putting new clothes on one's back.

So I went shopping and just as before, I stepped out of Barney's and saw Maria's sign shining out over Oak Street. And once again, for the life of me I don't know why, but I climbed those stairs. She told me that Jack Armstrong's money was tainted and would only bring me bad luck if I kept it. She told me that if I gave the money away, true love would follow.

With the wounds from Tag still fresh, I had no appetite for true love. But I couldn't stop thinking about all those women who toiled in sweatshops around the world. Of all the abuses they suffered. Giving the money to their cause was probably what Whitney would have done. I have no doubt it's what Tag would have done. But ouch! Ten million dollars?

I decided to donate one million to the Women and Children First Relief Fund. Certainly that was more than generous. But as I was filling out the check and looked at the one followed by six zeros, something about it felt all wrong. And though I could be considered even crazier than Shantel for what I did next, it was as if some invisible hand had taken hold of mine.

I added another zero to the sum.

What was it Oscar Wilde said? That anyone who lives within their means suffers from lack of imagination?

With a cadre of the country's best attorneys on her side, Suzanne Worthington plea-bargained and got five years for manslaughter. The case never even went to trial. As for Whitney's death, no one felt the sting of punishment for that. After all who could prove that someone was kidnapped and forced to take drugs in a foreign country? And Sokhom's death? And that of Annie Mitchell, the attorney who was trying to keep Chia in this country? Maybe they were just victims of hit-and-run drivers. Or maybe not.

When I saw the way our criminal justice system handled Tag's murder, I realized that the media could be controlled just as easily. So I decided to put the incriminating photos in a place where they could be the most effective. Why even bother with newsprint when there's the Internet? So I stopped at Starbucks to see my dear friend Marcel, who was only too tickled to give them their very own Web site. And he did it for free. I understand that there have been over a million hits on Dexter Worthington Sr. having his way with the helpless textile workers, and a resulting call for a worldwide boycott of Worthington Industries.

Last month, I was the honoree at a fund-raiser for Women and Children First. I tried to dodge the event (isn't giving ten million enough without having to suffer a bad meal?), but Theresa Armstrong insisted I attend. And a good thing it was. She seated me next to Richard "Skip" Tripton, the founder of an immensely successful hedge fund. Not only is he exceedingly rich, he is good-looking, rich, cultured, rich, my age, rich, and most important, available. And rich. He had lost his wife to a brain aneurysm a year before, and he told me that he never thought he would ever care for another woman again. But after meeting a genuinely generous woman such as myself, he had had a change of heart.

Last week he presented me with a Harry Winston diamond.

I decided to see Maria one last time, to hear what the psychic had to say about marrying Skip. But when I went up to her apartment it was shuttered with a "For Rent" sign in the window. I inquired at the dry cleaner below to see if anyone knew what had happened to her, and the woman behind the counter told me the couple had been arrested for burglary. Evidently, they had been running a big scam. Maria had been advising people to go out of town, and while they were gone her husband would break into their houses.

"Only fools and rich people have time for that psychic nonsense," she said, pulling a plastic bag down over a red floor-length gown that looked suspiciously familiar.

Acknowledgments

First, I must thank my agent, Helen Breitwieser, at Cornerstone Literary, for always looking out for me and my best interests.

Next, thanks and praise to my wonderful editor, Emily Krump, for doing such a fabulous job at catching a falling egg. Thanks also to the rest of the crew at Harper, especially Rachel Elinsky, Greg Kubie, and Claire Petrie, for their dedication and commitment to the written word.

On a more personal level, it's the gift of every writer to have a colorful family, and mine is no exception. Much love to my brothers, Tom O'Connell and Barney O'Connell, and my sister, Jane Davis. And to my brother-in-law, Tom Venrick, who probably has more stories than anyone.

To my cousin Ann O'Brien for help above and beyond the call of duty. And to my aunt Patricia O'Connell for being such a great reader.

To Donna Curry, Vita Konowich, and Roseann Moranetz for always being so supportive. And to Luky Seymour for saying that if you throw enough of it, some of it's going to stick.

To Chelsea Venrick and Lindsay Haigh for their invaluable input. And to my nephew Keith Venrick for his promotional assistance.

Thanks to Lisa Consiglio, Natalie Lacey, Jordan Dann, and Nicole Hernandez at the Aspen Writers' Foundation for all their work to help bring readers and writers together.

ACKNOWLEDGMENTS

More thanks to Amy Singh for her invaluable legal advice, Diane Whiteley for all her professional help, Roy Brandt for being a webmaster extraordinaire, and Michael Conniff for the on-the-air training.

Thanks to Dr. Tom Buesch for sharing his immense knowledge.

Thanks to Bill Getz for reasons he may never know.

And finally, thanks to my husband, Fred Venrick, for putting up with a writer.